...o often. An intelligent, well- — .en, ...th a perfectly structured plot arc and a ...he end. I would say I inhaled this in one, but ... holding my breath throughout. Bravo'
...ne Harris, author of *Chocolat*

'A chilling and beautiful masterpiece of suspense, cunningly plotted and written with the elegant imagination of a Shirley Jackson or a Sarah Waters. I was completely enthralled'
Joe Hill, author of *NOS4R2*

'Believe the hype. *The Last House on Needless Street* is not only a masterclass in horror, but in storytelling full stop. Up there with the best I've ever read. The most unsettling, beautiful, sad and wise book, it'll stay with me a long time. I'm in awe'
Kiran Millwood Hargrave, author of *The Mercies*

'The new face of literary dark fiction'
Sarah Pinborough, author of *Behind Her Eyes*

'A masterpiece. Beautiful, heartbreaking and quietly uplifting. One of the most powerful and well-executed novels I've read in years'
Alex North, author of *The Whisper Man*

'This book is tender rather than terrifying. Playful and sweet as well as sinister and thrilling, the creeping dread is tempered beautifully with humour and it ends being extremely emotionally impactful'
Emma Healey, author of *Elizabeth is Missing*

'This immersive modern gothic reads like a timeless classic as it lures you hook and sinker into its world'
Essie Fox, author of *Somnambulist*

The
Last
House
on
Needless
Street

CATRIONA WARD

First published in Great Britain in 2021 by
VIPER, part of Serpent's Tail,
an imprint of Profile Books Ltd
29 Cloth Fair
London
EC1A 7JQ
www.serpentstail.com

1 3 5 7 9 10 8 6 4 2

Printed and bound in Great Britain by
Clays Ltd, Elcograf S.p.A.

A CIP catalogue record for this book is available from the British Library.

ISBN 978 1 78816 6164
Export ISBN 978 1 78816 6171
eISBN 978 1 78283 7527

For my nephew River Emanuel Ward Enoch,
born 14 August, 2020

Ted Bannerman

Today is the anniversary of Little Girl With Popsicle. It happened by the lake, eleven years ago – she was there, and then she wasn't. So it's already a bad day when I discover that there is a Murderer among us.

Olivia lands heavily on my stomach first thing, making high-pitched sounds like clockwork. If there's anything better than a cat on the bed, I don't know about it. I fuss over her because when Lauren arrives later she will vanish. My daughter and my cat won't be in the same room.

'I'm up!' I say. 'It's your turn to make breakfast.' She looks at me with those yellow-green eyes then pads away. She finds a disc of sun, flings herself down and blinks in my direction. Cats don't get jokes.

I fetch the newspaper from the front step. I like the local because it has a rare bird alert – you can write in if you see something special, like a northern flicker or a Siberian accentor. Even this early, the dim air is as warm as soup. The street feels even quieter than usual. Hushed, like it's remembering.

When I see the front page my stomach goes into curls and knots. There she is. I forgot it was today. I'm not so good with time.

They always use the same picture. Her eyes are big in the shadow of her hat brim, the fingers clenched on the stick as if she thinks someone might take it away from her. Her hair lies wet and sheeny on her skull, short as a boy's. She has been swimming, but no one is wrapping her in a fluffy towel to dry her. I don't like that. She might catch cold. They don't print the other picture, the one of me. They got in big trouble for that. Though not big enough if you ask me.

She was six. Everyone was upset. We have a problem with that around here, especially by the lake, so things happened fast. The police searched the houses of everyone in the county who might hurt children.

I wasn't allowed to wait inside while they did it, so I stood out on the steps. It was summer, bright and hot as the surface of a star. My skin burned slowly as the afternoon wore on. I listened as they pushed back the ugly blue rug in the living room, tore up the floorboards and knocked a hole in the wall in the back of my closet because they thought it sounded hollow. Dogs went all over my yard, my bedroom, everything. I knew what kind of dogs they were. They had the white trees of death in their eyes. A thin man with a camera came and took pictures as I stood there. I didn't think to stop him.

'No picture, no story,' he said to me as he left. I didn't know what that meant but he waved goodbye in a cheerful way so I waved back.

'What is it, Mr Bannerman?' The woman detective looked like a possum. Very tired.

'Nothing.' I was shaking. *Got to be quiet, Little Teddy.* My teeth made little clicks like I was cold, but I was so hot.

'You were yelling my name. And the word "green", I believe.'

'I must have been thinking about this story I made up when I was a kid, about the lost boys who turned into green things, at the lake.' She gave me a look. I knew it well. I get that look all the time. I held tight to the trunk of the little oak in the front yard. The tree lent me its strength. Was there something to tell? If so it hovered just over the edge of my thoughts.

'Mr Bannerman, is this your only residence? No other property around here? No hunting cabin, nothing like that?' She wiped sweat off her top lip. Care pressed down on her, like an anvil on her back.

'No,' I said. 'No, no, no.' She wouldn't understand about the weekend place.

The police went away in the end. They had to, because I was at the 7-Eleven all afternoon and everyone says so. The security tape says so. What I used to do there was: I sat outside on the sidewalk by the sliding doors. When they parted with a whoosh and released people in a blast of cold air, I asked for candy. Sometimes if they had it they gave it to me, and sometimes they even bought it for me. Mommy would have been ashamed if she knew but I loved candy so much. I never went near the lake or Little Girl With Popsicle.

When they finally finished and let me back in the house I could smell them all over. Traces of cologne, sweat, squeaky rubber and chemicals. I was upset that they'd seen my precious things, like the picture of Mommy and Daddy. The photograph was fading even then, their features growing pale. They were leaving me, vanishing into white. Then there was the broken music box on the mantel – Mommy brought it from her faraway home. The music box didn't play. I broke it the same day I smashed the Russian dolls, the day of the thing with the mouse. The little ballerina was snapped from her stem, felled and dead. Maybe I felt worst about her. (I call her Eloise. I don't know why; she just looks like an Eloise.) I heard Mommy's beautiful voice in my ear. *You take everything from me, Theodore. Take, take, take.*

Those people had looked at all my stuff with their eyes and thoughts and the house didn't feel like mine any more.

I closed my eyes and breathed deeply to calm myself. When I opened them again the Russian doll smiled fatly back. Beside her sat the music box. Eloise the ballerina stood proud and upright, arms perfect and poised above her head. Mommy and Daddy smiled down from the photograph. My beautiful orange rug was like soft pills underfoot.

I felt better right away. Everything was OK. I was home.

Olivia's head butted my palm. I laughed and picked her up. That made me feel even better. But overhead in the attic, the green boys stirred.

The next day I was in the newspaper. The headline was SUSPECT'S HOUSE SEARCHED. And there I was, standing in front of the house. They searched other houses but the article made it sound like it was just mine and I guess those people were smart enough to cover their faces. *No picture, no story.* They put my photograph right alongside the one of Little Girl With Popsicle, which was a story in itself.

The picture didn't show the name of the street but people must have recognised it, I guess. Rocks and bricks came through the windows. So many. As soon as I replaced a pane another rock came through. I felt like I was going crazy. It happened so many times that I gave up and nailed plywood over the windows. It slowed them down. Not as much fun throwing rocks when there's nothing to break. I stopped going out during the day. That was a bad time.

I put Little Girl With Popsicle – the newspaper with her picture in it, I mean – in the closet under the stairs. I bend down to put it at the bottom of the pile. It's then that I see it on the shelf, half hidden behind the tower of newsprint – the tape recorder.

I recognise it immediately. It's Mommy's. I take the machine off the shelf. Touching it makes me feel strange, like someone's whispering nearby, just below the level of my hearing.

There's a tape already in the machine, part used – about half of one side has been recorded. It's old, with a striped yellow-and-black label. Her faded formal handwriting. *Notes.*

I don't listen to the tape. I know what's on it. She always spoke her notes aloud. Her voice had a slight hitch around the consonants; she couldn't quite get rid of it. You could hear the sea in her voice. She was born far away, Mommy, under a dark star.

I think, *Just leave it there, forget I've seen it.*

I ate a pickle and now I feel a lot better. After all, that stuff happened a long time ago. The light is growing and it's going to be a beautiful day. The birds will be arriving. Each morning they pour out of the forest and descend on my back yard. Yellowthroats, kinglets, buntings, red crossbills, sparrows, blackbirds, city pigeons. It's crowded and beautiful. I love to watch it. I made the peephole just the right size in just the right place in the plywood – I can see the whole back yard. I make sure the feeders are always full up and that there's water. Birds can suffer in this hot weather.

I am about to look out like I do every day, when my stomach lurches. Sometimes my insides know things before my mind does. This is wrong. The morning is too quiet. I tell myself not to be weird, take a deep breath and put my eye to the hole.

I see the jay first. He lies in the dead centre of the lawn. His bright mess of feathers shine like an oil slick. Twitching. One long wing strokes the air, desperate for flight. They look weird when they're grounded, birds. They're not meant to stay put for long.

My hands shake as I turn the keys in the three big locks on the back door. *Thunk, thunk, thunk.* Even now I take a moment to lock it behind me. The birds lie all over the yard, scattered on the parched grass. They twitch, caught helpless on what looks like pieces of tan paper. Many are dead, maybe twenty. Some are not. I count seven hearts still beating. They gasp, their narrow black tongues stiff with pain.

My mind runs like ants, everywhere. It takes me three breaths to make sense of what I see. In the night someone went to each feeding place and put glue traps down, wrapped them around the wire cages, attached them to the balls that hang from string. When the birds came to feed in the dawn their feet and beaks stuck to the adhesive.

All I can think is, *Murder, murder, murder ...* Who would do this to the birds? Then I think, *I have to clean up. I can't let Lauren see.*

That stray tabby cat crouches in the ivy by the wire fence, amber eyes intent.

'Go away!' I shout. I throw the nearest thing to hand, which is an empty beer can. The can flies wide and hits the fence post with a noise like *dunggg*. She goes slowly, in her uneven clawless limp, as if it is her own idea.

I collect the living birds. They stick together in my hands, bound into a twitching mass. They look like a monster from my bad dreams, legs and eyes everywhere, beaks drinking the air. When I try to separate them, feathers part from flesh. The birds make no sound. Maybe that's the worst part. Birds aren't like people. Pain makes them quiet.

I take them inside and try all the things I can think of to dissolve the glue. But it only takes a few tries with the solvent to see that I'm making it worse. The birds close their eyes and pant in the fumes. I don't know what to do now. This kind of stuck is for ever. The birds can't live but they're not dead. I think about drowning them and then hitting them on the head with a hammer. Each idea makes me feel weirder. I think about unlocking the laptop cupboard. Maybe the internet has an idea. But I can't figure out where to put the birds down. They stick to everything they touch.

Then I remember the thing I saw on TV. It is worth a try, and we have vinegar. Working with one hand, I cut a length of hose. I fetch a big Tupperware box, baking soda and the white vinegar from under the sink. I put the birds carefully in the box, seal it and pass the length of hose through the hole I pierce in the plastic lid. I mix the baking soda and vinegar in the bag and fasten it to the hose with a rubber band. Now it is a gas chamber. The air in the box begins to change, and the feathered twitching slows. I watch the whole thing, because death deserves a witness. Even a bird should have that. It doesn't take long. They had half given up already, from the heat and the fear. A pigeon is the last to die; the rise and fall of its plump chest grows shallow, and then it falls still.

The Murderer has made me into a murderer too.

I put the corpses in the trash out back. Limp, still-warm bodies, soft to the touch. A lawnmower starts somewhere on the block. The scent of cut grass crawls through the air. People are waking up.

'You OK, Ted?' It is the man with hair the colour of orange juice. He takes his big dog to the woods each day.

I say, 'Oh sure, fine.' The man is looking at my feet. I realise that I am not wearing shoes or socks. My feet are white and hairy. I cover one foot with the other but it doesn't make me feel any better. The dog pants and grins at me. Pets are better than their owners in general. I feel bad for all those dogs and cats and rabbits and mice. They have to live with people but, worse, they have to love them. Now, Olivia is not a pet. She's so much more than that. (I expect everyone feels this about their cat.)

When I think about a Murderer creeping around my house in the cold dark, laying traps in my yard – maybe even peering in, watching me, Lauren and Olivia with their dead beetle eyes – my heart stutters.

I come back. The Chihuahua lady is standing right up close. Her hand is on my shoulder. That's unusual. People don't like to touch me, as a rule. The dog under her arm trembles, stares about with bulging eyes.

I am standing in front of the Chihuahua lady's house, which is yellow with green trim. I feel I have just forgotten something, or am just about to know it. *Sharpen up,* I tell myself. *Don't be weird.* People notice weird. They remember.

'... your poor foot,' the woman is saying. 'Where are your shoes?' I know the tone. Small women want to take care of big men. It is a mystery. 'You got to look after yourself, Ted,' she says. 'Your mother would be worried sick about you.'

I see that my foot is leaking – a dark red trickle across the concrete. I must have stepped on something. 'I'm chasing that stray,' I say. 'I mean, I was chasing her. I don't want her to get the birds in my yard.' (I don't always get tenses right. Everything always feels like it's happening now and sometimes I forget it actually happened then.)

'It's a real shame, that cat,' she says. Interest lights up her eyes. I have given her something else to feel. 'The thing is a pest. The city should deal with stray cats like they do the other vermin.'

'Oh, I agree,' I say. 'Sure.'

(I don't recall names but I have my ways of judging and remembering people. The first one is: would they be kind to my cat? I would not let this woman near Olivia.)

'Anyway, thanks,' I say. 'I feel better now.'

'You bet,' she says. 'Come and have iced tea tomorrow. I'll make cookies.'

'I can't tomorrow.'

'Well, any time. We're neighbours. We have to look out for each other.'

'That's what I always say.' I am polite.

'You've got a nice smile, Ted, you know? You should use it more often.'

I wave and grin and limp away, miming pain I don't feel, favouring the bleeding foot until I am sure she has rounded the corner.

The Chihuahua lady didn't notice that I was gone, which is good. I lost time but not too much, I think. The sidewalk is still warm underfoot, not hot. The lawnmower still buzzes somewhere on the block, the scent of cut grass is sticky and green on the air. Maybe a couple of minutes. But it should not have happened in the street. And I should have put shoes on before I left the house. That was a mistake.

I clean my cut foot with disinfectant from a green plastic bottle. I think it was meant for floors or countertops, not for skin. The foot looks much worse after; the skin is red and raw. Looks like it would really hurt if I could feel it. But at least the cut is clean now. I wrap my foot in gauze. I have a lot of gauze and bandages about the place. Accidents happen in our house.

My hands are still sticky after, as if something clings to them, like gum or death. I recall reading something somewhere that birds have lice. Or maybe that's fish. I clean my hands with the floor stuff too. I am shaky. I take the pill that I should have taken a few hours ago.

Eleven years ago today Little Girl With Popsicle vanished. This morning someone killed my birds. Maybe these two things don't have anything to do with each other. The world is full of stuff that doesn't make sense. But maybe they are connected. How did the Murderer know that so many birds feed in my yard at dawn? Do they know the neighbourhood? These thoughts do not make me feel good.

I make a list. I write at the top: *The Murderer*. It is not a very long list.

Orange-Juice-Hair Man
Chihuahua Lady
A Stranger

I suck the end of my pencil. Trouble is, I don't know the neighbours so well. Mommy did. That was her thing, charming people. But they walk in the other direction when they see me coming. I have seen them actually turn around and hurry away. So the Murderer could be out there right now, a couple of houses down, eating pizza or whatever and laughing at me. I add to the list:

The Otter man or His wife or their Children
Men who live in Blue house together
Lady who Smells like Doughnuts

That is almost all the people on the street.

I don't really think any of them are the Murderer. Some, like the otter family, are on vacation right now.

Our street has a strange name. Sometimes people stop and take pictures of the dented street sign out front. Then they go away, because there's nothing but the woods beyond.

Slowly I add another name to the list. *Ted Bannerman*. You never know.

I unlock the closet where I keep the art supplies, and I hide the list carefully under an old box of chalk that Lauren never uses.

I judge people two ways – on how they treat animals, and on what they like to eat. If their favourite food is some kind of salad, they are definitely a bad person. Anything with cheese, they are probably OK.

It is not yet 10 a.m. – I can tell by how the sun shines in at the peepholes in the plywood, throwing coins of light across the floor – and it has been a very bad day already. So I decide to make myself an early lunch. It is my favourite lunch, the best in the world. OK, I should get the recording thingy for this.

Because I've been thinking – why shouldn't I use the tape recorder for my recipes? (Mommy wouldn't like it, I know. I have that hot feeling on the back of my neck which tells me I am about to be what she used to call *a nuisance*.)

I unwrap a fresh pack of cassettes. They smell good. I put a new one in the machine. I always wanted to play with it when I was little. The recorder has a big red button like a piano key, which makes a loud click when I press it. Now, I don't know what to do with Mommy's old tape, and that upsets me. I can't throw it away or destroy it – that's out of the question – but I don't want to keep it with my nice new cassettes. So I put it back in the closet under the stairs, slide it in there under the newspapers, under Little Girl With Popsicle. OK, ready!

Recipe for Cheese and Honey Sandwich, by Ted Bannerman. Heat oil in a frying pan until it smokes. Butter two slices of bread on both sides. Take some cheddar, I prefer the sliced kind, but you should use whatever you like best. It's your lunch. Take some honey and spread it over both pieces of bread on one side. Put the cheddar on top of the honey. Put slices of banana on top of the cheddar. Now close the sandwich and fry it in the pan until it's golden on both sides. When it's ready shake salt, pepper and chilli sauce all over. Cut it in half. Watch the cheese and honey ooze out. It's almost a shame to eat it. Ha, ha – almost.

My voice is horrible! Like a weird child with a frog in its belly. Well, I'll record the recipes but I definitely won't listen to them again unless I have to.

Recording stuff is the bug man's idea. He told me to keep a 'feelings diary'. Those words make me feel alarmed. He made it sound simple. *Talk about what happens and how it affects you.* Well, that's out of the question. But it's good to do the recipes in case I disappear one day and there is no one left to remember them. I'll do the vinegar and strawberry sandwich tomorrow.

Mommy had certain views on food, but I love it. Once I thought I could be a chef, run a lunch place, maybe. Ted's — imagine! Or write recipe books. I can't do any of that because of Lauren and Olivia. They can't be left alone.

It would be good to talk about these things with someone. (Not the bug man, obviously. It's very important I don't show the bug man who I am.) I'd like to share my recipes with a friend but I don't have any.

I sit on the couch with my sandwich and watch monster trucks. Monster trucks are great. They are loud and they go over things and through things. Nothing stops them. Cheese and trucks. I should be happy. But my mind is full of feathers and beaks. What if I get stuck on a glue trap? What if I just disappear? There is no one to be my witness.

I feel a gentle touch along my side. Olivia pushes her head into my hand then steps up onto my lap with her heavy little velvet feet. She turns and turns again, before settling on my knee. She always knows when I'm upset. Her purr shakes the couch.

'Come on, kitten,' I say to her. 'Time to go to your crate. Lauren is coming.' Her eyes close and her body goes limp with relaxation. She almost slips through my hands as I carry her, purring, to the kitchen. I lift the top on the old, broken chest freezer. I should have got rid of it years ago but Olivia loves this thing, God knows why. Like always, I check it's unplugged, even though it hasn't worked in years. I punched a couple more holes in the lid last week — I worry they don't get enough air. Killing things is hard, sure, but keeping them safe and alive is much more difficult. Oh boy, do I know about that.

Lauren and I are playing her favourite game. It has a lot of rules and involves riding the pink bicycle through the house at furious speed while shouting the names of capital cities. Lauren rings her bell twice for the right answer, and four times for the wrong one. It's a loud game but it's sort of educational so I go along with it. When the knock comes at the door, I clap my hand over the bell.

'Quiet while I answer that,' I say. 'I mean silent. Not a peep.' Lauren nods.

It's the Chihuahua lady. The dog's head pokes nervously out of her bag. Its eyes are glossy and wild.

'Sounds like someone's playing hard,' she says. 'Kids should be noisy, that's what I say.'

'My daughter's visiting,' I say. 'This isn't a good time.'

'I heard you had a daughter some years back,' the Chihuahua lady says. 'Who told me? Now, that I can't recall. But I remember hearing you had a daughter. I'd love to meet her. Neighbours should be friendly. I brought you some grapes. They're healthy, but they're sweet so everyone likes them. Even kids like grapes. They're nature's candy.'

'Thanks,' I say. 'But I have to go now. She and I don't get much time together. And you know, the place is a mess.'

'How are you doing, Ted?' she asks. 'Really, how are you?'

'I'm good.'

'How is your mother? I wish she would write.'

'She's good.'

'OK,' she says after about a minute. 'I guess I'll see you.'

'Hey, Dad!' Lauren shouts when the door is safely closed behind the Chihuahua lady. 'Chile!'

'Santiago!' I bawl.

Lauren screams and rides away, darting and swerving around the furniture. She sings loudly as she pedals, a song she made up about woodlice, and if I were not a parent I would never have believed that a song about a woodlouse could make me feel such joy. But that's what love does, it reaches right into you like a hand.

She stops suddenly, tyres squeaking on the wooden boards.

'Stop following, Ted,' she says.

'But we're playing a game.' My heart sinks. Here we go.

'I don't want to play any more. Go away, you're annoying me.'

'Sorry, kitten,' I say. 'I can't. You might need me.'

'I don't need you,' she says. 'And I want to ride on my own.' Her voice rises. 'I want to live in a house on my own, and eat on my own, and watch TV on my own, and never see anyone ever again. I want to go to Santiago, Chile.'

'I know,' I say. 'But kids can't do that on their own. An adult has to look after them.'

'One day I will,' she says.

'Now, kitten,' I say, as gently as I can. 'You know that can't ever happen.' I try to be as honest with her as possible.

'I hate you, Ted.' The words always feel the same, no matter how many times she says them: like being hit hard, at speed, from behind.

'Dad, not Ted,' I say. 'And you don't mean that.'

'I mean it,' she says, voice thin and quiet as a spider. 'Hate you.'

'Shall we have some ice cream?' I sound guilty even to me.

'I wish I'd never been born,' she says and pedals away, bell trilling, riding right over the drawing she made earlier, of a black cat with jewel-green eyes. Olivia.

I wasn't lying earlier; the place really is a mess. Lauren spilled some jelly in the kitchen then rode right through, leaving a sticky track through the house. There are broken crayons all over the couch and dirty dishes everywhere. One of Lauren's favourite games is to take each plate out of the cupboard one by one and lick it. Then she yells, 'Dad, all the plates are dirty.' Now she rolls off the bike onto the floor and starts pretending to be a tractor, growling and crawling. 'As long as she's happy,' I mutter to myself. Parenting.

I'm taking my noon pill with a drink of water when Lauren bumps into me. The water slops out of the glass onto the blue rug and the pill falls from my fingers, bounces, a tiny yellow airborne dot, and is gone. I kneel and peer under the couch. I can't see it anywhere. I'm running low, too.

'Damn it,' I say, without thinking. 'God damn.'

Lauren begins to scream. Her voice becomes a siren, rising until my head is ready to explode. 'You're *swearing*,' she weeps. 'You big, fat horrible man, don't swear!'

And I just snap. I don't mean to, but I do. I'd like to say that it wasn't the *big, fat* part that set me off, but I can't. 'That's it,' I shout. 'Time out, right now.'

'No.' She claws at my face, her sharp fingers seek my eyes.

'You can't play in here if you can't behave.' I manage to hold her back and eventually she stops fighting.

'I think you need some sleep, kitten,' I say. I put her down and start the record. The whisper of the turntable is soothing. The woman's pretty voice filters through the air. It's a winter night and no one has an extra bed, no one has any candy ... I can't recall the singer's name right now. Her eyes are full of compassion. She is like a mother, but one you don't have to be afraid of.

I pick up the crayons and felt-tip pens and count them. They are all there, good.

I sleep-trained Lauren with this music. She was a fussy child and she is growing into a difficult adolescent. What do they call it? A tween. Some days, like today, she seems very young and all she wants to do is ride her pink bicycle. I worry about what happened today. There is a lot to worry about.

First, and this is the big one: I've been going away more often. It happens when I'm stressed. What if I go away one day and I don't come back? Lauren and Olivia would be alone. I need stronger pills. I'll speak to the bug man. The beer is cold in my palm and hisses like a snake as I pull the tab. I take three dill pickles from the jar, slice them in half and top them with peanut butter. Crunchy. It's the best snack and it goes really well with the beer, but I can't enjoy it.

Second worry: noise. Our house is by the dead end; beyond, there's only forest. And the house on the left has been empty since for ever; the newspaper taped to the inside of the windows is yellow and curled. So I have relaxed my guard over the years. I let Lauren shout and sing. That needs thinking on. The Chihuahua lady heard her.

There is a black scatter of droppings under the kitchen table. That mouse is back. Lauren is still crying faintly but she's getting quieter, which is good. The music is doing its work. Hopefully she'll sleep for a while and then I can get her up for supper. I will make her favourite, hot dogs with spaghetti.

Third worry: how long will she like hot dogs and spaghetti? How long can I protect her? She needs watching all the time. Children are like a chain around your heart or neck, and they pull you in every direction. She's growing up too fast; I know every parent says this, but it's true.

Calm down, I tell myself. After all, Olivia learned to be happy with the situation in the end. When she was a kitten she would run for the door whenever I opened it. She could never have survived out there, but still she ran. Now she knows better. What we want isn't always what's best for us. If the cat can learn that, Lauren can, too. I hope.

The day draws to a close and after supper it's time for Lauren to go.

'Bye, kitten,' I say.

'Bye, Dad,' she says.

'See you next week.'

'Yup.' She plays with the strap of her backpack. She doesn't seem to care but I always hate this part. I have made it a rule not to show how upset I am. I put on the record again. The woman's voice winds through the hot dusk.

When I have a bad day, *now* and *then* get slippery. I catch Mommy and Daddy's voices in certain places around the house. Sometimes they're arguing over who goes to the store. Sometimes it's the ding and the whir of the old rotary phone in the hall, and then Mommy talking to the school, telling them I'm sick again. Sometimes I wake to her calling me for breakfast. It's clear as a bell. Then silence falls and I remember that they are both gone. Only the gods know where.

The gods are closer than you would think. They live among the trees, behind a skin so thin you could scratch it open with a fingernail.

Olivia

⁓

I was busy with my tongue doing the itchy part of my leg when Ted called for me. I thought, Darn it, this is not a good time. *But I heard that note in his voice, so I stopped and went to find him. All I had to do was follow the cord, which is a rich shining gold today.*

He was standing in the living room. His eyes were gone. 'Kitten,' he said over and over. The memories moved in him like worms under the skin. There was thunder in the air. This was a bad one.

I leant into him with my flank. He picked me up in shaking hands. His breath made roads in my fur. I purred against his cheek. The air began to calm, the electricity subsided. Ted's breathing slowed. I rubbed his face with mine. His feelings flooded into me. It was painful but I could take it. Cats don't hold onto things.

'Thanks, kitten,' he whispered.

You see? I was busy when he called but I went to him anyway. The LORD *has given me this purpose, and I do it gladly. A relationship is a very delicate business. You have to work at it every day.*

The lady ted is singing, mournful. I know each song by heart, the little hesitations in her voice, the tiny wrong note on that song about prairies. Her songs play on repeat, day and night, when Lauren isn't here. Ted seems to need the company. He thinks a cat doesn't count, I guess. If I were so inclined I might find that offensive. But teds are all needy and you can't take it personally. I'm speaking in general. I don't know any teds except Ted. And Lauren, I suppose.

I'll tell it from the beginning. About how he found me in the storm, the day the cord bound us together.

I remember being born. I wasn't there, and then I was, just like that. Pushed out from the warmth into the cold, kicking weak paws, tangled in strands of sticky membrane. I felt air on my fur for the first time, my mouth opened for the first time to cry. She bent over me, big as the sky. Warm tongue, warm mouth about my neck. Come, little kit, we're not safe here. Mamacat. The others we left in the mud. They hadn't survived the passage. The soft shapes I shared the dark with during all those months, now still and pelted by rain. Come. She was frightened. I could tell, even as little as I was.

The storm must have lasted for days. I don't know how many. We moved from place to place looking for warmth, shelter. My eyes weren't open yet so the memories are of scent and touch: the soft earthy place where we slept, the acrid tang of rat. Her fur on my nose as she curled tight around me, the slippery odour of holly leaves.

As my eyes began to open I could see dimly. Rain poured down like shining knives. The world crashed and shivered. I had never known anything different, so I thought there was always a storm.

I learned to stand and then walk, a little. I began to understand that something was wrong with Mamacat, in her body. Her movements were growing slower. Less milk came.

One night we took shelter in a gulley. Overhead, brambles shivered and lashed in the gale. She warmed me and fed me. She purred. The sound grew weak, her warmth faded. Then she was still. The cold began to creep into me.

There was a roaring noise and a blinding beam of light, not the shivering light of the sky, but a yellow circle. A thing like a spider of flesh, gleaming with rain. I had no word for hand, then. It enclosed me, lifted me from my mama.

'What's this?' The scent of wet earth was strong on him. His cuffs were slick with mud. A beast hummed nearby. He put me inside the beast. Rain hit the metal roof like little stones. He folded me up, warm. The blanket was yellow, with a pattern of blue butterflies. It held the scent of someone I knew, or longed to know. How could that be? I didn't know anyone, yet.

'Poor little kitten,' he said. 'I'm all alone, too.' I licked his thumb.

That is when it happened. A soft white glow gathered on his chest, over the place where his heart must be. The glow became a cord, reaching out through the air. The cord approached me. I rowed and struggled. But I was held fast. I felt the light encircle my neck, link me to his heart. It didn't hurt. It bound us together. I don't know if he felt it too – I like to think he did.

Then he brought me home to this nice warm house where I can sleep all the time and get stroked. I don't even have to look at the outside world if I don't want to! The windows are all boarded up. Ted made me an indoor cat and I've never had to worry about anything since. This is our house which is just for us, and no one else is allowed in. Apart from Night-time, of course, and the green boys and Lauren. I could do without some of them, to be honest.

I suppose I should describe us. That is what they do in stories. This is difficult. I can never tell the teds on TV apart. I don't know what details are relevant. I mean, my Ted is kind of a sandy colour? And he has patches of red fur on his face and thicker fur on his head, which is a somewhat darker shade, like varnished wood.

As for me, Ted always calls me 'you', or 'kitten'. But my name is Olivia. I have a thin slice of white down my chest, which sets off my coal-black coat. My tail is long and slim like a wand. My ears are large with a wide swivel and a delicate point. They are very sensitive. My eyes are the shape of almonds and green like cocktail olives. I think it's OK for me to say that I am beautiful.

Sometimes we're a great team and sometimes we fight. It's just the *way it goes. The TV says you have to accept everyone, teds and cats alike, for who they are. But you also have to have boundaries. Boundaries are important.*

That's enough for now. Feelings are very tiring.

I come out of my doze with a start, to the sound of faraway chimes, or a high voice calling.

I shake my head to clear it of the dream. But the noise goes on. Is there someone tiny singing somewhere? I don't like it. *EeeeeeEEEEeeeee.*

The orange rug is lovely on the pads of my paws, like walking on soft little pills. It's the colour of sun setting over the sea. Light dapples the walls through the peepholes. The walls in here are a restful deep red. Ted and I think it's a beautiful colour. We agree on some things! There's Ted's recliner, the leather worn shiny at the head and on the armrests. Silver duct tape covers the hole where he stabbed it with a steak knife during a dirt bike race. I like everything about this room except for two things that sit on the mantelpiece, next to the music box.

The first thing I hate is called a Russian doll. It holds a smaller version of itself inside it, and another inside that and so on. How awful. They are prisoners. I imagine them all screaming in the dark, unable to move or speak. The doll's face is broad and blankly smiling. It looks so happy to be holding its children captive.

The second thing I hate is the picture over the fireplace. The Parents, staring from behind glass. I hate everything about it. The frame is big, and silver, and has a pattern of grapes and flowers and squirrels. It's gross. The squirrels' faces look melted and burned black. It's like someone poured molten silver over living things and then let it cool. But the picture in the frame is the worst part. A lake, black and glassy in the background. Two people stand on a sandy beach. Their faces are just holes into nothing. The Parents were not nice to Ted. Whenever I come close to the picture I feel the empty tug of their souls.

I do like the music box, though. The little woman is stretched up so straight, like she's straining towards heaven.

EeeeEEeee. The high chiming sound is not coming from the Parents. I turn my back on them, lift my tail and show them my butt.

The pink bicycle lies in the middle of the living-room floor, training wheels imperceptibly turning. Lauren. She is Ted's small ted. Or maybe she belongs to another ted and he just looks after her? I forget. Her scent lingers on the rug, the arm of the chair, but it's quiet. She must have gone already. Good. But she never puts that god damn bike away. Oh dear. I really do try to say 'gd', not – ahem ahem. I don't like to take His name in vain.

I go to my crate when Lauren visits. There is room for my thoughts in there. It's always dark and good. I am sure the LORD would not approve of what I'm about to say, but – small teds are awful. You never know what they're going to do. And Lauren has some kind of *psychological issue*; I'm not clear on the details but it seems to involve being very rude and loud. Cats are sensitive to noise. We see with our ears and our noses. I mean, with our eyes too, obviously.

In the kitchen my crate stands against the wall. I put my ear to the cool side to listen, but the whining noise isn't coming from in there, I don't think. Ted has piled his weights on top of it again, so I can't get in. Annoying. Lauren has left scrawling, messy doodles all over the whiteboard by the refrigerator. *Blah blah blah*, she has written. *Ted is Ted. Olivia is a cat.* What GREAT observations. She'll go far. The refrigerator makes its rumble, there's a drip from the tap. But the little chime in my ears goes on, not matching either of these sounds.

In the room with all the humming, everything is as it should be. The cupboards are all secure. I can hear the machines purring quietly behind locked doors. Cellphone, laptop, printer. They sound alive and I always feel that they are about to speak to me, but they never do.

It goes on, the tiny sound like a chime or a high voice. The machines are not making the noise.

I go upstairs. I like going up stairs. It always feels like an improvement of some kind. I also like to sleep on the step that is exactly mid-flight. It makes me feel like I'm floating. The runner is black and I blend in well against it. Ted trips on me sometimes. He drinks too much.

The sound doesn't seem to get any louder or quieter as I move through the rooms, which is weird. I skirt the attic door, giving it a wide berth. Bad place. I stand on my hind legs to pull down the handle of the bedroom door. It gives with that robust *click* and swings wide. (Love doors. Just adore them.) There are five or six rolls of duct tape on Ted's bed. He buys the stuff by the yard. I don't know what on earth he uses it all for. I lick the tape. It tastes sticky and strong. The *eeeoooooeee* is still chiming softly in my ear. I *row* with impatience. Do I imagine this, or is the sound slightly metallic, hollow, like it's coming from a pipe?

In the bathroom I leap up to test the taps. No sound comes from them except the internal echo of air. I give the metal a lick and sniff the scum that covers the edges of the basin. Ted is not a very clean ted. His bathroom does not look like the bathrooms on TV.

The bathroom cabinet door is open. The tubes sit in long brown rows on the shelves. I stroke them with the tip of my tail, and then give a little nudge. The tubes fall in a clatter, pills raining from their mouths. Pink, white, blue. He never closes them properly, because they're safety caps and he can't get them off when he's drunk. The pills are all mixed up on the dirty tiles. A couple have landed in a puddle, left over from his morning shower. They are

24

already bleeding pink into the water. I bat a green-and-white capsule across the floor.

EEEEeoooeeee. The high song. It's a message, I know it, and it feels like it's just for me. But there's no more time to figure it out because it's time for *her*.

I am bound to Ted by the cord, and he is in my care as the LORD has decreed. But I do have a life outside him, you know? I have interests. Well, one. It's time for *her* now and that is very exciting.

I race down the stairs and to the window, avoiding the pink bike, taking another route behind the couch, leaving paw prints in the dust. I can't help being afraid that I'm late even though I know I'm not. But the circles of light are at *exactly* the right angle on the walls. I hop up on the small green macramé table. If I stand on my hind legs and stretch a little, I can just look out of the peephole that catches the street, through the little oak tree. The cord trails behind me in the air, a luminous silver.

The other peepholes are ted height and I can't reach them. This is my only glimpse of the outside. It's a small hole, the size of a quarter, maybe. I can't see much; a twisted stretch of oak trunk, some bare winter branches, through them a couple of feet of sidewalk. As I watch, the grey sky gives and snow starts to fall gently in the silence. Gradually the sidewalk vanishes under white, each tree branch bears a narrow line of snow.

This is all I know, this little coin of world. Do I mind? Do I miss going outside? Not at all. It's dangerous out there. This is enough for me, as long as I can see her.

I hope Ted doesn't move the macramé table. It would be just the kind of thing he might do. Then I'd have to get really mad and I hate being mad.

If she doesn't come I'll wait. That's what love is about, of course. Patience and endurance. The LORD taught me that.

Her scent precedes her, falls through the air like honey dripping onto toast. She comes around the corner with her graceful stride. How can I describe her? She's striped like a little dusty tiger. Her yellow eyes are the same colour as ripe gold apple skin, or pee. They're beautiful, is what I mean. She is beautiful. She stops and stretches, this way and that, extends her long black claws. She blinks as snowflakes come to rest on her nose. She has something silver sticking out of her mouth, a tail, maybe. A small fish like a sardine or an anchovy. I have always wondered what real fish tastes like. I get nacho cheese and leftover chicken nuggets, or old chuck from the discount aisle at the 7-Eleven. And when I'm really hungry I have to ask Night-time to hunt for me. (I abhor violence of any kind, but I didn't make the world and when I must, I must.)

I hope your fish is delicious, I tell the tabby silently. I stroke the plywood with a paw. *I love you.* The wind builds to a moan, the air is thick with whirling snow and she is gone in a flash of black and gold. Show's over. The LORD giveth, and he taketh away.

Usually after I see her I like to just sit and think for a spell. But the little whine is back, louder now. I rub my ear with my paw until it's glowing and sore. This makes no difference. Where the heck is it coming from? *OOoooeeeeooooee* it goes, on and on. How can I get anything done with that in my ear? It is like a little clock. Worse, because it almost feels like it's inside me and will not stop. This idea makes me uneasy. What is the little clock chiming for? What hour is come? I need guidance.

I go to my Bible. Well, it is mine now. I think it belonged to Ted's mother. But she went away and until she comes back, I don't feel bad using it. The pages are thin and whispery, like dried flower petals. It has gold on the cover, which catches the corner of the eye like a secret. Ted keeps it on a high table in the living room. It's wasted on him, honestly, he never opens it. The book is becoming somewhat battered, but after all, I must do my devotions.

I leap up beside the book. This part is fun because I always feel I am about to fall off. I tremble perilously in space. Then I push the book with a paw, nudging it over the edge.

It falls to the floor with a great crash, splayed open. I wait, because it's not over yet; a few moments later the house shakes and there is a rumble in the earth. The first time it happened I *yow*ed and hid under the couch. But I came to understand that these are His signs that I'm doing the right thing.

I leap down, landing neatly on all four paws and the LORD points my eyes at the verse He wants me to see.

> Beloved, let us love one another, for love is
> from God, and whoever loves has been born
> of God and knows God.

I tremble with the rightness of it. I love my Ted, my tabby, my house, my life. I am a lucky cat.

When I find a verse I like, I try to remember it – like that one I just said. But it can be hard to hold phrases in the mind whole. It's like oversetting a cup of marbles on a hard floor. They run in every direction into the dark.

The book is just a guide, really. I think the LORD is different for cats. He prefers to speak to us directly. We don't see things the way teds do.

I settle down on the couch in a disc of sunshine. I deliberately turn my back on the fallen Bible, so that Ted will know it's nothing to do with me. The whine has quieted some.

Now, why do I still have a bad feeling? What could be wrong? The Bible verse could not have been more positive. Anyway the trick to life is, if you don't like what is happening, go back to sleep until it stops.

Ted

I've been thinking that I should record some memories of Mommy. That way they won't disappear, even if I do. I don't want her to be forgotten. It's really hard to choose one, though. Most of my memories have secrets in them and are not suitable.

I have a great idea. What about that day by the lake? There are no secrets in that story. Can't find the recording thing at first; I'm sure I last had it in the kitchen. Eventually, after a hunt, I find it behind the couch in the living room. Weird. But that's my brain for you.

So. This is how I first got my love of birds. It was summer and we took a trip to the lake. I was six, I don't recall much from around that age but I remember how this felt.

Mommy wore the deep-blue dress that day, her favourite. It fluttered in the hot breeze that whistled through the cracked window. Her hair was pinned up but strands had escaped the bun. They whipped at her neck, which was long and white. Daddy drove and his hat was a black mountain range against the light. I lay on the back seat kicking my feet and watched the sky go by.

'Can I have a kitty?' I asked, as I did every so often. Maybe I thought I could surprise her into a different answer.

'No animals in the house, Teddy,' she said. 'You know how I feel about pets. It's cruel, keeping living things in captivity.' You could tell she wasn't from around here. Her voice still bore the faintest trace of her father's country. A pinched sound around the 'r's. But it was more how she held herself, as if waiting for a blow from behind.

'Daddy,' I said.

'You listen to your mother.'

I made a crying face at that, but only to myself. I didn't want to be a nuisance. I stroked my hand through the air and pretended I could feel silky fur under my hand, a solid head with enquiring ears. I had wanted a cat ever since I could remember. Mommy always said no. (I can't help but wonder, now, if she knew something I didn't, whether she saw the future, like a streak of red on the horizon.)

As we came close to the lake, the air took on the scent of deep water.

We got there early but the shore was already covered with families, blankets spread out like squares on a checkerboard on the white sand. Shadflies hung in clouds over the sheeny surface. The morning sun was strong; it tingled on my skin like vinegar.

'Keep your sweater vest on, Teddy,' Mommy said. It was hot but I knew better than to argue.

I played with Daddy in the water. Mommy sat in her chair, holding her blue silk parasol. The fringe rippled in the breeze. She didn't read. She just looked out through the forest and the land and the water, at something none of us could see. She seemed like she was dreaming, or watching for an enemy. Looking back, she was probably doing both.

The souvenir stand had little key rings carved from local forest pine. They were wonderful, shaped like dogs and fish and horses. They swung gently, looking at me with their wooden eyes, silver rings catching the light. I picked through them with water-wrinkled fingers. At the back of the rack I found her, a perfect little cat, sitting straight upright, paws together. Her tail was a question mark, her ears delicate. The carver had worked with the whorls and grain of the wood to make it look like a silky coat. I longed to have her. I felt like we were made for one another.

Mommy's hand fell on my shoulder. 'Put it back, Teddy.'

'But it's not real,' I said. 'It's just wooden. I could keep it in the house.'

'It is time for lunch,' she said. 'Come.'

She tied a napkin around my neck and handed me two small jars with blue-and-white labels — one of puréed apples, one of carrots — and a spoon. I imagined that eyes were on us, although they probably weren't. Around us other kids were eating hot dogs and sandwiches. Mommy saw me look.

'Those things are full of fat and preservatives,' she said. 'Our lunch is nutritionally complete. All the vitamins you need are in these jars. And it is inexpensive.' She spoke in her nursing voice, which was a little deeper than her regular voice, the consonants more clipped. Mommy looked after sick kids in her job at the hospital. She knew what she was talking about. So you didn't argue with the nurse voice. Daddy was between jobs. Like it was a dark gap he fell into, and now he couldn't climb out. He ate his prunes and rice pudding without a word. The jars looked tiny in his large brown hands. He took out his coffee Thermos.

Nearby, a baby was being fed by an impatient red woman. The label was blue and white. With a cold stab of horror I saw that the baby was eating the same creamed rice as my father. 'Put it away,' I said to Daddy. 'People will see!'

Mommy looked at me, but said nothing. 'Finish your lunch,' she told him gently.

When we were done Mommy put the jars away neatly in the cooler. 'You know where I am from, Teddy,' she said.

'Locronan,' I said, 'which is in Brittany. Which is in France.' That was all I knew. Mommy never spoke of that place.

'There was a boy in my village.' She looked out across the lake, and no longer seemed to be speaking to me. 'His parents had died in the big influenza. It cut through Locronan like a knife through butter. We all gave him what we could. But we did not have very much ourselves. He slept in our barn, with the donkey and the sheep. I don't recall his name. In the village they called him Pemoc'h, because he slept where the pig would sleep. Each morning Pemoc'h came to our kitchen door. I would give him a glass of milk, and half a loaf of bread. Sometimes I gave him dripping from the Sunday beef. Each evening he came again. I gave him scraps from the table. Turnip tops, cracked eggs. He always thanked me three times. Trugarez, trugarez, trugarez. I can never forget that. Sometimes he was so hungry that when he took the food his hands shook. For that poor food he worked all day for my father in the field. For years, he did this, and his thanks were never less than heartfelt. He was a grateful little boy. He knew how lucky he was.' She got up. 'I'm going to do my thirty minutes,' she said. Daddy nodded. She walked away, her dress blue against the blue sky. Mommy never felt too hot.

Despite the coffee Daddy fell into a deep sleep with his hat over his face. He slept a great deal, now. It seemed like every waking moment was exhausting to him. The red woman stared at us. She had noticed the three of us eating baby food for lunch. I tried to imagine that she was red because she had been fatally scalded and would die soon. I wished for her death with all my might, but the afternoon just went on. Small teal ducks played at the far edge of the lake, where the treeline marched right down to the water's edge. Daddy snored. He wasn't supposed to sleep while watching me.

Not long before, by this lake, a young boy had disappeared. They brought the kids from the group home there on weekends sometimes. Maybe they still do. This boy didn't get back on the bus at the end of the day. Sometimes I gave myself pleasant chills, imagining what happened to him. Maybe he chased a pretty red bird, or a deer, until he was out of sight of the crowds, by the deeper reaches of the lake. When he stumbled and fell into the cold there was no one to hear his cries. Or he wandered under the vast green canopy of the forest, until all his mind became green and he faded into the dappled light and became something else, something other than a boy. But he probably just hitched a ride back into the city. He was trouble, everyone said so.

'Here, Teddy.' Mommy's touch was soft on my head, but I gasped and started as if she had hit me. She put something into my hand and after a moment of sun blindness I saw what it was. The little cat seemed to arch her back in pleasure against my palm.

The rush of gladness was so strong it actually felt like pain. I stroked her with a finger. 'Oh,' I said, 'kitty, kitten!'

'Do you like it?' I could hear the smile in Mommy's voice.

'I love her,' I said. 'I'll take care of her so good.' Worry ran through my enjoyment like a vein. 'Was it expensive?' I knew that we were poor right now, and I knew I wasn't supposed to know.

'It is all right,' she said. 'Do not worry about that, for goodness' sake. Are you going to name her?'

'She's called Olivia,' I said. To me the name was classy and mysterious, exactly right for the wooden cat.

This small extravagance seemed to lift everyone up. I played with Olivia and I didn't care any more what other people thought about us. Mommy hummed, and even Daddy smiled and did his funny walks, pretending to trip over his own shoelaces and fall down in the sand.

Mommy's rule was always to get the most out of a trip, so we dawdled until almost everyone else had gone. The shadows lengthened and the hills began to eat the sun. Bats were darting through the dusk by the time we left. The car was a furnace, holding all the heat of the day. Daddy had to cover the scalding seats with a towel before I could sit down in back. I put Olivia carefully in my pants pocket.

'I will drive,' Mommy said gently to Daddy. 'You did it this morning. Fair is fair.'

Daddy touched her face and said, 'You are a queen among women.'

She smiled. Her eyes still held that distant look. It was years later that I noticed she never let Daddy drive after noon, after he started drinking from the coffee Thermos and doing the funny walks.

The car rumbled through the coming night and I felt happy. Everything was gentle, inside me and out. Only children can feel that kind of safety; I know that now. I must have drifted off because waking was like a slap to the head, shocking and sudden.

'Are we home?' I asked.

'No,' Mommy said.

I raised my head sleepily and looked out. By the beam of the headlights I saw that we were pulled over on the side of a dirt road. There were no people or sidewalk or other cars. Great ferns like ostrich feathers grazed the windscreen. Beyond that were the sounds and scents of trees talking, night insects making sounds like tick, tick, tick.

'Did we break down?' I asked.

Mommy turned around and looked at me. 'Get out, Teddy.'

'What are you doing?' The tone in Daddy's voice was fear, although I could not have named it so, at the time. All I knew then was that it made me feel disgusted with him.

'Go back to sleep.' To me she said, 'Teddy. Now, please.'

Outside the car the air felt solid, like wet cotton on my cheek. I felt small in the rolling dark. But another part of me thought it was exciting, to be in the forest at night with Mommy. She never did things the way other people did them. She took my hand and led me away from the car, from the light, into the trees. Her pale dress looked like it was suspended in the dark. She was like a sea creature floating across the ocean floor.

In the forest, even familiar things were strange. The constant wet patter of the night became the chilly drip of a dungeon. The creak of tree branches was the shifting of giant, scaly limbs. The snagging pull of a twig was bony fingers grasping at my sleeve — the fingers, maybe, of something that had once been a child, who wandered into the green light and never returned. I began to be scared. I squeezed Mommy's hand. She squeezed back.

'I am going to show you something important, Teddy.' She sounded normal, as if she were telling me what was in my sandwich that day, and I felt better. As my eyes adjusted, everything seemed to glow in the half-dark, as if the air itself held light.

34

We stopped beneath a towering fir tree. 'This will do,' she said. In the distance, through the crackling branches, I could still see the faint beam of our headlamps.

'I bought you that cat today,' Mommy said. I nodded. 'Do you love it?'

'Yes,' I said.

'How much?'

'I love it more than I love ... ice cream,' I said. I couldn't think how to explain my feelings for the little wooden cat.

'Do you love it more than you want Daddy to get a job?' she asked. 'Tell the truth.'

I thought about it. 'Yes,' I whispered. 'I do.'

'You know the little girl I look after at the hospital, who has cancer? Do you love the cat more than you want her to get better?'

'No,' I said. Surely I couldn't. That would make me a mean, mean boy.

She put a cool hand on my shoulder. 'Tell me the truth,' she said.

My throat felt like it was full of knives. I gave a single nod. 'I love the kitty more,' I said.

'Good,' she said. 'You are an honest child. Now take it out of your pocket. Put it on the ground right there.'

I laid her gently on a patch of moss at the foot of the tree. I could hardly bear to let go of her, even for a moment.

'Now, back to the car. We are going home.' Mommy held out her hand.

I made to pick Olivia up, but Mommy's fingers were like a cuff about my wrist. 'No,' she said. 'That stays here.'

'Why?' I whispered. I thought of how cold and alone she would be, here in the dark, how the rain would wet her and rot her, how squirrels would chew her beautiful head.

'It is practice,' Mommy said. 'You will thank me in the end. Everything in life is a rehearsal for loss. Only the smart people know it.'

She pulled me back through the forest towards the car. The world was a dark blur. I was crying so hard, my heart felt like it would burst in my chest.

'I want you to feel the power of it,' she said. 'Of walking away from something you love. Doesn't it make you feel strong?'

The spiny stars of the headlights drew closer and I heard the car door slam. My father smelled of what I thought was plum pudding and sweat. He held me tightly. 'Where did you go?' he asked Mommy. 'What's going on? He's crying.' Daddy turned my face this way and that, looking for hurt.

'No need for hysterics,' Mommy said with a little of the nurse. 'We tried to find an owl. They nest round here. Then he dropped that cat key ring and we could not find it in the dark. Therefore, the waterworks.'

'Oh, kiddo,' said my father. 'No big deal, huh?' His arms were no comfort.

I never asked for a kitty again. I told myself I didn't want one any more. If I loved her I might have to leave her in the woods. Or one day she'd die, which was almost the same thing.

So it was many years before it happened that Mommy began to prepare me for her departure. I understand her better, now. Now I'm a parent I know how afraid you get for your child. Sometimes when I think about Lauren I feel almost see-through with fear, like a pane of glass.

When we got home Mommy put me in the bath and gently checked me all over. She found a scratch on my calf where I leaked out red. She drew the flesh back together with two neat sutures from her kit. Breaking me, then mending me, over and over — that was my mother.

The next day Mommy set up the bird tables in the yard. She put up six wire feeders to attract the smaller birds. She hung them high from poles so the squirrels couldn't steal. She put out cheese for the ground feeders, wooden hutches filled with grain, plastic tubes to dispense sunflower seeds, balls of fat dangling from string, a block of rock salt.

'Birds are the descendants of giants,' Mommy said. 'Once they ruled the earth. When things got bad they made themselves small and agile and learned to live in treetops. The birds are a lesson in endurance. These are real, wild animals, Teddy — better than a key ring.'

At first I was afraid to feed or watch them. 'Are you going to take them away from me?' I asked her.

She said, surprised, 'How could I? They do not belong to you.' I saw that she was showing me something that was safe to love.

All that was before the thing with the mouse, of course — before Mommy began to be afraid of me. Now the Murderer has taken the birds away, even though Mommy said that it couldn't be done.

I had to stop because I'm getting upset.

All that happened fifteen years before Little Girl With Popsicle disappeared from that same beach on the lake. The lake, Little Girl With Popsicle, the Bird Murderer. I don't like to think that all these things are connected, but events have a way of echoing through. Maybe there are secrets in that story after all. No more recording memories. I didn't like that.

Dee

It happened on the second day of vacation. Dad took a couple of wrong turns on the drive up from Portland, but when they smelled water in the air they knew they were back on track.

Dee remembers the fine details best; the popsicle in Lulu's hand leaking sticky green onto her fingers, the drag of the wooden stick on her own purple tongue. There was sand in her shoes, and sand in her shorts, which she didn't like. There was another girl on a neighbouring blanket of about her age and they caught one another's eye. The other girl rolled her eyes and stuck a finger down her throat, gagging. Dee giggled. Families were so embarrassing.

Lulu came to Dee. The straps on her white flip-flops were twisted up. 'Please help, Dee Dee.' Both sisters had their mother's eyes; brown, shot through with muddy green, wide and black-lashed. Dee felt the familiar, helpless recognition, on looking into Lulu's eyes. She knew herself to be the lesser version.

'Sure,' Dee said. 'You big baby.'

Lulu squawked and hit her on the head, but Dee untwisted the straps and put the white flip-flops on her feet anyway, and made the moose face, and then they were friends again. Dee took her to the water fountain to drink, but Lulu didn't like it because the water tasted like pencils.

'Let's read minds,' Lulu said. It was her new thing that summer. Last year it had been ponies.

'Fine,' Dee said.

Lulu took ten steps away, out of whispering range. She kept her eyes fixed on Dee and made a cup of her hands. She murmured into them passionately. 'What did I say?' she asked. 'Did you hear anything?'

Dee thought. 'I think I did,' she said slowly.

'What, Dee Dee?' Lulu almost vibrated with yearning.

'It was so weird. I was just standing here, minding my own business, and then I heard your voice saying right in my ear, "I am such a pain and my big sister Dee is the best."'

'No! I never said that!'

'Weird,' said Dee. 'That's exactly what I heard.'

'That's not right!' Lulu was on the verge of tears. 'You have to do it properly, Dee Dee.'

Dee held her. She felt the shape of her sister, her small bones, her soft skin warmed by the sun. The nape of her exposed neck, soft dark hair as short as a boy's. Lulu hated her head to get hot. This summer she had wanted to shave it off. Their mother had only narrowly won that battle.

Dee was sorry she had teased. 'I'm just being silly,' she said. 'Let's try again.' Dee cupped her hands over her mouth. She felt her own warm breath fill her palms. 'I like my new dungarees, that I bought in the sale,' she whispered. 'But I can't wear them until the fall, because it's too hot for dungarees.' Dee imagined the words travelling to her sister's ear. She tried to do it properly.

'You're thinking of dancing school,' Lulu said. 'You dream about it and you think Mom and Dad are mean.'

Dee lowered her hands. 'No, I don't,' she said slowly.

'I read your mind,' said Lulu. 'Whisper me something else, Dee Dee.'

Dee lowered her lips into the warm cup of her palms.

'You're thinking about Greg in homeroom,' Lulu says. 'You want to French kiss with him.'

'I knew it,' Dee said with rising fury. 'You've been reading my diary. You little snoop.' If Lulu told Mom and Dad about the Greg thing, they would be mad. They might even reconsider the conservatory. Dee was due to start at Pacific in September. But she had to prove she could behave herself. That meant no boys, good grades, keeping to curfew and looking after her little sister.

'Don't, DeeDee,' Lulu said. 'You're not supposed to yell at me.' Her voice had gone up an octave and she sounded much younger. She knew that she had gone too far.

'That's it. Back to Mom and Dad. I don't know why I even try with you …'

'I don't want to go back yet! I'm still thirsty, and I want to pet the kitty.'

'You've had a drink of water and there's no kitty here,' Dee said. But for a moment she thought she saw a black tail like a question mark, disappearing behind a trash can. Black cats were supposed to be bad luck. Or was it good luck?

Lulu looked up at her sister with wide eyes. 'Don't be mean,' she said quietly.

They walked back in silence. Lulu put her hand into Dee's, and Dee took it because there were so many people around, but she held it as loosely as she could and didn't return the squeeze. Lulu's face was screwed up with sorrow. Her hurt made Dee feel good. Her heart was pounding. She thought of the diary, where she kept it in the floor vent. She screwed the vent back down each time. Lulu must have looked for it for a long time. She must have taken a screwdriver from Dad's toolbox to open the vent, read the diary, screwed the vent back up again … The thought made Dee want to slap her sister, see her cry. Lulu could *ruin* her life if she wanted.

Dee had wanted to go to Pacific since she was five. It had taken eleven years of pleading to get her parents to agree. It was mixed, boys and girls. Dee would live in a dorm at the school. Her parents' anxiety radiated off them whenever this fact was mentioned. Dee could see them half hoping that something would happen to prevent it. Her behaviour had to be perfect.

'I won't tell, Dee Dee,' said Lulu. 'I swear. And I won't read it again.' But Dee shook her head. Of course Lulu would tell, in the end. She might not mean to, but she would. She was like that. Dee would have to bury the diary in a random trash can and say Lulu was inventing things. She hoped that would be enough.

Lulu settled in the shade of the umbrella by Mom's feet. Mom dozed with her magazine clutched to her breast. Dad sat in the striped canvas chair reading his book and rubbing his eyes. He was tired too; his head nodded.

Lulu started digging with her bucket and spade, mouth pursed. 'I found a pretty pebble,' she announced. 'You want it, Dee Dee?' She offered it on the flat of her palm, eyes anxious.

Dee ignored her. 'Can I go swim?' she asked her father.

'Half an hour,' he said. 'If you're not back by then I'm calling the cops.'

'Fine,' Dee said. When his back was turned she rolled her eyes for form's sake, but actually she was surprised. He must be exhausted. He wouldn't normally let her wander unsupervised.

'Not so fast, Delilah,' she heard her mother call. 'You take your sister with you.'

Dee was a plausible distance away and she hurried on, pretending not to have heard. She wandered through the hedge maze of colourful blankets, beach umbrellas and windbreakers. She didn't know what, or who she was looking for, just that it was important to be alone so that things could happen.

She tried to move through the crowd like it was a dance. She put a reason behind each step she took. Dee had danced the part of the Caterpillar in *Alice in Wonderland* at the end of the semester in her ballet class. She still remembers how the steps, the *chaînés*, arabesques and *développés* became something different the moment she felt like a caterpillar. So now each step she took was a dance, heading towards a great romance. She imagined people (boys) watching her as she passed, though she couldn't see anyone actually watching. She imagined their thoughts. How long and glossy her hair was, how different she seemed to other girls, how mysterious, as if she had a secret. She imagined it really hard so that the other thoughts didn't come in, like about how her butt was too big and her chin was a weird shape.

She picked her way to the shoreline and sat down in the damp sand at the water's edge. In the shallows was a flotilla of bobbing toddlers in water wings. Farther out, by the buoys, the lake was still, showing back the treeline and the sky in dark, upside-down perfection. She could imagine monsters out there, lurking just below the sleek green surface. The air smelled of burgers grilling and Dee made her *yeeeugh* face. Her thing at the moment was to despise food. It seemed important to maintain it, even if only to herself. Ballerinas don't eat burgers.

'Hi.' Something loomed over her, throwing a tall shadow. Then it sat down, scuffing sand, and became human-sized. It was a guy. He was thin, yellow-headed. She could see swirls of white lotion on his pale skin.

'Hi,' said Dee. He had to be at least nineteen. She was suddenly aware that her palms were sweating and her heart was beating nervous and light. What would they talk about?

'I'm Trevor,' he said, and offered a hand to shake, which was very dorky and made Dee smirk. But she was also relieved because it made him seem familiar, what her mother would call 'raised right'.

Dee lifted one eyebrow, something she had just learned to do. 'How's it hanging?' She didn't take his hand.

Trevor blushed. 'OK,' he said, wiping his hand on his shorts as if that was what he meant to do all along. 'Are you here with your folks?'

Dee shrugged. 'I managed to lose them,' she said.

He smiled, like he appreciated the joke. 'Where are they?'

'All the way over by the lifeguard stand,' she said, pointing. 'They were sleeping and I was bored.'

'Your parents?'

'And my little sister.'

'How old is she?'

'Six,' Dee said. She didn't want to talk about her family any more. 'Where do you go to school?'

'UW,' he said.

'Cool.' So he was in college. 'I go to Pacific,' she said. It was nearly true.

'Cool,' he said, and she saw the interest warm his eyes. Guys liked ballerinas, she had discovered. They were feminine and mysterious. 'You want to go get some ice cream?' Trevor said.

Dee considered, shrugged, got up and dusted the sand off.

Trevor got up too then said, 'Um, you have a thing on you. On the back of your shorts.'

Dee twisted her head round to look. There was a dark stain on the white denim. Dee said, 'Oh, I must have sat on something.' She took her T-shirt off and tied it round her waist. 'You go ahead. I'll meet you there.'

She hurried to the women's restrooms, where there was a queue. People were taking their little kids into the stall with them, sometimes three at a time, and then they all had to go. It was taking a really long time. Dee could feel everything getting worse as she waited. She felt a snail of blood crawl down her inner thigh. She pulled out fistfuls of paper towel and swabbed at it. Eventually she said to the big, sweating woman in front of her, 'Um, do you by any chance have a sanitary pad?'

The woman stared at her. 'There's a machine,' she said. 'Right there on the wall.'

Dee left her place in line and went to the machine. It only took quarters. She had a dollar and some dimes. 'Does anyone have change for a dollar?'

A woman with a red-faced baby on her shoulder said, 'Where's your mom? She should be taking care of you.'

'Does anyone here have change, *please?*' Dee made her tone sarcastic and a little angry, so that they wouldn't see that she was literally about to cry.

A lady with a blonde bob gave her four quarters. But the machine was broken and the quarters tinkled back into the slot again and again. Blinking back tears, Dee returned them to the lady.

She cleaned herself up as best she could. The women in line watched as Dee rinsed her shorts in the sink. Jesus, she was just in her bathing suit like everyone else. She kept the T-shirt round her waist. It hid everything, so that was OK. She joined the line again and waited.

When she got to the ice-cream place Trevor wasn't there. She gave it a few minutes, but she knew he wasn't coming. Maybe she took too long in the restroom and he gave up. But probably he didn't want to buy ice cream for a girl who didn't even know when her period was coming.

She left the T-shirt on the shore and waded out, past the toddlers in water wings, knee-deep, then to her thighs, then her waist. She felt safer right away – hidden. In the heat of the day the cool lake water was like a sudden plummet, a shock that sent pinpricks up her spine. She trailed her fingertips on the broken mirrored surface, the skin of the water. The lake moved about her like a slow beast. She went deeper until the water lapped her chin and the gentle swell threatened to lift her feet from the stony bottom. Her cramps were

45

almost pleasurable, now, with the cold water and the sunshine and the distant roar of the summer crowd on the shore, the sound travelling eerie across the water. It didn't matter, suddenly, that the boy hadn't come back. Her body seemed like enough company. Lately its moods fascinated her. It behaved in new and surprising ways, like a friend she didn't know well yet. Pain and pleasure both had new faces. She was a story being told each minute. Dee closed her eyes under the lake's cold caress. Everything was happening now.

Something smooth glanced against her cheek. Again, again, like a playful push. Dee opened her eyes. Dark grey and black scales filled her vision, flowing. She held her breath. The snake's body was sunk a little beneath the surface but it held its head up, somewhat above the water, like a swan. The snake circled her slowly and curiously. It brushed her arm once as it swam. It was probably attracted to her body heat. What kind was it? Dee forced her juddering brain to think. It looked like a cottonmouth but surely you didn't get them around here. Another idea kept trying to slide into her mind and she had to work very hard to keep it out. *Rattlesnake*. It was then she realised there were two more heads periscoping out of the water to her left, then three or four. They were a group, a family perhaps. Several juveniles, young mature snakes and a large adult with its ancient head, its broad lipless smile. Exactly how many there were she could not say — her heart had stopped. A blunt head swooped gracefully towards her face. Dee closed her eyes and thought, *This is it, the end.* She waited for the needle fangs, the poison, for the carrion mouth to close on her. She thought she felt the feather kiss of a tongue on her jaw. Her life was thunder in her ears. She tried to hold herself still against the swell of the water, to be nothing alive, to be stone. Something brushed against her shoulder in a long caress.

Dee didn't know how long she stood there, time had expanded and collapsed. When at last she opened her eyes the water was smooth and empty. Maybe they were gone. But maybe they were writhing about her arms and legs out of sight, under the water. She seemed to feel their touch all over her body. She began to shiver uncontrollably, head baking in the bright day. Her legs buckled and she sank and gasped, mouth filling with tin. She turned and waded for the shore, water grabbing her, slowing her to a deathly pace. She could still feel them garlanding her limbs.

Dee reached the shore. She ploughed out of the water and the weight of her body descended on her again. She staggered and fell. The sand was good underneath, against her side. She made herself into a ball and cried, unobserved, among the running sunburned kids.

Dee slowly picked her way back through blankets and umbrellas. The air was hot with sugar and the sand sucked at her ankles. She didn't have her watch on but she knew she'd been gone longer than half an hour. All she wanted now was the sanctuary of her family. Her mother would shudder, cry out and take Dee in her arms. Lulu would look scared and excited at the same time and ask over and over, *How many snakes? What kind?* And her father would be furious, ask what the hell the lifeguard had been doing, and Dee would bask in the warmth of his anger, knowing she was cared for. It would become a story, one they all told in hushed voices sometimes. *Do you remember when Dee Dee got attacked by the snakes?* The story would live outside her then, and no longer run cold in her bones.

Even from a distance, Dee could see that that her parents were freaking out. Mom was screaming and Dad was shouting. Two lifeguards were there, and other men talking into radios. Dee cringed. How embarrassing. She was only a little late, for God's sake.

As she came closer, she heard her father saying, 'I just fell asleep for a minute. A minute.'

Dee came up to the blanket and sat down in the shade. 'Mom?' she said. 'I'm sorry ...'

'Quiet, Dee, please. Your father is trying to make these people *do* something.' Her mother's mouth trembled. Mascara ran down her face like black blood. 'Lulu!' She stood suddenly and screamed it out. Heads nearby turned. 'Lulu!' her mother screamed again.

'She has short hair,' Dad is saying over and over. 'People often think she's a boy. She won't grow it.'

Dee realised two things: first, they hadn't noticed how long she had been gone; and second, Lulu wasn't there. She sighed and tucked her hair behind her ear. The cramps were really bad now. She felt a stir of feeling. Lulu was being dramatic again. Now no one would comfort Dee and take the story of the snakes away.

As the long, hot afternoon wore on, more people came, and the real police. 'Laura Walters, Lulu for short,' everyone kept saying into radios, and then they started saying it to everyone on the shore, through the big speaker on the pole by the hot-dog stand. 'Laura Walters, six years old, brown hair, hazel eyes. Wearing a bathing suit, denim shorts and a red tank top.' It was only in the dusk, as the park emptied, that Dee began to under-stand that they weren't going to find Lulu that day. It took her much longer to understand that they would never find her. She had gone who knew where, with who knew whom, and she didn't come back.

Some weeks later, many miles away, a family from Connecticut found a white flip-flop mixed up in their beach stuff. No one could say how it got there, or even if it was Lulu's. It had been through the laundry with their clothes.

Lulu would be seventeen, now. *Is*, Dee corrects herself. *Lulu is seventeen*.

The last thing Lulu said to Dee was, *I found a pretty pebble*. Some days all Dee can think about is that pebble. What did it look like? Was it smooth or rough, grey or black? Was it sharp and angular or did it fill Lulu's small palm with its round weight? Dee will never know, because she got up and walked away without a glance.

The Walters family stayed in Washington for a month, hoping for news. But there was nothing for them to do and her father's boss was losing patience. So they went back to Portland. The house was strange without Lulu. Dee could never remember to lay three places for dinner, not four, and it always made her mother cry.

Her mother left soon after. Dee knew she couldn't stand the sight of Dee, the pale copy of her lost daughter. She emptied the checking account and was gone. Dee couldn't blame her, although her father felt differently. Then the other thing happened.

The night before, snow fell like ash from the quiet sky. Her father was building a model airplane below in the living room. Dee could smell the epoxy drifting up the stairs. He would sit there for hours, until his eyes were red-rimmed with fumes. He would not come up to bed until the night was almost worn out. *I'll talk to him tomorrow,* Dee thought. *I have to.*

She was a term late for Pacific, but she could catch up. Money was tight, but she could get a job, couldn't she? Her father didn't need her to make model airplanes and stare into the dark, after all. Dee breathed through the guilt that stabbed at her. The air was laden with mingled scents of hot glue and despair. She thought, *This cannot be my life. This is a ghost life.* Tears traced burning lines down her cheeks.

In the morning Dee made the special coffee to take to her father in bed. The special coffee was made with the fancy glass thing from San Francisco, and it took a long time to drip through. It was bitter and gritty like river sediment and her father loved it. Maybe he put all his love into the coffee maker because the bigger things were too painful. Dee hated the coffee maker because it reminded her of when they were all together. She poured the scalding water over the coffee grounds. The dark-brown scent filled the kitchen. This morning she was going to speak to him, she really was.

She pulled back her long sleeve and poured a little boiling water over her wrist, gasping. She watched the bracelet of red blisters rise on her flesh. That helped. She let the sleeve fall down to hide it, and finished putting everything on the tray. She would tell him today. He would be mad, he would be hurt. But she couldn't keep it to herself any longer. *Pretty pebble.*

She went into her father's room and put the tray on the table. She thought it would put him in a good mood, if the scent of coffee led him out of sleep. She opened the curtains to the white world. Houses, mailboxes, cars – the edges of everything were blunted with white snow. She turned to say, *Look how much fell in the night!* Then she saw him. His body lay very straight in bed, still in the blinding snowlight. His face wore an expression that for a moment she could not place. Then she recognised it as a welcome.

It was a stroke, they said. They didn't say it was brought on by Lulu's vanishing, and then Dee's mother leaving. They didn't need to. So the person who took Lulu also took Dee's mother, and then her father. Dee was taken too. For how much of her remains, after everything? She feels like a big, dark, empty room.

There was no ballet school because there was no money to pay for it. She didn't finish high school either. Dee got a job at the drugstore. But she had her real work, which was to look for the person who took her sister. All the men who had been at the lake that day, all the glances, the roll call of suspects. They are her job now.

She calls tired Karen each week, sometimes more. Tired Karen is the detective in charge of Lulu's case and she always sounds both exhausted and frantic. Her face is expressive; it shows all the hurt she has seen; every back she has patted, every tissue handed over, every screaming face pushed close to hers.

She and Dee were close, for a time. The detective felt sorry for Dee, a young girl with no one. *Call me Karen*. She told Dee things when she called. Now she just says, 'We're working on it.'

Ted

I can't always tell, but this time I'm pretty sure I am about to do something important. I am going to find a friend. I go away more and more, these days. Who will look after Lauren and Olivia if I don't come back, one day? I'm only one person, and it's not enough.

Mommy took me to the forest three times. The last time she sent me back alone. Yes, I still feel her under the dark canopy of leaves. She is in the scatter of light across the forest floor. And yes sometimes she's in the cupboard under the sink. But really, I have been on my own since that day.

I tell myself that this is for Lauren and Olivia, and that's true. But also it's because I don't want to be alone any more.

I pick a time when Lauren isn't around. If she knew what I was doing – well, that wouldn't be good. I take the padlock off the cupboard in the living room where I keep the laptop. The screen is a square of ghostly light in the dark room, like a door to the dead.

Finding a site is easy. There are hundreds of them. But what comes next? I scroll through. Faces race by, eyes and names and ages, little snatches of existence. I think hard about what I need, about what would be best for Lauren. Women are more nurturing than men, they say. So, a woman, I guess. But it has to be a very special woman who will understand our situation. A couple of them seem nice. This one, thirty-eight, likes surfing. Her eyes are chips of blue, as blue as the water behind her, and kind. Her skin is a little weathered by the sun and the sea. Her hair is the colour of butter, her teeth even and white. She has a happy smile. She looks like she cares about other people. The next one is all the colours of the forest. Brown, green, black. Her clothes are beautiful and cling to her. She works in PR. Her lipstick is like a slick of red oil.

I took the mirrors down some years ago because they upset Lauren. But I don't need a mirror to know how I look. Her words stung me. *Big, fat.* My belly is a rubber sack. It hangs like it has been strapped there. I'm getting bigger all the time. I can't keep track of it. I knock things over, I bounce off doorways. I'm not used to how much space I take up in the world. I don't go out much so my skin is pale. Lauren has this new habit of pulling my hair out by the handful and there are shiny pale patches of skull among the brown. I don't keep razors or scissors in the house and my beard spills down over my chest. For some reason it's a different colour and texture to the hair on my head; red and thick. It looks like a fake beard, like something an actor would wear to play a pirate. My hands and face are covered with scratches, my fingernails bitten to the quick. I haven't had the courage to look at my toenails in some time. The rest of me – well, I try not to think about that at all. There's a smell on me these days, like mush-rooms, earthy. My body is turning on me.

I scroll down. Somewhere in here there must be a friend. The women look out from the screen, skin glowing, eyes bright. They have fun interests and perky jokes on their profiles. I try to think of a way to describe myself. *Single dad,* I type. *Loves the outdoors.* Obeys the gods in the white trees … No. Who am I kidding?

Last week I went to the 7-Eleven for more beer. I felt faint so I sat down on the step outside the store, just for a second. Maybe it was old habit. But I was also just tired. I'm always tired. When I opened my eyes, a guy was putting down quarters by my feet. I gave a growl like a bear and he jumped and ran away. I kept the quarters. I can't imagine being in a room with these women.

I'm about to shut down the laptop when I hear something stir. The hair on the back of my neck stands up slowly. I don't close the computer, because I don't want to be alone in the dark. I have the sensation of eyes moving across my skull. The furniture lies quiet in unfamiliar shadow, in the screen's faint blue light. I can't shrug the feeling that it's watching me.

I have a twist in my belly. Where am I exactly? I get up quietly to look. The ugly blue rug is there, check. On the mantel the ballerina lies as if dead in the ruins of the music box. So I know where I am. But who else is here?

'Lauren?' My voice is a whisper. 'Is that you?' Silence follows. Stupid, I know she isn't here. 'Olivia?' But no, it wouldn't be.

Mommy's hand is cool on my neck, her voice soft in my ear. *You have to move them,* she says. *Don't let anyone find out what you are.*

'I don't want to,' I say to her. Even to myself I sound whiny like Lauren. 'It makes me scared and sad. Don't make me.'

Mommy's skirts rustle, her perfume fades. She is not gone, though – never that. Maybe she is spending a while in one of the memories that lie around the house, in drifts as deep as snow. Maybe she is curled up in the cupboard beneath the sink, where we keep the gallon jug of vinegar. I hate it when I find her there, grinning in the dark, blue organza floating around her face.

The fresh can is so cold it almost sticks to my palm. The hiss and crack as it opens is loud, comforting in the silent house. I keep scrolling down, down, through women's faces but Mommy's voice is singing through my head and it's no good. I go to find the shovel. It's time to go to the glade.

I'm back. Recording this, in case I forget how I hurt my arm. Sometimes I can't remember stuff and then I get scared.

I woke up to a hum. There was something walking on my lips. The morning was filled with clouds of flies, fresh-hatched. It was like a dream but I was awake. Early summer sun shone in the webs of orb spiders stretched between the trees. It made me think of that poem. '"Come into my web," said the spider to the fly.' You are supposed to sympathise with the fly, I think. But no one likes flies, really.

My arm was twisted at a bad angle. I think I fell. There was iron on my tongue. I must have bit down hard on it while I was out. I spat out the blood at the foot of a mountain ash. An offering to the birds, who were calling in the trees overhead. Blood for blood. They won't come to the garden since the murder. Birds tell one another about those things.

I got back home somehow. It was so good to hear the locks clicking into place. Safety.

My memory came back slowly. I had been trying to move the gods. They have laid in their resting place for a year or so now. They really shouldn't stay in one place more than a couple months — after that, they start drawing people to them. So I was on my way to dig them up. But the forest has its own ideas, especially at night. I should have remembered that. The ground shrugged, the roots turned under my feet. Or maybe I was too drunk. Anyway I fell. The last thing I recall is the crunching sound my shoulder made as it met the earth.

My face is scratched and my arm has black flowers all over it. It won't straighten. I made a sling out of an old T-shirt. I don't think it's broken. Getting hurt makes the body and brain weird, even if you don't feel the pain. My thoughts are everywhere right now.

When I went downstairs earlier Olivia couldn't leave me alone. Curious I guess. She licked my face. She has a real taste for blood, that cat.

Olivia

⌒

'Here, kitten.' Ted leans in the doorway, black against the light. Something is wrong with the way he's standing. He kind of falls into the house then turns to lock the door, hands shaking. It takes him a few tries to get all the locks.

'I had a weird one, kitten,' he says. His arm is bent at the wrong angle. He coughs and a little fleck of blood dances through the air. It lands on the orange carpet and rests, a dark globe.

'Got to sleep,' he says and goes upstairs.

I lick the dark spot on the carpet, taking in the faint taste of blood. *Oooooeeeeeeeeee, ooooooeee.* The whine is back.

Today when I leap up to my viewing spot, the tabby is already there, sitting on the unkempt verge by the sidewalk. The sight of her makes my heart burn. I purr and bat the glass with a paw. Her coat is all fluffed up with the cold. She looks twice her size. She pays me no mind, sniffs delicately around the oak tree in the front yard, at a patch of ice on the sidewalk. And then, finally, she looks straight at me. Our eyes hold. It's glorious; I could drown in her. I think she's waiting for me to break the silence. Of course, now I can't think of a single thing to say. So she turns away and it's agony but then it gets worse. That white cat comes strolling along the sidewalk. That big one with the bell on his collar. He speaks to her and tries to rub her cheek with his. I am hissing so hard that I sound like a kettle.

He's trying to get his scent on her, but my tabby knows better. Her back goes up into an arch and she retreats delicately out of sight. I could weep with relief, which quickly turns to sadness because she's gone. Each time the pain is sharp and penny-bright.

Let me tell you a couple of things about white cats. They are sneaky, they are mean, and they are below average intelligence. I am aware that you are not supposed to say stuff like that, that it is not POLITICALLY CORRECT but it's gd true and everyone knows.

I remember being born, of course, I have said that. But my real birth happened later. Do you want to know THE LORD? He wants to know you. Haha, just kidding, he probably doesn't. The LORD is quite choosy, actually. He doesn't show himself to everyone. When He picks you, wow, do you know about it.

It was the day I learned my purpose. All cats have one, just like all cats can turn invisible and read minds (we are particularly good at the last one).

I wasn't always grateful to Ted for rescuing me. For a while, I really didn't want to be an indoor cat. After Ted brought me home I was lonely, and I cried a lot. I missed my little kit sisters who had died at my side in the rain. I missed Mamacat, her big grinding purr and warm sides. We barely had a chance to know one another. I understood that they were dead, because I saw it happen, and it left a sadness in me like a heavy stone. But at the same time, I knew that they were not dead. I was convinced that if I could just get outside I could find them.

I looked and looked for ways to escape, but there weren't any. A couple of times I just ran straight at the door when it opened. I am not a natural planner. Ted scooped me back up in a friendly sort of way. Then we went to the couch and he stroked me or we played with a piece of yarn, until I stopped rowing and crying. 'There are bad people who would hurt you or try to take you away from me,' he said. 'Don't you want to stay here with me, kitten?' And I did. So I would forget about it for a while. But the happiness always passed, and then I was mad at myself for giving in to Ted, and sorrow consumed me once more.

So I had decided that this was the day, it really was. I had it all planned out; but the timing would have to be just right. It all depended on all the teds behaving exactly as they had behaved in the past. I had come to notice that they usually do.

The thing is, I know a lot about what goes on outside, even if it doesn't happen in front of my peephole. I can't see but I can hear and smell. So I know that at a certain time of day, a ted who smells like leather and clean skin goes along the street with his big brouhaha. He usually stops to pet it near our house. I don't know what they look like as I haven't actually seen them with my eyes, but judging by the smell the brouhaha is very ugly. The stink of it is like an old sock full of caca. I always hear the brouhaha writhing and whining, the jingle of its tags as it wriggles its butt. Cats' souls live in their tails and teds keep their selves behind their big wet eyes. But brouhahas keep their deepest feelings in their butts.

The ted talks to it like it can understand. 'Hey, Champ. You a good boy? Yes, yes you are, yes you are, oh yes, you big dumb lunk.' Only, often he doesn't say lunk. I hear the slopping of the brouhaha's tongue, smell the love coming out of its skin. This just proves the ted's point. Brouhahas really are big dumb ahem-ahems. Champ wants nothing more than to kill me. The old knowledge told me, the kind that is in our bodies. Teds don't have a lot of that knowledge left but cats have tons.

I waited until I had the timings off by heart. Ted goes to get candy and beer at a certain time each day. As he's coming up the steps, the brouhaha and the ted are sometimes passing in front of the house. Sometimes the ted says hi, and Ted kind of grunts back.

Today was the day and my heart was whirring like a hummingbird, but I knew it was going to work, I just knew it.

At this point, I was not yet very tall. I could still walk right under the couch, and the tips of my ears would not even graze the underside. So I hid myself in the umbrella stand in the hall. What a useless thing! How many umbrellas does Ted think he has? Anyway it is a good place to hide.

I heard Ted's footfall, the tinkle and crack of tiny pieces of the world breaking beneath his boot. He had started early, I could tell. This was also good. Ted would be slow. (There is a shuffling rhythm to his walk when he drinks. It is almost like a very simple dance – a square dance, maybe.) I crouched, my tail lashed. The cord stretched out in the air behind me. It was a burnt shade of orange that day, and it crackled like fire in a hearth as I moved.

I coiled myself to spring. Ted sang something under his breath and the keys clicked in the various locks. I could smell the outside, its earthy glow. I could smell the brouhaha, its breath like old broken eggs. A line of light broke the dark of the hall as the door began to open. I ran for it as hard as my small paws would carry me. My plan was to run for the oak tree in the front yard, and after that, well. I would be free.

I came skidding to a halt in the doorway, drowned in blinding white. I couldn't see anything at all. The world was a narrow crack of agonising light. I had lived most of my life in the dim of the house, I realised. My eyes couldn't handle the sun. I rowed and closed them tight. I felt strange freezing air touch my nose. Maybe I could do this with my eyes shut?

The door was opening wider. The air must have carried my scent out into the world; the big brouhaha exploded into a roar. I smelled the excitement coming from him, the anticipation of death. I heard the manic jingle of tags. I guessed the brouhaha was rearing and springing up the steps. Everything slowed, almost to a stop. In the blinding white fire I felt my death approach.

This was a terrible plan, I realised. I could never make it to the tree. I couldn't even open my eyes to see the tree. The brouhaha was close, I smelled his mouth, open like a long dirty cave, his rotten teeth. I felt a burning circle of fire spread around my neck. It was the cord, sizzling with heat. The cord burned and pulled me deep into the safe shadows of the house, as quick as a whiplash. I heard Ted slam the door closed.

I opened my eyes. I was inside again — safe. Outside, Ted was yelling. The brouhaha keened and whuffed, pressing his face to the bottom of the door. His stink drifted under, it was everywhere. I was horrified at myself. How could I have thought this was a good idea? I felt how tiny I was, each slender bone in my body, the delicacy of all my veins and fur and the beauty of my eyes. How could I have thought to risk all that in a world where a brouhaha could eat me in one bite?

'Hey,' Ted shouted. 'Get your dog under control.' He was angry. You don't want to mess with Ted when he's angry.

The barking and stink receded somewhat. The ted must have pulled his brouhaha away.

'My daughter's inside,' Ted said. 'That really scared her. You ought to be more careful.'

'Sorry,' the ted said. 'He just likes to play.'

'Keep him on a leash,' Ted said.

The scent of the brouhaha receded, blending with the distant scent of the forest. Then it was gone. Ted came in quickly. The locks went thunk, thunk, thunk. I was so glad to hear them.

'Poor kitten,' he said. 'Scary for you.'

I climbed into Ted's hands. I felt the fiery cord expand and enclose us in a blazing womb of light.

'That's why you have to stay indoors,' he said. 'It's dangerous out there.'

I'm sorry, I said to Ted. I didn't know.

He couldn't understand me, of course. I thought it was important to say it anyway. Warmth glowed around us. We were in a ball of warm yellow fire.

It was then that I saw Him. There was a third there with us, at the heart of the flame. He didn't look like anything I knew. He looked like everything. His face changed each moment. He looked like a yellow-beaked hawk, and then a red maple leaf, then a mosquito. I knew that my face was in there, too, somewhere among the many. I did not want to see it. I understood that would be the final thing. As I draw my last breath He will show Himself, and the face He wears will be mine.

Your place is here, *the LORD said to me*. I have saved you for a special purpose. You have to help one another, you and he.

I understand, *I said. It makes perfect sense. Ted does need a lot of help. He is such a mess.*

We have been a good team since then. We keep each other safe. I am pretty hungry now, so I will stop.

Dee

The rich man's eyes are deep and blue. 'Delilah,' he says. 'Good to meet you at last.' His hair is dazzling white, drawn into a low ponytail; his loose pants and shirt are linen. His deck sits high in the treetops, encircling the beautiful house, which is made of deep red cedar and glass. It is just the kind of place Dee would like to live. The air smells of sun on living green, mingling with the clean aroma of the lemonade in the jug beside them. Sprigs of mint float on its surface. The ice cubes make beautiful high sounds. His housekeeper brought it without a word the moment they sat down.

The yellow envelope sits on the table beside the lemonade. A drop of condensation has made its way down the jug's cold sides, has darkened the corner with moisture. Dee can't take her eyes off it, can't think about anything else. What if the contents are damaged?

'It is the only copy that I know of,' he says peacefully, following her gaze. 'The man who took it died of a heart attack some years ago. The newspaper is small, local, they don't keep records. So it may be the only copy in existence.' He doesn't move the envelope away from the water, and Dee forces herself not to reach for it.

'I'll take a look and be on my way,' she says. 'I've taken up enough of your day.'

He shakes his head. 'You can keep it. Take it with you. You will want a private moment.'

'Thank you,' she says, dazed. 'I mean – thank you.'

He says, 'I trust that you will not repeat the Oregon incident. You got carried away there. You were lucky to avoid jail.'

Dee winces. Of course, that is the kind of thing he would know about. The man from Oregon, who had been at the lake that day. Tired Karen let slip his details to Dee, the location of his hunting cabin.

Dee has the statistics by heart. The kind of person who took Lulu is an average of twenty-seven years old, unmarried. He is unemployed or works in unskilled labour. He is socially marginal. He is likely to have arrest records for violent crime. The primary motivation for stranger child abduction is— Dee does not allow herself to finish that thought. Over the years, she has acquired the art of making her brain go perfectly blank at will.

In all respects the man from Oregon was a perfect fit. Dee could not have known that he was miles away in Hoquiam with a flat tyre when Lulu went. That there were nine witnesses to it. The man did not press charges. But Karen was distant, after that.

'How much is it?' Dee asks, looking into the rich man's flat blue eyes.

The man watches her watch him. He slowly pours a glass of lemonade with a shaking hand. His frailty is a performance. His forearms are corded with muscle.

'Not money,' he says. 'I want something else.'

Her flesh begins to walk on her bones.

'No, no.' He smiles, indulgent. 'It's very simple. You know about my hobby. I collect all sorts of curios. But the meat of the collection, the heart of it, I keep in this house. I want you to look. Walk through it, just once.'

Dee says, 'I can pay you. Money.'

'Not enough,' he says gently. 'Be reasonable.'

She looks at the view over the trees, at his immaculate clothes, sees his assurance, built with money, and knows that he is right. She doesn't ask why she should trust him, or how she can be sure that the envelope contains what he says it contains. They are past such things.

She nods because she does not have a choice.

He leads her down into the centre of the house. At the bottom of the stairs he unlocks a door made of something that looks like, but surely cannot be, granite. Dee shivers. Perhaps he will lock the door behind her and leave her in there.

A long gallery stretches ahead running the length of the house. There are no windows. The air is cool, controlled to a fraction of a degree. Display cases and framed photographs line the walls, each lit by a single low spotlight. This is his collection; the museum, he calls it. She has heard of it. It is well known, if your interests lie in that direction. The man obtains things that most people can't. Things that no one should see. He collects the artefacts of death. Photographs, vials of blood stolen from evidence, letters in spiky Victorian copperplate, pieces of the unclaimed dead, the pieces the killer did not have time to eat before he was caught.

The room is a corridor of Dee's nightmares. Each object is a relic of something terrible that could have been done to Lulu. Dee glances at the black-and-white image on the wall to her left. She quickly looks away again.

'You must look,' he says. 'That's the deal.' He knows precisely what she feels. She can hear it in his voice.

Dee walks down the gallery. She looks at each display for exactly three seconds before moving on. She makes her mind white static. He walks beside her, intimately close. His skin exudes a faint odour of tin. He doesn't seem to breathe.

When Dee reaches the end of the dim corridor, she turns to him and holds out her hand. For a moment he is motionless, and his still blue gaze crawls all over her, head to foot. She understands that he is collecting her, and the moment. Not every memento can be housed in a glass case. She thinks, *It's going to happen now. I'm going to throw up.* Then he gives a little nod and puts the envelope into her hand.

The light and the air are blinding. She wants to weep with gratitude at the sight of trees. But she refuses to give him anything else.

'Drive safe,' he says, and goes back into his wooden palace. He has taken what he wanted and she holds no more interest. She goes to her car slowly, puts the envelope casually on the passenger seat beside her. She forces herself to drive away through the trees at a leisurely pace. He might still be watching. Dee's foot twitches on the gas, her breath comes fast.

As she turns out of the long forested drive, onto the road, she puts her foot down. The engine screams.

She lets the black ribbon of road take her on and on, until the forest changes to meadows and horses and barns, and they in turn give way to one-storey strip malls. Gasoline hangs heavy on the air. When she has put miles and miles between her and those freezing blue eyes she pulls into a rest stop. She lays her head on the steering wheel and breathes in ragged gasps. Vast trucks roar by, shaking the little car with their passage. She is grateful to them for covering the sounds she makes.

At length her breathing steadies somewhat. Dee sits up. It is time to find out what she has bought. She suppresses a swell of nausea, opens the envelope and draws out the photograph.

There it is, the familiar image, lacking only the caption: SUS-PECT'S HOUSE SEARCHED. And there he is, the suspect, shading his eyes against the sun. Dee knows this picture. She has asked Karen about it more than once.

This man had an alibi, tired Karen told Dee, and the search of his house turned up nothing. They had to move on with other lines of enquiry.

'But the people who saw him outside the grocery store might have been wrong,' Dee said. 'They were used to seeing him there, expected it. You know, they might fill in the blank place on the sidewalk with a familiar sight, even if he wasn't actually there.' Dee understands this, better than most.

'There's security tape,' Karen said.

'For the whole time?' Dee asked. 'Karen, for the whole afternoon?' Karen didn't answer but she didn't need to. Dee could see the *no* in the hunch of her shoulders. That was when Karen still gave Dee information, before the incident with the man from Oregon.

Karen would be concerned if she knew what Dee now holds in her hands. The photograph has not been cropped, as it was for publication in the newspaper. Perhaps it is the photographer's own print.

In this picture the view opens out, showing the hidden edges of the scene. Dee's heart pounds. She forces herself not to hurry, to look at each thing one by one; see it, know it, understand it.

There are trees in the distance behind the house. Thick, Pacific North West growth, clustering in, overrunning itself. There is a woman in a hat, back turned, walking away along the sidewalk, dragging a hairy terrier on a leash. There are small, pale, curious faces at the window of a farther house. Children.

Dee sees the most important thing last, as if her mind cannot absorb a success after so many years of trudging failure. The sign on the corner is in plain view, and can be easily read. Needless Street.

Dee understands for the first time why people faint and how it happens; like a white light going off in her brain, a flash, followed by a dark shock. She now knows where the suspect lived, maybe even still lives. She breathes shallow and fast. That would be enough, but it is not only that.

'We were there that day,' Dee whispers. 'Dad took a wrong turn.' Her mouth fills with the taste of memory and bubble-gum. She must have chewed thirty pieces on that long-ago ride. Dad was driving to the lake but he missed an exit and they ended up wandering, lost, through the endless grey suburbs that hemmed the forest. Then the rows of one-storeys thinned out and gave way to peeling Victorian houses, and the rank wild scent of the woods grew strong. These were streets that went nowhere. She recalls driving past that sign and thinking, *Yes, this craphole is totally needless.* The street was a dead end, she recalls. Dad wiped his brow and swore under his breath, and they turned around and retraced their steps.

They found Highway 101 again soon after, and the name of the street receded into the depths of Dee's mind, to be shelved with other useless information – what colour the attendant's uniform had been when they stopped for gas, who liked her best at school, who played bass in that band.

For a moment Dee considers whether this could be coincidence. But she rejects this idea with a strong mental shove. It must be connected, somehow. It must.

Did the suspect see them driving in their slow lost circles? Did he glimpse Lulu's bored face at the window, and did he then follow them to the lake? Did Dad even speak to him? Maybe he stopped to ask the suspect for directions. The suspect wouldn't have needed to follow, then. He would have known their destination, could have gone straight to the lake. Dee tries and tries to remember where Dad pulled over. But just as certain parts of that day are branded on her, charred into her flesh, others are soft and out of focus. It seemed like just another dead-end road. She and Lulu were kids; bored and hot. They didn't know that these were the last few moments of peace before lightning cracked open the world and everything changed for ever.

Reason dictates that Dee tell the police. She should call tired

Karen, who is still in charge of the case. Lulu is a missing person. No body has been found. (There was a time when Dee would have thought that missing was better than dead, but the long years have taught her better.)

'This is not supposed to happen,' Karen said once to Dee. 'Most of us spend our whole career without dealing with a stranger child abduction. It wears you thin, in ways you can't predict. Sometimes I think, why here? Why me?'

Dee said, 'I have a question. Why not do your job?' Karen went red.

'Lulu wasn't the first to disappear,' Dee said. 'I've looked into it. You've got a real problem around that lake.' Maybe that was when it really went sour between them. Sour or not, Dee should call her right away.

She won't. This is a particular gift, just for her. And she feels the silky-deep stirring of anger. If the police hadn't kept her out of everything maybe she would have remembered the street name and made the connection years ago. Wasted, wasted time.

The photograph has one more secret to yield. Dee peers hard at the suspect's shirt. Close to, it gets grainy and her eyes protest. But she can see writing there, embroidered across the breast pocket. They must have blurred it out for the newspaper. Dee can make out a name. Ed or maybe Ted, Banner something.

It feels like striking the last blow in a long, long fight. She has a name or part of one, and a street. Dee finds that she is crying, which doesn't make sense, because she is filled with fierce certainty. Just for a moment, for one beat of her heart, Dee feels Lulu beside her. The car fills with the scent of warm skin, suntan lotion. A soft, plump cheek brushes against hers. Dee catches the clean smell of her sister's hair, and the sugar on her breath.

'I'm coming,' Dee tells her.

Ted

It's the right day, so I go to see the bug man in the morning. I found him in the want ads online. He doesn't cost as much as the regular ones, so I can afford one session every two weeks. My appointment is always very early, before anyone else is awake — when no one else wants to go, I guess. I enjoy my visits to him. I tell him about Olivia, and how much I love her, and about TV I've watched and candy I've eaten and the birds in the dawn. I even talk about Mommy and Daddy sometimes. Not too much. I don't talk about the situation with Lauren or the gods, of course. Each time, I slip in real questions among the dumb stuff. I am slowly working my way up to the big one. I'll ask it soon. Things with Lauren are getting worse.

Sometimes talking to him even seems to help. Anyway he prescribes the pills, which definitely help.

It is a forty-five-minute walk, which I manage OK. It is not quite raining but a warm rotten mist hangs in the air. Headlights throw a musty sheen on the wet road and earthworms writhe pink and gleaming on the sidewalk.

The bug man's office is in a building that looks like a pile of children's blocks, carelessly stacked. The waiting room is empty and I settle happily on a chair. I like this kind of place, where you're in between one thing and another. Hallways, waiting rooms, lobbies and so on; rooms where nothing is actually supposed to happen. It relieves a lot of pressure and lets me think.

The air smells strongly of cleaning products, a chemical impression of a flowering meadow. At some point in the future, I guess, almost no one will know what real meadow smells like. Maybe by then there won't be any real meadows left and they'll have to make flowers in labs. Then of course they'll engineer them to smell like cleaning products, because they'll think that's right, and it will all go in a circle. These are the kinds of interesting thoughts I have while in waiting rooms and at crosswalks or standing in line at the grocery store.

The bug man appears and shows me in, adjusting his tie. I think I make him nervous. It's my size. He hides it well most of the time. He has a belly like a little round scatter cushion, the kind Mommy liked so much. His hair is sparse and blonde. Behind the glasses his eyes are blue and almost perfectly round.

Obviously I can't recall his name. He looks like a friendly little shield bug, or a stag beetle. So the bug man is how I think of him.

The office is pale, pastel, containing far more chairs than could ever be needed in here. They're all different sizes, shapes and colours. They put me in an agony of indecision. I wonder, is this the bug man's way of judging my mood? Sometimes I try to think like Lauren, and guess which chair she would pick. She'd probably just throw them around the place.

I choose a dented, metal fold-out. I hope this severe choice will show him that I am serious about my progress.

'You've lost some more hair,' the bug man says mildly.

'I think my cat pulls it out at night.'

'And your left arm looks badly bruised. What's up with that?'

I should have worn long sleeves, I wasn't thinking.

'I was out on a date,' I say. 'She shut the car door on my arm by accident.' I haven't actually been on a date yet, but I feel like it's more likely to happen if I say the words, like a spell that will force me to do it.

'That's unfortunate,' he says. 'Apart from that, did you feel the date went well?'

'Oh, yes,' I say. 'I had a great time. You know, I've been watching this new TV show. It's about a man who kills people, but only if they deserve it. Bad people, in other words.'

'What do you think appeals to you about this show?'

'It doesn't appeal to me,' I say. 'I think it's nonsense. You can't tell what people are like from what they do. You can do a bad thing even though you're not a bad person. Bad people could do good things accidentally. You can't really know, is my point.' I can see him drawing breath to ask me a question so I hurry on. 'And there was this other TV show where a man killed lots of people, but then he hurt his head in an accident, and when he woke up he thought it was ten years earlier. He didn't remember killing the people, or the new kinds of cellphone or his wife. He was a different person to the one who killed the women. So was it still his fault, even when it was out of his control?'

'Do you feel that your actions are sometimes out of your control?'

Careful, I think.

'And there's this other show,' I say, 'about a talking dog. That seems much more realistic to me, in a way, than being able to tell good people from bad. My cat can't actually speak – I admit that. But I always know what she wants. It's just as good as talking.'

'Your cat means a lot to you,' the bug man says.

'She's my best friend,' I say, which might be the first true thing I've said to him in the six months that I've been coming here. A silence falls, not uncomfortable. He writes on his yellow legal pad but it must be about groceries or something, because, really, I'm not giving him anything.

'But I am worried about her.' He glances up. 'I think she's …' I hesitate. 'I think my cat is, what would you say? Homosexual. Gay. I think my cat is attracted to female cats.'

'What makes you say that?'

'There's this other cat she watches, out the window. She watches her all the time. She loves her, I can just tell. My mother would be very upset if she knew I had a homosexual cat. She had very strong feelings about it.' The scent of vinegar fills the air for a moment and I think I might throw up. I didn't mean to say any of that.

'Do you think your cat——?'

'I can't talk about that any more,' I say.

'Well——'

'No,' I say. 'No, no, no, no, NO.'

'All right,' he says. 'How is your daughter?'

I wince. I mentioned Lauren once in passing, by accident. It was a big mistake because he has never let it go since. 'She's been spending a lot of time at school,' I say. 'I haven't seen her too much.'

'You know, Ted, this session is for you. It's private. You can say anything here. Some people feel it's the only place they can really express themselves. In our daily lives can be difficult to say what we think or feel to those closest to us. That is a very isolating experience. It can be lonely, keeping secrets. That's why it's important to have somewhere safe, like this. You can say anything to me.'

'Well,' I say. 'There are parts of my life I'd like to share with someone, one day. Not you, but someone.'

He raises his eyebrows.

'I was watching monster trucks on TV last night, and I was thinking, *Monster trucks are great. They're big and loud and fun. It would be so great if I could meet someone who has a love of big trucks, one day.*'

'That's a good goal.' His eyes are glazing over. They look like two blue marbles.

For weeks I store up my most boring thoughts to tell the bug man. It's hard work sometimes, thinking of enough things to fill an hour. But that last one just came to me spontaneously.

'In my book,' he says, 'I talk about how dissociation can actually *protect* us ...'

It's safe to tune out now, so I do. The bug man likes to talk about his book. It's not published or anything. I don't think it's even finished. He has been writing it since I've known him. We all have something that we care about more than anything else, I guess. For me it's Lauren and Olivia. For the bug man it's his never-ending book.

At the end of the hour he hands me a brown paper bag, just like a lunch bag a kid takes to school. I know there are four boxes of pills in there and it makes me feel a lot better.

What I'm doing with the bug man is pretty smart, I have to say. I got the idea some time ago, not long after Little Girl With Popsicle.

Lauren had been running a low-grade fever for some days. I wanted to get her antibiotics but I didn't know how. A doctor would never understand our situation. I hoped maybe she would get better on her own, but days went by and she didn't. In fact she got worse. I looked on the internet and I found a free clinic on the far side of town.

'How do you feel?' I asked Lauren. 'Tell me exactly.'

'I'm hot,' she said. 'There are bugs crawling on my skin. I can't think. All I want to do is sleep. Even talking to you makes me tired.' There was a little rasp in her voice. I listened very carefully to everything she said. I wrote it down and put the paper in my pocket.

After dark I walked into the city to the free clinic.

It took them a couple hours to see me but I didn't mind. The waiting room was bare and smelled somewhat like urine. But it was quiet. I settled in for some time with my thoughts. As I have said, I do some of my best thinking in waiting rooms.

When the angry lady called my name I took the note out of my pocket. I read it three times. I hoped I could remember it all. Then I went to a cubicle with a tired doctor in it. He asked me about my symptoms. I put a little rasp into my voice and spoke slowly. 'I'm hot,' I said. 'There are bugs crawling on my skin. I can't think. All I want to do is sleep. Even talking to you makes me tired.' I repeated what Lauren had said. I was word perfect. And it worked! He prescribed me antibiotics and bed rest. I went to the little pharmacy next door and filled the prescription. I was so relieved I almost danced in the aisles. I kept my head up as I walked back – I let myself watch the world around me. I saw a pretty neon sign with a flower on it, a stall selling fruit shaped like stars. I saw a woman with a tiny black dog in a big red handbag. I kept a tight hold of the paper bag with the antibiotics in it.

When I reached my street I was very tired. I had walked ten miles or more, to the clinic and back. I gave Lauren the antibiotics by hiding them in her food. She got better quickly after that. My plan worked!

When things with Lauren got bad I knew I had to get some answers. Not about her body but her mind. So that's how I got the idea to go to the bug man and pretend to talk about myself, while really asking him questions about Lauren. It's just like when I got the antibiotics except this time the medicine is information.

I come back. I am on my street. The house in front of me is yellow with green trim. I am in front of the Chihuahua lady's house again, and that same feeling is in me too, like I almost know something. It's like ants in my brain, marching with their little feet.

I see that there is something stapled to the telephone pole. I go to look, because it is usually a missing cat. Cats can seem very capable and independent, but they do need our help.

It is not a cat this time. One face is repeated in blurred photo-copy into the distance, pole after pole. It takes me a moment before I am sure. She looks much younger, sure, and there's no dog with her, but it's the Chihuahua lady. In the picture she is leaning against a wall in a sunny place, smiling. She looks happy.

The last time there were flyers on the telephone poles it was Little Girl With Popsicle.

Lauren is waiting when I get in.

'Where have you been?' She is breathing too fast.

'Calm down, kitten. You might pass out.' It has happened before.

'You are seeing a lady,' she screams. 'You're going to leave me.' She seizes my hand between her sharp teeth and bites.

Eventually I get her to sleep. I try to watch monster trucks but I am exhausted by the day. Feelings are hard.

I wake in the night-time, sudden and breathless. I feel the dark on my skin like a touch. The record player is supposed to be on constant repeat but it's old now or maybe I did something wrong. In the silence, I can hear Lauren crawling across the floor. Her sharp little teeth click.

'You bad man,' she whispers. 'Out, out, out.'

I try to soothe her and settle her again. She cries out and bites my hand again, this time drawing blood. She fights me, crying, all night.

I say, 'Even if I were seeing someone, I would still love you best.'

I know immediately that was the wrong thing to say.

'You are! You are!' Lauren scratches and fights until morning leaks grey into the room.

I meet the day tired and bruised. Lauren sleeps late. I use the time to update the diary. This is a habit Mommy instilled in me.

One day a week, she examined the house from top to bottom. The examination must be made twice, she was very clear about that, because of human error. She missed nothing. Each speck of dust, each spider, each cracked tile. She recorded everything in the book. Then she gave the book to my daddy so he could fix it during the week. She called it her *diary of broken things*. Her English was very nearly perfect; it was always a surprise when she missed the shade of a word's meaning. Daddy and I never corrected her.

So each Saturday morning after dawn, I take the book around the house. I do it again in the evening just before dusk. I do one circuit around the boundary of the property to make sure the fence is all good and so on, and then I come in for a tighter circle, to check the house for damage – loose nails, rat and snake holes, signs of termites, that kind of thing. It's not complicated but, like I said, it's important.

The three locks on the back door open loudly. *Thunk, thunk, thunk.* I wait. I never know what will wake Lauren. But she sleeps on. The day is blinding, the earth baked hard underfoot, cracked as old skin. The feeders hang empty. No breeze moves in the trees, each leaf is still and silent in the rotten heat. It is as if death has put its finger on the street and pinned it down. I lock the door again behind me and go to the tool shed around the side of the house.

In the lean-to it's cool and dim, filled with the scent of rust and oil. It is the scent of all tool sheds, everywhere. I must be careful – scent is a highway for memory. Too late; in a shadowed corner of the lean-to Daddy stands tall and silent. He reaches for a box of screws, and the brown bottle behind it. Little Teddy tugs at his hand. He wants to get in the car and go but Daddy has to deal with Mommy first.

I get the tools quickly and go, blinking with relief in the burning sun. I lock the tool shed. *You stay in there, Daddy. You too, Little Teddy. There is no place for you out here.*

I write everything in the book very clearly. It's not the same book, obviously. I keep my diary of broken things in an old textbook of Lauren's. I write on top of the maps.

Mouse in kitchen is back, I write carefully in the pale blue sea off the coast of Papua New Guinea. *Bathroom sink – faucet drips. Bible fell off table again?!?!? Why? Table legs uneven?!?!?!*

And so on. The hinges on the bedroom door are squeaking; they need oil. A sheet of plywood on one of the living-room windows is loose and needs nailing down. A couple shingles have come off the roof. It's raccoons; they're bad for shingle. But I like their small, clever black hands.

I do what I can now, and the rest I'll get to this week. I have to be both Mommy and Daddy for Lauren. I like repairing the house, fixing holes as if I'm making it watertight. Nothing gets in or out without my permission.

The chocolate-chip pancakes are ready just as Lauren is waking. Personally I find pancakes a waste of time, like eating pieces of hot washcloth. But she loves them.

I say, 'Wash up first. I've been working outside and you've been pedalling that bicycle with your hands.' She's so smart. She lies on her tummy on the seat and her arms go a-whirring. Lauren doesn't let anything get in her way.

'It's easier with my hands,' she says.

I kiss her. 'I know. And you go so fast, these days.'

We wash our hands at the kitchen sink, getting right under the nails with the brush.

Lauren is quiet as she eats. Yesterday was bad; she exhausted herself with anger. She goes back tomorrow and the prospect of her absence makes us both very gloomy. 'We can do anything you like today,' I say without thinking.

Her attention sharpens. 'I want to go camping.'

I feel the hot stroke of helplessness. We can't go camping. Lauren *knows* that. Why does she always have to push me? Always tugging, nagging like one of those little dogs at the heels of a bull. No wonder I get mad.

But sorrow tugs at me too. It is unfair. So many kids get to go to the woods and make fires and camp and so on. It's not even special for them. Maybe all the stuff with the Murderer has made me sad, maybe it's because I'm tired of the house, too, but I say, 'Sure. Let's go camping. We leave at dusk.'

'Really? Truly, Dad?'

'Sure,' I say. 'I said anything you like, right?'

Happiness shines out of her.

I put some supplies in a backpack. Flashlight, blanket, tarpaulin, energy bars, bottled water, toilet paper. Behind me I hear the dry sound of skirts rustling. Oh no. I squeeze my eyes closed really tight.

Her hand is like cold clay on the back of my neck. *Don't let anyone see who you are,* Mommy says.

'I won't,' I say. 'I just want to give Lauren a little treat. Only this once, I swear. I'll make sure she never wants to go again.'

You need to move them.

The sun falls slowly into the treeline. I watch through the western peephole that faces the forest. When the light is almost gone I shoulder the backpack and turn out the lights.

'Time to go,' I say. 'Pens and crayons, please.'

She counts them into my hand one by one, and I put them away. They are all accounted for.

'Do you need a drink of water before we go? Bathroom? Last chance.'

She shakes her head. I can almost see the excitement coming off her like a series of little explosions.

'You have to let me carry you.' The pink bicycle will be useless on the forest floor.

She says, 'Whatever.'

We go out the back door and I lock it after us. I check the street carefully before we come out from the shadow of the house. The road is empty. Midges dance around the buzzing yellow street-light. The neighbouring house stares with its newsprint eyes. Further down the block it's a different story. Sashes are pulled up, spilling noise and warm light. I catch the distant tone of a piano, the faint scent of pork chops cooking.

'We could go knock on a door,' Lauren says. 'Say hi. Maybe they'd ask us to stay for supper.'

'I thought you wanted to go camping?' I say. 'Come on, kitten.'

We turn away to where the trees are outlined against the purple sky. We duck through the wooden gate and here we are, among them. The flashlight casts a wide bloodless beam on the trail.

All signs of the city are soon behind us. We are enclosed by the forest. It is waking. The dark air is filled with hoots, clicks and song. Frogs, cicadas, bats. Lauren shivers and I feel her wonder. I love having her so close to me. I can't recall the last time she let me carry her like this without a fight. She hates to be helpless.

'What do you do if someone comes by?' I ask her again.

'I stay quiet and let you do the talking,' she replies. 'What's that stink?'

'Skunk,' I say. The animal wanders alongside us on the path for a time, curious, perhaps. Then it ambles off into the wooded dark and the scent fades.

We don't go far, about a mile. A couple hundred feet off the path there's the clearing. It's hidden by boulders and thick scrub and you have to know how to find it. I know the way well. This is where the gods live.

The scent of cedar and wild thyme is in the air, as strong as wine. But the trees that circle the clearing aren't cedar or fir. They are pale slender ghosts.

'Dad,' Lauren says in a whisper. 'Why are the trees white?'

'They're called paper birch trees,' I say. 'Or white birch. Look.' I peel a sliver of bark from a trunk and show it to her. She strokes its whispering surface. I don't tell her their true name, which is *bone trees*.

I find the spot I want in the north-west corner, where I spread the groundsheet over the earth, still warm from the day. We sit. I make her drink some water, eat an energy bar. Overhead, the branches show through the stars. Lauren is quiet. I know she feels them. The gods.

'This is nice,' I say. 'You and me together. It reminds me of when you were little. Those were wonderful times.'

'I don't remember it like that,' she says. I feel a spurt of frustration. She is always pushing me away. But I stay calm.

'I love you more than anyone else in the world,' I tell her. And I mean it. Lauren is special. I never showed any of the others the clearing. 'All I want is to keep you safe.'

She says, 'Dad, I can't live like this any more. Sometimes I don't want to live at all.'

When I can breathe again I say, in as regular a tone as I can manage, 'I'll tell you a secret, kitten. Everyone feels like that sometimes. Sometimes things get bad, and you can't see a future ahead. It's all cloudy, like the sky on a rainy day. But life moves very fast. Things never stay the same for ever, even the bad things. The clouds will blow away. They always do, I promise.'

'But I'm not like everyone else,' Lauren says. Her voice is so sharp it could slice me. 'Most people could have walked here on their own. I can't. That's not going to change or *blow away*. That's going to stay the same for ever. Right, Ted?'

I wince. There's no answer to this. I hate it when she calls me Ted. 'Let's just watch the stars, kitten.'

'You have to let me do stuff, Dad,' she says. 'You have to let me grow up.'

'Lauren,' I say, anger rising. 'That's not fair. I know you think you're all mature. But you still need looking after. Remember what happened at the mall?'

'That was years ago. It's different now. Look, we're outside and I'm being really good.'

She feels the first one soon after. 'Something bit me,' she says. Her voice has only surprise in it. No fear yet.

I am being stung too, on my leg, twice in quick succession. I don't feel it, of course, but I watch the flesh rise into red lumps. They're crawling all over us now. Lauren begins to scream. 'What are they? Oh, God, Dad, what's happening?'

'They're fire ants,' I say. 'We must be sitting on a nest.'

'Get them off,' she says. 'It hurts, get them off me!'

I grab the backpack and carry her through the trees at a run. The roots and brambles clutch my feet. When we reach the path I stop and brush us both down vigorously. I pour water over our exposed areas.

'Did any of them get inside your clothes?' I ask.

'No,' she says, 'I don't think so.' Her voice is full of tears. 'Can we go home, Dad?'

'Of course, my kitten.' I hold her tight all the way back. No more 'Ted', I notice.

She says, 'It was a dumb idea, camping. Thanks for getting us out of there.'

I say, 'That's my job.'

Lauren, tired out by it all, is unconscious before we reach the house. I put lotion on our bites, touching her sleeping skin with care. A line of vivid red pustules runs up her calf and into the crook of her knee, but that's it. We ran before any real damage was done. The young feel pain intensely, I think, because they don't know yet how deep it can go.

Morning, and it's time to say goodbye. Lauren clings. 'I love you, Dad.' Her breath is wet in my beard. 'I don't want to go.'

'I know.' I can taste her tears on my lips. Feeling rises like an ocean swell. It's so strong I have to close my eyes. 'I'll see you next week,' I say. 'Don't worry, kitten. You be good now. That will make the time go quickly and you'll be back before you know it.'

Each one of her sobs feels like I'm being hit with a wrench.

I sit on the couch and listen to the music and feel just miserable. After a time I feel the lightest touch of whiskers against the back of my hand. A silken head pushes into my palm.

Olivia has come out of hiding and she knows that I need her.

I walk out to the woods with a gallon jug of pyrethrin. The forest is different during the day. Scattered light lies on the ground like handfuls of thrown grain. A deer pokes its face out from the foliage, dark eyes wide, then flees. I soon see why, as I pass the orange-juice-hair man with his dog. The dog grins at me like always. It remembers that time Olivia tried to get out. Then I overtake a family hiking in matching red jackets. I think they're fighting. The children's faces are small and serious; the dad looks tired. The mother strides ahead as if she's alone.

I walk on past the place where I would normally leave the path for the clearing, and then sit on a stump to wait. They pass in silence. The father nods at me. They are definitely fighting. Families are complicated.

When their red jackets have vanished into the sunlit trees I circle back to the clearing. The groundsheet is still there. It lies wrinkled on the leaf mulch like the skin of a dead monster. Ants march busily across. It can't stay here. It might draw attention to this place. I take a long stick and poke the groundsheet together, into a kind of pile. Then I hook it up and drop it into the trash bag I brought with me.

I follow the marching trail of ants back to the main entrances to their nest. They're almost translucent in the sunlight, harmless-looking little things. You'd never think they could cause such pain. 'I'm sorry,' I say. I pour the pyrethrin over the nest, into the holes, and into the trash bag containing the groundsheet.

I didn't know whether the fire ant nest would still be here, in the north-west corner. But I thought it probably would. They're territorial creatures. It was difficult for me to listen to Lauren's cries, to hear her pain as they stung her. But it was necessary – she has to learn.

I have to admit that Lauren is much better, these days. There have been no repeats of that time at the mall.

I stand in the centre of the glade, which is also the centre of the pattern. A pool of sunlight falls there. I greet the gods and feel their power. They reach out from where they lie beneath the forest floor. It's like being tugged in different directions by slender threads. Mommy is right. As soon as my arm is better I have to find them a new home. People are beginning to feel them. That family got way too close.

As I climb my front steps I notice that they're bare. The wind has blown them clear of leaves and such. That won't do. If people come up to the house I need to hear it. What I do is, I crush a couple of Christmas ornaments and sprinkle them over the steps. This produces a crisp high tinkle that gives me plenty of warning of approaching visitors. It's not dangerous. People wear shoes. I mean, I know I went out in my bare feet the other day but most people don't. That's just a fact.

As I'm scattering the broken shards of fibreglass I catch movement at the corner of my eye. I turn to look, hoping I'm wrong. But I'm not. The newspaper is gone from one of the downstairs windows in the abandoned house next door. As I watch, a pale hand pulls more yellowing newsprint away, leaving the window unlidded like a dark deep eye. The sash is pushed up and a business-like hand dumps a panful of dust out of the window. Then there comes the sound of vigorous sweeping.

I go into my house and lock the front door behind me. I put my eye to the peephole that faces east, towards the vacant house. Overgrown timothy grass nods against the glass, but I still have a good enough view. I watch as a white truck pulls up. It says *EZ Moving* in orange letters on the side. A woman comes out the front door, lopes down the steps in easy strides and unhooks the gate at the back of the truck. She has a fixed look around her mouth. It makes her seem older than she probably is. She doesn't look like she sleeps much. A man in a brown uniform gets out of the driver's side of the truck. Together they begin to unload. Boxes, lamps, a toaster. An easy chair. Not much stuff.

The woman looks towards me, where I lie in wait. Her eyes seem to pierce through the screen of timothy into the dark room where I sit. I duck even though there is no way she can see me. This is very bad. People have eyes to look and ears to listen, and women look and listen more carefully than men.

I am so upset I have to go to the kitchen and make bullshots. I'm sad to say I didn't invent these. You can probably find the recipe but I've made some little changes of my own so I'll record this.

After a long hunt I find the machine under the bed. I kicked it there by accident I guess.

Recipe for Bannerman's bullshots. Boil up a little beef bouillon and season it with pepper and Tabasco. You can add a teaspoon of mustard. I like to add celery salt too. Then put in a shot of bourbon. Or two, maybe. You are supposed to add lemon juice but people who like lemon juice are the same kind of people who love salad. I won't have it in the house.

I have three before I feel any better. I follow it up with my pill, and before I know it I'm nodding pleasantly. Like Mommy used to say, if you have pain you take medicine. If you have a cut you get stitches. Everyone knows that.

Mommy used to tell me the story of the ankou, the god with many faces who lives in the graveyards of her home. It's so frightening to have more than one face. How can you know who you really are? When I was little I sometimes thought I saw the ankou in my room at night, hanging in the dark; an old man with a long knife, the blade reflected in his eyes. Then he was a horned stag, sharp prongs anointed with blood. Then a gazing owl, still as stone. He was my monster. I can't even remember exactly what Mommy told me about him – or which parts my mind added in the night. The thought of him still makes me tremble. But these days I have Olivia. When I stroke her fur or even just hear her little annoyed scufflings around the house, I remember that I am safe and the ankou is far away.

As I drift, the bug man's words go round and round in my head like ticker tape. *It can be lonely, keeping secrets.* It's weird because in one way I am very lonely, and in another I've got more company than I can handle.

I am almost asleep when the doorbell cuts through the air like a jackhammer.

Olivia

⌒

The gd doorbell is ringing, and Ted won't get up. He always sleeps late after he has been to the woods. I can hear him snoring like a snare drum. There it goes again. *BRRRRRRRRRR*. No, not like a snare drum. More like a saw or a nail gun to the head. Come on, the ted with opposable thumbs has to wake up and answer the doorbell. I can't, can I? I'm a cat. I mean, what the eff.

I race upstairs and walk on his face until he wakes up. He groans with the effort of dragging clothes onto his body. I tread the outline of his warm body in the sheets, as his steps retreat like thunderclaps down the stairs. There go the locks, *thunk, thunk, thunk*. He opens the door. Another voice says something pleading. I think it's a female ted. I wait confidently. Ted will tell this other ted where to go! He hates people ringing the doorbell. After all, other teds are dangerous. He has told me often enough.

But instead, to my horror, HE LETS THE OTHER TED IN. The door closes and the thunder comes. The whole house shakes. The carpet slides under me. I am *rowing* and scrabbling for clawholds. The timbers in the roof groan and scream, the walls judder. The fabric of everything threatens to spring apart.

Slowly the world settles. But I can't move from my place under the bed. I am frozen with horror, heart pounding. The new stink of her fills the house, fills my nostrils. It's like burning and black pepper. This ted is making me feel too much – who or what is she?

Below, the teds are talking like nothing's wrong. I think they're in the kitchen. I don't want to listen to them, of course I don't, but I can't help hearing. This lady ted is going to live next door. Then she says something about putting a cat in a washing machine. Oh my LORD. She's a gd psycho, like on the TV.

Ted's voice takes on a strange note. It is – interest? Happiness? Awful, anyway. What if he asks her back? What if this starts happening all the time? The conversation seems to go on for ever and I think, *Wow he should just ask her to move in here, the way he's going on.* At long, long last their voices move into the hall again. He shows her out.

As the lady ted leaves, she says, 'If you ever need help with anything,' and something about a broken arm that I don't really understand.

Finally he closes the door behind her.

Wow. That was not right. Bad, bad, bad. The whining reaches a pitch which makes me feel like my head will explode. That was a violation of all the trust between us – what do we have if we don't have TRUST? What if that lady ted is a murderer? What if she decides to come back? UNACCEPTABLE.

Ted comes upstairs and the bed creaks companionably above my head. Back to his nap, of course. He calls for me but I am completely upset and I run out of the bedroom. Obviously he has NO feelings because a few minutes later he is snoring again.

I pace the living room. The peepholes peer crazily at me, like eyes. Nothing feels safe. I knead the nice rug but even that can't comfort me like usual. I am so UPSET that even my eyes aren't working properly. Everything looks the wrong colour, the walls look green, the rug blue.

He has to be taught a lesson. Breaking stuff isn't enough, this time.

I leap crazily from the counter, aiming for the refrigerator door. Eventually I hook the handle with a paw and it swings open. I give a little *prrp* of satisfaction. Cold billows out. In this weather it will soon melt all over the floor. The beer will get warm. The milk and meat will spoil. Good. Look at my bowl! Empty! Let him see how it feels.

I feel better after that. When I go back in the living room I am relieved to see that my eyes are back to normal. I am able to curl up on the orange rug and have a little nap which to be honest I gd deserve, after all I've been through.

Dee

Something gives under her feet with a crack. There are bright shards among the leaves and dirt that cover the steps. It's as if a whole box of Christmas tree ornaments has shattered everywhere. It adds a hectic edge of unreality.

Dee wonders if she'll know, right away, when she sees him. Surely the truth will come off his flesh like a scent.

She rings the doorbell thirty or forty times. She sees movement at the window but there's no answer, and she wonders if she should leave. Part of her sags with relief at the thought. But she doesn't think she can put herself through all this again. *Get it done, Dee Dee.* Her father's voice in her head. Their grim credo during that long half-year when it was just them, alone. *Get through it, get it done*; no matter how unpleasant, however hard your heart pounds in the night, whatever dreams may come. *Get it done.* She straightens her spine a little, and that moment she hears a shuffling within the house. A small high noise – a cat, maybe? Then heavier sounds, a large body making impressions on stairs, walls, boards.

Three different locks click and the door opens a crack. A bleary brown eye presents itself, framed by a pale face which sprouts hair. His beard is red, much brighter than the lank brown strand that falls over his brow — the shade is attractive, it gives him a piratical, almost jaunty air.

'Hi,' she says.

'What is it?' His voice is higher than she expected.

'I'm your new neighbour. Dee. I wanted to say — well, hi, and I brought you some pie.' She winces and resists the urge to mention that she's a poet, but doesn't know it. Instead she holds out the box containing the out-of-season pumpkin pie she bought at the drugstore. The box has dust on it, she now sees.

'Pie,' he says. A pale hand snakes out and takes the pie. For a moment Dee expects his skin to sizzle in the sunlight. She doesn't let go of the moist cardboard, and for a moment they are caught in a gentle tug of war.

'I'm so sorry to bother you with this,' she says. 'But my water doesn't get switched on until this afternoon. Could I possibly use your bathroom? It was a long drive.'

The eye blinks. 'It's not convenient right now.'

'I know,' Dee says, smiling. 'The new neighbour only just got here, and she's already being a pain. Sorry. I already tried a couple houses on the street but I think everyone's out at work.'

The door swings wide. The man says stiffly, 'I guess, if you're quick.'

Dee steps into an underworld; a deep cave where lonely shafts of light fall on strange mounds, jagged broken things. Plywood is nailed over all the windows, with round circles cut out to let in light.

She peers to her left, into the living room. As her eyes adjust to the gloom she sees that piles of books and old rugs litter the wooden boards. There are bare patches on the yellowed walls, where pictures or mirrors once hung. The walls are a deep green, like a forest. She sees a beat-up lounger, a TV. There's a dirty blue rug on the floor that looks like it's made of little pills. The whole place smells of death; not of rot or blood but dry bone and dust; like an old grave, long forgotten. Everything is decaying. Even the latch on one of the back windows is rusted through. Flakes of dark red litter the sill. The tired detective Karen's voice is in Dee's head. *A chaotic home environment. Unmarried. Socially marginal.*

Behind her the front door closes. She hears the three locks click into place. Each hair on the back of her neck stands slowly, individually on end.

'Kids?' she asks, nodding at the pink bicycle, which lies on its side.

He says, 'Lauren. I don't get to see her as often as I'd like.'

'That's rough,' Dee says. He is younger than she had first thought, early thirties, maybe. Eleven years ago, he would have been just in his twenties.

'The bathroom is down the hall,' he says. 'This way.'

'Great music,' she says, following. The song that's playing somewhere in the house is another surprise, heartfelt country music, sung in a lovely voice. She sees that Ted has bare patches on the back of his head, as though handfuls of hair have been pulled out by small fists. For some reason this brings the light, airy graze of terror.

In the bathroom, Dee turns on both the taps. She can hear him waiting for her behind the door. His distress, his animal breathing. She's aware, in great detail, of her own body; her skin, so strong in some places, like on her heels and her callused fingertips, so thin in others, like her eyelids. She feels the delicate hair that stands up on her forearms, the soft globes of her eyes; her long tongue and throat, her purpled organs and muscled heart, which pumps the red blood through her. It is pumping fast, now. All these vulnerable things, which can be broken or punctured: the blood can spill; bone can become a cracked white edge; eyeballs can be burst by the pressure of two thumbs. She looks for a mirror, to reassure herself that she is whole, unharmed. But there isn't one above the basin or anywhere else in the dim, dirty bathroom.

She flushes the toilet, washes her hands and opens the door.

'Could I have a drink of water?' she asks. 'I'm parched. Is it always so warm around here? I thought this place was known for the rain!' He turns without a word and lumbers into the kitchen.

She looks about her as she drinks. 'Do you hunt? Fish?'

'No.' After a moment he asks, 'Why?'

'You must freeze a lot of stuff,' she says, 'to need two freezers.' Only the small combination fridge-freezer appears to be in use. The other – an old, industrial chest freezer – lies empty and open, lid resting against the wall.

He looks embarrassed. 'Olivia likes to sleep in there,' he says. 'My cat. I should have got rid of it when it broke, but the thing makes her happy, you know? She purrs and purrs. So I keep it. Dumb, I guess.'

She looks inside. The box is lined with soft things – blankets and pillows. On a cushion she can see a hair – it is brown, or reddish-brown. It doesn't look like a cat hair. 'Does Olivia live outside?' Dee asks. She can't see cat bowls for food or water anywhere in the kitchen.

'No,' he says, offended. 'Of course not, that would be dangerous. She's an indoor cat.'

'I love cats,' Dee says, smiling. 'But they're such assholes. Especially as they get older.'

He laughs, a startled stutter. 'I guess she is getting older,' he says. 'I've had her a long time. All I wanted, when I was a kid, was a cat.'

'Ours used to sleep in the dryer,' she says. 'It gave my dad nightmares. He was so scared he'd mistake her for a sweater and …' She mimes spinning, makes the face of a horrified cat, staring out through glass.

He gives another little choked laugh and she adds a kind of dance, like the cat paddling in the swirling laundry.

'You're funny,' he says. His smile looks lopsided, creaky, like it hasn't been used in some time. 'I was always afraid Olivia was going to get herself shut in. At least she can't suffocate, now.' He shows Dee the holes that are drilled in the lid.

'Pretty,' she says, running her finger across one of the blankets. It is yellow, with a pattern of blue butterflies on it, and it is like a duckling's back to the touch.

He closes the lid of the freezer slowly but steadily, so that she has to remove her hand. As he does, she notices the fading bruising on his forearm, his swollen hand.

'Hey, you're hurt,' she says. 'How'd that happen?'

'The car door closes on my arm,' he says. 'Closed, I mean. I was parked on a hill. At least it's not broken, I guess.'

She makes a wincing face. 'Still hurts, I bet. I broke my arm once. It was so awkward, you know, opening jars and stuff like that. Are you right-handed? If you need help, let me know.'

'Uh,' he says. She lets the ensuing silence stretch. 'What do you do?' he asks eventually.

'I wanted to be a dancer once,' Dee says. 'I'm nothing, now.' Strange that this is the first time she has allowed herself to admit it out loud.

He nods. 'I wanted to be a cook. Life.'

'Life,' she says.

At the door, she shakes his hand. 'Bye, Ted.'

'Did I tell you my name?' he asks. 'I don't remember doing that.'

'It's on your shirt.'

'I used to work at an auto shop,' he says. 'I guess I got used to the shirt.' *Manual labour or unemployed.*

'Anyway, thanks,' Dee says. 'You've been very neighbourly. I won't bother you again, I promise.'

'Any time.' Then he looks alarmed. He locks the door quickly behind her.

Thunk, thunk, thunk.

She walks back slowly across the parched yard. He's watching her as she goes, of course. She feels the weight of his eyes on her back. It takes all her restraint not to run. The encounter has shaken her more than she expected. She had been sure he wouldn't let her in.

Dee closes her front door behind her with trembling hands and sits down on the dusty floor with her back against it. She tries to breathe, to calm herself, but she seems to have handed her body over to someone else. Her hands clench and unclench. Hot tides crawl across her skull. A sawing gasp comes from her throat. Her heart thumps in her ears. *A panic attack*, she thinks vaguely. *Got to get it together.* But it's like sinking deeper and deeper into a sand dune; she can't just climb out.

At length it subsides. Dee coughs and breathes. She becomes aware of an acrid scent in the house, a mingling of dry grass and pepper trees, wattle and stinkbugs. The outdoors is coming inside where it doesn't belong. She gets up, weak as a kitten, and follows the scent to its source. In the dusty living room a pane of glass is missing from the window. Dry leaves have blown across the scarred boards. Something has been sleeping in here. Not a skunk, she doesn't think, but something. Possum or raccoon.

'Nope,' she whispers to the empty room. 'No room at the inn.' She pushes a small bookcase in front of the broken pane, blocking it. She'll probably have to get that fixed herself. Her landlord doesn't seem like the type to go to any trouble. She doesn't mind. The more he leaves her alone the better.

As an experiment, she looks around at the living room, walls brown with old cigarette smoke and corners hung with dust, and thinks, *This is my home*. It actually makes her laugh a little. She can't recall the last place she felt was home. In her early teens, perhaps, when Lulu still slept in the next room, thumb locked tight between her pursed lips, emitting her light, penetrating snores.

She is surprised to discover that the gas is connected. Dee makes steak, green beans and a baked potato in the hissing white stove in the kitchen. She eats quickly and without pleasure. She can't care about food, but she takes care of herself. She learned the importance of that the hard way. The stove still hisses after she switches it off and the kitchen smells faintly of gas. Another thing to get fixed. She'll do it tomorrow – or maybe she will die in the night. She decides to leave it up to fate.

Dee sits cross-legged on the living-room floor as dusk falls. The night flows in, pools in the corners, spreads across the floor like a tide. She looks at the dark and the dark looks back at her. The little circles in Ted's windows light up. Through one, colour and movement shiver – the TV, she guesses. Later the circles go dark downstairs, and for a few minutes two moons shine out upstairs. They go out at ten. Early to bed, then – no TV or book in bed either. She watches for a few moments longer. The house is dark but she cannot let go of the feeling that it is not at rest. There is something manic in its stillness. But she keeps watching and nothing happens. Her limbs are twitching with exhaustion; the dark revolves before her. She should sleep too. There is a long road ahead.

The bathroom is old white tile, mapped with cracks. A buzzing neon light hangs overhead, filled with the corpses of moths and flies. She puts blankets and pillows in the bathtub. *Safest place in an earthquake*, as her father used to say. Anyway, she doesn't have a bed. Dee lays the claw-hammer down beside her on the cold tile. She closes her eyes and practises reaching for it, reinforcing the muscle memory, imagining herself just woken from sleep, imagining a dark figure looming over her.

She pictures Lulu's face, the way expressions chased across it, clouds over the sun.

She reads *Wuthering Heights*. She is only a couple of pages from the end. When she finishes, she opens the book at random in the middle and continues reading. Dee only ever reads this one book. She likes to read, but you never know what books are going to do to you and she can't afford to be taken off guard. At least the people in *Wuthering Heights* understand that life is a terrible choice, which you must make each day. *Let me in,* Catherine pleads. *Let me in.*

When she turns out the light the dark is rich and complete. The house breathes about her like a person, boards groaning, releasing the stored heat of the day. Stars peer through the window. The house isn't really in the city at all – it is almost in the forest. She is so close to where it happened. The air holds the memory of the event, somehow. The particles of it are carried on the wind, lie in the earth, the old trees and dripping moss.

Her dreams are filled with burning sun and the fear of loss. Her parents walk through the desert, hand in hand, under a sky filled with stars. Dee watches as long as she can, but then the red birds take flight and the sky goes white, and the sound of their wings is a soft feathery scratching. She sits upright in the dark, heart pounding. Sweat trickles down her back and between her breasts. The sound has followed her out of the dream. From downstairs it comes again. Dee hears that it is not wings, but a scratch, like a long nail on wood.

Her palm is slippery on the rubber handle of the claw-hammer. She creeps downstairs. Each board cracks like a shot beneath her feet. The scratching continues, sharp claws or fingernails raking the wood. Dee understands that there has been some critical slippage between worlds. *Let me in – let me in.* Faint silver pours in through the uncurtained living-room windows. The scratching is faster now, insistent. Dee thinks she hears another sound behind the scrabbling – it is high, broken. Sobbing, perhaps. The book-case trembles, as if the force behind it were growing in fury and in strength.

'I'll let you in,' Dee whispers. She pulls the bookcase aside. It shifts with a groaning shriek. She sees what crouches outside the window, gazing in. The hammer falls to the floor. She kneels and comes face to face with it, the child, its silver-white flesh dappled in the moonlight, its mouth a black cherry, eyes gleaming like lamps, filled with the light of death, scalp stripped and wounded, where the birds have plucked the hair from her skull.

'Come in,' Dee whispers and puts out her hand.

The child hisses at her, an unearthly sound, and Dee gasps. Fear washes over her, so cold she thinks her heart will stop. The child's mouth opens, her hand whips out to grasp Dee's arm, to pull her out of this world and into whatever other awaits. Dee sees white teeth set like pearls in powerful jaws. She sees the blunt, crippled fingers. The small pale face seems to ripple in the uncertain light, as if through water.

She screams and the sound breaks the dream, or whatever it is. Dee sees that it is not a dead girl at the window. It's a cat, jaws hissing and wide, tabby coat bleached by moonlight. The cat swipes at Dee, and she sees that it has no claws in its maimed paws. She backs away, making a soothing noise. The cat turns to flee, but looks back at Dee for a moment, pointed face eerie in the dim. Then it is gone, melted nimble into the black garden.

Dee sits back on her heels, shaking. 'Just a stray cat,' she says. 'Don't read scary books before bed, huh, Dee Dee? No big deal. Nothing to worry about.' This is an old habit of hers – saying aloud what her dad would want to hear, while keeping her real feelings inside. There is no time to fall apart. She thinks of Lulu again and this works. Purpose calms her. Dee's heart slows its splashy beat.

Dee looks out over the tangled growth that swarms over her back yard. It's wild, impenetrable, scented in the night. Anything could be out there, hiding. It could creep close to the house, to the windows. And then, reaching out with a long finger … Some of the neighbours have razed their yards to the ground, she notices. Presumably to deter snakes and vermin from nesting there. Dee shivers. Ted's yard is chaos like hers. She stares at the under-growth that riots all over his garden. In the moonlight it seems to be moving, writhing gently. She shakes her head, nauseous. That day at the lake took almost everything from Dee but it left some-thing in her, too. *Ophidiophobia*, they call it; an overwhelming fear of snakes. Dee sees them everywhere, their shadowed coils. The terror slows her mind and heart to a glacial pace.

Slowly she cups her hands and then raises them to her lips, covering her mouth like a mask. She whispers into her palms, a name and a question, over and over. Clouds scud across the moon, throwing light and shadow on her face, gleaming on the wet sheen of tears.

The next morning she resumes her post by the living-room window. She keeps the curtains drawn at all times and does not turn on lights after dark. She knows how a lit window shines like a beacon in the night. Ted does too, it seems. The plywood-covered windows make it look as if his house has turned deliberately away from her, to face the forest.

She begins to learn his habits. Sometimes he goes to the woods, and he does not return for a night, or several. Other times he goes into town, and those visits are in general shorter, sometimes last-ing only hours, or an evening. Sometimes he returns very drunk. One morning he just stands in the front yard and eats what looks like a pickle spread with peanut butter. He stares ahead, blank, and his jaws move, mechanical. There are bird tables and hanging feeders in the yard, but no birds ever come. What do the birds know?

She finds out everything she can online. Ted sometimes sends in his sightings to the rare bird column in the local paper. His mother is a nurse. She is very beautiful, in an old-fashioned way that seems divorced from such things as flesh or food. In the grainy photograph she holds her certificate in delicate fingers. County Nurse of the Year. Dee wonders what it must do to you, to have a child like Ted. Does she still love him? Where is she?

The first time Dee tries to follow Ted into the forest, he stops at the trail head and waits in the dark. She hears him breathing there. She freezes. She is sure he can hear her heart. After a time he makes a sound like a slow beast and moves away into the forest. She knows she can't follow, not this time. He felt her there.

She is relieved despite herself. The dark forest seems full of the sliding passage of snakes. She goes home and throws up.

Dee watches the house, instead, after that. After all, it is not him she has come for. She waits, patient. *Wuthering Heights* lies open on her lap, but she does not look at it. She stares at the house without pause, memorises each flake of paint that peels away from the old clapboard, each rusty nail, each frond of horsetail and dandelion that bobs against its walls.

Two days later, she has almost given up. Then, beneath the cicadas and the bees and flies and the chirping of sparrows and the hum of distant lawnmowers, she hears something that sounds like the tinkle of breaking glass. Every fibre of her strains towards the sound. Did it come from Ted's house? She is almost certain that it did. So very nearly completely certain.

Dee rises from the floor, stiff from her long vigil. She decides that she will go over there. She thought she heard a window breaking, thought of burglars, she is just being neighbourly … It is a natural action.

As she does, Ted comes along the street. His walk is deliberately careful, like someone who is drunk or hurt. He carries a plastic bag by its handles.

Dee sits down again, quickly. At the sight of him, her vision goes dim at the edges, her palms are oily-slick. The body's reactions to fear are so similar to that of love.

Ted opens the door, moving with that eerie care. Moments later there is the sound of laughter. The TV, maybe. Through it, Dee hears a high, clear voice saying, 'I don't want to do algebra.'

There is the low rumble of a male voice. It could be Ted. Dee strains. Her head aches with effort. The stretch of summer air that lies between the houses now seems thick and impenetrable as dough. A young girl begins to sing a song about woodlice. In all her days of watching, Dee has seen no one but Ted come and go.

Relief and horror flood her, so strong she can taste them in her mouth like mud and water. Her worst fear and her best hope are confirmed. There is a child in that house who does not leave. *That's all you know right now,* she tells herself sternly. *Step by step, Dee Dee.* But she cannot help it. *Lauren,* she thinks. *Lulu.* Her given name, which is Laura. *Lulu, Laura, Lauren.* Such close sounds, lying almost atop one another.

To Dee, in that moment, the singing girl sounds exactly like her sister. The timbre, the little catch in her voice.

Ted

'I don't want to do algebra.' Lauren is pouting with that little jut of the lip that drives me crazy.

'No dice,' I say. 'And no whining, you hear? It's algebra and geography day, so no more singing, that's what we're doing. Kitchen table, books – now please.' It comes out sharper than I meant it to. I'm tired and I can't stand it when her voice gets that tone. She really picked a day. I'm a lot lower on the pills than I thought.

'My head hurts,' she says.

'Well, you got to stop pulling your hair like that.' She takes a thin strand of brown and gnaws on the end of it. Then she tugs it, hard. There are thin patches all over her skull, now. Her favourite thing is to tear hair out. Mine, hers. Makes no difference. 'You want me to send you back early? Behave, for goodness' sake.'

'Sorry, Dad.' She puts her head down over the page. She is probably not doing algebra, but at least she has the sense to pretend. We are quiet for a time, and then she says, 'Dad?'

'Yes?'

'I'll make dinner tonight. You look tired.'

'Thank you, Lauren.' I have to wipe a tear away before she sees it. I feel bad for being so grouchy. And I can't help hoping that she is beginning to take an interest in food.

She makes a mess, of course. She uses every pan in the kitchen, and when she burns the bottoms the corky acrid smell fills the house.

'Stop watching me, Dad,' she says. 'I can do it.'

I raise my hands and back away.

The pasta is only half cooked and the sauce is sloppy and tastes like nothing. It has little cold lumps of meat in it. I eat everything she gives me.

'Best dinner I ever had,' I tell her. 'Thank you, kitten. You used the new chuck I got today?'

She nods.

'Mmmmm,' I say. 'You're not eating much.'

'I'm not hungry,' she says.

'Mommy used to say, "The chef never has an appetite",' I tell her. 'Your grandmother. She said that a lot. Along with, "Never call a woman insane."'

'She wasn't my grandmother,' Lauren says quietly. I let that go because she has made such an effort today.

Afterwards I clean up, which takes some time, and we settle in for a quiet evening. Lauren sits in the middle of the kitchen floor. The night seems to be getting hotter, not cooler. Our skin is misted with sweat.

'Can I open a window, Dad?'

'You know we can't.' I wish we could, though. The air is solid heat.

She makes a disgusted *ugh* sound and takes off her blouse. Her undershirt is dirty; we need to do some laundry round here. The dry sound of marker on paper is soothing. When the sound stops I look up. There is a sea of crayons around her, a rainbow of markers, all with their caps off.

'Lauren!' I say. 'Caps back on, please. Markers don't grow on trees.' But she stares ahead, eyes glazed.

'Are you OK, kitten?' She doesn't reply, but gives a little gasp that makes my heart almost stop. When I put my hand on her brow it's cold and clammy, like the underside of a rock.

'Hey,' I say. 'Come upstairs, I'll put you to bed …'

She starts to answer but instead a hot stream of vomit darts from her mouth. Lauren doesn't even try to avoid the mess, she just lies down where she is. When I try to move her, things come out that shouldn't. I clean it up as best I can, I cool her with water, I try to give her aspirin and ibuprofen to keep her fever under control, but she throws them up straight away.

'Come on, kitten,' I say, but something strange is happening. My voice starts to sound very far away. A white-hot spear pierces me, runs through my guts. Things start to bubble and burn down there. Oh God. Black and red descend. We lie on the kitchen floor together, moaning as our insides twist.

Lauren and I are sick for a whole day and a night. We tremble and sweat. Time slows, stops and starts, inches by like a worm.

When it begins to lift I give her water and some sports drink thing I find in a cupboard. Later in the evening I butter saltines and feed them to her one by one. We hold on to one another.

'Nearly time to go,' I say to her. The roses have returned a little to her cheeks.

'Do I have to?' she whispers.

'Be good,' I say. 'See you in a week.' She lies still in my arms. Then she starts to scream. She scratches me and struggles. She knows I'm lying.

I hold her tight. 'It's for the best,' I say. 'Please, kitten, please don't fight.'

But she does and I lose my temper. 'You're grounded until I say different,' I say. 'You brought this on yourself.'

My head spins, my insides are molten. But I have to know. I look in the trash, where I dumped the chuck that was spoiled when I left the refrigerator door open. The white grubs writhe in the brown mess. There is considerably less in the bag than there was this morning. Something hot comes up in my throat, but I hold it back.

I take the trash out, which I should have done right away. The world staggers, the air seems solid. I have never felt so sick.

It has been years since Lauren tried anything like this. I feel like an idiot, because I thought we were friends. I shouldn't have let things get so slack.

The record scratches the silence. The woman's voice fills the air. I don't like this song. There's too much tambourine. But I leave it on.

I check everything carefully. The knife is in the high cupboard, where it should be. The padlock on the laptop cupboard is secure. But the metal looks … dull, somehow, as if it has been handled a lot with sweaty palms, as if someone has been clicking through combinations. I love my daughter. But I am pretty sure she tried to poison us both.

When I count the pens and crayons, a pink marker is missing. Worse, when I go to lock them up in their cupboard, I see my list of Murder suspects lies on top of the boxes of crayons. I didn't put it there. When I pick it up I see that another name has been added, in sickly pink marker.

Lauren, it reads in her shaky printing. This, of course, has been my fear all along.

I curl up on the couch like a woodlouse; blackness nudges the edge of my vision. My stomach writhes. Surely it all came up, surely it's finished now. Oh God.

Olivia

I know it's not her time but I'm peering through my peephole anyway. Love is also hope. Grey sky, patchy grass, a triangle of iced sidewalk. It looks pretty cold out there. It's not so bad being an indoor cat on a day like this.

Behind me the TV plays. Something about dawn streets and walking. Ted leaves it on sometimes to keep me company. Sometimes the set just turns itself on. It's pretty old. You can learn a lot from the television. I am also glad of it because it drowns out the screeching whine that is my constant companion, now. Eeeeeee, eeeee.

I must have dozed off because I start when a voice speaks to me. At first I think it's the LORD and I sit up quickly. Yes?

'We must investigate trauma,' the voice says. 'Get to its roots. Revisit it, in order to purge it.'

I yawn. This ted is on TV sometimes and he is very boring. I don't like his eyes. Round, like little blue peepholes. I always feel like I can smell him when he's on, which makes my tail tingle. He reeks of dust and sour milk. But how could that be? You can't smell teds on the TV!

Daytime TV is so bad. I think this is a public access channel or something. I wish I could change it.

I think I should have my own TV show, and actually it would be really fun. I would call it CATching up with Olivia, and I would describe everything I ate that day. I would talk all about my love and her tiger eyes *and her smooth stride. I would also investigate the type and quality of naps there are, because there are so many different kinds. Short and deep — I call that kind 'the wishing well'. The very light doze, kind of half under, which can go on for hours — I call those 'skateboards'. The sort you have in front of the TV when a good show is playing (NOT this show) and you kind of take in the plot but are also asleep — those are called 'whisperers'. When you are being stroked to sleep and the rumble of your purr blends with the deep voice of the earth … I don't have a name for those ones yet. But they're so good.*

Anyway I think it would be good to share my experience and all the valuable thoughts I have. Kind of like I'm doing now, but in a visual medium, because I am very camera-friendly.

Ted

⌒

I miss Lauren so much. Now the first shock is over, I know that
of course she cannot be the Murderer. Not that she wouldn't do
it, but she couldn't. She can't go outside. How would she have
got the traps? Laid them, without me knowing? No, it cannot be
Lauren. She wrote her name on the list to upset me. She likes to
do that.

She has to stay away for now, until I figure out what to do with
her.

By the time bug-man day comes around again, I have lost pounds
and pounds. I am shaky but I can walk down the street without
staggering. That's good. I have questions.

I start talking almost before he has closed the door.

'I've started watching this new TV show,' I say. 'It's really good.'

The bug man clears his throat. He pushes his glasses fussily up
his nose. They are square with thick black frames, probably expensive. I wonder what his life is like, if he ever gets sick of hearing
people talk about themselves all day.

'As I've said before, if you want to spend our time talking about
what you watched on television – it's your hour. But—'

'This show is about a girl,' I say, 'a teenager, who has these, well, these tendencies. What I mean is, she's violent. She likes to hurt people and animals. She has a mother who loves her a lot, and the mother is always trying to protect her and stop her from killing. One day the mother injures her so that she can't walk any more. I mean, it's an accident, the mother doesn't mean to do it, but the girl hates her for it. She thinks her mother did it on purpose. Which is very unfair, in my opinion. Anyway the girl has to live at home because of her disability. And she keeps trying to kill her mother. The mother spends her life trying to cover up her daughter's violence, and protect her while hiding her true nature.'

'Sounds complicated,' the bug man says.

'I was wondering – if this was happening in real life, could the mother do anything to make her daughter better? To stop her from being violent? Also, is it hereditary? I mean, did the mother make her angry? Or did it come from within?'

'Nature or nurture? These are big questions. I think I need to know a little more about the situation,' the bug man says. He's watching me intently, now, with his round cricket eyes. I can almost see the antennae waving above his head.

'Well, I don't know anything else. The show only just started, OK?'

'I understand,' he says. 'Do you think it would help, at this point, to talk about your daughter?'

'No!'

He looks at me. His round eyes seem flat now, like bad coins. 'There's a monster inside each of us,' he says. 'If you let yours out, Ted, it might not eat you.'

He looks like a completely different person, suddenly. A poisonous beetle, not a safe little bug. I can't breathe properly. How does he know? I've been so careful.

'I'm not as stupid as you think I am,' he says quietly. 'You depersonalise your daughter.'

'What does that mean?'

'Thinking of her as a person is overwhelming, so you deal with her feelings by attributing them to the cat.'

'If you can't help me, just say that.' I am shouting, I realise. I take a deep breath. The bug man is looking at me steadily, head on one side.

'Sorry,' I say. 'That was very rude. I'm in a bad mood. That stupid TV show has upset me.'

'This is a safe place in which you can express your anger,' he says. 'Let's continue.' He looks small and safe like always. I must have imagined the other thing. It's just the bug man.

The bug man carries on talking about trauma and memory, and all his usual stuff but I'm not listening. I keep trying to tell him I don't have any trauma but he won't listen. I've learned to tune him out at times like this.

I wish I had not shown him my temper. I got distracted and I didn't get the answers I needed. Lauren has worn me too thin. It's hard, living with someone who's trying to kill you.

The flyers are ragged on the telephone poles, tanned with weather. The Chihuahua lady's face is growing ghostly. I pass her house without looking. I'm afraid that it might look back at me. I hold tight to my little brown paper bag from the bug man.

Olivia

The windows show full dark, no stars or moon. Ted is still out. How long has it been? Two days? Three? I think it's kind of irresponsible.

In the kitchen, living things stir sluggish in my bowl. Well, I can't eat that. I lick some water from the dripping faucet. Something scuttles in the walls. I am so hungry.

There is something I can do, of course, to get food … I sigh. I don't like to let him in unless I have to. I'm a peaceful cat. I like patches of sunlight and sometimes stroking and the good feeling of sharpening my claws on the bannisters. I'm Ted's kitten and I try to make him happy because the LORD told me to, and that's what you do in a relationship, isn't it? I don't enjoy killing. But I'm so hungry.

I close my eyes, and feel him right away. He's always waiting, curled up in an inky pile in the back of my mind.

Is it my time, now? he asks.

Yes, I say, reluctant. *It's your time.*

I'm Ted's kitten, but I have my other nature. I can let that side take control, for a while. Maybe we all have a wild and secret self somewhere. Mine is called Night-time.

He gets up in one fluid movement. He's black, like me, but without the white stripe down his chest. It's hard to tell, because he's part of me, but I think he's larger, too. The size of a bobcat, maybe. It makes sense. He's a memory of what we once were. He's a killer.

Now I tell him, *Hunt*.

A pink tongue strokes Night-time's sharp white teeth. He comes out of the dark with his graceful stride.

I come to, retching. I'm in the bathroom, for some reason. The door is open and I can see the skylight over the hall. It's still pitch black outside, not yet pink in the east.

There's a pile of bloody bones before me on the tiles. They're picked clean. I'm full of night meat. I wonder what kind of animal it was. Maybe that mouse who's always singing in the kitchen walls. Or it could be a squirrel. There's a nest in the attic. Sometimes I hear them chittering, and running across the beams. I think they're squirrels, but they could be ghosts. I don't go into the attic. There are no windows there and I only like rooms with windows. Night-time doesn't care about things like that.

Thinking about the ghosts upsets me and makes me feel weird. The mess before me doesn't look like mouse remains any more. It looks like the bones of a small human hand.

Something crawls across the ceiling above. It sounds way too heavy to be a squirrel. I race downstairs as fast as I can and I put myself into my nice warm crate.

Ted doesn't know about Night-time – I mean, he can't tell the difference between us. I obviously can't explain it to him, there's a language barrier. And what would I say? Night-time is part of me; we are two natures that share a body. I guess it's a cat thing.

The night stretches ahead, and I am still hungry.

Is it my time, again?

It is your time.

Night-time comes forth once more, and his stride is full of joy.

Ted

The blonde woman said yes. I'm surprised. You'd think she'd be more careful. But people are trusting, I guess. We wrote each other all night. *It's so good to meet someone who loves the ocean as much as I do,* she writes. I might not have been completely honest about that but I'll explain when we meet.

But when and where *do* we meet? What do I wear? Will she actually show up? The questions come and suddenly everything is terrible. I look down at my clothes. My shirt is really old. It's from the auto shop where I used to work. The burgundy colour has faded almost to pink, the cotton is soft and thin as paper in places. And of course, it has my name across the pocket. This is handy in case I forget, ha, ha. But I don't think a woman would like it. My jeans are grey with age except where they are spattered with dark splashes of something, ketchup, I guess. There are holes in both knees but it doesn't look cool. Everything is so faded. I want to be colourful, like my nice bright orange rug.

The woman is making me feel terrible, with her blue eyes and blonde hair. How can she put me through this? Why did she pick me to talk to, to meet? I can already imagine her expression when she sees me. She'll probably just turn around and leave.

Mommy and Daddy watch from inside their silver frame. It's

heavy sterling silver. I've been putting this off but I think it's time. I take the photograph of Mommy and Daddy out carefully. I give it a kiss and then I roll it up and tuck it safely into the depths of the music box. The little ballerina lies broken and dead in her musical coffin.

I learned how to pawn things after Mommy went. Silver spoons; Daddy's pocket watch, which he got from his daddy. They are all gone, now. There are bare patches, empty places all over the house. The picture frame is the last thing.

The shop is dark on the warm dusty street. The man there gives me the money for the frame. It is much less than I need. But it will have to do. I like places where people don't ask questions. The bills feel good in my hand. I try not to think of Mommy's fading face, staring into the dark of the music box.

I walk west until I see a store with clothes in the window, and I go in. There is a lot of stuff here. Rods, flies, bait boxes, rubber boots, guns, bullets, flashlights, portable stoves, tents, water purifiers, yellow pants, green pants, red pants, blue shirts, check shirts, T-shirts, reflective jackets, big shoes, little shoes, brown boots, black boots ... I have only taken a quick look. My heart is going too fast. There's too much. I can't choose.

The man behind the counter wears a brown check shirt with brown jeans and a green coat thing but without sleeves. He has a beard like me, maybe even looks a little like me, so that's what gives me the idea.

'Can I buy those clothes?' I point.

'What?'

I am a patient person so I repeat myself.

He says, 'The ones I'm wearing? It's your lucky day, we have all this in stock. I guess I wear them well, huh?'

I don't like his clothes particularly. But so long as I don't have to go on a date with my name on my shirt like a kindergartener, fine.

'I'll take the ones you're wearing,' I say. 'If you just go take them off.'

His neck goes thick and his pupils go small. Mammals all look the same when they're angry. 'Listen, buddy—'

'Kidding,' I say quickly. 'Gotcha, buddy. Um, do you sell dresses? Like, maybe in different colours? Maybe blue?'

'We sell outdoor gear,' he says, giving me a long hard look. I have messed up bad, it seems. He fetches clothes from the rails in silence. I don't wait to try them on; I throw the dollars on the counter and go.

I get to the place early and take a seat at the bar. On either side of me are big guys who drive for a living, wearing trucker hats or leather. In my new clothes I look like one of them, which is why I picked this place. It's good to blend in.

The bar is just off the highway, with long benches out back. They do barbecue. I thought it would be good because it's been so hot lately. They put lights in the trees and it's pretty. Women like stuff like that. But I see quickly that it is the wrong place to meet her. It's raining tonight – a hot miserable thunderstorm. Everyone has been forced inside. And without the benches, the warm evening, the lights in the trees, this place looks very different. It's quiet apart from the occasional belch. There's no music, the fluorescents overhead are aching bright, casting glare on the aluminium tables which are littered with empty glasses and beer cans. The linoleum floor is slick with the tracks of muddy boots. I thought it was, you know, atmospheric, but now I see that it's not nice.

I order a boilermaker. There's a mirror behind the bar, which is another reason I chose this place and this particular seat. I can see the door perfectly.

She comes in, fresh with rain. I recognise her straight away. She looks just like her picture. Butter-yellow hair, kind blue eyes. She looks around and I see the place even more clearly, through her eyes. She's the only woman in here. There's a smell too, I hadn't noticed before. Kind of like a hamster cage that needs changing – or a mouse cage, perhaps. (No. Don't think of that.)

She goes to an aluminium table and sits. So she's optimistic or maybe desperate. I wondered if she'd leave straight away, when she saw that the guy with the white smile from the stock photo wasn't waiting for her. (I don't use my own picture; I learned that lesson quickly. I found mine on the website of some accounting firm. The man is pretending to sign a document, but also look-ing at the camera and smiling with big white teeth.) She orders something from the tired waitress. Club soda. Optimistic with common sense. Her hair falls, hiding her face in a creamy swing of blonde. And she's wearing a blue dress. Sometimes they come in jeans or check shirts, which isn't what I want. But this woman has done the right thing. It doesn't float, exactly, the dress, it's not organza, but made of some thicker fabric like corduroy or denim and she's wearing boots not sandals. But it's close enough.

I set it up carefully as we exchanged messages. I talked about that album by that woman, that singer – it's called *Blue*. It was my favourite album, I told her. And I loved the colour, because it was the colour of my daughter's eyes. When the talk got warmer between us I told her it was also because it was the colour of her own eyes. *Like a calm, kind sea,* I wrote. I was just telling the truth, they are nice eyes. She liked it, of course.

'Why don't we come dressed in blue when we meet?' I wrote then. 'So we can recognise each other.' She thought it was a great idea.

My flannel shirt is brown and yellow. I've got a green cap on. Even my jeans are brown. My new clothes are itchy but at least they don't have my name on! I couldn't stand the idea of her doing what the first one did – come in, take one look at me and walk out again. So I'm cheating. I feel bad about it. But I'll explain when I go over there, in just a second. Just like I'll explain that what I really need is a friend, not a date. I'll apologise and we'll laugh about it. Or maybe we won't. My head pounds with the stress of it all.

She looks at her phone. She thinks I'm not coming. Or rather that the man with the white teeth isn't coming. But she waits because it hasn't been twenty minutes yet, and you always give a late person twenty minutes, that's universal. And because hope is always the last thing to die. Or maybe she's just warming up before heading back out into the driving rain. She sips the club soda with a grimace. Not her usual drink. I order another boilermaker. *Nearly time to go over there,* I tell myself. I just need this one last drink, for courage.

After thirty-five minutes exactly she gets up. Her eyes are small with disappointment. I feel awful, having made her so sad. I mean to get up and stop her but somehow it doesn't happen. I watch in the mirror as she winds a blue silky thing around her neck. It's too narrow for a scarf, more like a ribbon or a necktie. She puts a five-dollar bill down on the table and goes. Her movements are decisive and she walks fast. She heads out into the vertical spears of rain.

The moment the door closes behind her, it's as if I'm released. I throw my drink down my throat, put my jacket on and follow. I'm so sorry I left her alone like that, let my nerves get the better of me. I want to make it right. I hurry, slipping on the wet linoleum. I mustn't let her get away. I can explain and she'll understand, I'm sure she will. Her eyes are so kind, so blue. I imagine the food I will cook for her. I'll make her my chocolate chicken curry. Not everyone appreciates it but I bet she will.

I run out into the storm.

It's still late afternoon but the cloud casts shadow over

everything so it looks like dusk. Rain hits the puddles like bullets. The lot is filled with trucks and vans and I can't see her anywhere. Then I do, at the far end of the lot, sitting in the warm-lit bubble of her small car. Her face is wet with rain, or she's crying. She still has her driver's side door open, as if even now she hasn't quite decided to leave. She adjusts the blue thing around her neck, fumbles in her purse and finds Kleenex. She dries her face, and blows her nose. I am very moved by her poise and her courage. She stood up to life by coming out to meet me – life knocked her down, of course, because I didn't show up – but look at her. She's drying her face, about to pick herself up again. That's the kind of person Olivia or Lauren could rely on. Those are the qualities I'm looking for in a friend. Someone who would be there for them, if I disappeared.

I bow my head into the billowing rain and go down the row of parked cars towards her.

Dee

'You said you would help,' Ted says.

'What?' It's early on a Sunday morning, and Ted is on Dee's doorstep. Her heart begins to pound, splashy and loud. In that moment she is convinced that he knows who she is and why she is here. *Get a grip, Dee Dee,* she tells herself. *Nobody gets murdered on a grey Sunday morning.* But they do, of course. She yawns to cover her fear, rubs the sleep from her eyes.

Ted shifts on his feet. His beard looks even thicker and redder than usual, skin whiter, eyes smaller and blearier. 'You said if there was something I couldn't do, uh, because of my arm, you would help out. Maybe you didn't mean it.'

'Sure,' she says. 'What's up?'

'It's this jar,' he says. 'I can't open it.'

'Hand it over.' Dee turns the lid hard, and it yields quickly. Inside the empty jar is a note. It reads, in neat block letters, LET'S GO OUT FOR DRINKS.

'Cute,' she says. She keeps her face still while her mind races.

'I mean as friends,' he says quickly. 'Tonight?'

'Uh,' she says.

'Only, I go away a lot.'

'Oh,' Dee says.

'I might be spending more time at my weekend place, soon.'

'A cabin?' Dee says.

'Kind of.'

'Up by the lake, I suppose.' Her heart is pounding. 'That's a lovely spot.'

'No,' he says. 'You wouldn't know it.'

'Well, we'd better have that drink before you disappear.'

'I'll meet you at that bar off the 101,' he says. 'Seven p.m.?'

'Sounds good,' she says. 'I'll see you there.'

'Cool,' he says. 'Great. Sayonara!' He stumbles a little as he backs away from her, and almost falls, but he recovers just in time.

'Well,' she says as she comes into her living room. 'I've got a date.'

The yellow-eyed cat lifts her head. She and Dee have a good understanding. Neither of them likes to be touched.

Dee says, 'It has to be tonight, before he fixes the window.' She wonders who she is trying to persuade. *Get it done.*

At 6.30 p.m., in the silvered near-dark, Dee is crouched in her living room by the shuttered window, watching Ted's house. In this light everything has a velvet quality. The world looks mythical and interesting. She waits, legs cramping, as she hears the turning of three locks next door. The back door opens and closes. The locks turn again. Ted's steps fade and she hears his truck start. She waits five minutes and then slides up the wall, muscles trembling. She goes quietly out of her back door and steps over the fence into Ted's back yard. She is somewhat screened from the alley by the timothy and pampas grass that grows wild, here. But she had better hurry. She goes to Ted's rear living-room window and takes the clawhammer from the pocket of her overalls. She pries the nails from the plywood that covers the window. They come out with little reluctant squeaks, but at last the sheet loosens and she pulls it free. The latch on this window has rusted through. She noticed it when she was in the house. He must have forgotten about it, after he boarded them up. She slides the sash upwards. Paint flakes scatter like snow or falling ash.

Let me in — let me in. But Dee is the ghost at the window now. She throws her leg over the sill. Inside, she is immediately filled with the sensation of being watched. She stands in the green living room, breathing the dust, and lets her eyes take in the dark. Ted's house smells strongly of vegetable soup and old, used-up air. If sorrow had a scent, she thinks, this is what it would be like.

'Here, kitty, kitty,' she says softly. 'Are you there, cat?' Nothing stirs. She should take Ted's cat with her when she goes, she thinks. This is no life for the poor thing. For a moment she catches the gleam of eyes, regarding her from the corner of the room, but it's just streetlight reflecting off a dented silver box. It's the only thing on the dusty mantel. There is a bare patch in the dust, as if a picture frame or something recently stood there.

She moves quickly; there isn't a lot of time. Through the living room, kitchen. The freezer lies open, door propped against the wall. There is no basement that she can see. She lifts the rugs and looks underneath, treads the boards carefully, looking for a trap door.

She heads upstairs. The carpet stops at the landing, which is dusty boards. Dee turns to sidle past the large wardrobe, which looms large in the tiny hallway. It is locked, and she can't see a key. No attic.

In the bedroom grocery bags line the walls. Clothing spills out of them. There's a closet containing one broken coat hanger, no clothes. It looks like Ted has just moved in, except that the mess has an air of timeless assurance. It has always been and will always be.

The bed is unmade, blankets still holding the moment when they were kicked away. There is a handful of pennies scattered across the sheets. When Dee comes closer she sees that it's not pennies, but dark drops of something. She makes herself smell it. Old iron. Blood.

The bathroom is as she remembers, sparsely furnished, a cracked sliver of soap, an electric shaver, various medications in amber drugstore tubes. The blank patch over the basin where the mirror used to be. She should have taken pictures, she thinks, but she didn't bring her phone or a camera. She tries to remember as much as she can. Her pulse is thundering.

There is a second bedroom containing an office chair and a desk. The couch has pink blankets on it and drawings of unicorns on the wall, of varying proficiency. The cupboards here are locked, too, with three-number combination padlocks. Dee bends to examine them. She touches the dial on one, gently.

A board sighs downstairs, and a hand clenches round Dee's heart. Something scutters by in the walls and she screams. It comes out as a gasp. The mouse feet scurry on. Actually, they sound bigger than a mouse. Maybe a rat. She leans against the wall, thinking as best as her thundering pulse will let her. How long will Ted wait in the bar, alone? She imagines him coming home, standing in the dark, watching her. She thinks of his blank eyes, his strong wrists. She should go.

She picks her way downstairs on tiptoe, every moment expecting to hear keys in the lock. Her breath is catching in little hiccups. She feels like she might faint, but also giddy with the strangeness of it all. Dee catches the barest glimpse of a dark slender shape, watching her from the corner of the living room and her heart stops for a moment.

'Here, kitty, kitty,' she whispers, to break the thick silence of the room. 'Have you seen a little girl?' But there's nothing in the corner but shadow and dust. Either the cat has slunk away or it was never there. Dee makes her way to the window, giving a little hoarse cry as the ugly, burry blue rug slips under her feet. She climbs out, swearing as she knocks her head against the frame, and pulls the sash down with relief, closing the house up behind her. The night air seems sweet and soft, the darkening sky is wonderful.

She raises the plywood with shaking hands. The old nails are bent, rusted and useless. Dee removes them gently. She nails the plywood back in place using the nails from her pocket. They are silver and sharp, fresh from the hardware store. The sound makes her think of coffins and she shakes herself. There is no time to lose focus. She must be precise hammering the new nails into the old holes. She must be quick, and finish while no one is passing to hear the blows or see her stumbling out of the creeper in the coming night.

When she gets back to her house she finds that she is shaking all over, like she has a fever. And in fact she does feel cold. She lights the wood burner and crouches by it, seized by cramps and chills. She used to think she was sick, when this came on. But she has come to know her body's ways of expelling distress.

Lulu is not in the house. Dee realises now that she had been thinking of her sister as very close. Had been imagining her breath-ing nearby. She has been reduced to wishing her sister a prisoner there. It seems so unfair, to have been driven to that. Feeling slices at her throat. She tries to order her mind. If Lulu is not there, she is somewhere else.

'The weekend place,' Dee whispers. That is the answer, it must be.

She clasps her hands before her mouth and whispers into them, watching the heat rise red behind the glass, the building flame.

I'm coming, she promises.

Olivia

I was at the window, looking for the tabby, when the sound began again. It's like bluebottles, only sharper, like a little needle in my head. I raced through the house. The tiny voice whined and stabbed. I bit open a couch cushion and clawed open a pillow in the bedroom. Where the heck is it?

I just played this back. I can hear the whine clearly on the tape. So it's not just in my head. It's a real thing. That's kind of a relief and also at the same time, not at all. I will get to the bottom of this. I think I could have been a good detective, you know, like the ones on the TV because I am very observant and—

The most awful thing just happened.

So, I was just sitting here, clawing at my head and trying to scratch the whine out of my ears, when I heard the repeating click of a key stabbing at the lock. It took several tries before it slid home. Thunk. The locks on the front door opened one by one. Thunk, chunk. Goodness, I thought, he's really steaming this time.

'Hey, Lauren,' he called. I purred and trotted to him. He stroked my head and tickled my ear. 'Sorry, kitten,' he said. 'I forgot. Olivia.' Wow, his breath.

I hope you don't go near any open flames, I told him. I always speak my mind to Ted. Honesty is important, even if he can't understand a gd word I say.

He weaved in, kissed the Parents where they stared from behind glass and went to sit on the couch. His eyes were half-closed. 'She didn't come,' he said. 'I waited for an hour. Everyone looking at me. Just this loser waiting in a bar. In a bar,' he said again as though this were the worst part. 'You're the only one who cares about me.' He swatted my head with a moist palm. 'Love you, kitten. You and me against the world. Standing me up. What goddamn kind of move is that?' He sighed. The question seemed to exhaust him. His eyes closed. His hand dropped to his side, palm up and fingers loosely curled as if in entreaty. His breath slowed to a heavy drag, in and out of his lungs. He looks younger when he sleeps.

Behind, in the hall, the front door swayed gently in the evening breeze. He didn't close it properly.

I leapt down. The cord was thin today, a stylish purple. I walked to the door, feeling it tighten about my neck. As I reached the threshold, I could still breathe, but only just. The open doorway burned, white light. A heavy hand fell on my head. Ted fondled my ears clumsily. He wasn't sound asleep.

'Hey,' he said. 'Wanna go outside, kitten? You know that's dangerous. It's bad out there and you should stay safe. But if you want to . . .'

I wasn't going to go outside, *I said.* The LORD told me not to, and I won't.

He laughed. 'First we got to make you pretty. Give you a makeover.'

I began to back away from him, I know this mood, but he seized me in strong hands, gripped me to his side like a vice. He locked the door, thunk, thunk, thunk, *then took me to the kitchen, the world swooping tipsily as he staggered. He reached up to a high cupboard and took something from it. The knife was broad and shining. I could hear the slight snick as the blade cut air. I fought hard, now, trying to reach him with my claws and teeth.*

He pinched the fur on the scruff of my neck, pulled it up. The knife made a soft pretty sound as it sawed through. The air was full of dark scatters of my silky coat. He sneezed but went on, cutting chunks of fur from my neck, my back, the tip of my tail. Somehow he was holding me and the knife and grabbing handfuls of fur all at once. He gets focused when he's drunk.

Then everything stopped. The arm holding me went rigid. Ted's face froze and his eyes were gone. I slipped from his grip, carefully avoiding the blade where it hovered, an inch from my spine. I left him standing in the kitchen like a statue, knife in his clenched fist. Soft tufts of fur floated on the air.

I crept away from him. The cord followed me, dirty yellow now and thin like an old shoelace.

The air is cold on the shorn patches in my coat. I can forgive his attacks on my dignity, on my feelings. The LORD would want me to. But there are limits. He should not have messed with my looks. I am stinking, stinking mad. Forgive me, LORD, but he is just a selfish piece of ess aitch eye tee. Ted must learn that his actions have consequences.

I go to the living room and jump up on the bookshelf. I push the bottle of bourbon off. It smashes on the floor in thousands of beautiful shards. The stink is strong as gas. My eyes water. For a moment it reminds me uncomfortably of something, some dream I had, maybe, about being locked up in a dark place, and a murderer was pouring acid onto me … My tail switches – whether it was a dream or a TV show, the memory makes me feel bad.

I jump up onto the mantel and knock the horrible fat monster doll to the floor. She falls with a crack, spilling her babies in the air as she goes. They shatter into splinters on the floor. It is a massacre. I try to knock the picture of the Parents down, too. I know it won't work, but I can't help myself. I am an optimist. I don't know what he has done to fix it so firmly – superglued it in place? The squirrels in the silver frame look more skull-like than ever. That thing is silver; I am surprised Ted hasn't sold it. Maybe he can't move it either!

Never mind, I have other ideas. I go quietly up to his bedroom and into his cupboard, where I pee in one of each pair of shoes.

I know the LORD won't like it but I must have justice.

Ted is calling for me now but I won't go to him, even though his voice is filled with black spikes.

Ted

I'm back, with the force of a blow — breathless, as if I have been punched in the guts. In one clenched fist I hold a knife. It's the big one that I keep hidden at the back of the high cupboard in the kitchen. No one knows about it except me. The blade is broad, polished to a high sheen. Grey daylight dances along its length and the edge gleams wickedly. It has been recently sharpened.

'Steady, Little Teddy,' I whisper. The rhyme makes me laugh.

Start with the basics. Where and when am I? *Where* is easy. I check the living room. Orange rug, bright and cheerful. Ballerina standing proud and upright on her music-box stage. The holes in the plywood are grey circles, filled with rain. OK, fine. I'm home, downstairs.

When is a little more difficult. In the refrigerator there is half a gallon of milk, yellowing and sour. A jar of pickles. Otherwise it's a bare white space. In the trash are sixteen empty cans. So, I ate and drank everything while I was away. I was surprisingly tidy, however. The kitchen's clean. I even smell bleach.

'Kitten,' I call. Olivia doesn't come. I am filled with bad ideas. Is she sick, or dead? The last thought brings horrible panic. I make myself breathe slowly. *Relax. She'll be hiding.*

I lost days, this time. At a guess, three. I check the TV. Yes, almost noon. So three days, more or less.

I go through the house, making sure of padlocks on the cupboards and the freezer, checking everything. I did some damage while I was out. Scratched up the orange rug, broke Mommy's Russian dolls into tiny shards. When I check my closet I find that some of my shoes are wet. Did it rain? Did I go through a river or something? *Or a lake,* my mind whispers. I shut that down real quick. I go to take a drink but apparently I broke the bourbon, too. Never mind. I get a fresh bottle and a pickle.

As I'm eating I drop the pickle. When I bend down to pick it up I see a gleam of white. There's something under the refrigerator. I know what it is. It shouldn't be down here.

Up in the attic there's the sound of weeping. It's the green boys. They've been quiet lately but now they're kicking up a storm. 'Shut up!' I yell. 'Shut up! I'm not scared of you!' But I am. I have nightmares that one day I will wake up in the attic, surrounded by the green boys and their long fingers and that I will slowly disappear, fading into the green. I hook the white flip-flop out from under the refrigerator and throw it in the trash. It's got bad memories all over it like fungus.

I don't put the knife back in the high cupboard. Instead I bury it in the back yard *under cover of dark.* Isn't that a wonderful expression? It makes the night sound like a warm blanket, littered with stars. I find a good place beneath a stand of blue elder.

I am still quite upset so I eat another pickle in front of the TV and slowly I calm down. I can't stop now. Those women weren't the right friends for me, I guess, but I'm not a quitter.

Olivia

Ted is gone again. Honestly, he is such a gadabout, these days.

The noise is very bad. *Eeeeeeeeeeee*. My head is a cavern of sound. I am in desperate need of guidance. I knock the Bible off the table with a paw. It falls open with a thump on the boards. I wait, eyes closed. When the crash comes it is so loud my ears want to burst. The house seems to tremble at its very foundations. There are great cracking sounds, as if the world or sky is breaking. It builds and builds to a scream and I think, *Is this the end of everything?* Horrible! Scary!

When at last it starts to die away I feel so relieved. I swear, I feel like a salt shaker that's just been used too hard. I have to sit for a moment to let my tummy settle.

I lean in. The verse that meets my eye is:

> And Ehud reached with his left hand, took the sword from his right thigh, and thrust it into his belly. And the hilt also went in after the blade, and the fat closed over the blade, for he did not pull the sword out of his belly; and the dung came out.

Well, if the LORD always made everything *perfectly* clear, there would be no point in faith, would there? The whining goes on and on. It almost sounds like a little bee, crying for help. The house feels wrong today, as if in the night someone moved everything an inch to the left for a prank.

Someone starts talking in the living room so I guess Ted left the TV on for me.

'We should revisit trauma,' the voice is saying. 'You know what they say. The only way out is through. Childhood abuse must be excavated and brought into the light.'

Maybe the whining sound is coming from the TV. I have checked the TV before, oh, hundreds of times. But I have to do *something*. The big Russian doll stares at me from the mantelpiece with its blank face, its round body. It looks happier than ever to have prisoned its little friends inside it. The Parents stare down from their horrible frame above the fireplace. *Go away,* I whisper at them, but they never do.

When I see who's on screen, I stop, ears flat. Him again. The round blue eyes stare out. He nods earnestly at some unheard question. The room is filled with that scent – spoiled milk and dust. I know he's only a picture on a screen but it feels like he's here, somehow. I sit down neatly and lick a paw. That always makes me feel better. *I could do this show so much better than you,* I tell him. *You have no charisma.*

He smiles as if in answer. I don't feel like talking to him any more after that. I don't know why – it's not like the TV can hear me. Can it? The smell is so strong, though. It's not like a ted smell, but like something left out of the refrigerator for too long.

And then, from the hall, I hear it. The tiny faint sounds of someone standing outside the front door. I pad over to it silently. I can sense someone behind. A male ted. He's not knocking, he's not ringing the doorbell. So what is he doing? And the reek is everywhere, seeping in around the door, invading my sensitive nose. It's the same smell that came off the TV. Somehow, the ted from the TV is also outside my house. The show must be pre-recorded.

The ted breathes into the place between the door and the jamb. Long, delicate inhalations. He must have his face pushed right into the crack. It's like he's smelling the front door. Can he smell me? Ted has warned me over and over about how dangerous outside is. I think this is what he meant. This feels dangerous. From the living room, from the TV, the ted's little blue coin eyes stare. 'Everyone has a monster inside them,' he says.

I need to be hidden. Somewhere dark. I creep up the stairs and along the landing. Overhead, one of the attic ghosts drags a long fingernail all along the length of the floor and now I run.

I gallop into Ted's room and shoot under the bed. I can still hear the celebrity ted downstairs on the TV, droning, talking about the bad things that people do to little teds, lecturing the empty room. Or is he talking through the door?

When I feel worried, I do one of two things. I consult the Bible, I break something of Ted's, or I go to sleep. Fine, three things. Well, I'm not going near that Bible again. It was scary. And I have already broken the Russian doll once this week and the music box twice. I feel kind of bad about it.

So I am going to need a long, long nap. I think I have to forgive Ted, too. I haven't really been speaking to him for the last couple days. But this has been a scary day and my tail's gone weird. I need to be stroked.

I can't sleep. I turn around and around and purr and close my eyes. But it all feels too wrong and my buzzing tail won't let me rest.

Ted

Olivia and I are sitting on the couch watching monster trucks when they come. I am a little worried about Olivia. She seems nervous, unlike herself. It makes me uneasy. Olivia is always OK. That's the thing about cats, isn't it? They don't hold on to things.

Maybe I'm imagining stuff because I miss Lauren so much today. I know she's better where she is, but it is very hard for a parent to be separated from their child. I call her but she's punishing me and doesn't answer. It's hurtful. It's worse than hurtful, it's a vice prying open my heart.

I am still very upset with that neighbour lady. It's not like I thought we would be friends right away. But I thought we could at least try. I wondered what she would look like in a dress. Something gauzy that floats around her ankles as she walks. Maybe blue. But I sat there at the bar and waited and she didn't come. I looked dumb. The search for a friend is not going too well in general.

Olivia hears it first. She vanishes under the couch. It takes me a moment longer to understand. The sound is not coming from the TV – it fills the air. Big engines are coming. Diggers, maybe, or tractors? Too loud, too close. What are they doing here? At this end of the street there are only two houses and then the forest. But they come on, closer and closer. I go to a peephole to watch them roaring by, yellow as death, great jaws crusted with earth. They don't stop. They go past the house, towards the woods. A man hops down out of the cab and takes the chains off the gates. There is something bad, something official about that action. He swings the gates open for the machines to pass through. Then the digger and the bulldozer roar and wheeze their way up the forest path.

I run out of the front door, and I am so upset I almost forget to triple-lock it behind me (but I do remember). The neighbour lady and some other neighbours are standing on the sidewalk, watching the two diggers fade into the trees with their terrible sound.

'What's going on?' I ask her. I am so worried I forget for a moment about how rude she is. 'They can't go up there. It's a wildlife reserve. It's protected.'

'They're making new rest stops off the trail,' she says. 'A picnic area. You know, so more hikers, more tourists will come. Hey, I got some more of your mail by mistake this morning. You want me to bring it round later?'

I ignore her. I run into the woods, following the grind of the engines. When I glimpse them, I follow at a distance. After a mile or so they turn off the path and start smashing into the under-growth. Saplings crack and give. It's like listening to children screaming. They are tearing up the earth less than three hundred feet from the clearing. They won't reach it today, but tomorrow they might. A man in a bright orange jacket turns and looks at me. I lift a friendly hand, then turn and walk away, trying to look like a normal person. The sound follows me down the path long after I am out of sight. Jaws, eating the forest.

I could kick myself. I knew it – I left the gods buried in the glade for too long. People sense them there, whether they know it or not. They are drawn to them as if on a string. I can't tell if my arm is all better yet. Some, I think. The bruising has gone down. Anyway there's no more time. I've got to move them tonight.

The afternoon is so long, it feels like years before the sun goes down. But at last it does, leaving crimson cuts across the sky.

Even in the kind darkness the woods don't feel like mine any more. I smell the diggers and the work site long before I see them – the black turned earth, the sap of murdered trees. The engines stand quiet among the ruins like big yellow grubs. I want to hurt them. I considered it. Hydrogen peroxide in the gas tank would do a good job. But that would hurt the forest too, and I don't want that.

In the glade I look around at the white trees. I feel so sad. This has been a good home for the gods. But if they stay, sooner or later they will be found. I might not be smart about some things, but I know this – no one would understand about the gods.

I take the shovel off my shoulder, unroll the pouch containing the tools, and dig. I buried them in a sacred formation, in fifteen different places. The location of each one burns in my mind like the pattern of the stars. I could never forget it.

I brush dirt gently from the rounded surface of the first god. The soil I lift it from is black and rich. The gods feed the earth. I put my ear close and listen. The god whispers secrets in a voice like rain. 'I hold you in my heart,' I whisper.

I put it gently into a trash bag and then into the backpack. I go to the next station. It is to the east, near the rock like a finger. This one is fragile. I put the shovel to one side and dig carefully with my hands. It's not buried deep. I like to dig this one up every now and again to look. I unwrap the plastic. The dress lies in my arms, a dark grey in the faint moonlight. I wish I could see it in the sunlight again, its true colour, the deep navy blue of the ocean in pictures. But of course I could never do this during the day. I wipe my hands on my jeans and stroke the fabric. The dress tells me things through the tips of my fingers. Each god holds different memories and brings its own feeling. My eyes feel tight and shining. This one always makes me sad. But also itchy, like a kind of excitement. 'I hold you in my heart,' I whisper, but it sounds so loud.

Next comes the vanity case, near the middle of the glade, to the left. I do this one as quickly as possible. It has sharp shining things in it and a voice like nettle or vinegar.

On and on I dig, and one by one each god fills the air with its voice. 'I hold you in my heart,' I whisper over and over. Each time, it is like going through it all again: the moment of the god-making, the sorrow.

At last the glade is empty. I am trembling. They are all in my heart now, and the sack is heavy. This part always makes me feel like I might explode. I fill in the holes and scatter debris over the soil until it looks like marmots have been here, or rabbits maybe. Nothing but nature taking its course. I pick up the sack gently.

We go deeper into the woods. The trees end at the lake to the west so I take a different direction. Even now, all these years later, I don't want to go near the lake.

I must find the right place. The gods can't live just anywhere. The beam of my flashlight dances over the ivy and dry brush. It's so warm tonight, the forest seems to be giving out heat. It spirals out from the trunks of the cedars, rises from the leaf litter. I take my sweater off. Midges and mosquitoes hover over my exposed arms and neck in grey clouds, but do not settle. Bats circle us, swooping so close their soft bodies graze my cheek. Tree branches spring away at my touch, clearing a passage before us. When I stop for a moment to catch my breath, a brown snake slides affection-ately over the toe of my boot. I am part of the forest, tonight. It holds me in its heart.

I hear the spring long before I see it, the glassy trickle of water on stone. I can't tell its direction; the sound seems to come from all around, as it often does, deep in the forest. I turn off the flashlight and stand in the dark. The sack shifts, uncomfortable against my back. Something sharp nudges me in the spine. The gods are eager. They want a home. I go where they tell me, through the catching bramble and bush. The half-moon is bright now; the clouds have cleared overhead. Without the flashlight I can see the forest in its night colours, silver-etched in delicate lines.

There is the gleam of pale bark ahead. White birches grow here, the bone trees. This is the sign I have been waiting for; I've found the place.

The spring leaps out of black wet stone, runs shrill and fast in its narrow channel, overhung by long fern fronds. Above, in the rock wall, there are dark crevices. Each hole is just the right size and shape to hold a god. One by one I slide them into their new homes. I shake a little as I do it – it's hard to hold so much power in my hands.

Dawn touches the sky with pink in the east by the time I'm done. I stand back and look at my work. Behind the rock wall I feel the gods hum, spreading their tendrils of power. The white birches stand tall in their clusters, watching. I'm so weary. Each time I do this I am destroyed. But it's my duty. I have to take care of them. Mommy has made that clear.

The woods are waking up. It is a long walk back in the new day, back to home and everyday things. I am carried on the furious joy of birdsong. 'I miss you,' I tell the birds. But at least they are safe from the Murderer here. I pass the yellow machines without a thought. Let them tear up the earth. The gods are safe in their new home.

Found the tape recorder in the refrigerator. I don't … nope, not even going to *try* to figure that one out.

No recipe. I thought maybe I should say, in case I forget — I moved them.

Maybe I'm just doing this because I want to talk to someone. Being with the gods makes me feel more alone than being alone. With Lauren gone, I need things that remind me who I am. I am so afraid that I'll just disappear and never come back.

This isn't making me feel any better. I feel stupid so I'll stop.

Dee

Everyone on Needless Street had a flyer through the door. Still, when yellow diggers come down the road like lions, she catches her breath. Their great metal mouths are still crusted with the dirt of old kills.

Dee comes out of her house to watch. It seems safer, somehow, than staying inside. A couple of the other neighbours are standing around, mouths and eyes wide.

A man with orange hair steps out in front of one of the diggers. He shouts to the driver. His big dog strains and whines so he takes it by the collar. 'I hope you're not going to use that neon paint to mark the trees,' he yells up at the driver. He is pointing at some canisters that sit in the truck. 'It's toxic.'

The driver shrugs and adjusts his hard hat.

'I'm a ranger,' the man says. In his hands the dog trembles with eagerness. 'It's terrible for the ecosystem.'

'Got to mark it somehow,' the man says comfortably. 'Neon stands out day and night.' He nods and the engine roars. The digger moves off like a dinosaur.

Breath tickles Dee's neck, lifts the hair on her nape. He is so close to her that when she turns, thrilling, his beard almost grazes her cheek. She can smell his distress, like crushed nettles on his skin. Ted sways. She realises that he is very drunk.

'No,' he says. 'They can't, they can't do this.'

He says some other things and Dee replies, she couldn't say what. She can't hear through the buzzing in her head. She knows that look, of a secret nearly revealed. Ted has it in his eyes.

When he runs up the trail after the diggers, she catches her breath. He's running towards something, she's sure of it. Something hidden in the forest. Dee knows she can't follow Ted. He'd see and then it would all be over. She must desperately hope that whatever is hidden cannot be accessed in daylight.

She goes indoors and sits at her post, biting her lower lip to shreds. Maybe she was wrong not to follow. Maybe she missed her chance and he's moving Lulu right now, taking her into the wild … Dee watches the forest with burning eyes.

Half an hour later, Ted comes back into view on the shadowed trail. Dee's heart burns and leaps. There is distress in his every movement. He shakes his head from side to side as if in passionate argument with himself. Whatever needs doing is still yet to be done. She hasn't missed it. There will be action, tonight.

Dee puts on hiking boots and lays out sweaters and a dark jacket, puts water and nuts in her pocket. Then she sits like a stone and watches Ted's house. Clouds pass and the sun sinks lower over the treeline. Dusk covers everything.

When she hears the distinctive triple thunk of the locks, the creak of the back door, she is ready. She feels, rather than sees him leave the house in the black. As he passes under the streetlight she sees the backpack. It is full of something that bulges in odd angles and curves. Tools, a pick, a shovel? He moves along the road into shadow. Now there are no more lights, just soft night and the moon overhead, shining like half a dime.

She follows at a distance; his flashlight guides her like a star. When he stops at the entrance to the woods and looks around, she stops too, sheltering behind a tree trunk. He waits for a long time, but she lets the night speak, lets it tell him that he is alone. When he goes on into the forest, she follows.

As they pass the work site, Dee hears Ted come to a halt ahead. The trees are thinning, perhaps into a clearing. She crouches among the bulldozers. Ahead, to the east, she hears the sound of a shovel cutting the earth. She hears whispering. She shivers. It must be Ted, but his voice sounds strange, like leaves rustling or the creak of living wood. Her calves and thighs cramp but she doesn't dare move. If she can hear Ted, he can hear her. The moon climbs and the night seems to grow warmer. Perfect weather for snakes. *Shut up, brain,* Dee thinks grimly. What can Ted be doing? She thinks about trying to edge closer but her every movement sounds loud as a gun-shot. She sits and listens. Time passes, she doesn't know how much, it might be an hour or longer. His whispering and the rhythmic cut of the shovel mingle with the night sounds of the forest.

At last there comes the sound of boots approaching and Dee starts. She has been teetering on the edge of sleep. She crawls quickly on numb legs under a digger. The moon is behind a gauzy screen of cloud but she can see enough. Ted carries something heavy on his back. The shovel in his hand is crusted with earth. He has dug something up. She struggles to her feet as silently as she can.

At the top of the rise to the west the moon gleams on still water. The lake, no more than a mile distant. *An hour's hike between Ted's house and the place where Lulu went missing,* Dee thinks, burning inwardly. Tonight Ted has proved that he can cover ground quickly with a heavy load. Yet the police just let him go. No matter what she tells them, they'll probably just let him go again. They don't care. Lazy, burnt out, incompetent ... Dee realises that she is trembling. She reaches out blindly, and grasps a slender branch for support. The forest seems full of sibilant whispers. The dry scratching of a long belly sliding over leaves. *Ophidiophobia,* she tells herself. *That's all it is, Dee Dee.* But now even the word is like a snake. It makes coils in her mouth.

She tries to take the next step. Tries not to think of what might be lying in wait on the ground in front of her. *There are no snakes here,* she repeats firmly to herself. *All the snakes are asleep underground. They are more afraid of you than you are of them.* But her breath comes fast. Her feet are welded to the ground. She is scared of the forest, of being lost in the trees, of being alone in the dark with a murderer. Most of all she is scared of the tree roots, which seem to twitch, looking at her with vertical pupils in the moonlight.

Don't be stupid. Walk, she commands her legs. *They aren't goddamn snakes.* Still she is paralysed, still as marble. Something rustles in the leaf mould close by. She can almost feel the long body approaching. *Walk,* she thinks, with every inch of her will.

Ahead, Ted's dancing light flickers and then vanishes among the trees. Dee is alone with whatever is coming through the dark. Soft, constant sound of a muscular body sliding.

Dee opens her mouth wider, wider, until her jaw strains and cracks. She screams in silence. She turns and runs for home. The whispering sound follows her, slithering fast, almost on her heels.

She locks the doors and windows. She takes the claw-hammer in hand and sits at her post. Her breathing is hoarse in the empty room. She looks at the old food wrappers and empty yoghurt pots that litter the floor. Ants crawl in and out of them. *I'm getting like him,* she thinks, trembling, disgusted. *And I am just as much of a coward.*

Ted comes home in the dawn. He unlocks his back door. As he goes in, she hears him calling, 'Here, kitten.' His voice is relaxed and friendly. Dee makes a list of things to get. It will be difficult, her mind will fight her, but next time Ted goes to the forest she won't fail.

Olivia

~

Lauren hasn't been around the last few weeks. I think she's on holiday with her mama ted or something? I don't know, I tend to tune out when he talks about her. No pink bike sprawled in the living room like a dead cow, no notes on the whiteboard, no screaming, no mess. The quiet, the peace — my stars! It's been great.

It's good that Lauren's not here because Ted has really been getting out there. Lauren hates it when he dates. She screams at him. My goodness, she is the most unpleasant little ted.

There's been no sign or scent of the TV ted with the eyes like dead blue coins. I think I let my imagination get the better of me, there. I do have such a rich and wonderful imagination, it's not surprising that it went a little too far.

Everything would be perfect if the whine would get out of my head. It's like an object lodged there, like a tintack or a knife. EEEEooooeeee.

I think I feel calm enough to consult with the Bible again. I am a little nervous, after last time — the house shook so hard. It was so scary I haven't dared since. But I can't leave it much longer. The LORD *would not like that. I have to be brave! Wish me luck, tape machine!*

I push the book off with my eyes tightly closed, braced for impact. But the crash and the tremors, when they come, are far away and deep in the earth. When the page falls open I read:

...if the salt has lost its taste, how shall its salt-
iness be restored? It is no longer good for anything except to be thrown out and trampled
under people's feet.

I can smell the salt and fat, now. I race upstairs to find Ted. Sure
enough, he is in bed, eating French fries with one hand. I leap on
him with high abandon, landing foursquare on his belly. The LORD
never lets me down.

He gasps. 'You startled me, kitten.' He drops what he has been
playing with in his other hand. A blue thing, too thin for a scarf,
more like a silky necktie or something. I settle on his stomach for
a purr. Ted and I are very happy together these days. Yes, I think
everything is returning to normal.

Ted

The past is close tonight. The membrane of time bulges and strains. I hear Mommy in the kitchen, talking to the Chihuahua lady. Mommy's telling her about the thing with the mouse. That was where all this started. I stop up my ears and turn the TV up, but I can still hear her voice. I remember everything about the thing with the mouse, which is unusual. My memory is Swiss cheese, in general.

Each homeroom had a pet. It was like a mascot. One homeroom had a startled-looking corn snake, which was so cool, and obviously better than a white mouse with bloody little eyes.

The kid with the moles was supposed to take the mouse home that weekend, but he hadn't been in school on Friday. His mother said he had a cold but everyone knew that he was getting the moles on his face removed. Anyway he couldn't take the mouse and I was next in the alphabet. Snowball, that was his name. The mouse, not the boy.

I took Snowball home. I had to sneak him into the house. Mommy would never have permitted it. Domesticated animals were slavery. Then the thing happened, and I did not bring him back on Monday.

I didn't get in trouble. There was nothing anyone could do or say. It had been an accident, after all – the cage door had come loose. I was really upset about it, but there were other feelings, too, which were more pleasant. I had discovered a new part of myself. I remember the look in my teacher's eye, that Monday. It had new reserve in it. He saw me for who I was. That I was dangerous.

Our homeroom got a hamster to replace Snowball. My teacher changed the system for taking the hamster home for weekends – it was random, now, pulled from a baseball cap. Somehow my name never came out of the hat. He became the principal, in the end, that homeroom teacher. It was years later, when I punched someone in the hall by my locker, that he found his chance. I can't even remember who it was that I punched. Was it a punch, or a kick? But it was my third strike, that's the point, and the school expelled me. I knew that teacher had been waiting for his chance to get me out, ever since the thing with the mouse.

I look at the cassette tapes. They sit in a neat row on the bookshelf. I think of the tape I hid in the hall closet. Maybe if I were braver I would listen. Her last words.

Thoughts are a door that the dead walk through. I feel her now, cold fingers walking up my neck. *Mommy, please leave me alone.*

I have to focus. I shake my hands loose and turn my palms upwards. I look at my hand – each finger, the pillowy base of the thumb, the palm as dry as leather. I take a deep breath for each part. This is something the bug man suggested I try, and surprisingly, it works.

I unlock the laptop cupboard and start the computer. The photograph of the man behind a desk comes up, grinning. It doesn't look like a real picture at all. But if people are lonely enough, they don't care about what's real and what isn't. Once again I feel bad for using a fake picture but no one would meet me if I used my own.

I look at the rows and rows of women. There are so many. The search hasn't been going well but it's important not to give up.

Maybe I've been doing this wrong. I've been focusing on

butter-blonde hair and blue eyes and so on, whereas what I really need is someone with whom I have more in common. A single parent. I change my search and the faces disappear, replaced by new ones. These are older, mostly. I try a couple, but they seem more wary than women without children, less responsive.

Finally I find one. She's willing to meet tonight. She answers quickly, within three seconds, which even I can tell is a mistake. It's too eager. She will meet me at a coffee shop after work. She does look nice, actually. She has a soft face and her jawline is doughy. Her dye job is old, grey shows at the roots, interrupting the dull black. It's late, but she'll try to get her sister to babysit. She has a twelve-year-old daughter.

I have a daughter myself, I tell her. *Lauren. What's yours called?*

She tells me and I type, *That's a pretty name. It's so great to talk to another single parent. It can be lonely at times.*

I know! she replies. *Some days I could just cry.*

If your sister can't sit, you could bring your daughter along, I tell the woman. *I'd love to meet her. I could bring Lauren, too.* (I can't bring Lauren, of course. But I can always say she is feeling sick.)

Wow, that is so understanding, she says. *I can tell you're a good person.*

I'll wear a blue shirt, I type. *Maybe you could wear blue too, so I can recognise you.*

Sure, that sounds fun.

Maybe not blue jeans, because everyone will be wearing those.

OK ...

Do you have a blue dress?

⁓

I haven't showered in a while so I do that, harmonising along with the beautiful melody the woman sings. I take a couple more pills, too. I don't want to mess this one up.

I have a quick beer before I go. I drink it in one, standing in front of the open refrigerator. There are trails of black droppings on the kitchen counters. The mouse problem is getting worse. I don't mind mice if the cats can deal with them, but not here. Sometimes, with problems you do nothing and they go away. Other times it is the opposite. I should get the diary out and note it. But there's no time!

The street is dark and quiet as I leave the house, triple-locking the door behind me. The Chihuahua lady's house is still empty. It pulls at me as I pass, that strange tug, like the house wants me to go in, like a god sending out tendrils of power.

Olivia

Ted is gone again. It has been a day and a night. I long for my nice dark crate but he has piled the weights on top of it. So thoughtless. I have licked my bowl so much my tongue tastes like metal. Oh, and of course, of course, that whining sound is here, filling my brain. It rises and falls but never goes away, these days. I can almost imagine I hear words in it, sometimes. Just now it's bearable. The hunger is worse. It gnaws at my stomach.

The TV is on, some creepy thing about a murderer stalking a girl in a parking lot. It's dark, raining. The actress playing the girl is pretty good. She looks scared. I don't like stuff like that so I leave the room. But I can still hear it: the running, the screams. I hope she gets away. Honestly, who watches this trash? There are sick people in the world, let me tell you. I thank the LORD that my Ted is nothing like that.

So hungry.

I stalk around the house. The cord floats behind me. It is sagging and grey today, which seems appropriate. You can't eat it. I've tried. I have eaten everything there is to eat in this place. I even knocked the lid off the trash can, but there were only dirty tissues in there. Since the Bad Dinner, Ted takes out the trash twice a day. Anyway, I ate the tissues.

I patrol the house, scenting for blood. I even go to the basement workshop, which I don't like too much because it has no windows. The engine sits like a shining sea creature on the workbench, under the spotlight. Boxes line the walls. I climb over them and into them. They are mostly empty, or filled with old parts. Even in my anxious state, the cardboard makes me purr a little. I have to make a big effort not to settle down for a comfortable doze.

I creep under the couch and peer behind radiators. I go under Ted's bed where beer cans roll about among the dust bunnies. I pull open his drawers and dig through his socks and boxers and undershirts. I scrabble about in the back of the closet. I don't find anything. No blood, and not even the scent of Lauren.

I stop before the attic door, my tail straight and scared. There is no sound. I force myself to come closer. I put my delicate velvet nose to the crack under the door and I breathe. Dust, dust and nothing. I listen, but all is quiet. I picture the still air, the thick beams sighing, abandoned objects spilling out of boxes. I shiver. There's something horrible about the thought of an empty room, in the dark. *OOoooeeeeeee,* goes the singing in my brain. If the LORD has a purpose for this almost constant noise, I wish he would reveal it pretty darn quick.

I realise I haven't looked under the refrigerator. Sure enough after a couple of tries I hook out a stale cracker with a claw. Ugh. Soft.

I am chewing when I glimpse something else in the dusty dark. I gently slide my paw, delicately extend my claws to their full length and reach in among the bottle caps and soft grey fluff. I sink a claw into the thing. It is a yielding surface, the claw goes right through. *A little body*, is my first thought. *A mouse? Ooh* ... But it's not flesh, something thinner and more porous. I pull the thing into the light. It's a child's white flip-flop. It must be one of Lauren's. Lauren can't walk but she likes to wear shoes sometimes anyway.

Well, no big deal, I say to myself, *it's just a flip-flop.* The iron-rich scent that fills my nostrils tells another story. Reluctantly I nose it over, and there it is on the other side. The sole is stiff, caked with dried, dark-brown matter. So I think, *Maybe it's jelly or ketchup or something, maybe it's not blood.* But my mouth is filling up with the scent. I want to eat it. The whining rises in pitch and volume.

I drop the flip-flop between my front paws and stare at it, as if there's an answer written there. It's probably nothing to do with me. Lauren must have hurt herself. She doesn't have any feeling in her feet, she's rough with them. But I can't help thinking about tiny bones, and the taste Night-time leaves at the back of my throat. About how often he has taken over, recently – how often I have let him. My tail blows up into a bottlebrush of unease. Normally this is exactly the kind of situation in which I would look to the LORD for guidance. But I don't. Somehow I don't want His attention on me, right now.

There is no blood anywhere else in the kitchen. I am sure of that. In fact, it is unusually clean. I can smell bleach. Now, that is really weird, because Ted never cleans.

Are you there? I ask.

His eyes glow green in the darkness. *Is it my time?*

No.

Maybe it is. He comes forward, a little playful, trying to take control. I fight him back – but honestly, it is more difficult than I remember. Is he getting stronger?

Did you ... I pause and lick my chops. My tongue feels kind of dry and woody. *Did we hurt Lauren?*

No, he says, and there comes that dark ripple through my body that happens when Night-time laughs. *Of course not.*

Phew. But my relief can only be short-lived. *Then why,* I ask Night-time, *is there a bloody flip-flop under the refrigerator?*

He shrugs, and the whole inside of my mind moves up and down like the swell of the ocean. *Hurt herself?* he suggests. *Kids.*

Maybe, I say. *But why hasn't she been around lately?*

Not my job to explain things to you, he says. *Ask someone else.* He turns to go back into the dark.

Well, what a gd help you are! I shout after him. Who the hell else am I supposed to ask?

I don't feel reassured. The opposite, actually. Night-time was so strong. The hair stands up on the ruff of my neck.

Ted sways into the kitchen. The light blazes up. I hadn't realised it had gotten dark.

'What have you found?' He takes the bloody little flip-flop from me, and goes still, looking at it. 'I thought I threw that away,' he says. 'Why won't it stay gone? I don't want it down here, I don't want you to see it.' He puts the flip-flop in his pocket and picks me up. His breath is a warm blast through my fur. I writhe and scream but it's no good.

He puts me in the crate. The lid comes down. I hear him piling things on top. He NEVER does that while I am in here. I *row* politely, because clearly there has been some kind of mistake. I won't be able to get out. But he carries on. Ted is trapping me! Why would he do that?

I *row* and *row*, but I am answered by silence. Ted is gone. He has locked me here in the dark. I try not to panic. He'll get over it and let me out. Besides, I love my crate, don't I?

I can't sleep. Every so often I twitch awake, convinced there is someone in here with me. I feel them along my side, stirring in the dark.

Ted

⌒

I cannot remember exactly how old I was when I realised that my Mommy was beautiful. No more than five, I think. I understood it not by looking at her but from the other kids' and parents' expressions. When she picked me up from school the parking lot was always full, and they all looked.

It gave me complicated feelings. It was obvious that the other mommies weren't like her. My mommy had smooth skin and big eyes that seemed to see only you when they looked. She didn't wear big jeans or sweaters. She wore a blue dress with a skirt that swished about her calves like the sea, or sometimes sheer blouses, which showed glimpses of the warm shadowed caverns of her. She spoke really softly and gently, she never yelled like other moms. Her pointed consonants and flat vowels were exotic. I was proud that they looked at her. But the glances also made a little hot place in my belly fire up. I both wanted them to look and didn't. It was better after I started taking the bus.

I was protective of her at school. But I was always most jealous when Mommy came home from her shift. I was scared that all the other kids she looked after at the hospital would use her up and there would be nothing left for me.

In a way, that was what happened. She was heartbroken when they let her go. There were cutbacks everywhere, everyone knew that. Money was tight. Daddy told me to keep out of Mommy's hair. She needed some space, he said. And she did seem diminished, somehow. Her easy glow was dimmed. I was fourteen or so then, maybe.

The Chihuahua lady and Mommy were tight. Every morning, if they weren't on shift, Mommy would walk over to her house. They would drink black coffee and smoke Virginia Slims and talk. If it was nice they sat on the screen porch. If it was dull or cold, which it usually was, they sat at the dinner table until the air grew so thick with smoke and secrets that you could have sliced it with a knife. I knew all this because sometimes on the weekends they lost track of time and I had to go fetch Mommy to make lunch. Maybe it was only opening jars of baby food, but it was still women's work, Daddy said. He was drinking a lot by then.

After Mommy was fired the Chihuahua lady was outraged, way more upset than Mommy. Chihuahua lady tried to get her to fight it. 'You're the best,' she said. 'You have such a way with the kids. They're crazy to lose you. It's a crime.' Her wide brown eyes were pools of belief. The Chihuahua lady always hummed with energy. 'You can write to the hospital board,' she said to Mommy. 'Come on. You can't take it lying down. You are an asset.'

Daddy and I both echoed her. 'You're the best, Mommy,' I said. 'They don't know how good they have it with you.'

'It's just the way of things,' Mommy said in her gentle way. 'You accept misfortune with grace.'

My problems at school had already started, but my parents had not yet begun to take them seriously. I guess I was so well behaved at home, they must have thought there was some mistake. I was helpful and polite, or at least I always tried to be. 'Teddy seems to have skipped being a teenager,' Mommy would say, stroking my cheek. 'We are lucky.'

One morning the Chihuahua lady came to the house before I left for school. I was eating cereal at the kitchen counter. Mommy was wearing her blue gauzy dress that floated behind her when she moved. The Chihuahua lady settled herself on a stool and poured three sachets of sweetener into her coffee. Steam wreathed about her head. She liked her coffee molten hot and sweet enough to kill. She took her dog out of her bag and put him on the counter. He had a little smooth, dark face, intelligent. He sniffed delicately at the coffee cups and blinked in the blue haze of cigarette smoke.

'How can you do it?' Mommy asked. 'How can you keep that poor creature in captivity? Can't you see the suffering in his eyes? It's monstrous to breed and keep wild animals.'

'You're soft-hearted,' the Chihuahua lady said. (Of course, I realise now, this was pre-Chihuahua. She was the dachshund lady, then, so I'll call her that.)

The dachshund lady gave her a look and Mommy said, 'Let's go in the other room. Teddy, finish that math homework.'

They went to the living room and she shut the kitchen door. I heard her say, 'Oh, that dog. I can't bear to look at him. And don't let him sit on my upholstered dining chairs! It's not hygienic.'

I got out my math homework. I had a headache. It had been sitting there for a few days now, like a toad at the front of my skull. I stared at the page, which throbbed and swam. It was hard to concentrate with my brain pulsing like this. I seemed to have at least attempted some of the math problems last night, although I could also see that I had got most of them wrong. I sighed and took out my eraser. The dachshund lady's voice drifted in and out. The kitchen door was thin pine board.

'Something stinks,' she said. 'All week there have been these big meetings, and yesterday the cops came. They're interviewing us all, one by one in the nurses' lounge. It's not very convenient. It means we have to go to the cafeteria for coffee. That's three whole floors down in the elevator, and three floors back up again. It uses up all my break.'

'Goodness,' Mommy said. 'What in heavens is that all about?'

'I don't know. They didn't get to me yet; they're going alphabetically. The girls won't say. They all looked kind of upset when they came out.'

'You know,' Mommy said, 'it doesn't surprise me.'

'No?' I can almost hear the dachshund lady lean forward, anticipating.

'Think about it. All that business with money. Where's the money going, I'd like to know? We're running the same ward we always have, on the same budget. Why is there suddenly so little to go around?'

'Wow,' says the dachshund lady on an indrawn breath. 'Do you think there's some kind of ... scam or something going on at the hospital?'

'It is not for me to say,' Mommy said in her gentlest voice. 'But I wonder, that is all.'

I heard the dachshund lady make a clicking sound with her tongue. 'It never made sense to me, that they fired you,' she said. 'If I said it once I said it a million times. Now, that would explain things.'

Mommy didn't answer and I imagined her shaking her head with her gentle, quizzical smile.

I started to feel upset, I didn't know why. So I got into the old chest freezer. I pulled the lid down on top of me and I felt better straight away.

I lost some time after that. When I came back I was still in the freezer, or there again more probably. I heard the dachshund lady's voice, and the scent of cigarette smoke trickled under the kitchen door from the living room. The kitchen was a little different.

The tulips that had been on the windowsill were gone. The walls looked dirtier.

'It's a scandal.' Mommy's voice. 'Throwing stones! They have broken every streetlight on this road. I blame the parents. Kids need discipline.'

I pushed open the kitchen door. The two women looked up at me in surprise. Mommy was wearing a green blouse and slacks. Through the window the day was cold, framed by bare twigs. The shaggy terrier sitting by the dachshund lady wasn't a dachshund. It raised its brown-and-white head, blinking in the cigarette smoke. She was the terrier lady, now.

'Go on, Teddy,' Mommy said, gentle. 'There is nothing to worry about. Finish the job application.' I closed the door and went back to the kitchen where the application for the auto shop in town sat half finished on the counter.

It wasn't the same day and I didn't go to school any more. I had been kicked out for punching the boy by the lockers. Mommy thought it was better I stay home anyway. I was a help to her. I had never before lost so much time at once. I tried to collect the brief flashes of memory that gleamed in my mind. I was twenty or twenty-one, I thought, Mommy worked at the daycare, now, not the hospital. But actually she didn't any more, because she had just been fired again, because people were mean.

I felt the difference in my body. I was bigger. Like, a lot bigger. My arms and legs were heavy. There was reddish hair on my face. And there were more scars. I could feel them on my back, itching under my T-shirt.

'Meheeeeeco,' the terrier lady is saying through the door. 'I'm going to have a cocktail with breakfast every day. One with an umbrella.' She has been looking forward to her vacation for weeks. 'That nice Henry is coming with me. The one who packs the bags at the Stop and Go. Twenty-five years old, what do you think about that?'

'You're terrible,' Mommy says. It sounds like a compliment and a judgement at the same time. I think about how old twenty-five is, and then how old the terrier lady is. Gross. She must be almost forty.

'Sylvia thinks so too,' the terrier lady says. She sounds sad, suddenly. 'I never thought my daughter would grow up to be so judgemental. She was the sweetest baby.'

'I am very lucky with Teddy,' Mommy says, and I am filled with love for her. 'He is always respectful.'

I wonder where Daddy is, and then I remember. Daddy left because I punched him in the head. I recall the crack of the bone against my knuckles, and look of the bruises on my hand. It is one of the many times I have been grateful that I do not feel pain. He felt it. I know that Daddy deserved it, but I have to search for the reasons why. It comes back to me in flashes. I had to hit him because he was yelling at Mommy. Calling her bad names, saying she was insane.

'Tsk,' Mommy says, breaking into my thoughts. I look up at her, grateful that she is there. 'You have cut yourself on that knife, Teddy.'

I start and put the knife back in the drawer. I didn't remember taking it out. 'It's fine, Mommy.'

'Don't take risks with your health,' she says. 'It needs disinfecting, and a couple stitches. I'll get my kit.'

No, that didn't happen then. I am in the wrong memory, now. *Never call a woman insane.* The feel of Mommy's cool hands on my face and the sappy green scent of the woods in the springtime. No, that is not right, either. I try to find the thread of that day. I am almost panting with frustration. There was something important about it. But it is gone.

The second time Mommy brought me to the forest was for Snow-ball the mouse. I was in the living room, crying over the cage. What was left of him lay gleaming in a corner. The sawdust was brown and hung together in clumps. A lot of blood in such a small thing. I remember the taste of snot and fear. I clutched my yellow blanket to my face and it was soaking wet; the blue butterflies glistened with sadness.

I looked up and there she was in the doorway, watching me in silence. She was wearing her blue dress, the floating one she called her tea dress. I didn't know what to do. How could I explain?

'Don't look at me,' I said. 'I didn't do it.'

'Yes, you did.'

I screamed and seized the Russian doll from the mantelpiece. I threw it at her. Tiny dolls flew in every direction. They all missed her head. They splintered on the wall behind. I screamed again and picked up the music box. But I was frightened of the bad feelings writhing through me. I let the box fall to the floor. It broke with a deep twang.

'Look what you have done.' She was calm. 'You take everything from me, Theodore. Take, take, take. Are you quite finished?'

I nodded.

'Get a shoebox from my closet,' she said. 'Take the shoes out first. Then dump everything from the cage into the box.' It was good that she gave exact instructions. I needed them, I couldn't think. My brain was lit up with shame and excitement both. Poor Snowball. But I had found a deep and secret thing.

I carried the shoebox in one careful hand. Mommy held the other. She pulled me along, not unkindly. 'Quickly now,' she said. Out the front door, down the street.

'You didn't lock it,' I said. 'What if someone goes into the house? What if they steal things?'

'Let them,' she said. 'Only you and I matter.'

What about Daddy? I thought, but did not say.

When we reached the gate to the woods I pulled back. 'I don't want to go in there.' I started to cry again. 'I'm afraid of the trees.' I remembered what had happened with the little wooden cat. What would I be asked to leave behind, today? Maybe Mommy would have to stay and I would be forced to return alone. That was the worst idea.

'You don't need to be afraid, Teddy,' she said. 'You are more frightening than anything that lives in these woods. Besides, you will feel better out of the heat.' She squeezed my hand. In her other hand she held her gardening trowel, the one with the pink handle.

We followed the path, which was a leopard skin of light and shade. She was right, I did feel better here, under the cool trees. I was still sorry, though. The mouse had been so little and I knew that we owe kindness to little things. So I cried again.

We reached a glade lined with boulders and silver trees like bolts of water or light. I knew, as soon as I stepped into that circle, that something would happen here. This was a place of transformation, where the wall between worlds was thin. I could feel it.

Mommy dug a hole with her pink trowel in a patch of sunshine, and we buried what was left of the mouse. The bones were picked clean; they shone almost translucent against the young grass. As the rich earth fell on top of the shoebox, covering it, something happened. I saw that what had been just a mouse was changed. Its remains became precious and powerful. It was part of death and of the earth now. It had become a god.

She sat and patted the earth beside her. I remember the scent of sap and her hands as she cradled my face. It must have been spring. 'You think I am hard on you,' she said. 'You don't like it that I have rules, and remind you of the reality of things. That I take care of your health, and don't let you keep pets or eat hot dogs like

American boys, that we cannot afford doctors and I sew up your cuts myself. And I do all this anyway, despite your complaints. I take care of your health because it is my duty. As I care for your body I must also tend your mind. We have discovered today that you have a sickness, there.

'You are probably promising yourself that you will never do such a thing again. You are thinking that you gave in just this once … And maybe that will prove true. But I do not think so. Yours is an old sickness, which has been in our family for a long time. My father – your grandfather – had it. I hoped that it had died with him. Maybe I thought that I could atone for it. A new world, a new life. I became a nurse because I wanted to save people's lives.'

'What is it? The sickness.'

She looked at me and the beam of her attention was like a warm sea. 'It makes you want to hurt living things,' she said. 'I saw that, the night that I followed Father to the old place, the tombs under the *iliz*. I saw what he kept there …' Mommy put her hand over her mouth. She breathed hard into her palm.

'What is *iliz*?' It sounded bad, like the name of a demon.

'It means church,' she said. '*Iliz*,' she said again softly, as though her tongue were remembering. I had never before heard her speak anything but English. I understood then that there was another, shadowy her, made of the past – like a ghost and a living person bound together.

'Did you like it there?' I asked. 'Do you miss it?'

She shook her head, impatient. '"Like", "miss" – these are soft words. Such places just are. It does not matter what you feel about them.

'In this country, all the people are afraid of death. But death is what we are. It is at the centre of things. That was the way in Locronan. In the *iliz* the ankou was carved on the altar. We left milk by the graves for him to drink, with one of his many faces.

The cemetery was the heart of the village. It was there we came to talk, to court and argue. There were no playgrounds or parks for children. Instead, we played hide and seek among the gravestones. Life was conducted amid death, side by side.

'But those two things can lie too close together. The line between them fades. So when the people heard the sounds from the *iliz* at night they said nothing because that was the way of things. When the dogs went missing, they said, "That is the way of things." Death in life, life in death. But I did not accept that.' She paused. 'One morning the boy who slept with the animals, Pemoc'h, did not come to the door for his cup of milk and his crust of bread. I went to look for him. He was not in the stable. There was blood in the straw. All day I hunted for him. He had no one to care what happened to him, except me. I looked in ditches in case he had been knocked there by a passing car, and in the hen-house in case he had fallen asleep among the warm bodies – and, oh, many other places. I did not find him.

'My father found me in the grain store in the afternoon and cuffed me round the ears. "There is the cooking and the laundry. You should not be idle."

'"I am looking for the boy Pemoc'h," I said. "I am afraid that something has happened to him."

'"Go to the kitchen," my father said. "You are neglecting your duty. I am ashamed." My father looked at me. I saw that behind each of his eyes there burned a tiny candle.

'When he went out that night, I followed him across the field, into the village, into the graveyard, to the place under the church. And there I saw his true nature.

'What did you see in the church?' I whispered. 'Mommy, what?'

'I saw them in the cages.' She did not look at me. 'Father's pets. I saw what had become of Pemoc'h.

'On Sunday, I denounced him in the church. I stood up before the congregation and I told them all what he had done. I told them to go and look, if they did not believe me. They did not go to look. So I saw that they already knew.' She paused. 'They preferred to close their eyes, to lose a stray dog, even a stray child, every so often. It had always been so. It was the way of things. People who have lived together for many generations share a special kind of madness. But when I spoke the truth aloud, they were forced to act at last.

'I woke that night to fire. There were five of them, with kerchiefs over their faces and torches in their hands. They took me from my bed, dragged me outside. My father, they bound to his bed. Then they set the house alight. The ankou wore my father's face that night.

'I dropped to my knees and I thanked them. But then the world went black. I think they hit me on the head. The next thing I knew was that we were rattling along the road in my father's van. It still smelled of his tobacco. They drove me through the night. By morning we had reached a town. "You are insane," they said. "Tell your tales to the cobbles and the mud. We good men have no time for them." And then they left me there, on the streets of that strange town. No money, no friends. I did not even speak the language, only the old tongue.'

'Why did they do that?' I wanted to hurt them. 'That wasn't fair!'

'Fair!' she smiled. 'I had broken the silence of Locronan. I understood their actions.'

'What happened to you?' I asked. 'What did you eat and where did you sleep?'

'I used what I had,' she said. 'My face, my health, my mind, my will. I had some talent with helping the sick, and a neat stitch. So I did not fare as badly as I might have done. But anyone may kick a stray dog in the street, and that is what I was, until your father came through the town. I would be in that place still, but for him. He brought me here.

'I felt the ankou follow me across the ocean, across the land, to this far coast. Once he has seen you he will not let you go. We know these things in Locronan. This so-called new world has forgotten them. On the day he comes to me with open arms, wearing my face, I will be ready.'

I wasn't upset by what she was saying, because it was clear to me that Mommy could never die. My fears were for myself. I looked at the disturbed earth, under which there lay the little god that had once been Snowball. 'What is going to happen to me?' I whispered.

'One day, maybe soon, or maybe when you are a big man, you will want to do that again. You may resist but in the end you will give in to the wanting, over and over. And in time you will hunger for sport bigger than a mouse. Perhaps it will be dogs, and then cattle, and then people. That is how it goes – I have seen it. However it progresses, it will become all that you are, and you will grow careless. That will be your undoing. One day, after you have gone far, far beyond the reach of reason, they will get you. The police, the courts, the prisons. You are not clever enough to avoid them. They will find out your nature, and they will hurt you and lock you up. I know that you could not survive it. Therefore, you must take care. You must never, ever let them see who you really are.'

It was a relief, in a way, to hear her say these things. I had always felt that there was something wrong with me. I was like one of the tracings I did on her baking paper, a bad one, where the comic book underneath slipped; the lines slewed across the page, and the picture became a monstrous version of itself.

'Do you understand?' she asked. Her fingers on my cheek, light and cool. 'You must never tell anyone about this. Not your friends at school, and not your father. It must be a secret between you and me alone.'

I nodded.

'Do not cry,' Mommy said. 'Come with me.' She pulled me up with a strong arm.

'Where are we going?'

'We are not *going* anywhere. We are *walking*,' she said. 'When your feelings get too big, you must come to the woods and walk.' The nurse tone crept into her voice somewhat. 'Exercise is good for the mind and the body. Thirty minutes each day is recommended. It will help you to master yourself.'

We marched along the trail in silence for a time. Mommy's blue dress flew out behind her in the breeze. She looked like something from a myth, here among the trees.

'They would call you "insane" if they knew what you were,' she said. 'That word. I abhor it. Promise me that you will never call a woman insane, Theodore.'

'I promise,' I said. 'Can we go home now?' I thought of Snowball's pink paws and eyes. The tears rose again. There was still a lot of feeling left in me.

'Not yet,' Mommy said. 'We keep walking until the need to cry has passed. You will tell me when that is.'

I took hold of her skirt and clung to it with both fists as we walked. My hands were still dirty from the grave we had dug. They left finger marks on the blue organza. 'Thank you for not being mad at me,' I said. I meant the dress, the mouse, everything.

'Mad,' she said, thoughtful. 'No, I am not mad. For a long time, I have feared that this was in you. Now it is confirmed. I find that it is a relief. I no longer need to think of you as my son. No longer must I search my heart for a love that I cannot feel.'

I cried out and tears welled hot in my eyes. 'You can't mean that,' I said. 'Please don't say that.'

'It is the truth.' She did look down at me, now. Her eyes were remote and serious. 'You are monstrous. However, you are my responsibility. I will continue to do what I can for you, because that is my duty, and I have never been afraid of my duty. I will not permit you to be called "insane". In this country, in particular, they love to throw that word around like a ball.'

She waited patiently as I cried. When the tears slowed she offered me a tissue, and her hand. 'Come,' she said. 'Walk.'

We did not turn for home until my feet were sore.

I tried to mend the dolls and even the music box, with crazy glue and a book about clocks. Both were broken beyond repair. Mommy kept the music box but she put the dolls in the trash and they are gone for ever; another part of her I can never get back, another thing I broke that cannot be mended.

I keep meaning to record the recipe for my vinegar strawberry sandwich, but I don't have the heart for it now.

Olivia

Light, at last. Ted's hands on me, lifting me out of the dark. Bourbon hangs thick on his breath.

'Hey, kitten,' he breathes into my fur. 'You ready to behave? I hope so. I missed you so much. Come watch TV with me. Tell you something, I'll do the stroking and you do the purring, doesn't that sound good?'

I twist out of his hands and rake my claws across his face. I slash at his arms and chest, feel cotton and flesh part, feel the blood come. Then I run and hide beneath the couch.

He calls to me. 'Please,' he says. 'Come out, kitten.' He fetches a plate with two chicken fingers on it, and puts it in the centre of the room by the recliner. He chirps and calls me, 'Here, kitty, kitty, kitty ...' The chicken fingers smell really good but I stay put. I'm hungry and thirsty, but my anger is stronger.

I feel like I don't even know *you any more,* I say, though of course all he hears is a hiss. In the end he gives up, which is typical. He can never take responsibility for anything.

As he goes, something falls out of the cuff of his pants. It is little and white, but I can't quite make it out. The thing bounces and my tail twitches. I want to chase it. Ted doesn't notice.

In the kitchen, I hear the hollow crack of a beer being opened, the clicking of his throat as he swallows, and his heavy tread as he climbs the stairs. The record player blares into life. The sad woman begins to sing in long elongated vowels about dancing. He'll lie in bed now, music playing low, drinking until there's nothing left to drink.

Right now I'm hiding under the couch, even though the dust bunnies tickle my nose very badly. I have to record this.

So, obviously, I had to go get the thing that fell out of the cuff of Ted's pants. It was irresistible. Cats and curiosity and all that, you know?

I stalked towards it, belly flat to the floor. The scent came from it in waves. It was the scent I lick off my paws and jaws after Night-time has been with me. It was the scent that came from the little white flip-flop. That's when I knew this was bad, bad.

I took the thing in my mouth. It turned out to be a square of paper, folded so many times that it was like a hard little pellet. I thought, Why would Ted carry it in his pants cuff? Weird.

I got safely back under the couch and teased the note open with a claw. It wasn't paper, actually, but a scrap of white tree bark, thin and beautiful. But it had been used as paper. I saw there was a word, written in pink marker on the creamy surface. I froze because I know those messy letters. I have seen them often enough on the whiteboard in the kitchen.

It's Lauren's writing. Above the word in pink marker, like outlying islands, are three irregular patches of brown. My nose tells me what they are. Splashes of blood.

Several times I pushed the note away and tried to pretend it didn't exist. Then I retrieved it and I read it again, each time hoping that it would say something different. But it didn't. There it was, just that one word.

Help.

Ted

I'm drinking bourbon from the bottle, no time for glass or ice. The liquor courses down my face, my eyes sting from the fumes. Disaster, disaster, disaster. I must stop everything. I am being watched. Invaded, even. I might not have known if Mommy hadn't trained me so well. I missed it my first morning round with the diary, which goes to show that she was right. Everything seemed fine. The windows were all secure, the plywood nailed down tight over them, the portholes were clear. I was in a really good mood.

I was in a hurry during the evening check. I had some donuts and a new bottle of bourbon waiting for me and there was a big monster truck rally on TV at six. So I was looking forward to the end of the day and I skimped my inspection a little. Who could blame me? I was heading back inside when I caught it in the corner of my eye.

Maybe I wouldn't have noticed anything if the sun hadn't come out from behind a cloud at just that moment, at that exact angle. But it did and so I did. There it was, gleaming silver. A pinprick of light, a little drop of brightness against the weather-stained plywood that covers the living-room window.

I waded into the thick mess of briars and weeds that cling to the house. I clutched the diary to me, trying to protect it. Is there anything on this planet that doesn't want to scratch me? But it wasn't as hard to fight through them as I had expected. Some

175

of the briars were snapped and hung sadly as if something had recently forced its way through. Others lay broken on the dirt, as if trampled underfoot. Unease stirred.

When I reached the window I tugged at the plywood but it was solid, still nailed fast. I stood back again and looked. Something was wrong, but what? Then the sun came out again. It caught the nail heads. They shone, store-bright.

I knew then — someone had been here. They crawled up to the house, through thorns and poison oak and brambles. They carefully dug the nails out of the window frame and lifted the plywood off. And after that, I have to assume they lifted the sash and went inside. Later, they came out again and hammered it back in place and left. They did a good job. I might never have known. But they didn't think to reuse the old nails. Instead, they put these shiny things in. It's impossible to know when. These thoughts were like being punched repeatedly in the neck.

Were they watching right now? I looked about me, but it was still. A lawnmower growled somewhere.

I made my way out of the briars and towards the back door. I felt the weight of unseen eyes. I didn't run — though I wanted to, every muscle wanted to, my skin itched with the urge to run. Once inside I closed the door gently behind me and locked the locks. *Thunk, thunk, thunk.* But the sound didn't mean safety any more. I went to the living-room window. My fingers sought the latch on top of the sash. It was loose in my hand. As I turned it, the latch came right off in a little shower of brown dust. At some point over the years the metal catch rusted through. Anyone could have got in.

I never open the windows, of course. I forgot that they did open. That was a mistake. There was a gasping sound somewhere, and I realised it was coming from me. I paced up and down the living room, kicking uselessly at the bobbly blue rug. I always feared this day might come. Mommy told me it would, in the forest, after the thing with the mouse. The day she understood my true nature. *They'll come for you, Teddy.* I hoped so hard that she was wrong.

What did they see, this intruder? Did they watch me? As I made my chicken and grape salad, or as I watched TV, or slept? The only real question, of course, is, did they see Lauren and Olivia? They can't have done. I would know by now. There would have been consequences.

Mommy would say, look for the variable. My neighbours, the police – they haven't bothered me for years. So what has changed?

The neighbour lady. She is new. She is the variable. She didn't want to be my friend. She stood me up at the bar. I stare at her house and think.

I was going to unground Lauren and let her come home this weekend – but that can't happen obviously. And there can be no more dates, for now. It's not safe.

'Lauren can't come out to play,' I sing along to the music. Then I realise that's kind of mean, so I stop. I have been very stupid but I will take care from now on.

Deal with things one at a time. Lauren first, then I'll see about the intruder. Maybe it's the neighbour lady, maybe not.

I think I hear a Chihuahua barking in the street and I put my eye to the peephole to look. Maybe she's back! That would be one less thing to worry about. The bark comes again – it's much deeper and louder than a Chihuahua. The man with the orange-juice hair comes into view, walking his dog to the woods. He looks at my house and for a second it's like our eyes meet, like he sees me. But he can't see me through the peephole, I tell myself. Then I think, he doesn't live on our street, so why is he always here? Is he the Bird Murderer, or the intruder, or both? I sit down with my back against the wall, heart galloping. My nerves are singing like struck metal.

Bourbon, just to calm me down. I drink it standing out in the yard, watching the neighbour lady's house. Let her see me.

Dee

She has not had the dream since she moved to Needless Street. To-night it begins immediately, as if in response to some long-awaited cue.

Dee is walking by the lake. The trees lean over, casting dark, glassy reflections. Damselflies kiss the surface of the water, send-ing out shining circles. The sky above is an aching nothing. The sand beneath her feet is sharp, a million tiny shards of glass. She bleeds but feels no pain. Or perhaps there is so much pain in her that she doesn't notice the cuts. She keeps walking. Dee would give anything to stop, to turn, to wake. But she has to get to the trees and the birds and the nests, that's how it goes. She has to see it.

The treeline draws nearer, the air is shuddering with the force of everything. She sees the birds now, small and beautiful, darts of colour among the trees. They do not call. They are silent as fish in a pond. The lake falls away behind her and she is in the shad-owed place beneath the trees. Pine needles litter the forest floor. It is soft underfoot, soft as grave earth, freshly dug. Overhead the birds glide and dart. Dee comes into the clearing beneath the ter-rible sky and there it is, the white tree. It is a silver birch, slender and lovely. She remembers that sometimes they're called paper birches. Strange, the thoughts that come to you in dreams. There is an intricate nest built at the juncture of two branches. A crimson bird with golden eyes and a golden beak lands. She carefully weaves the strand of dried grass she has brought into the soft inside of the nest where she will lay her eggs.

Dee begins to moan. She tries to wake herself because the next part is the worst. But she can't. Against her will she is drawn closer to the tree, to the nest, to the bird. She covers her dream mouth with her dream hand. Even in a dream, it seems, a stomach can feel sick to death.

She tries to turn, to run. But everywhere she turns there are silent crimson birds fluttering among the trees of bone, bearing in their beaks the wisps of grass that are not grass, lining their nests with her dead sister's hair.

Dee wakes to a soft tapping on her cheek, her forehead, her nose. When she opens her eyes all she can see is fur and whiskers. The tabby cat is very close; her nose nearly touches Dee's. The cat taps Dee's nose once more with her velvet fist, to make sure that Dee has really stopped screaming.

'Sorry, cat,' she says, then starts. 'What are you doing in here?'

The cat sits back on her haunches and looks steadily at her. She is thin and ragged, ears torn from fighting. Her eyes are a soft tawny brown. Dee could not call her a beautiful cat. But she is a survivor.

The tabby puts her head on one side and makes an interrogative *pprrrrp?*

'Really?' asks Dee in disbelief. But the cat continues to regard her fixedly, and everyone knows what that look means, from a cat.

Dee finds a can of tuna in a cupboard in the kitchen. She empties it onto a saucer. The cat eats delicately, stirring the air with her tail.

'Do you have a name?' Dee asks. The cat ignores her. She licks her lips with a small pink tongue and strolls into the living room. Dee rinses the saucer before following. It only takes a moment but when she comes through she can't see the cat anywhere. It has left.

Dee knows that her sister has not come back to her as a mangy alley cat. Of course not. That would be crazy. But she can't help the feeling that the cat pulled her out of the dream. That it is helping her, somehow.

Dee goes to her post at the window. The world is lit by a dim and secret light. She is not sure if it's dawn or dusk. She hasn't slept on a regular schedule for some time. She gasps, her heart flurries with shock.

Ted is standing in his front yard. Bourbon drips from his beard. He lifts a slow hand, a pointing finger. His eyes seem to pierce the shadows. Dee wriggles as if his gaze is a touch.

She knows he can't see through the glass, into the dark house. But she feels the feather brush of fear like red bird wings. With it comes a rush of defiance. *I'm coming for you,* she tells Ted silently. *You feel it, too.*

She yelps and jumps as her cellphone rings. She's surprised it's charged and switched on. It has been so long since she used it. Dee checks the number. She makes a face and answers.

'Hi,' she says.

'Delilah.' Karen sounds even more tired than usual. 'How are you doing?'

'Oh, you know,' Dee says. She doesn't offer anything else. She makes Karen work for it.

'Where are you, these days?'

'I keep moving,' Dee says. 'If I stay put I start to think.' Tears rise as she says this. She hadn't meant to. She brushes her stinging eyes angrily. Truth is as slippery as mercury. It always seems to find a way to escape. *Get a grip, Dee Dee. Get it done.* 'I'm in Colorado, right now.' Colorado seems safely distant from here.

'You need anything, you let me know.'

Words cluster, stinging in her throat but Dee bites them back. Karen has failed again and again to give Dee the only thing she really needs. Lulu.

'How are you?' she says instead.

'We're having a heatwave up here in Washington,' Karen says. 'It hasn't been this hot in years.' Not since the year Lulu went missing, but neither of them says that. 'Anyway I know this time of year is difficult for you. I thought I'd check in.'

'Check in on me or check up on me?' Dee says. She knows Karen is thinking of the man in Oregon.

'What?'

'Nothing. I appreciate it, Karen.'

'You've been on my mind. I could have sworn I saw you in a grocery store in town the other day. The mind plays tricks, huh?'

'That it does,' Dee says. Her heart is racing. 'That part of the world won't hold me, Karen. I wouldn't come back.'

'I understand.' Karen sighs. 'You promise me you'll call, Dee, if you need help?'

'I do.'

'Take care of yourself.' The line goes dead.

Dee shivers and curses her luck. Could Karen trace her cellphone? Maybe, but why would she? Dee has done nothing wrong.

She's got to be more careful. It would mess everything up if Karen knew she was here. No more going out in the day. She'll take the bus into the city to do her groceries. She swears to herself in a hiss. When Dee looks out of the window again, Ted is gone.

Ted

Is the intruder the Murderer? I think and think but I can't work it out.

I haven't been so scared since that time at the mall. That was the last time I came this close to being found out – to being seen for what I am.

Lauren cried and showed me the holes in her socks. She had outgrown all her clothes and she hated the stuff I chose for her. What dad can refuse his daughter clothes? So even though I knew it was a mistake, I said yes.

I picked an older mall, one slightly further out of town, and we went on a Monday afternoon, in the hope that it wouldn't be too crowded. Lauren was so excited before we left that I thought she would pee herself. She wanted to wear all kinds of crazy pink things in her hair, but I thought there should be limits.

'I simply couldn't be seen with you,' I said to her in a fancy lady's voice, and she giggled, which showed what a good mood she was in, because she never laughs at my jokes. I wore a baseball cap, sunglasses, and regular clothes in neutral colours. I knew that this shopping trip was a risk, and I was anxious that we should attract as little attention as possible.

Lauren was good on the drive there, looking out of the window and singing to herself, the song about woodlice. There was none of the nonsense that she had tried in the past, trying to grab the wheel and steer us into a ditch or a wall. I allowed myself to hope that this would go well.

When we got to the mall we couldn't even see it at first, the parking lot was so huge, and we had picked a spot right at the far end. Lauren was impatient and didn't want to get back in the car, so we walked. It must have been a quarter of a mile, and the morning was close. The big square box of the building got bigger and bigger as we approached. It had fancy writing across it, huge like a giant's signature. Lauren pulled me on.

'Faster,' she said. 'Come *on*, Dad.'

I was sweating heavily by the time we reached the doors. The cool air and marble floors were a relief. I had picked a good place; there was hardly anyone else here. Some angry women with small children. Bitten-looking men who didn't look like they had anything else to do with the day.

There was a big plastic board with a map on it, and I stood in front of it for a while trying to make sense of the floor plan. But I was too anxious and it all dissolved into lines and colours (those were the days before I had the bug man and the pills). Lauren was no help, she was all over the place, peering this way and that, trying to look at everything at once.

I went up to a lady in a brown uniform, with a badge on her chest, and asked, 'Excuse me, where is Contempo Casuals?'

The woman shook her head. 'That store closed down,' she said. 'Years ago, as I recall. Why would you want that?'

'My daughter, she's thirteen,' I said. 'She wants to get some clothes.'

'And she asked for Contempo Casuals? Has she been in a coma?'

The woman was being very rude so I walked off. 'They don't have that store here,' I told Lauren.

'It doesn't matter,' she said. 'Isn't this great, Dad?' Her voice was loud and I saw one of the tired mothers look over at us.

'If this is going to work, you have to be smart,' I told her. 'You don't talk. Keep close, no tantrums, do everything I say. Deal?'

She smiled and nodded and didn't say a word. Lauren has her faults but she's not slow.

We walked along the storefronts, looking at all the stuff. There was so much to see, we could have spent all day there. Piano music came out of the white pillars and echoed on the marble floor. There was a fountain playing somewhere. I could tell Lauren loved it, and if I'm honest, I did too. It was great to just walk around together, out in the open, like a regular father and daughter. I got us an Orange Julius in the deserted food court. Burnt sugar and soy sauce fought uneasily in the air. The tables were all messy like people had just left, burger wrappers and plastic forks and crumbs all over the place. But there was no one in sight.

We went into an empty, echoing department store and I picked up some socks and undervests. All boring white for me, pink and yellow for Lauren. The undervests had unicorns on them.

To entertain her, I started making up names and histories for the bored-looking clerks standing behind their counters. The buck-toothed girl was Mabel Worthington, working extra hours to help her little brother realise his dream of becoming an ice dancer. The guy with two big moles was Monty Miles, and he had just arrived here, straight from his little ice-fishing village in Canada.

'Those two blonde girls are sisters,' I said. 'They were separated by foster care, and they've just found each other again.'

'I don't like that one,' Lauren whispered, unhappy. 'That's not nice, Dad. Change it.'

'You're a fussy kitten today, aren't you?' I was trying to think of a good one for those two when Lauren tugged my hand hard. I turned and saw a pair of leggings hanging on a nearby rack. They were bright blue with shiny gold lightning bolts on them. Lauren held her breath as she looked at them.

'I guess you can try them on,' I said. 'I have to come with you into the changing room, though.'

All the leggings on the rack were too small. I looked around hopelessly. The two sales girls came over to us. Close up they didn't look much alike, after all. They were both blonde, that was all.

The taller one said, 'Can I help you?'

'Is this all you have in stock?' I asked.

'I think so,' she said.

'Are you sure?' I could tell how much Lauren loved those leggings and how disappointed she would be if she couldn't get them. 'Don't you have more in back?' I gave her my best smile and told her the size Lauren needed. The short one smirked.

'Something funny?' I asked. In that moment I hoped the smirking girl actually had been raised in foster care and separated from her family. Luckily Lauren's attention had wandered back to the leggings and she didn't see.

The taller woman ignored her friend and said in a professional tone, 'I can check.' I noticed that she had a twitch in her left eyelid, some kind of tic. Maybe living with this had made her a nicer person. After a while she came back with more pairs of leggings draped over her forearm, like a fancy waiter carrying a white napkin. 'These might work,' she said.

The changing room was long and quiet, hung with white curtains.

'Go away, Dad,' Lauren said when we were inside a cubicle.

'You know I can't do that, kitten.'

'At least – don't look. PLEASE.' So I closed my eyes. There was rustling and silence. Then she said sadly, 'They don't fit.'

'I'm so sorry, my kitten,' I said. I really was. 'We'll find you something else.'

'No,' she said. 'I'm tired, now. Let's go home.'

We left the leggings where they lay on the floor in a sad pile of blue sky and lightning. We followed the green exit signs through what seemed like miles of empty aisles: leather goods, lingerie, then into home furnishings.

As we reached the store exit I heard running feet. Someone yelled, 'Stop!' When I turned, the tall blonde girl was running towards us through the display living room.

'Excuse me,' she said. 'Is this some kind of joke?' Her voice shook. Her eyelid was twitching furiously.

'Is something wrong?' I asked her.

She held out a handful of blue and gold fabric. 'This,' she said, and turned the leggings inside out. They were lined with white stretchy stuff. Lauren had treated this lining like a piece of blank paper. On it she had written, in her favourite pink marker:

Plaes help. Ted is a kidnaper. He cals me Lauren but taht is not my nam.

And then underneath, she had drawn a map to our house. It was pretty good. She must have been watching carefully as we drove.

'That shit is not funny,' the woman said. 'Do you think missing children are a joke?'

I could feel Lauren starting to get upset by her shouting, and by the cursing, so I said, 'I'm so sorry. I don't know how that happened. Obviously I'll pay for them.' I put a twenty and a ten in the blonde clerk's hand, which was much more than the pants cost, and took them from her. She shook her head at us and her mouth was a grim little line.

We walked back through the desert of the parking lot. The sun was high in the sky, now, and heat was shimmering off the asphalt. When we reached the car I said, 'Get in please, and fasten your seatbelt.' Lauren obeyed in silence.

I turned on the AC. The cool air began to dry the sweat on my brow, and I let it soothe me. When I could at last trust myself to speak I said, 'You must have been planning that one for a long time. Give me the marker.'

'I left it in the store,' Lauren said.

'No,' I replied. 'You didn't.'

She pulled the marker out of her sock and handed it to me. Then she started crying silently. That hurt, it was like a skewer to my heart. 'You have to learn that your actions have consequences,' I said.

Lauren's back heaved with huge sobs. The tears ran in a steady stream down her face. 'Please,' she said. 'Don't send me away.'

I took a deep breath and said, 'Six months. You can't come home for six months.'

Lauren moaned. It was a bad sound that made tears poke out in my own eyes.

'It's for your own good,' I told her. 'It hurts me as much as it hurts you. I've tried to raise you right. But I've failed. I see that. Defacing property and downright lying. You have to learn that you can't pull that kind of stunt. What if that woman had believed you?'

The separation that followed was so painful that I have tried to erase it from my mind. We do not speak of it. During those months the birds in the mornings became an even greater comfort. I needed something to love.

After that dark time was over and Lauren returned, I put precautions in place. I always triple-lock the door and lock up the laptop. I always count the marker pens before I put them away. It is not easy but I keep her safe.

Lauren seemed changed afterwards. She was still loud but it was empty, somehow, the temper of a much younger child. My daughter had learned her lesson, I thought.

I am very upset this evening so I make mint hot chocolate.

Recipe for Mint Hot Chocolate, by Ted Bannerman. Warm the milk. Break pieces of chocolate into it and melt them. Add crème de menthe, as much as you like. You can add bourbon too. It's night, you're not going anywhere! It should all come together in a smooth goo. You can put chopped fresh mint in too, if you like. Pour it into a tall glass with a handle. If you don't have one, a mug is fine. (I don't have one.) Then top with whipped cream and chocolate chips or smashed-up pieces of cookie. You need a spoon to eat this.

I like to make this slowly, stirring the chocolate, thinking about things, which is what I'm doing when I put my hand in my pocket. I often do that, to think, and my fingers meet a piece of paper. I draw it out, wincing. *The Murderer.* It is the list of suspects I made after the birds were killed. I left it under Lauren's chalks, locked up in the cupboard. How did it get in my pocket? A name has been added to the list, below Lauren's. I don't recognise the writing.

Mommy

Well, that is a very cruel and scary joke. If there is one person who could not have killed the birds, it is Mommy. She's gone.

I tear up the list and throw it in the trash. Even mint hot chocolate doesn't help, now.

Lauren

⁓

Please come and arrest Ted for murder, and other things. They have the death penalty in this state, I know that. He makes me do my social studies homework. When I'm done, I'm going to try to throw this cassette out the mail slot. I hope someone finds it.

Ted always takes the knife when he goes to the woods. Maybe I will do it to him, maybe he will do it to me. But it will finish in the woods, where he put the others. Out we will go like a little candle, leaving nothing but the peaceful dark. I kind of look forward to it. I am made with pain, for it, of it. I don't have any other purpose, except to die.

He doesn't think I can hear him when I'm down there, but I can. Or maybe he forgets I exist as soon as he closes the door. He's such a dork with his dumb recipes. He didn't invent the strawberry and vinegar sandwich thing. Even I know that, from the cooking network. I heard him talking to the cat about making a — what? — a feelings diary. SUCH a dork. But that's how I got this idea, so I guess it was lucky. I'm not what they call book smart but I can make plans.

I found the tape recorder in the hall closet. It's the only closet he doesn't keep locked. I guess because there's nothing in here, just piles of old news-papers. But then I found the machine, with the tape in and I thought, Here's my chance.

I'm sitting here right now in the dark, so I can put everything back where I found it, if he comes. The tape is really old, with a yellow-and-black label. It had her writing on it. Notes. I didn't listen to it; I know what's on there. There's a hot feeling in my tummy. I feel good about recording over her. I'm afraid, too, though.

I wonder what it's like being a regular person — not being afraid all the time. Maybe everyone is afraid all the ti— Oh God, he's coming n—

Olivia

I keep trying to record my thoughts but the whine is so loud. It has become a scream. My head feels like it will split. I can't, I just can't.

Oooeeeeeooo, metal dragging on metal, torture to my poor brain, my soft ears, my delicate bones … It's a hammer of sound in my skull. So when the voice starts speaking, running underneath it, I don't hear at first.

'Olivia,' says the voice. 'Olivia.' It's no louder than a butterfly's wing. *Ooooooeeeeeooo.*

Hello? I ease out from under the couch. *Where are you?* I ask, which is just as useless as me talking to the TV, I guess, because it's definitely a ted saying my name, and they don't understand.

'Olivia, in here.'

My heart is beating really loudly. I am on the edge of something. If I do this I can never give back the knowledge. Part of me wants to get back under the couch and forget about it. But I can't. That wouldn't be right.

I recognise the voice and where it's coming from. I have never hoped harder to be wrong.

I go to my crate, in the kitchen. It's not a crate of course, I just call it that. It's one of those old chest freezers. I like to sleep in it – the dark, the quiet. But sometimes Ted piles stuff on top of it. Weights. Like now.

I put my ear close. The whine is high like a lady singing opera. But I can still hear her voice, underneath it.

'Hello?' she says, tearful, a bare whisper. 'Olivia?' The words are faint, she sounds weak and sad, but there is no mistake. I picture her curled up in the dark, in there. I can hear her wet breathing.

'He's mad that I made a bad dinner,' Lauren says, her voice coming eerie through the air holes. 'So mad. The only time I remember him being this angry was after that time at the mall …' She's doing that slight, involuntary gasping that happens when people are tired out from crying.

My mind won't work properly, it races like that mouse in the walls. My fur stands up in quills.

Calm down, Olivia, I tell myself. *So she got herself locked in the freezer somehow. Careless kid …*

'I didn't lock myself in,' Lauren says.

I leap a little in the air. *You can hear me?* I ask. *You understand cat? Oh my* LORD!

'Listen. Ted shut me in …'

What a silly accident, I say, relieved. *I bet he'll feel terrible when he realises … OK. Easy! I'll go wake Ted, and he can let you out.*

'No, please don't wake him.' Her voice is like a scream, if a scream could also be a whisper. It's horrible. It has little bloody flip-flops and scrawls saying *help* in it. I feel cold marching up my tail, into my spine. Lauren gives a series of hard little gasps like she's trying to get herself together.

You can't stay in there for ever, Lauren, I say, reasonable. *That's my place. It's a little selfish of you, actually. Anyway, your mom will come looking for you, or the school … Is it a school you go to? Sorry, I forget.*

'No, Olivia,' she whispers. 'Think. Please.' I look at the freezer, its size. I look at the air holes Ted pierced in the lid for me. Or were they for me? I feel the answer ebbing through the thick metal door, the rubber seal. The knowledge twists through my organs, flesh and bones.

You don't go anywhere, when you go away, I say. *You stay right here.*

'When you can't get in, that means I'm here,' she says. 'We take turns, I guess.'

I think of it: Lauren lying quiet in the dark, listening as Ted and I go about our business. *I haven't seen you for over a month,* I say.

'Has it been that long? Time drifts here in the dark, it's hard to tell whether you are dead or not. I wondered. But then I heard you through the wall, and I thought, no, not yet ...'

Oh, I say. *Oh, oh.*

'I've been trying to speak to you,' she says. 'Had to find a time when he didn't stop my mouth too tight, when he was asleep and the music wasn't too loud. I wrote notes. I slipped them into his pocket, his pants, anywhere I could reach ... You didn't find them I guess but he didn't either so that's good. Lucky he's so drunk, always.'

I *row* uselessly and turn in circles. *I'm sorry, I'm so, so sorry ...*

She sighs and I hear the wet catch in her breath. 'You're always sorry,' she says, sounding more like her old self. 'Always trying to make him feel better.'

Oh, how could he? I say. *To lock up his own daughter like this ...*

She gives a tired little laugh. 'Grow up, Olivia. I'm not his daughter.'

But you call him Dad.

'He calls me kitten when I'm good — does that mean I'm a cat?'

I shudder and my tail lashes. *He calls me kitten,* I say.

'I know,' she says. 'There have been lots of kittens over the years.'

I think back to the night Ted found me, a kit in the woods, the night when the cord bound us together. His cuffs covered in fresh mud. The elusive scent in the back of the car, as if the seat had just been vacated. Soft fabric, yellow with blue butterflies. He wrapped me in a child's blanket. I guess maybe I should have wondered what was he doing at night in the woods, with mud on his cuffs and a child's blanket.

I ask, *How long have you been here?*

'I don't know,' she says. 'Since I was little.'

All this time, I say. It's like looking in a mirror, to find it's really a door. I could really hurt Ted, I could. *Oh Lord,* I whisper, *how awful.*

'You don't know what awful is.' Lauren takes a deep breath. 'I'll tell this once and then never again.'

'Once upon a time I lived with my family. I don't recall that too well. It was long ago and I was little. I don't remember much about the day he took me, except that it was hot enough to fry an egg on the sidewalk. I think my mom used to say that, but I'm not sure. Lauren's not my real name. I don't remember that either.

'I do remember when he brought me here. I liked the house, it was dusty and dirty, and Mom never let me play in the dirt. I liked the peepholes in the plywood; I thought they were like portholes in a ship. I said so, and he told me I was very smart. He told me his name was Ted and that he was taking care of me while my parents were out. I didn't think anything was wrong. Why would I? It had happened before, me being left with people, neighbours and such. My parents went to a lot of parties. My mother always used to come into my room to kiss me goodnight, before she left for the evening. I remember her scent. Geraniums. I used to call them "germamiums". God, I was so dumb when I was little. I guess that's how I ended up here. What was I talking about?'

You were telling me about the day Ted ... took ... you, I say. Each word feels like a little piece of gravel on my tongue.

'Yeah,' says Lauren. 'I was so hot, that day, my bathing suit or underwear or whatever itched. I complained to Ted, said I was boiling. Maybe that was what gave him the idea. He told me there was ice cream in the freezer in the kitchen, and that I could go and get it. The kitchen was a mess, a pile of unwashed plates in the sink, old takeout food piled high on the counters. I liked it, it seemed like he wasn't a regular grown-up.

'It was in the corner, a big chest freezer with a padlock on it. I'd seen ones like it in garages and basements. Never in a kitchen before, though. The padlock was undone so I lifted the lid. I was expecting a rush of freezing air on my face, but it didn't come. Then I saw the freezer was unplugged at the wall. I felt hands under my arms and I was flying up and over down into the freezer, onto the soft blankets. I had my own blanket with me too. He let me keep that. It's yellow with blue butterflies. Soft. The butterflies are faded now. I still wasn't afraid, even though it smelled like old chicken inside there. But then the lid came down and I was alone. There were stars in the black, like stab wounds in the sky. It was the air holes he had pierced in the lid. I shouted for the man to let me out.

'"You're safe, now," he said. "This is for your own good."

'I remembered his name, and I knew that names were real important to grown-ups, so I tried to say, "Please, let me out, Ted." But I had trouble saying my 'd's, back then. So it came out "Teb". And when he wouldn't let me out I thought that was why – I got his name wrong, and that made him mad. It took me a while to figure out that he would never let me go, no matter how I said it.

'At first, for a long time, I lived in the box. He trickled water through the holes and I opened my mouth and drank it. He gave me pieces of candy the same way. Sometimes cookies or a chicken finger. He played the music really loud, all day and all night. The sad woman who sings. I thought that maybe I was in the hell they used to warn us about, at Sunday school. But hell was supposed to be full of fire, and it was very wet and cold, where I was, cold to the bone. After a while I didn't notice any of it any more, not even the smell. Time stopped being a line and flattened out.

'I had to learn a new language, for my body and my mind. The language of the box. It meant instead of walking, I just moved my feet an inch or two. That was a journey. Instead of jumping up and down or dancing, which I had once liked to do, I clenched and unclenched my fists. Sometimes I bit my cheek, to taste blood. I pretended it was food.

'If I made noise or kicked at the sides of the box, boiling water came through the holes. I couldn't see, but I knew the burns were bad, because of the way my skin came off. Kind of like snakeskin. It smelled bad and I wanted to die with how bad it hurt.

'One day the music stopped. Above me, there was an explosion of light. I had to keep my eyes closed, it was too bright, I had been in the dark for too long. I heard him say, "Let's get you clean."

'He lifted me out of the box. I cried because I thought there would be more boiling water, but it was cool, from the faucet. I think he bathed me standing in the sink. Afterwards he put something soothing on my burns and covered them with gauze.

'"I put boards up over the windows for you," he said. "It's dim in here. You can try opening your eyes."

'I did – just a crack at first, and then a squint. The house was dim and huge. Everything juddered and shook. My eyes had forgotten how to see distances, because I had been in the box for so long.

'He gave me a sandwich – ham, cheese and tomato. It was the first vegetable I had eaten in weeks and my body lit up with it. I used to push the tomato round my plate, before, in my old life. Makes me laugh, now. While I ate he cleaned up the box and put new blankets in there. I shivered at that – I wanted to scream. It meant I was going back in. The second I finished my sandwich, he put the music back on. That woman. How I hate her.

'"Get in," he said. I shook my head. "I made it all nice for you. Get in." When I wouldn't he poured something from a gallon jug into the bottom of the box. It had a sour smell that made my throat tingle. "The blankets are all soaking wet now," he said. "What a waste of my time." Then he picked me up, put me back in the box and closed the lid. I'll never forget the sound of the padlock closing, right next to my ear. *Snick*, like a blade through an apple.

'The bottom of the freezer was filled with vinegar. It was like fire on my burned skin. The fumes caught in my throat and made my eyes water. He poured more hot water in through the air holes. That was bad, it seemed like the air had turned to acid.

'"When the music plays, you get in and stay there, quiet," he said. "No dilly-dallying. No argument. Every moment it plays, you stay inside, being quiet and good."

'I don't know how many times we went through it. I was slow to learn, I guess. In the end it wasn't so much that I gave in. It was like, my body just started obeying him. Now I can't get out of here when the music is on, no matter how much I want to. If the house was on fire, I couldn't do it.

'I can take more than the others, so I've lasted longer than usual,' Lauren says. For a moment her voice has an edge of pride. 'Ted says it's because of my *psychological issues*. But it's not enough to survive. I want to live. I'm going to get out and you're going to help me.'

My brain reels with everything she's telling me. I try to focus. *Of course I'll help,* I say. *We'll get you out.*

'Well, we have to try,' she says. She sounds so adult and exhausted. It makes it all real. I feel it in my tail, the horror.

Up in the bedroom, Ted groans. His head must be very sore. The bed creaks as he turns over. His feet hit the floor with a thump. I hear him shuffling, bare feet on tile. The shower comes on.

'Olivia,' he calls, thick. 'Kitten.' The music grows louder.

'You have to go to him,' Lauren says. 'You have to act normal.' I hear a very small sound that could be a sob. She tries really hard not to let it out.

I pad upstairs and into the bathroom. Steam wreathes, water beats the tile. Some cats don't like water, I know, but I've always loved it here. The interesting scents, the steam that frames the air in delicate wisps, the taste of warm drips from the tap.

Ted stands under the running water, hair flat and shining like a seal. Water strikes him in metal darts. He is in his undershirt and underwear, as always. Wet fabric is gathered in translucent rucks over him like an ill-fitting second skin. His body never sees the light. The scars show through in ridges. Drunkenness comes off him in waves, I can almost see it, mingling with the steam.

I search and search for a sign, some indication of the great change that has taken place between us. But he seems just as usual, like he gets when he goes back into the past and gets stuck.

'Teddy went to the lake with Mommy and Daddy,' he says, resting his forehead against the wall. His voice is small and far away. 'And the Coca-Cola was cold and freezy in the glass. The ice made music on the rim. And Daddy said, "Drink it all up, Teddy, it's good for you."'

He turns off the shower, groaning as if it is a painful act. He goes into the bedroom. I follow, watching as closely as if I had never met him before. Maybe I haven't. He bends his head and his back heaves. I think he's crying.

Now it's my job to purr and wind myself around him and nudge him with my head until he laughs. But now the walls seem to hum and buckle. Bad things scuttle through my mind and everywhere. Hatred for him washes over me so strongly that I become a tall arch and my fur stands up in quills. I wish the cord had bound me to anyone except him.

Why are you doing this to Lauren? I ask, wondering if he'll reply.

There isn't a good answer, and I can't stand to think about the bad ones.

But I have to be normal. I have to try. I purr and nudge my head into his hand. Each place our flesh meets is cold. He turns the music up loud.

So, this is why the LORD asked me to stay here, that day when I almost escaped. I thought it was to help Ted, but it was for Lauren.

Ted

I am kind of crazy today. The green boys were loud in the attic last night. So it's no surprise that this morning I went away for a little. Stress.

When I came back I knew where I was before I even opened my eyes. I could smell the street and the forest, the asphalt, the rotting scent of trash in the bins. Garbage day. I knew what I would see when I opened them. And there I was, like I knew I would be, in front of the yellow house with the green trim, the blinds down, the emptiness of it seeming to echo out into the street, and all through the world.

Maybe Chihuahua lady is dead. Maybe it's her ghost that keeps making me go to her house. I am imagining it now. My eyes blank and gone, her grey, transparent hand taking mine, leading me to that spot on the sidewalk in front of her house, making me go there again and again until I realise – what?

The only way to end the stress is to figure stuff out with Lauren. So I have to ask the bug man the question. I've been trying to lead up to it carefully, but things are getting out of hand. I have to figure out what Lauren is. What they are, I guess.

In the meantime, I have made a decision: I can't keep putting my life on hold for my daughter and my cat. I have to do something for myself occasionally, or I'll be unhappy, and an unhappy parent isn't a good parent.

So I have a date tomorrow. Something to look forward to!

Olivia

⁓

I have to wait a few days before I can speak to her again. Ted always seems to be around, drinking and singing along to sad songs. When I *row* through the freezer door she doesn't answer.

Three nights later, he goes out. He's whistling and his shirt is clean. The door closes behind him and the three locks *thunk* into place. Where is he going?

I count to one hundred, to give him time to get far away, or to come back for his wallet or whatever. The lady on the record player moans quietly about her home town. I race to the kitchen and scratch on the freezer.

Are you OK? I am *row*ing in distress. *Are you there?*

'I'm here.' Her voice is faint under the record. 'Is he really gone?'

Yes, I said. *He had a clean shirt on. That usually means he's on a date.*

'Gone hunting,' Lauren says. She hates it when he dates. Now I know why.

So, I say, stalking up and down. *Let's go through our options. Can you shout for help?*

'I do,' Lauren says. 'Or I used to. But no one came. The walls are thick. I don't think much sound gets through. You have cat ears, remember? I started to think that even you would never hear me.'

Hm, I say. *You're right. Cross that off the list.*

'What's the next option?' she asks.

Now I feel terrible because actually I only had one option. *That's the end of the list.*

'It's not your fault.' Lauren is trying to comfort me, and somehow that makes my tail hurt most of all. 'It's not so bad, sometimes,' she says. 'I like my pink bike and I can ride it around the house. There's TV. He gives me food unless he's angry.' Lauren giggles. 'Sometimes he lets me look at the internet, even. If I am "supervised".'

The feelings in my throat and tail are worse than a hairball. What can I do? I *row* miserably. I was always so happy to be a cat but now I'm not sure. *If I had hands I could get you out,* I say.

'If I still had feet I could get myself out,' Lauren says. 'But you can help, Olivia. You just have to do one thing.'

Anything, I tell her.

'Make him turn down the music,' Lauren breathes. 'That's all you have to do. I can't do anything with the music on. He made sure of that, long ago. You hear? It has to be off, or at least so low I can barely hear it.'

OK! What happens then?

Piles of lead weights and counterweights are stacked on top, like abandoned castles in a bad land.

'You can get me out, Olivia. Just do what you do with the Bible.'

It would be good to record all this in case something happens to me. But I don't dare.

Ted watches cars screaming through the dirt on the TV and the level of the bourbon bottle dips steadily. He leaves the record player on while he watches. Under the roar of engines there is a banjo playing and the woman sings about bars and love. He is fading. Bourbon and exhaustion twine their arms about him, pulling him earthwards.

I *prrp* and go to him. But then I stop and my tail blows out. I become a tall arch. When the banjo strikes, I *yow*.

'What's up?' He reaches for me.

The banjo tinkles and I speed beneath the couch.

'You're such a dumdum,' he says. He changes the song; it becomes something mournful sung by that pretty voice. I cry along to the music, as loud as I can.

'You dumb kitten,' he says. The banjo twangs and I *row* with it, a long note.

'Oh man, really?' He turns the record down so that the piano and the woman are ghosts of themselves, whispering into the air.

I *row*. I don't come out.

'Hey, Olivia,' he says, exasperated, 'what am I? Your butler?' But he turns it down even further. I think this is as good as it's going to get.

I emerge from under the couch.

'Oh,' he says warmly. 'There you are. Decided to honour us, did you?'

I start slowly doing all the things, the way I know he likes them. I circle his ankles in a figure of eight, purring. He bends to tickle my ears. I rear up to rub my head against his face. For a moment I wonder if it's a trick. Perhaps he'll take my head and twist it, now, until my neck breaks.

'Hey,' he says. 'Kitten.' The fondness in his voice gives me a broken feeling in my spine, all along my tail. He is familiar to me as my own silky coat, or Night-time. I thought he saved me. I thought we were part of one another, almost. The thought makes me cough again in my throat.

'What's up? Got a bone stuck or something? Let me take a look.' He lifts me gently onto his lap and parts my jaws.

'No,' he says. 'You're OK, kitten.' I purr and knead and he runs a gentle hand up and down my back. 'I've been away too much,' he says. 'We've spent too much time apart. I'm going to be home more often, I promise. Starting now.'

I *row* furiously and purr.

'You want me to turn off the TV?' he asks.

I purr louder. *We're going to get away from you,* I start to say and then I think better of it. What if he's like Lauren and understands cat? A horrible thought – that all this time he has been listening to me.

'Got to turn the music up again,' he says sleepily, but I stroke the underside of his chin with my tail. I know just what to do to give him peace, I always have, and his eyes close, as I knew they would. His breathing becomes slow and regular and his chin meets his chest. I watch for a moment, searching for a way to feel. I guess something or someone made him the way he is, but that doesn't matter now.

He looks so much younger when he sleeps.

I did it, I say to Lauren. *He's asleep.*

'Is he really out?' Lauren asks. 'Is it really safe?'

I listen. Ted's breathing in the far room is heavy and regular. I think it's now or never. *OOoooeeeeeooo.* The whining in my head is back, a mad wasp in my ears.

Yes, I tell her. I hope I'm right. I shake my head and rub my ears.

She says, 'You see where the freezer sits close up against the kitchen counter?'

Yes.

'Knock the top weight off the pile. It'll make some noise, but not too much. Don't let it fall on the floor. Then push it off the freezer, onto the counter. Got it?'

I nod, forgetting she can't see me. *Got it,* I say.

The first weight comes off the pile with a clang. It's small and wants to roll. I bat it back with my paws and push it onto the counter. Then the next. The one after that is heavy. I push it too hard and it slides off the freezer onto the floor, with a leaden thunk that seems to shake the world. We are both as still as death. I listen. It's difficult through the shrieking drone in my ears. Lauren's breath shudders in and out. In the next room, Ted snores. *He's still sleeping,* I say, weak with relief.

After a moment Lauren says. 'Don't drop them, OK, Olivia?'

No, I whisper. *I won't.* I'm very, very careful after that. The last weight, the one at the bottom of the pile, is so heavy that it hurts my paws to push it. Each inch is a miserable struggle. But at last it slides onto the countertop, clunking against the others.

They're all off, I say.

'All right,' she says. 'I'm coming.'

I close my eyes tight and make a sad little *row*. For some reason I am afraid. What will she be like?

You know, Lauren, I say, eyes still tightly closed, *I don't think I have ever even seen you in real life. Isn't that weird? We have kind of always taken it in turns being out here, I guess!*

There is no answer.

I hear the freezer begin to open, slowly, effortful, as if the hand that lifts the lid is shaking and fragile. I hear the lid thud against the wall. There is wet stirring, a sigh. The stench of misery and terror comes in waves. I think of white thin hands like claws and flesh shiny with scars. It makes me want to *row* and curl up in a ball.

Come on, cat, I tell myself sternly. *Don't make things worse for the poor girl.*

I open my eyes. The freezer lies open, a dark grave. I stand on two hind legs and peer into the depths.

It is empty.

Ooooooooeeeee, goes the whine.

Where are you? I whisper. Something is very badly wrong. The whining in my head rises to a scream, and I *row* and claw my head. I want to run headfirst into a wall, just to make it stop.

'Hey, cat,' Lauren says, next to my ear. The screaming rises. Through it I can hear my breath, my heart chopping like an axe on a block.

'Olivia,' she says, 'try not to freak out.'

What in heavens, I say. *I'm going insane . . . Why aren't you in the freezer?*

'I was never in there,' she says.

I can feel her, somehow, the warm outline of her, or smell her maybe. Or maybe there's no word yet invented for the sense I am using. I'm on the very knife-edge of losing my mind.

Lauren? I say. *Where are you? What the eff is going on? Why can't I see you? It feels — and I know this can't be true, but it's what it feels like, nevertheless — it feels like you're inside me.*

'It's the other way around, Olivia,' she says. 'You're inside me.' And now a horrible thing happens. My body seems to stutter and shift. Instead of my lovely tail and paws I feel for a moment that there are hungry pink starfish at the end of my limbs. My silky coat is gone, my eyes are small and weak . . .

What, I say, *what . . . Let me go. None of this is happening. Let me go back into my nice crate . . .*

'Look at it,' she says. 'The thing you call a crate. The truth is right there. But you have to choose to see it.'

I look at the chest freezer, the open lid resting against the wall, the holes punched in the lid for air.

'I left you a note,' Lauren says. 'But what kind of cat can read? What kind of cat can talk?' The screeching rises again. *OOooooeeeeoo.*

I'm imagining this, I row. *If only that gd noise would stop I could think . . .*

'One of us is imaginary,' she says. 'It's not me.'

Go away! Stop it! Stop that noise!

'Olivia,' she says, 'look at what you're doing.'

My paw is outstretched, claws extended. It rakes across the side of the metal freezer, making a scream like terrible suffering.

Eeeeeeeooooooeeeee, go my claws, screeching across the metal. The noise was me, all the time. But how can that be?

'I've been trying to get your attention for such a long time,' Lauren says.

The screeching of claws on steel rises. The world seems to flicker. Instead of my paw there is a hand with long dirty nails, dragging, dragging ... *eeeeeeeeeeeooooeeee*. Claws on metal. *Fingernails on metal,* a voice whispers and I *yow* and scream but even that can't rise above the screeching; it builds until it becomes a physical thing, a wall inside me that breaks with a terrible crack.

I come to with Lauren stroking my back. But somehow, once again, she's doing it from the inside. I start to cry, little piteous mewlings like a kit.

'Shhh,' she says. 'Let it out quietly, if you can.'

Leave me alone, I say. I curl up tightly. But it feels like she's wrapped around me.

'I can't do that,' she says. 'You really don't get it, do you?' She strokes me again. 'The first time I tried to run,' she says, 'he took my feet. He broke them between two boards with a mallet. The second time I tried, you came out of my mind.

'I was half way to the door when he took me by the hair. I knew I would rather die than go back into the freezer, so I made up my mind to do that. But instead, something else happened. I went away. I don't know how. It was like my mind was a deep cave and I was pulled back into it. You walked out of the emptiness, and came to the front. I could see you, feel what you were doing. I could still hear what he was saying. But it was like watching TV. I wasn't in our body. You were. You purred and sat in his lap and made him calm again. You were made from darkness, to save me.

No, I say. *I remember being born. It wasn't like that.*

'I know the story,' Lauren says. 'I can see your memories. Or what you think are your memories. You were in a ditch with your Mamacat ...'

Yes, I say, relieved to hear something I recognise.

'It never happened,' Lauren says. 'The mind is clever. It knows how to tell you something that you can accept, when life gets too hard. If a man who calls you kitten keeps you prisoner – why, your mind might tell you that you *are* a kitten. It might make up a story about a stormy night and how he saved you. But you weren't born in the forest. You were born inside me.'

It was real, I say. *It must be. My dead little kit sisters, the rain ...*

'It's real in a way,' she says sadly. 'There are dead kittens buried in the forest. Ted put them there.'

I think about the earth that clings to Ted's boots, some nights when he comes in from the woods. The scent of bone on him. I can't seem to get enough air, even when I open my mouth wide to breathe. Truth has weight. It leaves footprints in your mind. Lauren strokes me and murmurs until the blood stops pounding in my ears.

Why did you pretend to be in the freezer?

'I knew you wouldn't believe me,' she says. 'I had to find a way to show you that we're one person.'

Oh, I say, helpless. *I'm your psychological issue.*

'Don't feel bad,' she says. 'Things got better after you came. He began to let you out regularly, feed you. You calm him. You're his pet. You like the freezer. You feel safe in there. And the happier you made him, the kinder he was to both of us. There is no more hot water and vinegar. He sends me to sleep and you come forward.'

I help keep us here, I say. *I care for him, I let him stroke us ...*

'You made sure we survived,' Lauren says. Warmth spreads throughout my mind. 'I'm hugging you. Can you feel it?'

Yes, I say. The feeling is just like being enclosed in loving arms. We sit for a while, holding each other.

In the living room, Ted groans.

'He's coming,' she says. 'I have to go. I'll try and come back soon.'

She touches me gently, comforting. 'You opened the door between us, Olivia. It will be different now.' And then she is gone.

I used to spend all my time wishing Ted would come home. Now all I want is for him to stay away.

I feel weird because even though it is such an awful situation, I love having Lauren around. She is fun to talk to. We talk or play or just sit together. It is really nice, like having one of the kits in my litter with me again. I suppose that's what Lauren is. She can make it feel like she's stroking me or hugging me, though it's just in our mind. The music stops her from using our body. It's like being tied up but not gagged, she says, and I shudder at her matter-of-fact tone, because she sounds so young, and no one should know how those things feel.

Tonight we are curled up together on the couch in the dark house. Outside, the trees spread fingers against the moonlight. The cord is a soft black, invisible against the night. Ted is passed out, the stone-dead kind of passed out, upstairs. We whisper to each other.

'If I still had my feet we could run away,' Lauren says. 'Just run.'

Can you see me? I ask. *I can't see you. I wish I could. I want to know what you look like.*

Ted has made sure that there are no reflective surfaces in the house.

'I'm glad you can't,' she says. 'Too much has been done to our body. I feel you, though. You're warm — it's nice, like someone is sitting by my side.'

I try not to think about the body, Lauren's body, that she says we both live in. I kind of only half believe her. I can feel my fur, my whiskers, my tail. How can that not be real?

You know, there's another one, I say. *There are three of us. He's called Night-time.*

'I think there are more than three,' she says. 'I hear them sometimes, when I'm very deep down. I try not to. I don't like it when the little ones cry.'

Deep down?

'There are other levels. I need to show you all that.'

Fear strokes me, a dark feather. I purr anxiously to make the feeling stop.

'Don't you think, Olivia,' and I can hear the wet catch in her voice, 'that it would be better if none of us had been born?'

No, I say. *I think we're lucky to have been born. And we're luckier still to be alive. But I don't know what being born or being alive means any more. What am I? It seems like everything I knew is wrong. I thought I saw the* LORD, *once. He spoke to me. Did that happen?*

'There are no gods except Ted's gods,' she says. 'The ones he makes in the forest.' The cold feather strokes on, up my tail, down my spine.

We won't let that happen, I say. *We are going to get out of here.*

'You keep saying that,' she snaps. For a moment she sounds like the old Lauren, shrill and unkind. Then she softens again. 'What will you do when we're free? I'm going to wear a skirt and pink barrettes in my hair. He never lets me.'

I want to eat real fish. (Privately, to myself, I think, *I will go and find my tabby love.*) *What about your family?* I ask Lauren. *Maybe you can find them.*

After a pause she says, 'I don't want them to see me like this. It's better if they keep thinking I'm dead.'

But where will you live?

'Here, I guess.' Her voice sounds like it doesn't matter. 'I can manage without Ted. I want to be alone.'

Everyone needs someone, Lauren, I say sternly. *Even I know that. A person to stroke you and tell you nice things and get annoyed with you sometimes.*

'I have you.'

That's true, I say, in surprise. *I hadn't thought.* I tickle her strongly with my tail and she laughs. Luckily, I am an optimist and I think we're going to need that.

Lauren sighs, the way she does when she's about to say something I won't like. 'It has to be you,' she says. 'When the time comes. You know that, right, Olivia? You have to do it. I can't use the body.'

Do what? But I know.

She doesn't answer.

I won't, I say. *I can't.*

'You have to,' she says sadly. 'Or Ted will put us under the ground like the other kittens.'

I think about all those little girls. They must have sung songs too, and had pink barrettes and played games. They must have had families and pets and ideas and they either liked swimming, or didn't; maybe they were afraid of the dark; maybe they cried when they fell off their bikes. Maybe they were really good at math or art. They would have grown up to do other things – have jobs and dislike apples and get tired of their own children and go on long car rides and read books and paint pictures. Later they would have died in car wrecks or at home with their families or in a distant desert war. But that will never happen, now. They are not even stories with endings, those girls. They are just abandoned under the earth.

I say, *I know where he keeps the big knife. He thinks no one knows, but I do.*

She holds me tight. 'Thank you,' she whispers, and I feel her breath in my fur.

Suddenly I cannot bear to wait. *I'll do it now, today,* I say. *Enough.*

I leap up onto the counter and stand on my hind legs. I open the cupboard. At first I can't believe my senses. *It's not here,* I say. But it must be. I nose in and search the dusty interior. But the knife is gone.

'Oh.' I hear the deep wound of disappointment in her voice and I would do anything to make it better. 'Don't worry about it, Olivia.'

I'll find it, I tell her. *I swear, I'll find it …*

She gives a little sound, and I can tell she's trying not to cry. But I feel her tears running hot through the fur on my cheeks.

What can I do to make it better? I whisper to her. *I'll do anything.*

She sniffs. 'You probably can't,' she says. 'You would have to use the hands.'

I'll try, I whisper even though the thought of it makes me ill.

The cupboard under the stairs is dusty and smells pleasantly of fatty engine oil. There are dusty rugs piled in the corner, a stack of old newspapers, part of a vacuum cleaner, boxes of nails, a beach parasol … My ears are wide and alert, my tail raised with expectation. This is just the kind of place I love. I sniff the delicious trickle of black oil that runs across the floor.

'Focus, Olivia,' Lauren says. 'I hid it under those newspapers.'

I nose into them and I smell something that is not newspaper. Bland, smoother. Plastic.

'It's a cassette tape,' Lauren says. 'Pick it up. No, that won't work, use your hands. You don't really have paws.' Her frustration rises. 'You live in my body. We are a girl. Not a cat. You just have to realise that.'

I try to feel my *hands*. But I can't. I know the shape of myself. I walk delicately balanced on four velvet paws. My tail is a lash or a question mark, depending on my mood. I have eyes as green as cocktail olives, and I am beautiful …

'We don't have time for all this, Olivia,' Lauren says. 'Just pick it up in your mouth. You can do that, right?'

Yes! I take the cassette gently in my jaws.

'Let's go to the mail slot, OK?'

OK!

On our way past the living room I see something that makes me stop for a second.

'Is something wrong, Olivia?' she asks.

Yes, I say. *I mean ... no.*

'Then hurry up!'

I nose the mail flap open. The metal is heavy and cold on my delicate velvet nose. The outside world smells of dawn frost. White light hits my eyes.

'Toss the cassette out into the street,' Lauren says. 'As far as you can.'

I jerk my head and throw the cassette. I can't see anything, but I hear it bounce.

'It went into the bushes,' Lauren whispers. I hear the dismay in her voice.

Sorry, I say. *Sorry.*

'It was supposed to land on the sidewalk so someone could find it,' Lauren says. She starts to cry. 'How will anyone find it there? You wasted our chance.'

I feel terrible, Lauren, I say. *I really do!*

'You aren't trying,' she says. 'You don't want us to get out. You like it here, being his prisoner.'

No! I say, agonised. *I don't, I want to help! It was an accident!*

'You have to take this seriously,' she says. 'Our lives depend on it, Olivia. You can't go on pretending you don't have hands. You have to use them ...'

I know, I say. *For the knife. I'll practise. I won't mess up again.* I nose her and rub my head against her where I feel her in my mind. *You rest now,* I tell her. *I'll watch.* We curl up on the burry orange rug and I purr. I feel her beside me, inside me. She gives a deep sigh and I feel her slip gently down and away into the peaceful dark. My tail is filled with worry. Lauren never likes to talk about after, when we're free. I have a bad feeling she doesn't care about being free. Worse – that she doesn't want to be alive. But I will help her. I will keep us safe.

She has enough to deal with, so I didn't mention it, but the weirdest thing just happened. As I walked to the front door just now, with the tape in my mouth, I glanced into the living room. And I swear that for a moment, this rug had changed from orange to blue.

Dee

Dee sits by the window looking out at the dark. She strokes the clawless tabby with a gentle hand and wishes she still smoked. 'Pretty pebble,' she whispers to herself. The cat looks up at her sharply. It's late, Ted's windows are all dark. But Dee fears sleep. The red birds will come flying into her head, with you-know-what in their beaks. Or it will be the other dream, where she sees her mother and father walking hand in hand across a desert under a blanket of stars, still looking, still calling their younger daughter's name. Her memories cannot be kept at bay. They are nested inside one another. *Like one of those Russian dolls,* she thinks.

It's getting harder and harder, the long waiting, the endless watching. Sometimes she wants to scream. Sometimes she wants to get a crowbar, go over there and break down the door – and finish it. Other times like now she just wants to get in her car and drive. Why does it fall to her, this terrible task? But this is how it is. Dee owes it to Lulu, and to all the others. She has seen the newspaper articles, blurry columns lit by the dirty glow of microfiche. Children go to that lake and don't come back. Seven or eight, at least, over the years. Children without families or anyone to care. That's why there hasn't been much notice taken. Recently there have been no more disappearances. None since Lulu, in fact – and there might be a reason for that. Maybe he learned it was better to keep a child than risk taking them, over and over.

The sun is rising through milky cloud over the trees. Pink touches the sky in the east, like a finger.

Something stirs the air at the front of Ted's house. A rectangular object hurtles out of the mail slot and sails through the air. It makes a crack as it bounces off two steps, then falls silently into the rhododendron bushes that spring up about the steps, glossy and green. The mail slot opens again with a faint creak.

Every one of Dee's senses is alight. She starts for the door. Her heart is so loud in her ears that she can't hear anything else. She forces herself to breathe deeply. Her hand is on her door handle, turning it, when she hears the familiar *thunk*, *thunk*, *thunk* of the locks.

Dee freezes for a moment. Then she goes to the window. Ted comes out onto the front steps. He looks slightly neater than usual. He seems to have combed his beard.

As Ted goes down the steps he glances to his left, stops and bends to pick something out of the glossy green leaves. Everything stops inside Dee. Too late. Whatever it was, he has found it.

Ted stands up. He has a little pinecone in his hand. He turns it this way and that, looking at it closely in the morning light.

When he has been gone twenty minutes Dee walks over to his house. She follows her plan carefully. She rings the doorbell. When there is no answer, she lifts the mail flap.

'Hello?' she calls into the bowels. The mood of the house strokes her face. It is dust and old despair.

'Hello,' she calls again. 'Neighbour, here to help!' It took her a while to come up with the right phrasing. Something the little girl would understand, but would also sound innocuous to anyone else listening. The house breathes at her. But there is no other sound.

Then Dee puts her lips to the aperture and whispers, 'Lulu?' She waits for a minute, and then two. But the silence of the house only thickens.

The day is getting brighter. Some guy passes, walking his dog. There can be no breaking and entering. Sooner or later someone might start to wonder why she's loitering on Ted's steps.

She takes out her flashlight, gets on all fours and crawls quickly into the rhododendron. Cobwebs cling to her face like tiny hands. Adrenaline punches her heart. It makes her feel good, alive.

The cassette lies half buried in dry leaves. A beetle sits atop it, waving curious horns. Dee brushes the beetle off and puts the cassette in her bra. She backs slowly out of the bush. The rush is seeping away and she feels cold. To her right something moves through the leaf litter in a long thin line. She gasps and backs out of the undergrowth, hitting her shin painfully on the edge of a step. She beats her head frantically with her hands, feeling the phantom weight of a scaled body clinging and coiling in her hair. She runs, panting, to her front door.

Ted

It's bug-man day at last. I have to see it through. I have to do this for Lauren. But I should not have yelled at him last time. I saw the light come on in his eyes.

The walk is nice. Not too hot. I stroke the little pinecone in my pocket. I found it by the front steps. I love pinecones. They have very individual personalities.

I stop with my hand on the door handle. The bug man is talking in his office. It's the first time I've ever seen or heard another patient, here!

'Goddamn small minds,' I hear the bug man say. 'Small towns.' It makes me feel weird. I knock so he knows I'm there. I really respect privacy. He stops muttering and says, 'Come in!'

The bug man's round eyes are calm behind his spectacles. There is no one else in the room.

'I'm glad to see you, Ted,' he says. 'I thought you might not show up. There are more scratches on your hands and face, I see.'

'It's my cat,' I say. 'She's going through a rough patch.' (Nails on my face, her screams as I put her in the crate.)

'So,' he says. 'How are things?'

'I'm good,' I say. 'The pills are good. Only, I run low real fast.

I was thinking maybe I could have a prescription I could refill, instead of getting them from you.'

'We can talk about increasing the dosage. But I would rather you continue to get the pills from me. And you would have to pay to fill a prescription. You don't want that, do you?'

'I guess not,' I say.

'Have you been keeping your feelings diary?' he asks.

'Sure,' I say politely. 'All that is great. Your suggestions have been very helpful.'

'Has the diary helped you to identify some triggers?'

'Well,' I say. 'I am very worried about my cat.'

'Your gay cat.'

'Yes. She shakes her head all the time, and she claws at her ears like there's something in them. Nothing seems to help her.'

'So,' the bug man says, 'that makes you feel powerless?'

'Yes,' I say. 'I don't want her to be in pain.'

'Is there any action you can take? Could you take her to the veterinarian, for instance?'

'Oh,' I say. 'No. I don't think they would understand her at the animal clinic. Not at all. She's a very particular kind of cat.'

'Well,' he says. 'You'll never know if you don't try, hmm?'

'Actually,' I say, 'I have been wondering about something else.'

'Yes?' He looks expectant. I almost feel bad. He's been waiting so long for me to give him something.

'Do you remember the TV show I was telling you about – with the mother and daughter?'

He nods. His pen is still. His eyes are flat blue circles, fixed on me.

'I am still watching it. The plot has been getting more complicated. The angry girl, you know, the one who keeps trying to kill her mother – well, it turns out she has another … nature, kind of?'

The bug man doesn't stir. His eyes are fixed on me. 'That can happen,' he says slowly. 'It's rare … and it doesn't work like it does in the movies.'

'This movie wasn't like those other movies,' I say.

'I thought you said it was a TV show.'

'That's what I meant, a TV show. So in this show, sometimes the daughter is a young girl – but at certain times she seems completely … different.'

'As if another personality takes over?' he asks.

'Yes,' I say. 'Like there are two people inside her.' Two different species, actually, but I think I've told him enough.

The bug man says, 'I think you're talking about dissociative identity disorder, or DID.'

Dissociative identity disorder. It sounds like something that goes wrong with a TV or a stereo. It doesn't sound like anything to do with Lauren.

The bug man is watching me closely, and I realise that I am murmuring to myself. Being weird. I fix him with a firm gaze. 'That's very interesting.'

'It used to be known as multiple personality disorder,' he says. 'DID is a new term – but we still don't really understand it. I deal with it extensively in my book. In fact, you might say the whole *thesis*—'

'So what do we understand?' I say, keeping him to the point. I know from experience that if I don't he'll just talk about his book for ever.

'The girl in your TV show would probably have been subject to systematic abuse, physical or emotional,' he says. 'So her mind fragmented. It formed a new personality to deal with the trauma. It's rather beautiful. An intelligent child's elegant solution to suffering.' He leans forward. His eyes are bright behind his glasses. 'Is that what you saw, on the show? Abuse?'

'I don't know,' I say. 'Maybe I missed that part while I was getting popcorn. Anyway the mother doesn't know what to do about it. What should she do? In your professional opinion.'

'There are two schools of thought on this,' he says. 'The first sets as its goal a state known as co-consciousness.' He sees my look, and says, 'A therapist would try to help the alternate personalities, or alters, to find a way to live harmoniously with one another.'

I almost laugh out loud. Lauren could never live harmoniously with anyone. 'That wouldn't work,' I say. 'On the show the two people don't know that they're one person.'

'Her imagination could be made to work for her,' he says. 'She doesn't have to be at its mercy. She should construct a place inside herself. A real structure. A lot of children use castles, or mansions. But it can be anything. A room, a barn. Big, with enough room for everyone. Then she can invite the different parts to congregate there safely. They can get to know one another.'

'They *really* don't like each other,' I say.

'I can recommend some reading,' he says. 'That could help you understand this approach better.'

'What's the other school of thought?'

'Integration. The alters are subsumed into the primary personality. Effectively, they disappear.'

'Like dying.' Like murder.

He looks at me carefully over his glasses. 'In a way,' he says. 'It's a long therapeutic process, which can take years. Some practitioners think it is the best solution. I don't know. To merge fully evolved personalities into one another might be difficult – inadvisable. Some practitioners consider these personalities, these alters, to be people in their own right. They have lives, thoughts. For want of a better word, they have souls. It would be like trying to merge you and me.'

'But it can be done,' I say.

'Ted,' he says. 'If you know – someone – with this condition, they are going to need help with this. A lot of help. I could guide her ...'

His left hand rests in his lap. His right hand lies palm down on the small table at his side, an inch or so from his mobile phone. I pick up a pen from the table and play with it, watching his right hand, the one near the phone, very carefully. I wait for him to make the next mental leap. I wait for him to reach for the phone. I hope he doesn't. Strangely, I have grown fond of him.

'Such a rich puzzle,' he says dreamily, and I can tell that he's not really talking to me any more. 'It's a question I ask in my book. Of what does the self consist? You know, there is a philosophical argument that DID could hold the secret to existence. It theorises that each living thing and object, each stone and blade of grass, has a soul, and all these souls together form a single consciousness. Every single thing is a living, component part of a breathing, sentient universe ... In that sense we are all alternate personalities – of God, essentially. Isn't that an idea?'

'Neat,' I say. 'Could you give me the names of those books, please?' I am as polite as possible. 'About the integration thing.'

'Oh – sure.' He tears a page out of his notebook and scribbles.

'Please think about it, Ted,' he says, eyes on the page. 'I think it could be really helpful if I could talk to her.' His eyes are full of safe abstractions. He is lit up with the thrill of it. I keep the pen hidden in my fist, held like a dagger.

If only he knew. I think of the dark nights with Lauren, the clinging moistness of her hands, her sharp teeth and nails, which leave neat scores in my flesh. I think of Mommy.

I come back from that place. There is a sound like mice running in the walls. The pen nib is buried deep in my palm. The sound is not mouse feet but blood, trickling in patterns onto the pale rug. The bug man stares. His face is empty and white. As I watch, it begins to fill with horror. My own face is not making the correct shapes for pain and it's too late, now, to pretend that I feel it. The bug man has seen something of who truly I am at last. I pull the pen gently from where it is embedded in my palm. It comes out with a gentle sucking sound, like a lollipop between firm lips. I staunch the wound with Kleenex from his desk.

'Thank you,' I say, taking the piece of paper from his fingers. He tries not to, but he shrinks away from me. I know it well: that withdrawal, as if the flesh of his hand is trying to creep away from mine. It is how my mother touched me.

I stumble out of the office, slamming the door behind me and fall into the plastic waiting room, with its reek of synthetic blossom. That did not go well. But at least I have a name for it, now. I stop long enough to write it down. *Dissociative identity disorder*. I hear the office door opening behind me and I run again, stumbling against empty plastic blue chairs. Why is there never anyone else waiting here? It doesn't matter now, I won't be coming back.

Olivia

I am beginning to wonder if Ted has thrown the knife in the trash. Or maybe he carries it with him, wherever he goes on those long nights, when he comes home smelling of earth and old bone.

We considered other approaches. But it must be the knife, because it is sharp and fast. Lauren's body is not strong. There is nothing to eat in the house, poisonous or otherwise. Ted has learned his lesson.

I don't want to tell Lauren this, but I think Ted is up to something. He brought home some new books, today. The titles make my whiskers ache. But I think they are about us. I try and mask these thoughts, keep them from her. She can't hear if I sink them deep enough. Once again I thank the LORD for keeping me here. Lauren needs me.

'Maybe I can make a knife,' Lauren says, doubtful. 'Like they do on TV, in jail. I wish there was some food. It might help me think.'

I can feel her hunger. It adds to my own, deepening the ache in our stomach. Night-time growls and shakes himself in the deep places of us like the beating of black wings. I force him down again. He's hungry like the rest of us.

It's not your time, I tell him.

He snarls but he is still too deep down for me to catch it. It is either, *Now, now, now,* or, *No, no, no.* I cannot be sure which.

We hunt through drawers and cupboards. All we find is dust. To keep us entertained, Lauren makes up songs. The best one is about a woodlouse. It is really, really good.

We are exhausted. I curl up on the floor under the couch. The cord lies in a pile beside me. It is pale yellow and delicate today.

Even if we found the knife I couldn't use it on Ted. Apart from one brief flash, when Lauren took down the wall between us, I have not been able to control the hands, the head, the arms like a ted. I just feel like a cat. And there's something else, too. I wish I didn't but I still feel the old pull when I think of Ted. Love doesn't die easily. It kicks and fights.

Lauren says, 'You have to keep practising, Olivia.'

I'm tired, I say. In my head I think, *Practice is horrible and I hate it.*

'I heard that,' she says. 'How do you think we're going to get out of here if you can't use the body, you stupid cat?'

You are quite rude sometimes.

'At least I don't go back on my promises, Olivia. You said you'd try.'

I *row* with unhappiness, because I know she's right.

She sighs. 'Let's start again. Go to the bottom of the stairs. What can you see?'

I see the stairs, I say, tentative. (I always feel like my answers are wrong.) *I see the carpet. The bannister, running up. At the top, I can just see the landing. And if I turn around I can see the front door, the umbrella stand, the door to the kitchen, into the living room a little ...*

'OK,' she says. 'Enough. So, we'll call this "Night-time". He can see what's down here, but nothing more. Think about that. Imagine him here at the bottom of the stairs. Now, let's go up top.'

On the last stair but one, before the landing, she pulls me up. 'What do you see?'

I can see the bathroom door, I say, *and Ted's room and your room and the roof light ...*

'All the upstairs stuff, right?'

Yes.

'But can you see anything downstairs? The hall? The front door, the umbrella stand ...'

No.

'So, let's call this "Lauren". That's what I can see. Got it?'

Not really, I say, but she's not listening.

'Go down again.'

When I am precisely half way down the stairs, Lauren says, 'Stop.' I am on the step where I like to nap. There are seven stairs below me and seven above. 'Now what do you see?' Lauren asks.

I can still see the bannister, I say. *I can still see the stairs and the carpet on the landing. If I look down I can see the floor of the hall and if I crouch I can see a little of the front door. And if I look up, towards the top of the stairs I can see the window, the bathroom door and the roof light on the landing.*

'So you can see a little of what's above you and some of what's below. This is you, Olivia. Night-time at the bottom, and me in the upstairs and you in the middle, joining us. You are the connecting point. Only one person is going to save us. You.'

The cord glows positively rose-gold as I swell with pride.

'All you have to do is go up,' Lauren says. 'Try.'

But ...

'I don't mean literally go upstairs,' she says, impatient. 'I mean, it's not like any of this is real.'

OMG. WHAT DO YOU MEA—

'Never mind that now. Again.'

I shudder. I feel the old stair carpet, rough under the velvet pads of my paws. I like my paws. I don't want to be a ted. I want to be me.

I'm scared, I say. *I can't move, Lauren.*

'Tell yourself a story,' Lauren says. I can tell from her voice that she knows what it's like, to be pinned by fear. 'Pretend something you really want is up there and go to it.'

I think about the LORD, and his many shifting faces, and how good he is. I try to picture him on the landing above me. My heart fills with love. I can almost see him, with his tawny body and tiger's tail. His eyes are golden.

I climb up one stair. For a moment the walls shiver around me. I feel utterly sick, like I'm falling from a great height.

'Good,' Lauren says, voice cracking with excitement. 'That's great, Olivia.'

I look up at the LORD. He smiles. Then I see that he wears Ted's face. Why is he wearing Ted's face?

I turn and run back down the stairs, *rowing* in distress. Lauren is shouting indistinctly in our head.

I can't do it, I say to Lauren. *Please don't make me. It is horrible.*

'You don't love me,' Lauren says sadly. 'If you loved me you'd really try.'

I do, I do love you! I say, with a little *row*. *I didn't mean to upset you.*

'You've done it before, Olivia, I feel it. You take down the barrier and come up. It happens every time you knock the Bible off the table. There's thunder, right, and the house moves? You do it when you make your recordings. Remember when you opened the refrigerator door? The meat really went bad! You just have to learn to do it on purpose.'

I remember but I don't understand. Of course the meat spoiled – I left the fridge door open.

'What colour was the rug that day, Olivia?'

It's not surprising, I guess, after what she's been through – Lauren has lost it.

Lauren says, 'I guess I have, but try anyway?' Weird having someone hear what you're thinking. I'm not used to it yet.

'Please.' She sounds so sad that I am ashamed of myself.

All right, I say. *I will!*

I try again and again, but no matter how hard I wish all I can feel is my silky black coat and my four padding paws.

After what seems like for ever, Lauren says, 'Stop.'

I sit on the stairs with some relief and begin to groom.

'You don't want to help me.' Tears fill Lauren's voice.

I do, I say. *Oh, Lauren, I want to help more than anything. It's just – I can't do it.*

'No,' she says quietly. 'You don't want to.' My tail feels funny. Warm, somehow. I twitch it to feel the cool air along its length. But the warm feeling grows. It becomes hot.

'I can stroke you,' Lauren says. 'But I can also do this.'

Pain glows red all along my vertebrae. It builds into flames. My tail becomes a red-hot poker. I am crying with it.

Please make it stop, Lauren!

Lauren says, 'It doesn't matter what I do to an imaginary cat.'

Oh, please, it hurts! Pain pulses through my brain, my fur, my bones.

'You think you're beautiful,' Lauren says in the same, dreamy voice. 'He took down the mirrors – you can't see what you really are – so I'll tell you. You are small, twisted, wizened. You are half the size you should be. Each one of your ribs stands out like a knife blade. You don't have many teeth left. Your hair grows in stringy patches on your bald head. As the burns on your face and hands healed, over and over, the scar tissue grew so thick that it twisted your face. It pulled your nose aside, and it grew over your eyes so one of them is almost sealed shut by scars. You think you are stalking around the house on four elegant feet. That's not what's happening. You are crawling on your hands and knees, dragging your useless broken feet behind you, like an ugly fish. No wonder you don't want to live in this body. You helped him make it and

233

then afterwards you climbed into his lap and purred. You are pathetic.'

She stops, and says in a different voice, 'Oh, Olivia, I'm so sorry.'

I am running, *rowing* with horror. The aftershock of pain still rolls through me. Her words hurt more.

'Please,' she calls. 'I'm sorry. I just get so angry, sometimes.'

I know how to hurt her back. I know the place she fears more than anywhere else.

I leap into the chest freezer and hook my claws into the lid, pulling it down over us with a crash. The dark closes over, welcome, and I close my ears to Lauren's screams. I let soft nothing take me. I go away into the deep.

How many times can someone bend before they break for ever? You have to take care, dealing with broken things; sometimes they give way, and break others in their turn.

Ted

I go back to the bar with the lights in the trees where I met the butter-haired woman with the blue eyes. It is a warm day so I sit out back at a long table and breathe the smell of barbecue and think of her for a while. There's country music playing from somewhere, mountain music, and it's nice. This is the date we should have had. The real one didn't go well. *Don't think about that.*

Around me, men mill and flow. They are focused, energy comes off them, but no one's talking much. Once again there are no women here. I wish I could keep that part of my brain turned off, to be honest. I feel bad about what happened with the butter-haired lady. The day is warm and calm begins to steal through me, almost as if I were in a waiting room. I drink six or seven boilermakers. Who's counting? I will be walking home later. 'Didn't drive here. That would be irresponsible!' I realise I am speaking aloud, and people are looking. I sink my face into my beer and keep quiet after that. Plus I remember now, I sold the truck a while ago.

As dusk falls more men arrive. After their shifts, I guess. There is a lot of to and fro but people leave me alone. I begin to understand why there are no women here – it's not for them. What would Mommy have said if she saw me in a place like this? Her mouth narrowing with disgust. *It's against science.* I shiver. *But Mommy can't see you*, I remind myself. *She's gone.*

I don't realise how drunk I am until I get up from the bench. The lights in the trees burn like comets. The dark hums and time stops moving, or maybe it's going so fast I can't feel it any more. *That's why I drink,* I say to myself, *to control time and space.* It seems the truest thought I've ever had. Faces tip and slur.

I wander through the pools of light and dark, across the patio, past the tree. I'm looking for something I can't name. I see an outbuilding squat against the sky, a lighted doorway. I go through it, and find myself in a mineral-smelling room with plank walls and lined with urinals. It's full of guys laughing. They're passing something small from hand to hand and telling a story about a friend who has a horse. Or who is a horse. Or who does horse. But then they go and I am alone with the peaceful dripping and the bare bulb swinging in the air. I go into the stall and bolt the door so I can sit down in peace with no eyes on me. It's the butter-haired woman's fault, coming here has reminded me of her and that is why I'm upset – normally I am cautious, I only drink this much at home. I have to get out of here, I have to get to my house. But just at this second I can't figure out how to do that. The walls pulse.

Two people enter the bathroom. Their movements and words have furry edges, they're very drunk – this is obvious even to me.

'They belonged to my uncle,' a voice says. 'And were my grand-father's before that. And his father's. And his father wore them in the War of Northern Aggression. So just give them back, man. The sleeve-links, I mean cufflinks. I can't replace them. And they were red and silver, my favourite colours.'

'I didn't take anything from you,' a voice says. It's familiar. The tone sets my sluggish synapses firing. There is an idea in my brain but I can't seem to have it. 'And you know I didn't. You're just trying to make me give you money. I see straight through you.'

'You were sitting beside me at the bar,' the cufflinks guy says, 'I took them off for just a second. And then they were gone. That's a fact.'

'You're unstable,' the familiar voice says, sympathetic. 'I understand that you don't want to believe you lost those cufflinks. You want someone to blame. I understand. But deep down, you know I'm not responsible.'

The other man starts crying. 'Please,' he says. 'You know it's not right.'

'Please stop visiting your delusions on me. Go find someone else.'

There's a thud and a crack. Someone just hit the tile. I am curious by now, and that feeling is cutting through the drunk. Plus, I am nearly certain that I know who the second voice belongs to.

I push open the stall door and the two men look at me, startled. One has his fist pulled back, about to hit the other, who lies on the floor. They look like the cover of a Hardy Boys book or a poster for an old movie. I can't help laughing.

The bug man blinks up at me. He has a smear of dirt across his nose. I hope it's dirt, anyway. 'Hi, Ted,' he says.

'Hey,' I say. I give him my hand. The guy who lost his cufflinks and knocked him down is already out the door. Sometimes, very occasionally, my size works in my favour.

I help the bug man off the floor. The back of his shirt is slick and brown. 'Ugh,' he says, resigned. 'Maybe we should go. I think he'll be back, maybe with friends. He seems to have those, inexplicably.'

'Sure,' I say. 'Let's go.'

The road is a tunnel of amber light. I can't remember which way my house is and it doesn't seem very important. 'What shall we do?' I ask.

'I want to drink some more,' the bug man says. We walk towards a lighted sign in the distance. It seems to advance and recede as we approach but in the end we get there – it is a gas station, which sells beer, so we buy some from the sleepy man who minds the store. Then we sit at the table on the roadside, by the pumps. It's quiet. Only the occasional car goes by.

I give the bug man a paper napkin. 'There's something on your face,' I say. He cleans himself up without comment.

'We're having a beer together,' I say. 'It is so weird!'

'I guess that's right,' he says. 'This kind of thing is not supposed to happen between therapist and client, obviously. Are you going to keep coming to see me, Ted?'

'Yes,' I say. Of course I'm not.

'Good. I was going to bring this up at our next session, but you should give me your real address, you know. For our files. I checked and the one you gave me isn't even a house. It's a 7-Eleven.'

'Made a mistake,' I say. 'I get numbers wrong sometimes.'

He just waves a hand as if it's not important.

'Where do *you* live?' I ask.

'That's not how it works,' he says curtly.

'Why did that guy think you had his cufflinks?'

'I'm not sure. Can you imagine me stealing them?'

'No,' I say, because I really can't. 'Why did you pick your job? Isn't it boring, listening to people for hours and hours?'

'Sometimes,' he says. 'But I'm hoping it's about to get much more interesting.'

We drink together for a time, I don't know how long. We say things but they're all lost in the ether after that. Occasionally the lights of cars sweep white across our faces. I feel very fond of him.

He leans in close. 'Lots of people saw us leave together, tonight. The guy in the gas station is looking at us right now. He'd remember you. You're pretty memorable.'

'Sure,' I say.

'So let's talk honestly,' he says. 'For once. Why did you stop coming to see me?'

'You cured me,' I say, giggling.

'That was quite some stunt, impaling yourself with that pen.'

'I have a high pain threshold, I guess.'

He hiccups, gently. 'You were pretty shaken up. You left in a hurry. So you didn't notice that I followed. You like to keep your home private, don't you? But it's harder to muffle sound. Children's voices are so penetrating.'

The darkness is shot through with a hectic red. The bug man suddenly doesn't seem as drunk as before. A terrible feeling begins in me.

'She's not really your daughter, is she?' he asks. 'Just as your cat isn't really a cat. You thought you were so subtle, leading me onto dissociative identity disorder. But I read people for a living, Ted. You can't fool me. DID is caused by trauma. Abuse. Tell me, what's the real reason Lauren – or Olivia, if you prefer – doesn't leave the house?'

I make myself laugh. I make myself sound drunk and friendly. 'You're so smart,' I say. 'Did you follow me to the bar tonight?'

'It was really bad luck that guy came into the bathroom,' the bug man says, dreamily. 'You would not have known otherwise. I've been watching you for a while.'

I have been careless and blind. I let him see who I am.

'You broke into my house,' I say. 'It wasn't that neighbour lady, like I thought. But you made a mistake. You used different nails.'

'I have no idea what you're talking about, there,' he says, sounding injured. If I didn't know better, I would believe him. 'Ted, this is an opportunity. We can both benefit.'

'How?' I ask. 'I can't pay you more money.'

'There can be money for both of us!' he says. 'The thing is,' he leans close, 'I was meant for more than a crappy little practice, listening to middle-aged housewives talk about how they've lost their self-esteem. I was top of my class, you know? I had that little hiccup, true, but I got my licence back, didn't I? I deserve more than this. What's the difference between me and those guys on the bestseller lists? Opportunity, that's all.

'When I met you, I knew I'd found something special – my case study. I had been posting those ads for cheap therapy for months. My dad used to say, if you wait long enough, evil always shows up. I think you can give me what I deserve. You're at the centre of my book, Ted. Don't worry, no one will ever know it's you. I'll change your name – Ed Flagman or something. I just need you to be honest with me – really honest.'

'What do you want me to say?' I wish he would stop talking. I'm going to have to do something I don't like.

'Let's start at the beginning,' he says. 'The girl, Lauren, or Olivia, whatever you like to call her. Is she the first?'

'The first what?'

'The first of your "daughters",' he says. I can hear the quote marks around the word. 'Is that the right word? Daughters? Wives? Or maybe you just call them kittens …'

'You're so dumb,' I say, furious. 'I thought I was the dumb one!' But he's smart enough to be dangerous.

His bloodshot eyes narrow. 'Why do you go to that bar, Ted?' he asks. 'For your cat?'

I take him in my arms. 'Don't try to tell me what I am,' I whisper in his ear. He gives a terrified belch. I hug him and hug him, panting and gripping tighter until I feel the sawing crack of his ribcage and the bug man seems to turn to water. His hand unclenches. Two small objects fall onto the table, catching the light. It is a pair of cufflinks, silver, inlaid with stone as red as blood, picked out gleaming under the neon. I stare at them for a moment. 'You're just a thief,' I say into his ear, squeezing. 'You steal everything – even thoughts. You can't even write your own book.' He moans.

There is a shout from behind me and someone comes out of the store; the sleepy man who sold us the beer.

I drop the bug man and he slumps onto the table. I run across the road into the welcoming arms of the woods. Branches whip my face, I stumble, ankle-deep in leaf mould. More than once I fall but I don't stop, I push myself up on the slippery forest floor and I run and run towards home. The roar builds, stacking up in my throat, but I don't let it out, not yet.

The front door closes behind me. I lock it with trembling hands. Then I ball my fists and I scream and scream until my throat is sore and my voice hoarse. Then I take a couple of deep breaths. I shove two yellow pills into my mouth and swallow them dry. They stick in my throat, clicking like two little stones. I choke them down. The bug man wasn't dead, I don't think. I have to pray he wasn't. There is no time for feelings, and no time for fancy preparation. We have to go.

I pack quickly. Sleeping bag, tent, lighter. Water-purifying tablets, a coil of wire. I gather all the canned food in the house. It's not much. Peaches, black beans, soup. After a moment of staring at it, I seize the bottle of bourbon and add it to the pack. I shove my warmest sweaters in. When the pack is full I put two jackets on, one over the other, and two pairs of socks. It will be too warm, but I've got to wear everything I don't carry. I put all my pills in my pockets, rattling in their amber tubes. If ever there was a time to keep calm, this is it.

Then I go to the garden and dig up the knife. I shake it free of earth and hang it on my belt.

Olivia

Lauren's voice reaches deep into my dream. It has the biting edge of panic. 'Help,' she hisses. 'Olivia, he's taking us away.'

I twitch an ear. The dark is quiet around me. I had been dreaming of sweet cream and it was very pleasant. I am not perhaps at my most receptive.

What?

'Ted,' she says. 'He's taking us outside, to the woods. You have to help.'

Oh, I say coldly. *I'm just a stupid cat, I'm afraid. I can't help.*

'Please,' she says. 'Please, you have to. I'm afraid.' Her voice is like scratched glass. 'Please, Olivia. It's happening now. He's making us into gods. This is our last chance.'

I say, *I don't exist. So that sounds like a* you *problem.*

She starts to cry, in broken ragged sobs. 'Don't you understand that if he kills me, you die too? I don't want to die.' She sniffs. And despite myself I feel a little sorry for her. She is a hurt child. She didn't mean what she said.

I'll try, I say slowly. *But I can't promise anything. Now leave me alone. I have to focus.*

As usual, everyone is relying on the gd cat. Honestly, teds are gd *useless*.

I crouch in the dark. I am hoping it will help. The crate was a sort of door between Lauren and me, once. Perhaps it can be opened again. I listen to the sound of the house — the drip of the tap, boards creaking, a fly caught in between plywood and glass. I smell the linoleum in the kitchen, and the air freshener Ted uses when he remembers. I sheathe and unsheathe my claws. They curve out in beautiful wicked points. I don't want to wear the horrible ted-suit and have hands. Horrible. Got to.

Right, I mutter. *Time.*

I look up at the landing and try to think about something I love. I try to think about the LORD, and then I try to think about the cream that coated my tongue all lovely and white and thick in the dream. But I can't concentrate. My tail lashes and my whiskers twitch. My thoughts are everywhere.

Come on, I whisper, closing my eyes.

All I can think of is Lauren. Not how she looks, because I have never seen her. I think of how clever she is, making this plan to save us, and how annoying, especially when she calls me *stupid cat.*

Nothing happens. No good. I tried my best! I should really go back to my nap. Bad things are happening, and it seems best to sleep until they stop.

But each time I close my eyes and try to sink back into my comfortable doze, doubt needles me wide awake again.

I have tried everything, I say out loud. *I can't do anything else!* I am answered only by silence. But I can feel His opinion. I *row* with unhappiness because I know the LORD disapproves of dishonesty.

I push with my head and the freezer door lifts up an inch. A slice of light greets me, blinding.

As soon as I'm out, I can hear Lauren screaming. Her voice fills the walls, runs through the carpet under my feet. Her fear comes in through the portholes in the plywood, and I can hear it running out of the faucet in the kitchen. I have to help her.

The thought of climbing inside the Lauren-sack is truly horrible. My tail stiffens in distaste. So gross! That smooth piggy pink skin in place of my nice coat. Those creepy things instead of paws! I hiss, horrified at the violent intimacy of it. But she's counting on me. *Think, cat.*

I go to the Bible. I nudge it off the table. As it falls to the floor with a great crash, I feel the house shake. It's like an echo, but louder.

> Ask, and it will be given to you; seek, and you will find; knock, and it will be opened to you. For everyone who asks receives, and the one who seeks finds, and to the one who knocks it will be opened.

Gd it. Sometimes it's annoying, being right. An idea has been forming in my mind for a while. I may be just an indoor cat, but I have seen the many faces of the LORD, and I know there are strange things in the world. Lauren thinks she knows everything, but she doesn't. We are not like a staircase. We're like the horrible doll on the mantelpiece. Lauren and I fit inside one another. When you tap on one it reverberates through all of them.

Think, think!

When I opened the refrigerator door I was angry. Maybe angrier than I have ever been. I didn't feel the cord connecting me to Ted. I was myself, alone.

So I make myself angry. It's not hard. I think about Ted and what he's done to Lauren. It's really difficult to think about. She was right about one thing; what a stupid cat I am, really. I believed his lies, didn't want to know the truth. I just wanted to sleep and be stroked. I was a coward. But I don't want to be a coward any more. I'm going to save her.

My tail bristles, becomes a spike of rage. The fire begins at the tip, spreads down the length of my switching tail, into me. It's not like the heat when Lauren hurt me. I made this feeling. It's my fire.

The walls begin to shudder. The crashing sound begins far away, and then it is all around me. The hall shivers like a bad TV picture. The floor is a sea, tossing.

I pad to the front door, slipping and *yow*ing. Just because I am deciding to be brave doesn't mean I'm not scared. I am so scared. What I see through my peephole isn't really the outdoors. I understand that now. Now, I see with a shiver that the three locks are not fast. The door is unlocked, of course. I don't have to go up, I have to go out. And everyone knows how you get in and out of a house. I give a little *row*. I didn't really want to be right. I stand on my hind legs and pull on the handle with my paws. The door swings wide. The white flame greets me. I am blinded; it's like being inside a star. The cord is a line of fire, burning about my neck. What will happen? Will I burn up? I kind of hope so. I don't know what's out there.

I step out of the house. The cord burns hot as a furnace, surrounds me in a forge of white heat. The world tosses and flips. Blinding stars suck me out into nothing. Nausea rises and I choke. All the air is crushed from my lungs.

The blinding white retreats; the stars shrink to small holes in the hot dark, through which I catch flashes of movement, colour, pale light. Moonlight, I think. So that's what it looks like.

The world tosses like a boat on rough seas. Ted's familiar scent fills my nose. We are being carried on his back, in a bag I think, or a sack – there are small holes stabbed in it, for air I suppose. I am too big. My skin is exposed and hairless like some kind of worm. My paws have become long fleshy spiders. My nose is not an adorable soft bump but a horrible pointy thing. Worst of all, where my tail should be there is a blank nothing.

246

Oh Lord. I wriggle but I can't move. I think we're restrained, tied up maybe. All around, there is sound. Leaves, owls, frogs. Other things I don't know the name of. It all has a clarity I have never heard before. The air is different too. I can feel that, even through the bag. It's cooler, sharper somehow – and it's moving.

Lauren sobs, and I feel it burst up through my unfamiliar chest, my cavernous ribcage. I feel the tears coming from my tiny weak eyes. It's just as horrible as I thought it would be.

I made it, I tell her silently. *I'm in the body.*

'Thank you, Olivia.' She squeezes me tightly, and I squeeze back. *Lauren, why is the air moving, like it's alive?*

'It's wind,' she whispers. 'That's wind, Olivia. We're outside.'

Oh my goodness. Oh gosh. For a moment I am too overwhelmed to think. Then I ask, *Where are we?*

'We're in the woods,' she says. 'Can't you smell it?'

As she says it, the scent hits me too. It is incredible. Like minerals and beetles and fresh water and hot earth and trees – God, the scent of the trees. Up close, it's like a symphony. I could never have dreamed it.

'He has the knife,' Lauren says. 'Can you believe it? He buried it.'

Maybe he's just taking us for a walk, I say, hopefully. *Maybe he's got the knife because he's scared of bears.*

'Kittens don't come back from the woods,' she says.

We are quiet after that. More than anything I want to go back inside. But I can't leave Lauren alone. I have to be brave.

He walks for an hour on rough ground. He climbs steep rock faces and wades across streams, goes through valleys and over hills. Very quickly we are in the wild.

He stops in a place that smells of stone where trees speak to one another in the night, over the sound of running water. From what I can see through the tiny opening at the neck of the sack, we're in a shallow gulley with a waterfall at the end. Ted makes camp with a lot of rustling and groaning. Light flickers through the dark fabric that contains us. Fire. Overhead, I can hear the wind stroke the leaves.

I can't see much but I can feel the vastness of the air. Wind crashing into clouds. *I wish I'd never known the truth,* I say to Lauren. *The outside is terrifying. There are no walls. It goes on and on. How far does it go, the world?*

She says, 'It's round, so I guess it goes on until it comes back to you again.'

That's terrible, I say. *I think that's the worst thing I've ever heard. Oh* LORD, *preserve me ...*

'Focus, Olivia,' she says.

Is he going to let us out of this bag? I ask. *To pee or whatever?*

'No,' she says. 'I don't think he will.' I can hear her mind running furiously. 'It's a change of plan,' she whispers. 'That's all it is. We pivot. We adjust. He has the knife. I felt it against his hip. So you get it from him, is all, and kill him. Same plan. Better, actually, because we're in the middle of nowhere and no one will come to help. We can make his plan work for us, see?' I wonder if she's been at Ted's bourbon because she sounds exactly like he does when he's drunk. Fear can make you slur your words as badly as drink does, I guess.

I think of the body, our weak, thin body, against Ted's bulk, his might. The wind strokes my fur with cold fingers. I breathe it in. It is both ancient and young at once. I wonder if it is the last thing I will feel.

Wind is lovely, I say. *I'm glad I got to feel it. I wish I had got to taste real fish, though.*

'I wish you had too,' she says.

I can't do it, Lauren. I thought I could but I can't.

'It's not only for us, Olivia,' Lauren says. 'It's for him. Do you think he wants to be like this? Do you think he's happy, being a monster? He's a prisoner too. You have to help him, cat. Help him one last time.'

Oh, I say, *oh dear ...*

'OK then,' Lauren says, soft and resigned. 'Maybe it won't be so bad.'

I think about the round world, which if you travel far enough, only brings you back to the same place.

Be a brave cat, I whisper to myself. *This is why the* LORD *put you here.* I take a deep breath. *I'll do it. I'll get the knife, and then I'll kill him.*

'Clever cat,' she says. Her breath comes fast. 'You have to be quick. You only get one chance.'

I know.

Beneath, in the dark, Night-time growls. I feel his great flanks writhing as he strains against his bonds.

What is your problem? I ask, terse. *I'm busy. I don't have time for you right now.*

His answer is a roar that rings in my ears, sends shocks down my spine. *It is my time, it is my time, it is my time,* he roars. But I have him pinned down tight; he won't get free.

Ted is restless. He keeps us close, tied up against his back. The fire glows hot, sending red needlepoints of light through the sack. I feel the rumble of his voice as he speaks softly to himself.

'Mommy, are you still here?'

As dawn is about to break he drifts into an uneasy doze. I feel the deep give and take of his breath. He is at peace. Above, the sky holds its breath.

Can you see anything? I ask.

'It's in his left hand,' she murmurs. I reach out with ours. It is revolting, using the hand – like wearing a glove of rotten meat. I take the knife from his loose palm. It is lighter than I expected.

I reach around and drive it into his stomach. The point punctures flesh with a crisp sound like an apple bitten into. I thought it would be soft, flesh, but inside Ted is a mess of objects and textures. There is resistance; it is hard to thrust the blade in. It is even more horrible than I could have imagined. I hardly hear myself crying, over Ted's screaming. The sound drives a bird from a nearby bush, plummeting upwards into the sky. I wish I could go with it.

The first thing is the pain. The nerves in our body are alight with it. The black cloth drops away. Lauren and I fall face first onto the rough floor of the forest. Our cheek is thurst hard into the mess of slick leaves and twigs; we're half in and half out of the stream; water runs cold over our legs. Our heart chugs unevenly, like a car about to stall.

Lauren? I say. *Why are we bleeding? Why can't we get up?*

Dee

Dee puts the tape recorder on the table. It was not easy to find. None of the electronics outlets stock them. In the end she overpaid for this one in a vinyl store downtown.

She puts the cassette in and presses play with a trembling finger.

'Please come and arrest Ted for murder,' a little, anxious voice says. 'And other things. They have the death penalty in this state, I know that ...'

It's a short recording, lasting maybe a minute. Dee listens without breathing. Then she rewinds and listens to it again. Then she listens further, in case there is another recording after this one. But it's just some medical student's notes. A woman with a slight accent Dee cannot place, and a voice like a clear bell.

She sits back. It is Lulu. Older, yes. But Dee cannot mistake her sister's tones. Now that the moment has arrived and she has proof, Dee does not know what to do. She puts a hand on her heart, which is pounding. It feels swollen, likely to burst.

She should tell tired Karen about all this, take her the tape. She will, as soon as she can lift her head from her hands.

There comes a familiar sound from outside. *Thunk, thunk, thunk.*

Dee's body becomes electric. She goes to the darkened window. Ted has come out into the back yard. He stands for a moment, listening. He looks around. Dee stays still as a post. She hopes the moonlight reflecting on the windowpane will hide her silhouette. Apparently it does, because Ted nods to himself, and goes to the tangle of blue elder that overruns the eastern corner of the yard. He digs with his hands.

Ted takes something from the ground. He shakes it free of earth, and then slides it briefly from its sheath. A long hunting knife. The blade reflects the moonlight. He puts the knife on his belt and goes into the house.

When he emerges again some minutes later, he has a bag on his back. He goes slowly out of his yard, towards the forest. As Dee watches, the bag seems to move. She is sure it's twitching in the faint light.

Dee's mind clears. Everything becomes cold and hard. There is no time for Karen. Lulu must be saved – and there is a monster to be dealt with. *Get it done, Dee Dee,* she thinks.

Dee runs to the closet and grabs the spray can of fluorescent paint, the claw-hammer and the thick, snake-proof boots she bought for this moment. She throws on her hoodie, jacket, ties the laces with shaking hands. She emerges from her house and closes the door quietly behind her, in time to see Ted vanish under the trees. His flashlight dances on the night air.

Dee bends low to the ground and runs after him on silent feet. This time nothing will stop her.

Fifty feet into the forest, where the streetlight can still be glimpsed through the branches, she stops and blazes the trunk of a beech tree with the reflective yellow paint. Branches brush her face and drag at her legs. The forest at night is slippery, it clings. She tries to quiet her breath.

The words she heard on the tape run through her mind over and over. *Nothing but the peaceful dark.* Lulu.

Ted leaves the path, and overhead the moon is obscured by reaching branches. Dee blazes a trunk every fifty feet. She keeps Ted's flashlight in her sights, focusing on it so hard that it blurs into a starry glow. After a time she feels the woods change. Dee is no longer in the place where families walk. She is in the wild, where bears roam and hikers' bones are never found.

The whisper of leaf to leaf begins to sound like a rattle shaken by a sinuous tail. *Shut UP*, she thinks, exhausted. *There is no god-DAMN rattlesnake.* How long has she been a prisoner of fear, she wonders? Years and years. It is time to be free.

Dee's foot slips on a muddy branch. The branch slides under her foot in a muscular movement. At the same moment her torch beam catches it, just ahead of her right toe on the forest floor. The diamond pattern is all too familiar. The sharp, light rattle, like dried rice shaken in a bag. The snake rears back slowly with the grace of a nightmare, poises to strike, eyes reflecting green. It is about four feet long, young. Dee's torchlight dances crazily over the cairn of rock behind, which most likely serves as its home.

Fear spreads through her veins like ink. She screams but it comes out as a slight whistle. The snake sways. Perhaps it is sluggish having just awakened, maybe it is blinded by the flashlight, but it gives Dee the moment she needs.

Keeping the beam steady, she steps forward and swings. She knows that if she misses, she is dead.

The claw-hammer hits the snake's blunt, swaying head with a crack. At her second blow the snake drops limp to the forest floor. Dee leans over it, panting. 'Take that,' she whispers.

She pokes the long body with a finger. It is cool to the touch, limp and powerless, now. She picks up the dead snake. She wants to remember this for ever. 'I'm going to make a belt out of you,' she says. Joy rolls through her. She feels transformed.

As she lifts the dead snake, meaning to put it in her pocket, the head twitches and turns. Dee sees it happen in slow motion – the snake's head lunging, burying its fangs in her forearm. Dee feels her mouth widen to a silent scream. She shakes her arm, trying to detach it. The long limp body shakes too, lashing in mimicry of life. Some things survive death. The pain of the bite is bad. But it is nothing to the horror of having the thing attached to her, like a monstrous part of herself.

At last Dee hooks the claw-hammer into the dead jaws and pries them open. The fangs are pale and translucent in the torch-light. She throws the mangled body into the forest, as far as she can.

Something bubbles up inside her. *Don't scream,* she tells herself. But it's laughter. She is racked with it, wheezing with it. Tears stream down her face. There *was* a snake, after all.

She doesn't want to look, but she has to. The flesh around the bite is already swollen and discoloured like a week-old bruise.

Get it done, Dee Dee. Still giggling, she rips her sleeve off at the shoulder to relieve the pressure on her ballooning flesh. She is a good hour away from help. The only thing to do is go on, and finish it. Ahead, Ted's light dances away through the trees. Unbelievably, the encounter with the rattlesnake took less than a minute. Dee stumbles after his light.

She begins to feel sick. Other things happen, too. It seems to her that the trees are becoming whiter, and there are red birds darting among the trunks. She gasps and tries to blink the image away. This is not a dream. There is no nest of human hair. Her arm pulses, like it has its own heart. She knows that if you are bitten, you are not supposed to move. It spreads the poison. Too late, she thinks. The poison got me long ago.

She follows Ted westward. She turns off her flashlight. The moon is bright enough. Ted keeps his on. It must be difficult, keeping his footing with all that weight on his back. Maybe the weight is moving, fighting him.

With her good hand she fingers the claw-hammer in her pocket. It is sticky with drying snake blood. She burns; her anger leaps and licks at her insides. Ted will pay. Every fifty feet she blazes another tree with reflective yellow. She has to believe that she will be coming back this way, with her sister.

She follows as close as she dares. Even so, she loses him. His light dances out of sight, and then he's gone. The ground begins to fall sharply, and Dee stumbles, panics. But then logic reasserts itself. She can hear water running somewhere below. He will probably stop by water. Dawn is not far off, she can smell it in the air. Dee leans against a slippery trunk and breathes. She just needs to be patient for a little longer. She can't risk falling in the dark. She needs dawn. She knows it won't be long.

Dull sunrise paints the world pewter. Dee staggers down a rocky escarpment towards the sound of water. She comes to the lip of a deep defile. At the bottom, a stream runs hard and silver over the rock. By the narrow shooting water, there is a sleeping bag, open like a slack mouth. A dying fire sends up threads of smoke in the dawn-grey air.

So this is the weekend place. Now that the moment is upon her, Dee feels solemn. It seems almost holy, the end of so many things.

She picks her way down, shakily. Her arm feels heavy as stone, weighed down by venom. The rock by the stream is spattered with dark drops. Blood. Something has happened here.

She follows the drying blood into the stand of birches. *That's right,* she thinks. *Animals go into hiding to die.* But which one, Ted or Lulu? It is familiar, the dim dappled tree light. The quiet conversation, leaf to leaf. This has happened before. Dee went into the trees and when she came out, someone was dead. This time overlays that, like a drawing on tracing paper. But of course, it was a summer afternoon, that time, by the lake. And it was pines that day, not silver birch. She drops white static over these thoughts.

She does not see it at first, the body. Then she glimpses a hiking boot, half torn off a foot, poking out from a tangle of briar. He is splayed at an angle, face down. Dark stuff leaks from his mouth. She thinks, *Oh, she got away and he is dead,* and joy surges through her. Then she thinks, *But* I *wanted to kill him.*

Ted groans and turns, slow as a world revolving. Dirt and leaf mould cover his flesh like a dark tattoo. The knife is still stuck in his abdomen. Blood bubbles up around it, pulses out in a glossy stream. He sees her, and his expression of surprise is almost comical. He has no idea how well she knows him, how closely she has watched, how intertwined are their fates. 'Help me,' he says. 'You're hurt too.' He is looking at her arm.

'Rattler,' Dee says, absently. She stares at him in fascination. She knows how the snake feels, now, approaching the mouse.

'My bag, by the stream, surgical glue. There's a snakebite kit too. Don't know if it works.' She finds it wonderful that at this moment he's concerned for her well-being. Of course, he thinks she's going to help – he needs her.

'I'm going to watch you die,' she says. She watches as disbelief spreads over his face.

'Why?' he whispers. Blood trickles from the corner of his mouth.

'It's what you deserve,' Dee says. 'No, it's just a little of what you deserve, after what you've done.' She looks around in the dim air. Nothing else stirs between the trees. 'Where is she?' Dee asks. 'Tell me where she is and I will make it quick. Help you end it.' She thinks of Lulu, alone and frightened, under the big uncaring sky. She wags a finger back and forth in front of his face. His eyes follow it. 'Time is running out for you,' she says. 'Tick-tock.'

Ted gasps and red bubbles form at his lips. He makes a sound. It is a sob.

'So sorry for yourself,' Dee says furiously. 'You didn't have any pity to spare for her.' She stands. The world sways and greys at the edges, but she steadies herself. 'I'm going to find her.' Lulu will come home to live with her. Dee will have the patience for the years of healing she will need. They will heal one another. 'Die, monster,' she says and turns away, towards the sound of the waterfall, towards the day, where the sun is breaking gold through the cloud.

Behind her, a little girl's voice whispers, 'Don't call him that.'

Dee turns, thrilling. There is no one there but her and the dying man.

'He's not a monster,' the girl's voice says, coming reedy and weak through Ted's blue lips. It is the same voice that was recorded on the cassette tape. 'I had to kill him – but that is between Daddy and me. You keep out of it.'

'Who are you?' Dee asks. The rushing of red wings fills her ears.

'Lauren,' the little girl says through the big man's mouth.

'Don't try to trick me,' Dee says firmly. It must be a hallucination, some side effect of the poison. 'He took Lulu. He takes little girls.' This must be true, or everything collapses.

'He never did that,' the girl says. 'We're part of one another, he and I.'

The world tips as Dee limps towards Ted's body. 'Shhhh,' she says. 'Be quiet. You're not real.' She presses her palm over his nose and mouth. He squirms and struggles, kicking up leaves and dirt with his heels. She holds her hand fast until he goes still. It's hard to tell through the mess but she thinks he has stopped breathing. She stands, wearier than death. The world goes grey at the edges. Her arm is shiny, blackened and swollen.

She stumbles to Ted's backpack, through wisps of white cloud. She finds a yellow pouch. The snake on the label rears out at her and she flinches, gasping. The instructions swim before her eyes. She puts the tourniquet on and places the suction cup on the mouth of the wound. The flesh there is pudgy and dark. It hurts. She pumps and blood fills the chamber. Perhaps it is wishful thinking, but she feels better already, steadier, more alert. She pumps a couple more times, then gets up. That will have to do.

She sees the surgical glue tucked into a pocket of the backpack. She throws it into the fast-running stream. 'Just in case,' she whispers. After all, dead rattlesnakes still bite.

She thinks of her hand over Ted's nose and mouth as he fought for breath. It's fine, because he deserved it. Everything will work out. As for the moment when the man spoke with a little girl's voice, that was just confusion caused by the poison. Her vision blurs, but she quests patiently, until she sees her yellow blaze on a distant tree trunk, marking the path out of the valley. She stumbles towards it. Dee will find Lulu and give her a place to live, and they will be so happy, and hunt for pebbles together. But not at a lake. Never there.

'Lulu,' Dee whispers. 'I'm coming.' She staggers through the forest, through pillars of dark and light. Behind her she hears a dog baying. She hurries on.

Olivia

It's not your body, Lauren. I am crying now. It's his. We live in Ted.

'Yes,' she says with a sigh. 'But not for much longer. Thank God.'

Why, why? I am rowing like a kit. You made me kill us. All of us.

'I needed your help to end it. I couldn't do it on my own.'

I thought I was so smart — but Lauren led me so easily down this path, to this moment, to our death.

You lied, I say. All that stuff you said, about the vinegar and the freezer ...

'That was all true,' she says. 'Though it happened to him and me both. You don't know what we have been through. Life is a long tunnel, Olivia. The light only comes at the end.'

I can see her in my mind, now. Lauren is slight with big brown eyes. Everything she said about her body is true. Murderer, I say to her.

Somewhere, Ted is panting. There is a really bad sound in it, a wet red whistle. He raises our hand, where it has been clutched against the wound in his abdomen. We all watch as our blood runs down our palm, hot and stinking slick. It drips to the ground and the earth drinks it. Ted's body, our body, is failing.

Oh, Ted, I say, trying to reach him. I am sorry, so sorry. Please forgive me, I didn't mean to hurt you ...

'You can't hurt him,' Lauren says, voice both a whisper and a scream. 'We take his pain. You take it from his heart, I take it from the body.'

Be quiet, I say. *You've done enough talking. Ted,* I call. *Ted? How do I fix it?*

He is bleeding from the mouth, a thin line of red. The words are slurred but I know him well so I understand. 'Listen to them,' he says. All around, in the dawn, the birds are singing in the trees.

The cord is white and soft, glowing. It connects the three of us, heart to heart. Then the white light grows, spreads over the earth, and I see at last that actually the cord runs not only through us, but also through the trees, the birds, the grass and everything, out across the world. Somewhere, a big dog bays.

The sun has risen. The air turns warm and golden. The LORD is here, before me, a burning flame. He has four delicate paws. His voice is soft. *Cat,* He says. *You were supposed to protect.* I cannot bring myself to look up into the LORD's face. I know that, today, it will be my own.

Ted

Dimly, above, someone is pressing their hands to the hole in my stomach. Someone's breath is warm by my ear. He presses down harder and harder but the blood comes out all slippery anyway. He curses to himself. He is trying to draw me back up from the black, into the sunny morning.

We could have told him it was no good. We are dying, our flesh is cooling to clay. We feel it as it happens, each one of us. Our blood comes in slow pumps, spilling out all our colours and thoughts onto the forest floor; each breath is harder, slower, leaving us colder. The safe tattoo of our heartbeat is broken; now it beats like a kitten playing or a bad drum: growing fainter, more irregular.

There is no time for goodbye, there is only the cold stillness that creeps over our fingers and hands, our feet and ankles. Crawling up our legs, inch by inch. The little ones are crying, deep down in the pit. They never did anything to anyone, the little ones. They never had a chance. The bright burning world falls into darkness.

Sun lies in long stripes across the bloodied forest floor. Nearby, far away, a dog whines.

Now nothing.

Olivia

I'm back in the house, I don't know how and it doesn't matter. There is no time to feel relief at having my lovely ears and tail again. It's anything but safe here.

The walls are giving in like lungs collapsing. Plaster falls in chunks from the ceiling. Windows explode inwards in a hail of icy splinters. I run to hide under the couch, but the couch is gone, instead there is a great wet mouth with broken teeth. Through the portholes there falls thunderlight. Black hands reach up from the floor. The cord is tight around my neck. It is transparent, now, the colour of death. There is no scent at all, and perhaps it is that which makes me understand that I am going to die.

I think about fish, and how I will never know its taste, and I think about my beautiful tabby, and how I will never see her again. Then I think about Ted and what I did to him and I am really crying, now. I know, in the way I know my own tail, that the others are already gone. For the first time I am all alone. And soon I will be gone too.

I can feel it all, now, the body. The heart, the bones, the delicate clouds of nerve endings, the fingernails. What a moving thing a fingernail is. I see that it doesn't matter what shape the body is, that it doesn't have fur or a tail. It still belongs to us.

Time to stop being a kitten, I say to myself. *Come on, cat. Maybe if I help the body, the others can come back.*

But when I look there is a seething mass of shining blades where the front door should be. They whir and snick through the air. There is no way out there.

I'll try up, then. At the top of the stairs, the landing and the bedroom and roof are gone. The house is open to a raging sky, the storm which beats and whirls overhead. It is made of tar and lightning. There are brouhahas with great saggy jaws, baying. They tumble and race through the clouds, eyes like points of fire.

My fur is on end, my heart pounds. Every fibre of me wants to turn, to run and hide somewhere quiet, and wait to die. But if I do that it's over.

Be brave, cat. I put my paws on the first step, and then the second. Maybe this will be OK!

The staircase caves in with a great sound. Rubble lands all around me, and there is choking dust and ropes of the sticky black tar that burn and blind me. When the dust clears, I can only see rubble, brick. The walls are caved in, closing off the stairs. Everything is quiet. I am sealed in.

No, I whisper, tail lashing. *No, no, no!* But I am trapped, the crumbling house my tomb. I am finished, we are all finished.

I call on the LORD. He does not answer.

There is a deep stirring somewhere and I start, tail bristling. In the darkest corner of the living room Night-time groans. He raises his head. His ears are ragged and there are deep slashes along his flanks, as if made by a knife. Dying, yes. But not dead. Not yet.

I think furiously. I can't go up or out, but perhaps there is somewhere left to go, after all.

Hurt, he says, in a deep growl.

I know, I say. *I am sorry. But I need your help. We all do. Can you take me down, to your place?*

264

He hisses, a sound as deep as a geyser. I can't blame him. He tried to warn me about Lauren.

Please, I say. *Now, more than ever — now it is your time.*

Night-time comes forward, no longer graceful, but limping and painfully slow. He stands over me and I hear his breath sawing in and out. He opens his jaws wide and I think, *This is it, he will finish me.* Part of me is glad. But instead he closes his mouth about my scruff and picks me up, gentle as a mamacat.

My time, he says, and the house is gone. We hurtle down, down through the dark. Something hits me with a terrible blow and now we are somewhere else entirely.

Night-time's place is worse than I could have imagined. There is nothing but old, old dark. Great plains and expanses and canyons of black nothing. I understand that there is no such thing as distance here — it all goes on for ever. This world is not round and you never come back to yourself.

Here, he says, putting me down.

I gasp, my lungs almost crushed by loneliness. Or maybe it is the last life draining from us.

No, I say. *We have to go further down.*

He says nothing, but I feel his fear. There are deep places even Night-time cannot go.

Do it, I say.

He snarls and bites me, deep in the throat. Blood gushes forth, freezes in a stony spray in the cold dead air. Bodies don't work the same way down here.

I snarl and bite him back, my small teeth puncturing him in the cheek. He starts in surprise. *We die if we go down,* he says.

We have to go down, I say. *Or we will certainly die.*

He shakes his head and grabs me by the scruff and we sink into the black earth.

It is like sinking to the very depths of a dark ocean. The pressure becomes unbearable. Night-time forces us deeper into the dark ground, rasping in distress at my side. We are pressed together so tightly that our bodies and our bones begin to break and our eyes explode. Our blood is frozen to sludge and bursts out of our veins. We are crushed, bodies mangled to jagged ends of bone. The weight of everything obliterates us. We are crushed until we are no more than particles, dust. There is no more Olivia, and no more Night-time. *Please*, I think, *it must be over now*. The agony cannot go on. We must be dead. I can't feel him any more. But somehow I am still here.

A gleam of light ahead, like the first evening star. We struggle towards it, weeping and gasping. Somewhere, Night-time raises his head and roars. To my amazement, I feel it rumbling in my chest.

I am powerful and sleek, my great flanks heave. *Where are you? I say. Where am I?*

Nowhere, he says, *and here.*

Are you still Night-time?

No.

I'm not Olivia any more, I say, certain.

I roar and run towards the light. I tear at the dark with my great paws, clawing at the point of light until it rips and grows. I fight with all my strength until I burst out of the black, into the barred sunlight. I cannot move, I lie trapped in the cold and bloodied corpse on the forest floor, with the red-haired man's hand pressed down hard on the wound. The blood has slowed almost to a stop.

I take a deep breath and spread myself throughout the body, running through all its cold bone and veins and flesh. *Come back. Wake up.*

Our heart twitches faintly.

The first beat is like thunder, echoing through the silent body.

Another, then another, and the roaring begins, blood hurtling through the arteries. We gasp, we take his breath in a great heaving sigh. The body lights up cell by cell, reawakening. It begins to sing with life.

Dee

⌒

Dee runs into the dawn. The bite on her arm is a ragged hole, edges brown with dirt. She knows she needs a hospital. The pump seems to have got the venom out, but the bite might be infected. She tries not to think about that. All that matters is finding Lulu.

She stumbles on through the forest, seeing faces in the patterns of light and shade. She shouts her sister's name. Sometimes her voice is loud, sometimes it is a dry whisper. Ahead, she catches a little sound. It could be a blackbird, or a child's whimper. Dee hurries on, faster. Lulu must be scared.

Murderer. The word is like a bell, ringing through her head. Is that what she is? Dee knows she can never go back to Needless Street. She left bloody traces of herself all through the forest, all over his body. If one thing comes to light, others follow. They are like that, secrets, they move in flocks like birds.

She runs on through the forest. It becomes difficult to see the path ahead; the past is everywhere, overlaying the dawnlit world. Images come, and voices. She sees a ponytail flying between two tree trunks, hears her name whispered in a frightened voice. The tired detective's face swims before her, the last time they spoke face to face.

'Are you sure you've told me everything about that day, Delilah? You were just a kid, you know. People would understand.'

Karen's eyes were kind. Dee nearly told her right then and there, she really did. She has never been closer to telling.

It was Lulu's white flip-flop that made Karen suspect, of course. The woman from the bathroom was certain she hadn't picked it up by mistake and put it in her own bag. She was sure it must have been put there by someone else. Dee was furious with herself for that. Who knew the woman would be so sharp?

'You can't prove anything,' Dee hissed. Karen's careworn eyes moved over her, the creases deepened at the edges, like volcanic land.

'It will eat at you until there's nothing left,' she said finally. 'Believe me, it would be better to let it out.' That was when it went sour, of course.

Dee stops, retching. She crouches, her mind yawns up colours and memory. Her breath is coming too fast. She tries to summon the white static, make it cover the thoughts that teem in. But it's no good. The air smells like cold water, sunscreen on warm skin.

Dee walks across the lake-shore, away from her family, navigating the chequerboard maze of blankets.

The yellow-headed boy says, 'Hi.' She sees the swirls of white lotion on his pale skin. When he smiles his front two teeth overlap slightly. It gives him a feral, intriguing air.

'Hi,' says Dee. He has to be at least eighteen, probably in college. She watches him watching her and understands, for the first time, that he sees both predator and prey. It is complicated and exciting. So when Trevor offers a hand to shake she smirks. She sees the flash of anger, of hurt. His pale skin flushes.

'Are you here with your folks?' This is retaliation. What he means is, *You are a baby who comes to the lake with her family.*

Dee shrugs. 'I managed to lose them,' she says. 'Except for this one.'

He smiles, like he appreciates the joke. 'Where are your parents?'

'All the way over by the lifeguard stand,' she says, pointing. 'They were all sleeping and I was bored.'

'Is this your little sister?'

'She ran after me,' Dee says. 'I couldn't stop her.' Lulu swings, bored, from Dee's hand. She says something to herself under her breath. She squints in the sun, eyes serious and far away. In one sweaty palm she clutches her straw sun hat with the pink ribbon tied around it.

'How old is she?'

'Six,' Dee says. 'Put your hat on or you'll burn,' she tells Lulu.

'No.' Lulu loves her hat but it is an object to be treasured, not worn.

Loathing strokes Dee, feather light. Why does she have such an annoying family? She takes the hat from her sister and puts it roughly on her head. Lulu's face crumples.

Trevor bends down and addresses Lulu. 'You want to go get some ice cream?'

Lulu nods twenty or thirty times.

Dee considers, shrugs. They queue. Trevor and Dee don't get ice cream. Lulu gets chocolate, which Dee knows will spread all over her face and clothes, and then her mother will scream at them both. But right now she finds that she does not care. Trevor's hand hangs a millimetre from hers, then brushes, finger to finger. Something is coming, it is in the air like heat haze, like thunder.

Dee does not argue when Trevor steers them away from the ice-cream stand, through from the burger-scented, colourful crowds, towards the trees. Dee thinks of what her parents would say, but defiance wins out. *Just this once,* she thinks, *I want to do something all my own.*

In the pine-striped shadows the three of them move soft as tigers. The crowded beach falls behind them quickly, is lost in the tapestry of hushing leaves. Soon there is only the sound of the black water kissing stones. They track the pebbled shore, climbing over rocks, fallen branches, nests of briars. Even Lulu is quiet, excited, possessed by the sense of trespass. Her white flip-flops are too flimsy for the rough terrain. But she doesn't complain as her feet and ankles become beaded with scratches. The yellow-headed boy lifts Lulu when she cannot get over.

Dee grows impatient. She pushes on ahead, pulling him by the hand. They come to a place where the trees open out somewhat, where the pine needles look soft and there aren't too many thorns. A rock shaped like a canoe pushes out into the water. Dee and the boy look at one another. The time has come for whatever is coming.

'I want to go home,' Lulu says, scrubbing one eye with a fist. Her cheeks are pink, sunstruck. Somewhere in the shadowed pines she has lost her hat.

'You can't,' Dee tells her sister. 'You followed me so now you have to wait. And if you tell about this, I'll say you're lying. Now go play by the lake.' Lulu bites her lip and looks like she might cry. She doesn't, though. She knows Dee is still mad at her, so she does what she is told.

Dee turns to the boy. What is his name again? Her heart is racing. She knows she is risking everything. Lulu is a true tattle-tale. *Doesn't matter,* she tells herself. *This is real, it is happening.* She will figure out how to silence her sister.

The boy leans in close. Now he is no longer a face but a series of features, giant and individual. His lips are wet and trembling. Dee thinks, *Is this French kissing?* There are moments, flashes of excitement which make it seem like they are just about to get good at it, but then they both miss the moment and it goes on, mouths pushed against one another, spitty and loose. He tastes faintly of hot dog. Dee thinks maybe it doesn't get good until you do the other stuff so she puts his hand up her top. Her bathing suit is a little wet and his hand is warm. It's nice, so she considers that a success. Next, his hand makes its way into the tight confines of her denim shorts. It is too tight, his hand gets stuck there, so she unbuttons them and wriggles them down. They are both still for a moment, aware that they are moving quickly into unfamiliar territory. She giggles because it is so weird to be in her swimsuit in a forest with a boy looking at her.

Dee hears a sound. It is like a spoon tapping an egg, just once. Dee pulls her shorts up, calling, 'Lulu?' There is no answer. Dee runs towards the shore. The boy follows her, stumbling on his jeans.

Lulu is lying half in and half out of the lapping waves, submerged to the waist, as if she was trying to dive back onto land. Blood clouds and blooms in the water. Dee is not aware of jumping in, but somehow she is standing, waist deep in the water, beside her sister's small form. The sound it made was quiet, but her skull must have hit the boulder with great force. It is dented, as if punched by a fist. Dee tries not to look at that part.

She presses her lips to Lulu's and breathes, in a half-remembered impression of first-aid classes at school. But she thinks it's too late. Lulu's skin is changing, even as Dee watches. Her face grows pale and waxy. Threads of blood trickle out of her hair. They look kind of like red birds in flight; the way children draw birds, lines against a white sky.

The yellow-headed boy whose name Dee still cannot recall begins to breathe fast, like a woman giving birth. He runs from them, crashing away through the forest.

Dee touches Lulu's hand where it lies on the gritty sand. Loosely grasped in Lulu's palm is a deep green stone, shot through with veins of white. It is oval and planed smooth by water and time. *Pretty pebble.* Dee moans. Threads of fresh blood seep from Lulu's head into the water. They blow up into crimson clouds.

Dee's legs and arms are slick with lake water, with blood. She bends again and breathes into Lulu's mouth. A sound comes from Lulu's chest. It is deep like the creak of a tree branch.

From under Lulu's body there comes a flexing thing, a line of dark. The snake curls over Lulu and brushes against Dee's thighs. It looks like a cottonmouth, but there are no cottonmouths round here. Small shadows follow it. Young hatchlings. Now Dee sees the puncture wounds on Lulu's swollen ankles. That's why she fell.

Dee is a stone in the water. She feels the bodies glancing gently against her thighs. The snakes seem to regard her as part of the lake or the land. Then she hurls herself up and out, throwing great sheets of spray. She claws up across the warm rock. A very small snake is coiled six inches from her hand. It opens a white mouth at her then flows away, down into a dark crack in the rock. Dee screams and runs blindly, leaving Lulu where she lies, half in, and half out of the water.

Dee can't see; there's something in front of her eyes like a cloud of flies or a hurricane. She tries to blink it away but she can't so she slows, and then stops. The cold trickles of bloody lake water keep coming down the backs of her legs, and she is panting. She thinks she might faint so she stops for a moment. She leans against a broken stump, silvered and dead with age. All she can see at her feet are snakes. *Stop,* she commands her body and mind. *Stop. No snakes here.* She has to think.

A new little voice speaks in her mind. *At least Lulu can't tell Mom and Dad on you now.* She sobs. How can she even think such a horrible thing?

Gnats swarm greedily at the blood on her. She tries to scrub it off. But she is shaking and it has stained her shorts. Instead she ties her sweater round her waist to hide it as best she can. *Blood, blood,* Dee thinks in a fog. Fresh threads of blood. The next thought shines out, knifes through her hard and quick. Lulu was still bleeding. Dee has watched enough TV to know what that means. She is not dead.

Dee turns and runs hard, back towards Lulu. Her lungs are bursting with effort and the scalding air. How could she have left her like that? But Dee will make it right, she swears. She will stay by Lulu's side and scream until someone comes. It is not too late. Events are not yet final. But she has to be fast.

Dee feels like she has been running and climbing and stumbling back towards her sister for her whole life. But eventually the undergrowth thins and the canoe-shaped rock comes into view. Dee goes even faster, taking long hare-like leaps over the shore debris. She falls more than once, skinning palms and knees and elbows. She does not notice, pushes herself up and runs on. When she comes to the rock she stops for a moment, too frightened to set foot on the rock.

'Come on, Dee Dee,' she mutters. 'You baby.' She climbs over the canoe rock.

In its shadow, where Lulu should be lying, there is nothing. Water laps cold at the granite. Gnats buzz above the water, grey punctuation marks. No Lulu, alive or dead.

Maybe this isn't the right place, Dee tells herself. But it is. On the rock she can see a slender thread of drying blood. In the water, one white flip-flop bobs. Then Dee sees that there is a footprint at the muddy edge. The heel is already filling with brown lake water. The footprint is big, much too large to be Lulu's, or Dee's. It could be the boy's, maybe. But somehow Dee knows it's not.

From nearby there comes a familiar, homely sound – it takes Dee a moment to place it in this nightmare. A car engine starts, then idles. A door slams closed.

Dee runs across the clearing where, what seems like a lifetime ago, she fooled around with the boy. She pushes through a stand of brush, and falls out onto a dirt road. Dust billows and dances in the air as if recently kicked up by tyres. Dee thinks she glimpses a car bumper vanishing down the track. The roaring in Dee's ears almost drowns the engine, her ragged screams for the driver to stop, stop, and let her sister go. But the car is gone. At Dee's feet, in the dust, lies a deep green stone; a perfect oval shot through with veins of white.

A short distance away through the scrub, sun gleams on ranks of chrome and glass. Dee wants to shriek with laughter. They thought they were so far from everything, but they were right by the parking lot.

In the bathroom, the women look at her, disapproving. She leans against the white-tiled wall. Over the roar of the hand dryers, she tries to understand what has happened. It is impossible. She retches briefly into a basin, and earns herself more disapproval from the line. *I have to tell someone,* she thinks, and the thought is cold and numbing.

She pictures the expression her mother's face will wear as she tells her parents. Tries to imagine the tone of her father's voice as he tries to forgive her.

The little voice says, *If you tell, there will be no Pacific ballet school.* Even through her fear for Lulu, Dee feels the molten creep of fury. They have always loved Lulu best, ever since she was born. Dee has always known it. It is so unfair. She didn't do anything wrong, not really. This is real life, not one of those old books where a girl makes out with a boy and then someone has to *die* because it's so *sinful.* She knows, deep down, that making out with the boy wasn't what she did wrong.

What can she tell them, anyway? Dee does not have any real information. She couldn't even see the car through the dust. Was there a car? She is not sure, now. Maybe Lulu's body floated away in the lake. Or it was taken away by an animal. Like, a bear. Maybe Lulu woke up and went back to Mom and Dad. *Yes,* Dee thinks with a rush of relief. *That's it.* Dee will go back to her family and Lulu will be sitting on the blanket playing with pebbles. She will greet Dee with an affronted look, because Dee left her alone, to do boring big-kid stuff. But Dee will tickle her and Lulu will forgive her in the end. So there really is no point in telling.

A fresh snail of watery blood crawls out of Dee's shorts, down her leg. 'Does anyone have a sanitary towel?' Dee tries to sound pissed off instead of scared, which she is. She takes her shorts off in the bathroom in front of all the women and rinses them at the basin. She makes a big deal out of it, so they will remember her later. Dee was here, and nowhere else. She doesn't ask herself why this is necessary, if Lulu is waiting with Mom and Dad. The word *alibi* drifts through her mind. She banishes it, firmly.

Her period, she tells herself over and over. That is where the blood comes from. It is like rehearsing a dance – putting a story into the steps. Can she make herself believe it? She constructs, carefully in her mind, a day where the yellow-haired boy stood her up for ice cream, where Lulu never followed her into the woods.

Once the decision is made, everything becomes simple. A tired-looking woman washes her hands at the neighbouring basin, while her three children jump up and grab her sleeves. At the woman's feet is a wicker basket, from which spill tissues, granola bars, buckets, spades, toys and sunscreen. Dee takes the white flip-flop out of her pocket and slips it into the woman's bag where it blends with the chaos. It will go home with the woman and she will assume she picked it up by accident with her kids' stuff. It will never be connected with Lulu. Dee knows that if the shoe is found by the canoe-shaped rock, they will do police stuff, like forensics and they will know that Dee was there.

As she heads back towards her parents, she tosses the smooth green stone into the thick brush that hems the beach.

Dee wipes her mouth with the back of her hand and gets up. She seems to be in a different part of the forest, now. It is darker, denser. Groundsel and ivy are knee-deep. She must remember to keep blazing the trees. A giant fern brushes her face. She thrusts it away, impatient. Why does everything in this part of the world have to be so wild and scary?

She can hear feet ahead, frightened, uneven. A child running.

'Lulu,' she calls. 'Stop!'

Lulu laughs. Dee smiles. It's good that she's having fun. Dee doesn't mind playing tag for a while longer.

Later, when Dee had time to think, the horror of what she had not told settled into her like disease. *It's too late to tell now,* the little voice said. *They'll send you to jail.* After her mother left and her father died there was no point in Dee telling, because there was no one left to forgive her.

Dee realised what she had to do. She had to find the person who took Lulu. If she could do that, there was a chance she could be a good person again. It was something to cling to. But tired Karen kept clearing people of Lulu's disappearance. And as the years went by the possibilities, the list of suspects, was whittled down and down. Dee grew desperate.

She had almost given up, until Ted.

Karen said that Ted had an alibi. Dee didn't believe it. She suspected that Karen was trying to throw her off the scent, stop her repeating the Oregon incident. Dee knew she had to be careful. She would watch him. She would get proof before she acted, this time. Dee got a little ahead of herself, however. She may as well admit that.

It was the anniversary that pushed her over the edge. 10 July, every year, the day Lulu went missing; that day is always a black hole for Dee. It's all she can do not to get sucked down into the dark. Sometimes she isn't strong enough to resist. That was what happened in Oregon. Loss had Dee in its black grip and someone had to be punished.

She had been watching Ted for some days before she moved in. She saw his eyes in the hole in the plywood, every morning at first light, watching as the birds descended. She saw the care he took with the feeders, the water. There's a lot Dee doesn't know but she knows what love looks like. So she knew what to do.

She needed Ted to feel something of her savage grief. That was why she killed the birds. She didn't like doing it. She retched as she put out the traps. But she couldn't stop. She kept thinking, *Eleven years today. Eleven years that Lulu never had.*

Afterwards she watched as Ted cried over the birds. His bent back, his hands covering his face. She felt the sorrow deeply in herself. It was awful, what she had been forced to do.

Now, Dee stumbles on after Lulu. She grabs at the slender sappy branches, pulling herself along.

'Stop,' she calls. 'Come on, Lulu. No need to be afraid. It's Dee Dee.'

The sky turns red and the sun becomes a burning ball, sinking into the horizon. Dee's breath comes short and her fingers are swollen where they grip the branch. She blinks to clear her vision of the black edges.

Come on, Dee Dee.

She vomits but there is no time to stop. Instead Dee starts to run again, even faster this time, careening gracefully through the trees, speeding so smoothly over the uneven ground, the fallen branches that her feet leave the earth. She flies silent and fast, piercing the air like an arrow. All she can hear is wind and the tapestry of forest sound: cicadas, doves, leaves. *Why didn't I know I could fly?* she thinks. *I'll teach Lulu how and we can fly all over, never landing. We can be together and they won't catch me. I'll have time to explain to her why I did what I did.*

Dee sees Lulu at the top of the next rise, silhouetted against the low sun. The little figure, the sun hat. Dee can just make out the white flip-flops on her feet. Dee hurtles through the air towards her. She comes to rest lightly on the grassy rise.

Lulu turns and Dee sees that she has no face. Red birds explode from her head in a cloud. Dee shrieks and covers her eyes with her hand.

When at last she dares to look, she is alone in the forest. Night has come again. Dee looks about her in terror. Where is she? How long has she been walking? She sinks to her knees. What has it all been for? Where is Lulu? Where are the answers that are her due? Dee screams out her horror and her sorrow. But her screams are no louder than papery whispers against the patter of rain. Her cheek is cold. She is lying on the forest floor, slick with rain. Her arm is swollen dark and heavy as a block of stone. *I'm dying,* she thinks. *I just wanted there to be some kind of justice in the world.*

As her vision clouds to black and her heart slows, she thinks she feels the lightest touch on her head. She seems to catch the scent of sunscreen, warm hair, sugar. 'Lulu,' she tries to say, 'I'm sorry,' but her heart stops beating and Dee is gone.

The thing that was once Dee lies far from any trail. The can of yellow spray paint is still held in what was her hand, swollen black with venom.

The birds and the foxes come, the coyotes, bears and rats. What was Dee feeds the earth. Her scattered bones sink into the rich changing humus. No ghost walks under the spreading trees. What's done is done.

Ted

I am not dead, I can tell, because there is a strand of spaghetti on the green tile floor. What happens after death may be bad or good but there won't be spilled spaghetti. The white hospital bed is hard, the walls are scuffed, and everything smells like lunch. The man is looking at me. The light glints on his orange-juice hair. 'Hi,' he says.

'Where's the woman?' I ask. 'The neighbour lady? She was saying the girl's name. She was sick.' Her arm looked snake-bit. I think she used the kit from my bag, but everyone knows those kits don't do anything. I don't know why I carry it. The memories are very confused, but there was something wrong with the neighbour lady – inside and out.

'You were alone when I found you,' he says. The man stares at me and I stare back. How are you supposed to talk to the person who saved your life?

'How did you find me?' I ask.

'Someone had been blazing young trees with yellow paint. I'm a park ranger up in King County, so I didn't like that. It's toxic. I followed the trail, to tell them to stop. The dog got a blood scent. That was you.'

The doctor comes and the orange-haired man goes into the hall, out of earshot. The doctor is young, tired-looking.

'You seem better. Let's take a look.' He does everything gently. 'I want to ask you about the pills they found with you,' he says.

'Oh,' I say, anxiety settling on me like a cloak. 'I need them. They keep me calm.'

'Well,' he says, 'I'm not sure about that. Did a doctor prescribe them?'

'Yes,' I say, 'He gave them to me in his office.'

'I don't know where your doctor got them – but I would stop taking them, if I were you. They stopped manufacturing these pills about ten years ago. They have extreme side effects. Hallucinations, memory loss. Some people experience rapid weight gain. I am happy to recommend an alternative.'

'Oh,' I say. 'I won't be able to afford that.'

He sighs and sits on the bed, which I *know* they're not supposed to do. Mommy would have been upset. But he looks exhausted, so I don't say anything. 'It's tough,' he says. 'There's not enough support or funding. But I'll bring you the forms. You might be eligible for aid.' He hesitates. 'It's not just the medication that concerns me. There is a great deal of burn scarring on your back, legs and arms. There are also many scars from sutured incisions. That would normally indicate many hospitalisations in childhood. But your medical records don't reflect that. They don't seem to reflect any medical intervention at all.' He looks at me and says, 'Somebody should have caught this. Somebody should have stopped what was being done to you.'

It never before occurred to me that Mommy could have been stopped. I consider. 'I don't think they could have,' I say. But it's nice that it matters to him.

'I can give you the name of someone who can go over your medical history in detail, someone you can talk to about … what happened. It's never too late.'

He sounds unsure and I understand why. Sometimes it is too late. I think I finally understand the difference between now and then. 'Maybe some other time,' I say. 'Right now I'm kind of tired of therapy.'

He looks like he wants to say more but he doesn't, and I'm so grateful to him for that that I just start crying.

The orange-haired man brings me a toothbrush from the gift shop, sweatpants, a T-shirt and some underwear. It's kind of embarrassing that he bought me underwear, but I need it. All my clothes were ruined by blood.

Doctors come and give me the stuff that makes the world go underwater. It keeps the others in here quiet, too. For the first time in many years, there is silence. But I know that they are there. We all move gently in and out of time.

Through the window I can see tall buildings, gleaming in the sun. I feel how far I am from the forest. I ask to have the window open, but the nurse says no, that the heatwave is over. This part of the world is returning to its cool, deep-green self. I feel like I'm coming home after a war.

The nurses are nice to me, amused. I'm just some clumsy guy who slipped and fell on his hunting knife, early one morning in the woods.

The orange-haired man is still here when I wake again. It should be weird, having a stranger in the room. But it isn't. He is a peaceful person.

'How are you feeling?' he asks.

'Better,' I say. And it's true.

'I have to ask,' he says. 'Did you really slip on that knife, or not? There was something in your eyes while I was trying to stop the bleeding. It looked like maybe you weren't sorry to be – you know. Dying.'

'It's complicated,' I say.

'I'm no stranger to complicated.' He takes off his cap and rubs his head so his hair stands up in red spikes. He looks exhausted. 'You know what they say. If you save someone's life, you're responsible for them.'

If I tell him the truth, I guess I won't see him again. But I am so tired of hiding what I am. My brain and my heart and my bones are exhausted by it. Mommy's rules haven't done me any good. What do I have to lose?

Lauren stirs, watchful.

I ask her, 'Do you want to start?'

Lauren

⁓

This is how it went, the thing with the mouse – how Ted found the inside place.

Night-times were the most special times for Little Teddy. He loved sleeping by his mother's warm, white-clad form. But before that, she would tend to his injuries. It used to be once a month, maybe, but lately Teddy hurt himself so badly and so often that Mommy had to spend all night sewing up his cuts. They did not look bad to Ted, some were barely scratches. And some of the cuts were the invisible kind, he couldn't see or feel them at all. Mommy told him that these were the most dangerous kinds of wounds. She opened these cuts again, cleaned them and sewed them back up.

Teddy knew that Mommy had to do it, that it was his fault for being so clumsy. But he dreaded the moment when she turned on the bedside lamp and angled it just so. Then she set out the tray. The things gleamed there, the scissors and the scalpel. Balls of cotton, the bottle that smelled like Daddy's drink. Mommy put on white gloves like skin, and she then went to work.

I don't think Ted really liked me, especially in the beginning. Ted is a polite, peaceable boy. I am loud. I get very angry. Rage flows through me in waves. But it is not my job to make him like me. It is my job to protect him from hurt. I took some of his pain – I came forward so that we shared it. I couldn't make it go away altogether. Sometimes the pain wasn't even the worst part – it was the sounds. The little noise as the flesh parted. He really didn't like that.

That night, as the tip of the scalpel met his back, I came forward as usual to share it with him.

'Stay still, please, Theodore,' said Mommy. 'You are making this very difficult.' Then she continued her dictation, pressing the red piano-key button down with a click. 'The third incision,' she said, 'is superficial, outer dermis only.' Her hand followed the words.

Ted knew that Mommy was right – this only got worse if he fought it. He knew if he stepped out of line Mommy would put him in the old chest freezer, in the disinfecting bath of vinegar and hot water. So Ted tried to let it happen. He tried to be a good boy. But the pain and the noises got so bad, Ted was afraid he wouldn't be able to stop himself making a sound – even though he knew what happened if he did that.

We were lying alongside one another, and I felt all his thoughts and fears. It was hard to take at the same time as everything that was happening to the body.

And Ted did it, he let out a little high *ahh*, barely a sound at all, really. But it fell into the quiet like a pebble into a pond. We both held our breath. Mommy stopped what she was doing. 'You're making this very hard for both of us,' she said, and went to make the vinegar bath ready.

As she lowered us into the freezer, Ted started crying properly. He wasn't as strong as me.

The dark closed over. Our skin was a gulf of flame. Ted was breathing too fast and coughing. I knew I had to protect him. He couldn't take much more of this.

'Get out of here, Ted,' I said. 'Go.'

'Where?' he asked.

'Do what I do. Leave. Stop being.'

'I can't!' His voice was really high.

I pushed him. 'Go away, you big baby.'

'I can't!'

'Well, maybe Mommy will go too far this time,' I said, 'and we will die.' This neat solution had never occurred to me before. 'Ted! I just had an idea!'

But Teddy was gone. He had found his door.

Ted

The air changed around me, somehow. I was standing by the front door to our house. But there was no street, no forest, no oak tree. Instead everything was white like the inside of a cloud. It wasn't scary. It felt safe. I opened the door and stepped into the house, which was shrouded in a warm, dim calm. I locked the door behind me, quickly. *Thunk, thunk, thunk*. Mommy couldn't come here, I knew.

The air was suddenly filled with the sound of purring. A soft tail stroked my legs. I looked down and caught my breath. I could hardly believe it. I was staring into a pair of beautiful green eyes, the size and shape of cocktail olives. She regarded me, delicate ears alert and questioning. I crouched and reached for her, half expecting her to vanish into nothing. Her coat was like silky coal. I stroked her, ran my finger down the slice of white on her chest.

'Hi, kitty,' I said, and she purred. 'Hi, Olivia.' She weaved herself in a figure of eight about my legs. I went to the living room, where the light was yellow-warm and the couch was soft, and took her on my lap. The house looked almost exactly like the one upstairs – it was just a little different. The cold blue rug I had always hated was orange down here, a beautiful deep shade, like the sun settling on a winter highway.

As I sat on the couch stroking Olivia, I heard it. The long, even passage of breath, great flanks rising and falling. I wasn't afraid. I peered into the shadows and I saw him, lying in a great pile, watching me with eyes like lamps. I offered out my hand and Night-time came padding out of the dark.

So I got my kitty in the end. Actually it was even better than I had hoped, because I got two.

And that's how I found the inside place. I can go down when I like, but it's easier if I use the freezer as the door. I guess I could have made the inside place a castle or a mansion or something. But how would I know where everything was, in a castle or a mansion?

I am Big Ted now but Little Teddy is still here. When I go away, it's because he has come forward. He does not use the face in the same way that grown-ups use their faces. So he can look scary. But he would never hurt anyone. It was Little Teddy who picked up the blue scarf and tried to give it back to the lady as she sat crying in her car, in the parking lot of the bar. She screamed when she saw Little Teddy. He ran after her, but she drove away fast through the rain.

Lauren

⁓

Ted was gone and all the pain that had been shared between us rushed into me. I had not known the body was capable of standing so much. I tried to follow him down, inside. But he had locked the door against me. I wonder if he could hear me screaming, from down there. I expect he could.

Mommy put us back in our little bed when she was done. The gauze was itchy over the stitches but I knew better than to scratch. The room was full of moving shadow and the mouse's pink eyes gleamed where it watched from its cage.

I'm scared, I tried to tell Teddy. Teddy didn't answer. He was deep in a good place full of black tails and green eyes and soft coats. I tried not to cry but I couldn't help it.

I felt Ted soften towards me. 'You can sleep now, Lauren,' he said. 'Someone else will watch.'

I heard the pad of great paws as Night-time came upstairs. I sank into the soft black.

I was woken in the morning by his weeping. Ted had found Snowball's bloody bones in the cage. He was so sorry about it. 'Poor Snowball,' he whispered over and over. 'It isn't fair.' He cried more about that mouse than he did about the new little railway of black sutures that ran down our back. He wasn't there when it was done, I guess. He didn't feel it. I did, each one.

Ted knew it wasn't Night-time's fault. Night-time was just obeying his nature. Ted told Mommy that the mouse got out of its cage, and a stray cat got it. It was true, in a way. Of course, Mommy didn't believe him. She took Teddy to the woods and told him to hide who he was. She thought he had a hunger in him. Ted was afraid that she would find a way to take Olivia and Night-time away. (And then it would be just me and him. He didn't want *that*.) So he let her think it was the old sickness, the one her father had, the one who kept his pets in the crypt beneath the *iliz*.

I had begun to understand what Ted could not – what he would not allow himself to know. Each time the thought bobbed up he pushed it down harder, harder. Up it came again like a cork or a corpse surfacing. The sickness had indeed been passed down, though not to Ted. I wonder what the people of Locronan would say, if you asked them why they cast Mommy out. Maybe they have a different story to hers. Maybe it wasn't her father who had the sickness.

At school they sensed that something had changed in Ted. He was like a mask with no one behind. Everyone stopped talking to him. He didn't care. He could go inside, now, with the kitties. For the first time he could recall, he told me, he did not feel alone.

To me, who had been with him for all of Mommy's repairs. He said that to *me*.

Teddy began calling the inside house his weekend place, because there was no work or school down there. Soon he found that he could add to it. He couldn't keep his job at the auto shop in Auburn, so he made a basement where he could work on engines. He liked engines. It was a good workshop, full of tools in shining boxes and the scent of motor oil. He put white socks in the drawers, the kind that Mommy would never let him wear, because she said they were for girls. He put a window in the ceiling on the landing, where he could watch the sky all night, if he wanted, but no one could look back at him except the moon. He fixed the music box and put the Russian dolls back on the mantelpiece. Down here, he can fix everything he breaks. The picture of Mommy and Daddy can never be taken off the wall. Olivia walked through it all, her tail held curious and high. He made sure she had a peephole all her own. For her, it is always winter outside: Ted's favourite season.

Ted made sure that Night-time only hunted downstairs, after the thing with Snowball. He put lots of mice in the weekend place to keep Night-time happy. Ted didn't want any more suffering.

He added an attic, which he kept locked. He could put memories and thoughts in there and close the door. He didn't like some of the inhabitants of the house. The long-fingered, green things, which had once been boys. He was afraid that the green boys were the ones who went missing from the lake. But that was just fine, because he put them in the attic, too. Sometimes they could be heard in the night, dragging their bony stick fingers on the boards, and weeping.

The more time Teddy spent inside, the clearer and more detailed it got. Soon he found that he could go there whenever he wanted. He began to lose time, there. The TV played anything he wanted. He could even watch what was happening in the upstairs house. If he saw something good was happening, like Mommy had got ice cream, he could open the front door and he would be up there again. Usually he found himself lying in the freezer in the acid-scented dark, with the air holes shining above him like stars. He went up less and less as the years went on.

More and more, he left me alone with Mommy. When she

angled the light just so, Teddy went down to the weekend place and stroked his kitty.

I came to hate that smug cat. Ted knew it. Sometimes when I tried to come down he kept me suspended between the two places, in the black, vinegar-smelling freezer, because the cat was downstairs. Then when she went away it was my turn. If I did something he didn't like, he found he could keep me in the dark freezer all the time.

I can't come forward fully when we're outside the house, unless Ted lets me. I can do little things – scribble a note, maybe, on the inside of some leggings, or make him lose concentration for a couple seconds. And of course it has to be stuff that doesn't require the use of working legs. I don't know why Ted's broken mind made me like this but it did. He has to carry me through the world, maimed and powerless. I think that's why he sometimes forgets that it was my strength that kept us alive.

Ted couldn't say boo to a goose, or so I thought. I soon found out how wrong I was.

One day we were looking for mints in Mommy's drawers. She didn't like candy but she liked her breath to be fresh, so she would put one in her mouth for a few moments then spit it into a handkerchief. She moved the hiding place but sometimes we found it. We knew to eat just one, no matter how hungry we were. Mommy counted, but one mint was *a plausible margin of error*.

Mommy kept interesting things in her drawers. An old song book with bears on the front, a single white child's flip-flop. Teddy was careless today. He pawed through her hose with damp hands.

'She'll notice, Teddy,' I said. 'Sheesh. You'll tear them!' He looked up and I caught our reflection in the mirror on the vanity. I saw it then, in his face. He didn't care any more. Mommy would punish us and make the body cry. She would put us in the big box with vinegar. But Teddy could just go downstairs. It was me who would feel it.

'Ted,' I said. 'You wouldn't ...'

He shrugged and took the box of mints from where it was neatly folded inside a camisole. Slowly, dreamily, he opened the tin and put it to his lips. He tipped it so that the mints flowed into his mouth. Some spilled from his lips and fell bouncing to the floor.

'Ted,' I whispered. 'Stop! You can't be serious, she will hurt the body for that.'

He shook the last mints into his mouth, which was already crammed with round white shapes. Even in my panic I could taste them, my mouth was filled with sweetness ... I shook myself. I had to stop him.

'I'll scream,' I said. 'I'll bring her.'

'So what?' he said, through a mouthful of clicking mints. 'Bring her. You'll feel it, not me.'

'There are more ways to hurt than the body,' I said. 'I'll tell her about your weekend place, and those cats. She will find a way to deal with that. I don't know what it will be, but you know I'm right. Mommy knows how to make brains do things, not just bodies.'

He growled and shook his head at me in the mirror. Suddenly there was nothing in my mouth. The taste was gone. He had cut me off from our senses. He looked as surprised as me. We hadn't known that was possible.

'You can stop me eating mints but you can't stop me telling,' I said.

Ted took a pin from the cushion on the dresser. Slowly he drove the tip into the fleshy part of his thumb.

A red line of fire ran through me and I screamed and wept.

Ted stood before the mirror. His face held Mommy's expression of clinical interest. Again and again he drove the needle home. 'I'll stop when you promise,' he said.

I promised.

I understand something about life that Ted never has: it is too painful. No one can take so much unhappiness. I tried to explain it to him. *It's bad, Teddy. Mommy is nuts, you know that. She's lost it. She'll go too far and end us one day. Better to choose our own way out. We don't have to feel bad all the time. Take the knife, knot the rope. Go hide in the lake. Walk into the woods, until everything goes green. The kindness of ending.* Teddy tried to block his ears, but of course he could not shut me out altogether. We are two parts of the whole. Or we were supposed to be.

Shortly after that I tried to kill us for the first time. It wasn't a very good try but it showed Teddy that he didn't want to die. He found a way to silence me. He started playing Mommy's music when he gave me pain. He gave me so much pain that the music became it, weaving through the air. The agony only stopped when I slipped half way down, into the dark freezer, leaving the body empty. I quickly learned to vanish as soon as the first note was plucked on the guitar.

Ted doesn't know everything. I still fight him. And I am stronger than he thinks. Sometimes when he goes away, it is not Little Teddy who comes. It is me. When he finds himself with a knife in his hand – those times it is me, trying to do what should be done.

But I wasn't strong enough. Ted had too good a hold on me. I had to make the cat do it. And that's how we come to be where we are.

Ted

She must have suspected that it was all about to come down around her. The police had come to the hospital, to Mommy's old work, asking questions. The children at the kindergarten where she worked now had got so clumsy. Previously Teddy had been the clumsiest and she had saved the big stuff, the stuff that left marks, for him. But recently Teddy wasn't enough any more. There were too many children being stitched up who hadn't fallen down.

Mommy had taken a long time to fix me, the night before. I was still shivering in the aftershock. I came into the kitchen for a glass of water. Mommy was standing on her tiptoes on a chair. She had a length of laundry line in her hands. On rainy days like today Mommy ran the washing line across the kitchen, to dry her stockings. Not pantyhose, she would never wear that.

'Teddy,' she said. 'You are tall. Help me get this up here. The goddamn thing won't go over the beam.' It was funny to hear her swear in that elegant, accented voice. I climbed up on the chair and threw the line over the crossbeam.

'Thank you,' she said, formally. 'Now go and get some ice cream from the store.' I looked at her, startled. We had ice cream once a year, on her birthday.

'But it will rot our teeth,' I said.

'Please do not argue with me, Theodore. When you get back, there will be some chores for you. Can you remember everything I am about to say? You must not write it down. And I am going out almost immediately, so I will not be able to tell you again.'

'I think I can remember,' I said.

'There is something I need you to dispose of. I will leave it here, in the kitchen. You must take it out to the woods. You will have to wait until dark to remove it from the house, because you are not allowed to bury things in the woods.'

'Yes, Mommy,' I said. She gave me ten dollars, way too much for ice cream.

As I closed the front door behind me I heard her say, in a low voice, '*Ya, ma ankou.*' It was all getting weirder and weirder.

I got vanilla ice cream. That was the only flavour she liked. I can still feel the numbness of my fingertips where they met the cold tub, see the delicate sediment of ice that covered the lid.

I come into the kitchen and see her. In a way, it is all I have seen, ever since. The sight is inside my eyelids. My mother is floating in air, swaying gently. She is a dreadful pendulum. The laundry line creaks as she moves. Her teeth bite her blue lower lip as if caught in a last moment of doubt.

Her favourite possessions are stacked neatly by her drifting feet. Her little vanity case, packed with the gauzy blue dress, her nightgown, perfume. Her soft suede handbag, the colour of a doe's belly. A note lies on the case, in her formal French schoolchild's copperplate. *To be taken to the woods,* it says.

I had to wait until night. She had told me that. But I did not want to leave her hanging there. I was afraid someone would knock on the door and insist on coming in. Then they would see her. I was not afraid of getting in trouble. But she looked so exposed up there, with her twisted blue face. I did not want other eyes on her.

So I took her down. It was difficult to touch her. She was still warm. I folded her up small and put her in the cupboard beneath the sink. 'Sorry,' I said to her, again and again. I cleaned the floor, which had mess on it beneath where she had hung.

I wanted to send all her clothes with her, but I couldn't find her big suitcase. I did my best by adding a couple of things to the little overnight vanity – everyday things she might need in the woods. I put in her suture kit. I packed the copy of *Aesop's Fables* that lay by her bed. She could never fall asleep without a book and I worried about her, lying wakeful in the cold forest.

Night came like a blanket. I put Mommy and her things on my back, and carried her into the trees. She had grown stiff and clammy. Things seeped out of her. She would have hated that. I knew I needed to get her to the forest. As soon as we were under the trees I felt better.

She seemed to grow heavier as we went through the night forest. I gasped and stumbled. My spine felt as though it were being crushed, my knees trembled. I welcomed those things. It was right that this should be a difficult journey.

I buried her in the centre of the glade, near Snowball the mouse. I buried her blue dress in the south corner, her favourite leather handbag to the west, her perfume in the east. As the earth took each thing it became a god. As I laid her down in the hole I felt the earth take her in its arms. 'I hold you in my heart,' I whispered. She started to transform. The white trees watched like a hundred eyes.

Lauren whispered in my ear, 'Get in. We can lie down with her.'

For a moment I thought about it. But then I remembered that if I died, Olivia died too, and Lauren and Night-time, and the little ones. And I found that I didn't want to do it.

When all the gods were safely in their homes I piled earth back on top of them. Even after they were buried I could still feel them radiating. They shone without light beneath the earth.

Mommy had acted just in time. The police came two days later. I stood outside, under a sun like a burning star. I became a picture for the man for the newspaper. When they searched the house they found nothing, of course. There was a case missing, and some clothes.

Where did she go? they asked me. I shook my head, because I really did not know.

Before she did it, Mommy had mailed a letter to the Chihuahua-dachshund-terrier lady. The woman was on vacation in Mexico but she read the letter when she got back. The letter said that Mommy was going away for her health. She was a very private woman, my mother. She was thorough. She did not want to be known, even in death. Perhaps that is the only thing that I ever truly understood about her.

So Mommy is gone, and has never been found. The little girl is still gone too. I do not think that they are in the same place, however.

Lauren was six years old when she first came to me, and she stayed that age for a long time. I never thought of it before, but it's the same age Little Girl With Popsicle was when she went.

Eventually Lauren started to grow up. She grew slower than me, but she grew. Her anger grew with her. It was bad.

'I don't have anywhere to put all the feelings,' she kept saying. And I felt so bad, because it was the pain she took from me. I loved her for that, no matter what she did. She hates the body. It's too big and hairy and weird for her. She can't even wear the clothes she likes, star-spangled leggings, little pink shoes. They never fit. They don't make those things in the right sizes. Maybe that time at the mall was the worst. It was so sad for her. I feel as protective towards her as a father. I promised that I would try to be that, for her. I know I'm failing. I'm too messed up to help anyone.

I went to the inside house when I needed comfort. Olivia with her little feet and her curious tail was always waiting. Olivia didn't know anything about the world outside. I was glad of that. When I was with her I didn't need to know either.

Nothing is perfect, of course. Not even the weekend place. Sometimes things show up I don't expect. White flip-flops, long-lost boys crying behind the attic door.

I fall silent. We seem to have reached the end. Lauren is gone. I am so tired I feel I might evaporate like water.

'Maybe I should have guessed,' he said. 'Champ knew.'

'What do you mean?'

'He likes you. But that day he just went crazy, barking at you in the street. I thought I saw something in your eyes, just for a second. Like someone else was in there. I thought I imagined it.'

'That was Olivia, my cat,' I say. 'She was trying to get out. Never mind. We'll get to that another time.'

The man gets up to leave, as I knew he would.

'Who's looking after your dog?' I guess I want to keep him there a moment longer, because I won't see him again.

'What?'

'Your dog,' I say. 'You've been here for a night and a day. You shouldn't leave a dog alone all that time. It's not right.'

'I wouldn't,' he says. 'Linda Moreno is taking care of Champ.' He sees my look of puzzlement. 'The woman with the Chihuahua.'

'I thought she was gone,' I say. 'I saw flyers on the telephone poles. They had her face on them.'

'Went on an Atlantic cruise,' he says. 'With a younger man.

Didn't want her daughter to know. The daughter got worried. But she's back now. Got a nice tan, too.'

'That's good,' I say. I felt a spurt of happiness. I'd been worried about the Chihuahua lady. It was good someone was doing ok.

'See you tomorrow,' he says, though I won't, of course. Then he is gone. He never seems to use an unnecessary word.

The dark comes, or the closest you get to dark in the city. I don't turn on the lamp by my bed. I watch the lights from the parking lot make yellow squares across the ceiling. When the nurse comes in she shocks me awake in a blaze of white neon. She gives me water, and the name of the hospital is printed on the plastic cup she puts to my lips. I'm not so good with names, and I'm dazed with sleep and painkillers, so it takes me a moment, before I realise – this is her hospital. Mommy worked here, was fired from here for the things she did to the children. It is one of those strange circles in time. But I can't tell whether I'm at the beginning or the end. The nurse goes, leaving me in the dark again. It comes to me, for the first time, perhaps, that my mother is really dead.

'It turns out you can't kill me,' I say to Lauren. 'And I can't kill you. So we have to find another way of doing things.'

I feel for her, try to take her hand. But she's not there. She's sleeping, or shutting me out, or maybe just quiet. There's no way to tell whether she hears me or not.

I think about the Chihuahua lady. I hope she had a good vacation with her young boyfriend. I hope she's relaxing in her nice yellow house with the green trim.

I turn the cup in my hand. The name of the hospital revolves. Mommy's place. But she isn't here. She is at home, waiting for me in the cupboard under the sink.

Something is teasing, tugging at my brain. Something about the Chihuahua lady and her trip to Mexico. I shake my head. That is not right. The Chihuahua lady went on a cruise, not to Mexico.

She was in Mexico the first time. The familiar tug in my mind, of having forgotten something. But it is gone.

The orange-haired man appears as I am being discharged. I have to look twice to check, but yes, it is him. I am very surprised and weirdly shy. We told him so much, the other night. I feel sort of naked.

'I thought you might need a ride,' he says.

I smell the forest as we approach. It is such a relief to see my street, the dented sign, trees crowding the horizon.

But I don't want the man to see my sad house; the plywood over the windows, the dusty dark rooms where I live alone with all my others. I want him to go. Instead he helps me out of the car and indoors. He does it quickly and efficiently, not asking me to acknowledge it.

Even when we're inside, he still hovers in the hall, not seeming to notice the cobwebs and the brokenness of it all. So now I have to offer him something. The refrigerator yields the sour stench of old milk. I feel a twinge of despair.

'Beer,' he suggests, looking at the contents.

'Sure,' I say, feeling immediately more cheerful. I take a look in the cupboards. 'I bet you've never had a pickle with peanut butter.'

'You would win that bet,' he says.

We sit in the broken lawn chairs out back. It is a beautiful day. Dandelion clocks dance in the low sun. The trees whisper in the slight breeze. I turn my face up to it. For a moment I feel almost normal – sitting in my yard in the late summer heat, just like anyone might, having a beer with a friend.

'Hospital,' he says. 'You must have missed being outside. You like the woods.'

'I did,' I say.

'Hey,' he says, but not to me. The tabby cat steps out of the undergrowth. She looks even thinner than usual. 'What's up?' She slides and curves around the rusty chair legs. He puts some peanut butter on the ground for her and she licks it, purring. 'Poor girl,' he says. 'She belonged to someone, once. They took her claws out then they abandoned her. People.' The cat lies down at his feet. The sun shows up the dust in her fur.

I try to think of a question a normal person would ask. 'What's it like, being a park ranger?'

'It's good,' he says. 'I always wanted to work outdoors, ever since I was a kid. I grew up in the city.' I can't imagine him among tall buildings, on busy sidewalks. He seems designed for great distances and solitude.

'You and I have talked before,' he says. 'At the bar we say hi sometimes.'

'Oh,' I say. I am too embarrassed to tell him that I don't remember much about the times at the bar. I think Little Teddy took over towards the end. He's not good at talking to grown-ups. Or maybe I was just drunk. 'I picked that bar to take women to,' I say. 'How dumb is that?' I tell him about my date with the woman in blue.

'But you kept going there, on your own. Even after you realised what kind of place it was.'

'Oh,' I say. 'Yeah, to drink.'

Something is happening to the air between us where we sit. Time seems to stretch out somewhat. I can't stop looking at his forearm, where it rests on the rusty chair. Pale skin, covered in fine hair that glows in the sun like burning wire.

Fear ripples through me. 'I'm not like a regular person,' I say. 'It's hard being me. Maybe even harder being around me.'

'What's a regular person?' he says. 'We do what we can.'

I think of Mommy's narrowed mouth and her disgust. I think

of the bug man, who wants to write a book about how messed up I am. 'Right now,' I say, 'what you can do is go.'

I reach the car, limping, as he puts on his seatbelt.

'I didn't mean it,' I say. 'Sorry. It's been a bad month. Year. Life, even.'

He raises his eyebrows.

'Please, come back. Have another beer,' I say. 'Let's talk about you, now.'

'You just got out of hospital. Probably need to rest.'

'Don't make me chase your car down the street,' I say. 'I just got out of hospital.'

He thinks and then he turns off the engine. 'OK,' he says. 'I got some weird stories, too.'

His name is Rob and he has a twin brother. Growing up, they did all the usual twin stuff. They confused their mother and pretended to be one another, even went to each other's classes in high school sometimes. Rob was better at sciences and Eddie was better at artsy stuff, English Lit and so forth. So they both got good grades. They stopped swapping around on their parents, though, when they got older, and they never did it to girlfriends. It was a mean trick, they agreed, not to be practised on those you love. Then Rob stopped having girlfriends. He didn't tell Eddie, even when he met a man who worked in a restaurant in town who made his heart beat fast. They started seeing one another.

One evening the man from the restaurant saw Rob across the street. He was filled with love so he crossed the street and took Rob in his arms. As soon as he touched him, he knew it wasn't Rob. But it was too late. Eddie beat him until he couldn't see out of either eye.

The man from the restaurant moved away. His brother won't

speak to him, and Rob says he wouldn't want him to, anyway. 'Even so,' he says, 'it's like a missing leg. I had to learn how to walk again without him. I stopped seeing people for a time. Only wanted my dog and the woods. I like early mornings best, when no one is around.'

I think about the story for a time.

I say, 'If all that hadn't happened to you, I would be dead.'

'Well,' he says, surprised. 'I guess that's right.' We look at each other briefly. Then we sit in silence.

He goes home as evening is sneaking in. The sun falls low, purple shadow wraps around things, readying for night. As I pick up the beer cans I catch a flash of yellow overhead, in my beech tree. Goldfinch song fills the dusk. The birds are coming back.

Night Olivia

⁓

Hello, everyone. Welcome to the first episode of CATching up with Night Olivia. *We've got a great show ahead. We're going to be talking about light — types of sunshine, kinds of darkness — what's best for naps, what will illuminate your eyes like unearthly lamps in the dusk, and so on, plus: what shadows work best for concealing you, as you stalk your prey like a black bolt of death in the night.*

But first, let's address the elephant in the room. We need to talk about the upstairs world, the so-called real world. I think we can all agree that it is not as good as the one inside. It is grey and everything smells bad. I don't like the colour of the rug, which up here is not a beautiful shout of orange, but the shade of dead teds. Anyway I do come up here sometimes, despite my reservations, because one should always know what one is dealing with. Sometimes I even go outside. I am not an indoor cat any more. I see and feel the world, where once I just smelled and heard it, from downstairs in the inside place. Now, if I want, I can come upstairs and be with Ted as he walks in the fall leaves, feel the chilly bite of first frost in the shortening days.

But yes, outside is quite disappointing. It is no big deal, I would say. There is a tabby cat up here, but she is not the one I love. When I first saw her I thought, You poor thing. *Her eyes are dull brown — when I look into them I see only a hungry animal. She is small and thin, has no claws and walks with a staggering limp. She does not shine. The orange-headed* ted insists on feeding her. That ted looks like a lumberjack but he is actually very sentimental. Also he smells very strongly of his big brouhaha, which is disgusting. Ted keeps telling me the brouhaha scented the blood and found us in the woods but I refuse to believe that I was saved in such a fashion. Anyway, I was wondering how Ted would cope without Olivia. He seems to be doing fine.

I love to go down to the weekend place and watch the other one, the beautiful one, through the window as she grooms and preens. She stares like a snake with her apple-yellow eyes. She is one of us, of course. Another part. Maybe I should have guessed that earlier. She chooses not to talk. But I hope that one day she will speak to me. In the meantime I will worship her and wait. I will do that for ever, if necessary. I can always keep an eye on what is happening upstairs through the TV.

Sometimes the LORD comes walking through the kitchen wall or floating up the stairs towards the roof light on the landing. He turns to look down at me with his round fish eyes, or the mirrored gaze of a fly. He's a fragment of Ted's imagination. Mommy talked so much about the ankou that the ankou came. Mommy's god found his way from her faraway village in Brittany, through Ted, into Olivia's world. That's how gods travel, through minds.

The LORD never made Olivia help Ted or Lauren. She just wanted to be kind. She was a nice cat. I am nice, but I am other things too.

There is no cord any more, binding me to Ted. I kind of miss it, now it's gone. He and I are bound to one another and the cord was a reflection of that. It was honest and showed how things truly are. I find that the upper world holds few such helpful signs. It is a cold bleak place. Our big fleshy body lumbers through it, with us inside like badly nested Russian dolls. Disgusting, in my opinion.

However, we can all be together upstairs, now — Ted, Lauren and me, and some of the others whose names I don't know yet. They are just beginning to come up into the light. We can talk or fight or whatever just as well as we can downstairs in my place. Sometimes I forget to go back down for days at a time. So I guess in some ways the upstairs is now my home too.

Ted

The path winds up into the fall day. The air has mushrooms and red leaves in it. The trees are thin-fingered against the sky. Rob is warm at my side, hair escaping from his hat like tufts of flame. It has been three months since that morning in the forest, but it could be a lifetime ago.

The stories all fit inside each other. They echo through. It started with her, Little Girl With Popsicle. And she deserves a witness, so that's why we're here.

It is only a quarter-mile or so from the parking lot to the water, but it takes us a while. I shuffle rather than walk, mindful of my healing wound. You can really damage yourself, if you can't feel pain. 'Put your scarf on,' I tell Rob. I wanted a friend to look after us. The weird thing is, now that I have one, all I want to do is to look after him.

The trees open out and we are at the water's edge. It is cool today; the sand looks dirty and dull under the grey sky. There are some hikers, some dogs. Not many. The lake gleams, black glass. The water is too still, like a painting or a trick. It's smaller than I remember. But of course it's me who's changed.

'I don't know what to do,' I say to Rob. What can the living say to the dead? Little Girl With Popsicle is gone and we don't know where. Mommy isn't really under the sink, and Daddy isn't in the tool shed.

'Maybe we don't do anything,' he says.

So I just try to focus really hard on the little girl, and remember that she was here once and she isn't any more. Rob's hand is on my back. I send my best thoughts for her out into the water and the sky and the dry fall leaves and the sand and the pebbles under us. *I hold you in my heart,* I think at Little Girl With Popsicle, because it feels like someone should.

I take my shoes off, even though it's raining. Rob does the same. We bury our feet in the damp sand. We watch the lake, where the drops strike circles on the glossy black skin of the water, which grow, move out and out into infinity.

At last Rob says, 'It's really cold.' He is a practical person.

I shake my head. I don't know what I expected. There's nothing here.

We walk back towards the car in silence. The path winds downhill, back towards the parking lot. There is something bright on the rain-spattered trail. I bend to pick it up. A long, oval shape, rounded and smooth to the touch. It is green as moss, shot through with veins of white. 'Look,' I say, 'what a pretty pebble.' I turn to show Rob. As I do the ground suddenly gives way beneath my foot with a graceful slide. Loose earth and stones skid away from my feet and the world is upturned. I fall, striking the earth hard.

Something tears inside me. It is like being killed again. But this time I feel the shockwave, deep and purple and black. Sharp notes are played hard and raw on my nerves. The feeling bursts through, fills each living cell of me.

Rob leans over me, mouth twisted with distress. He says things about the hospital.

'In a minute,' I say. 'Let me feel it.' I would laugh, but it hurts too much.

It is the pain that lets him through, I think. The barriers between us are coming down.

I put it in our pocket, he says to me, clear and young.

Little Teddy?

In our POCKET but you THREW it in the TRASH.

I get a hand into my pants pocket. There is blood coming from somewhere. It has made a mess of this shirt.

'What are you doing?' Rob says. Cold grey threads of fear run through his voice. 'You're *bleeding*.' He takes out his phone.

'Stop.' I am almost yelling at him and that hurts a lot. 'Wait!'

My fingers meet paper. I take it out. *The Murderer.* My list has been taped back together. The last name stares at me. *Mommy.*

Little Teddy does not mean the murderer of the birds. He probably doesn't even know about that. He is talking about another murder.

I been TRYING to show you, Little Teddy says. *But you didn't want to know.*

His memory hurtles towards me, carried on the pain. A rush of feeling, colour, wet earth, moonlight on empty streets. It's like watching a movie with scent and touch.

Little Teddy

We share it out between us – the time and hurt. Big Ted took Mommy to the woods so she could become a god. But I saw what happened the night BEFORE.

I am in the living room. Daddy has been gone some years now. Little Girl With Popsicle vanished from the lake the other day. Everyone is VERY upset.

There is a paper on the table in front of me. It is a job application. I draw a picture of myself on it in yellow crayon, humming. The smells of cigarette smoke and burnt coffee creep under the kitchen door. The terrier lady is talking.

'Half a can in the mornings, dry food at night,' she is saying to Mommy. 'But only after his walk. Heavens, I nearly forgot. The potted ferns need water three times a week. No more, no less. Some people would say that's too much but the soil should always be a little damp, I think, for ferns.'

'You can depend on me,' Mommy says gently.

'I know I can,' the terrier lady says. There is the sound of keys chinking. 'The one with the green ribbon is for the front door; this is for the back door, down to the storm cellar. I don't open it, in general. Oof, Meheeco. I'm going to have a cocktail with breakfast every day. One with an umbrella. I'm going to swim and lay in the sun and I'm not going to think about work once. Nope.'

'You deserve it,' Mommy says warmly. 'The strain you've been under.'

'You said it.'

There is silence and rustling, the sound of a cheek being kissed. The terrier lady is hugging Mommy. I press my ear harder against the door. I'm jealous, I am FILLED with vinegar.

I am at my window watching when Mommy leaves the house after dark. She has a big suitcase and I am afraid that she is going to Me-heeeeeco to join the terrier lady. I don't want to be left behind. But the suitcase is empty, she swings it at arm's length as she goes. I stare because I've NEVER seen her like this. Mommy is NOT playful. I know she would not want me or anyone to see it. The streetlights are all out, tonight. It's lucky for Mommy that those kids threw the stones and broke them, I guess.

Mommy goes to the woods. She is gone a long time and I almost start crying, because she is really GONE, this time.

I wait, and wait.

It seems like many hours, but it's probably one or two. Mommy comes out of the forest. She walks through the long dark shadows of branches where they stretch across the sidewalk. When she goes through the breaks of silver moonlight, I see that the suitcase is heavy now. She pulls it slowly along the sidewalk on its little wheels. She goes right past our house without looking or stopping! I am surprised. Where CAN she be going?

The green trim on the terrier lady's house looks grey in the moonlight. Mommy goes around the back of the house. I get into my bed and hide under my covers but I do NOT sleep. She comes in quietly, a long while later. I hear running water in the bathroom, the sound of her brushing her teeth. Then there comes another tiny sound. Mommy is humming.

In the morning she is as usual. She gives me a small jar of applesauce for breakfast, and a piece of bread. Her hands smell like damp cellar earth. I never see the big suitcase again, so I guess she sent it on to Meheeco without her. I hear her ask Big Ted to go to the store for ice cream.

I kept TRYING to tell Big Ted. I took him back to the yellow house with the green trim again and again but he still didn't get it. I think he always knew somewhere deep down that it was Mommy. But he hoped so hard it wasn't. Now he can't avoid the truth any more. Bam, POW, like being hit with a punch.

I can hear Big Ted crying.

Ted

⁀

'Don't move. You'll make it worse.' Rob's face is hung above me in the sky. It is even paler than usual.

'We have to tell someone.' My beard is wet with tears. 'I know where she is. Please, please, we have to go *now*.' Another good thing about Rob is that he does not waste time on questions.

Everything happens both quickly and slowly. We stagger back to the car, and Rob drives us to a police station. We have to wait there for a long time. I am still bleeding a little but I won't let Rob take me to a hospital. *No*, I say, *no, no, no, no, NO*. As the 'NO's get louder Rob backs away, startled. At last a tired man with pouches under his eyes comes out. I tell him what Little Teddy saw. He makes some phone calls.

We wait for someone else to arrive. It is her day off. She hurries in, wearing fishing waders. She has been on her boat. The detective looks very tired and kind of like a possum. I recognise her from when they searched my house, eleven years ago. I am pleased by this. Brain is really coming through for me today! But the possum detective looks less and less tired the longer I talk.

I wait on another plastic chair. Still the police station? No, this is full of hurt people. Hospital. In the end it is my turn, and they

317

staple me up, which is weird. I refuse the painkiller. I want to feel it. So short, this life.

By the time Rob drives me home, it is dawn. As we turn into my street I see a van stopped outside her house. Cars with beautiful red and blue lights, which play on the green trim and the yellow clapboard. The lady is crying and she holds her Chihuahua tight, for comfort. The dog licks her nose. I feel bad for her. She was always nice. Mommy never hurt the Chihuahua lady's body, but she hurt her all the same.

They put up big white screens around the Chihuahua lady's house, so that no one can see anything. I stay at the living-room window, watching, even though there is nothing to see. It takes some hours. I guess they have to dig deep. Mommy was thorough. We all stay there, awake and alert in the body, watching the white screens. Little Teddy cries silently.

We know when they bring her out, Little Girl With Popsicle. We feel her as she passes. She is in the air like the scent of rain.

The next-door-neighbour lady has not come back. She was calling the little girl's name as she ran from me into the woods. That made me think. I told the possum detective about her. When they looked through her house and all her things I felt bad for her – even after everything. It was her turn to have all those eyes on her stuff. Then they found out she was the sister of Little Girl With Popsicle. When I heard, I thought, *Now they're both dead*. I felt sure. I don't know why.

They found Mommy's yellow cassette tape in the sister's house. It had her notes on Little Girl With Popsicle. The possum detective says it sounds like she was already dead when Mommy got her. Still, I can't think about it.

I'm sure Mommy mistook the Little Girl for a boy. Mommy never messed with girls. So Mommy took her because of all those chances coming together. A haircut, a trip to the lake, a wrong turn. It makes my heart hurt and that feeling will never go away, I don't think. Like a cut that never heals.

The possum detective and I are drinking sodas in my back yard. Our fingers ache after yanking out so many nails. Plywood lies in broken stacks all around us. The house is so strange with its windows uncovered. I keep expecting it to blink. It's still warm in the sunshine, but cold in the shade. The leaves are thick on the ground, red and orange and brown, all the shades of Rob's hair. Soon it will be winter. I love winter.

I like the possum detective but I'm not ready to let her in the house. Other people's eyes make it a place I don't recognise. She seems to understand that.

'Do you know where your mother is?' The possum detective asks the question suddenly, in the middle of another conversation about sea otters (she actually knows a fair amount about them). I smile because I can see that she is enjoying the conversation about sea otters, but also using it to be a detective and try to surprise me into telling her the truth. I like it; that she's so good at her job. 'Should I still be looking for her?' she says. 'You have to tell me, Ted.'

I think about what to say. She waits, watching.

I don't know much about the world but I know what would happen if they find the bones. The excavation, the pictures in the newspaper, the TV. Mommy, resurrected. Kids will go to the waterfall at night to scare each other, they'll tell stories of the murder nurse. Mommy will remain a god.

No. She has to really die this time. And that means be forgotten.

'She's gone,' I say. 'She's dead. I promise. That's all.'

The possum woman looks at me for a long time. 'Well then,' she says. 'We never had this talk.'

I walk the possum detective to her car. As I'm going back to the house, I notice that the last 's' on the street sign is wearing away. If you squint it might not be there at all. *Needles Street.* I shiver and go inside quickly.

The bug man is gone. His office is cleared out. I went to see. Now I talk to the bug woman. The young doctor from the hospital fixed me up with her. The bug woman comes to the house sometimes and sometimes I go to her office, which is like the inside of an iceberg, cool and white. It contains a normal amount of chairs. She is very nice and doesn't look like a bug at all. But I still have trouble with names. And so much has changed. Maybe I need one tiny thing to stay the same.

She suggested that I play back my recordings to see what I have forgotten. I'm surprised to find I've used up twelve cassettes. I really didn't think I recorded that much but that's why I need the tapes, isn't it? Because my memory's so bad.

They're numbered so I start with 1. The first twenty minutes or so is what I expected. There are a couple recipes, and some stuff about the glade, the lake. Then there's a pause. I think maybe it's finished, so I'm reaching over to switch off the recorder, when someone starts breathing into the silence of the tape. In and out. Cold walks up my arms and legs. That's not my breath.

Then a hesitant, prim voice starts to speak.

I'm busy with my tongue, she says, *doing the itchy part of my leg when Ted calls for me. Darn it, this is not a good time.*

My heart leaps up into my mouth. It can't be – oh, but it is. *Olivia,* my beautiful lost kitten. I never knew she could speak. No wonder I could never find the tape recorder. She sounds sweet, worried and teacher-like. Hearing her is wonderful and sad, like seeing a picture of yourself as a baby. I wish we could have talked. It's too late now. I listen on and on. I don't know why I'm crying.

It is called integration, the bug woman tells me. It happens, some-times, in situations like ours. Integration sounds like something that happens in a factory. I think they just wanted to be together, Olivia and the other one. Anyway, Olivia is gone and she won't be back.

The bug woman always tells me to let feelings in, not shut them out, so that is what I try to do. It hurts.

There are other voices, among Olivia's recordings – ones that I don't know. Some don't use language, but grunts and long pauses and clicks and high songs. Those are the ones that move through me moaning like cold little ghosts. In the past I tried to shut them in the attic. Now I take time to listen. I've spent too long covering my ears.

Dawn wakes me these days. I surface slowly from a dream full of red and yellow feathers. My mind echoes with green sounds and thoughts that are not my own. I can taste blood in my mouth. I never know whose dreams I am going to get in the night. But the body actually gets to rest, these days, instead of being used by someone else while I sleep. So it's worth it.

Other things are different too. Three days a week I work in the kitchen of a diner across town. I like the walk, watching the city slowly grow up around me. Right now I just wash dishes, but they tell me that maybe soon I can start helping the fry cooks. There is no work today – today is just for us.

Without plywood over the windows, the house seems made of light. I get out of bed, careful not to tear the staples that run down my side. Our body is a landscape, of scars and new wounds both. I stand and for a moment there is a wrestling in the depths of us. The body sways dangerously and we all feel sick. Sulky, Lauren lets me take control. I steady us with a hand on the wall, breathing deeply. The day is full of these seismic, nauseous struggles. We are learning. It is not easy to hold everyone in your heart at once.

Later today, maybe Lauren will take the body. She will ride her bike and draw, or we will go to the woods. Not to the glade, though, or the waterfall. We don't go there. The blue dress of rotting organza, her old vanity case, her bones — they must be left alone so that they stop being gods and return to being just old things.

We will walk under the trees and listen to the sounds of the forest in autumn.

The tired possum detective and the police are searching the woods near the lake. They want to find the little boys Mommy took. They think there might have been as many as six, over the years. It's hard to say because children do wander off. They were mostly boys from sad families, or who had no families. Mommy would have chosen the ones who wouldn't be missed. Little Girl With Popsicle was a big deal because she had parents.

Maybe one day the boys will be found. Until then I hope they are peaceful under the forest green, held by the kind earth.

In the late afternoon perhaps Night Olivia and I will doze on the couch, watching the big trucks. When darkness falls they will hunt. A moment of unease travels through me, like the brush of a wet leaf on the back of my neck. Night Olivia is large and strong.

Well, it's a beautiful day, and it is breakfast time. As we pass the living room I peer in, and take a moment to admire my new rug. It's the colour of everything — yellow, green, ochre, magenta, pink. I love it. I could have thrown away that old blue rug any time since Mommy left, I guess. Strange that it never occurred to me until after everything happened.

We go into the kitchen. So far we have only discovered one thing that all of us like to eat. We have it together in the morning, sometimes. I always describe what I'm doing as I do it, so that we all remember. I don't need to record my recipes any more.

'We're going to make it like this,' I say. 'Take fresh strawberries from the refrigerator. Wash them in cold running water. Put them in a bowl.' We watch them gleam in the morning sun. 'We can dry them with a cloth,' I say, 'or we can wait for the sun to do its work. It is our choice.'

I used to saw the strawberries into quarters with a blunt knife, because there was nothing sharp in the house. But now I keep a set of chef's knives in a block on the counter. 'This is called trust,' I say as I slice. 'Some of us have a lot to learn about it. See my point?' I guess that is what Lauren calls a dad joke.

The blade reflects the red flesh of the fruit as it slides through. The scent is sweet and earthy. I feel some of them stir with pleasure within. 'Can you smell that?' I have to be careful with the knife near my fingers. I don't give my pain to the others any more. 'So we slice the strawberries as thin as we can and pour over balsamic vinegar. It should be the kind that is old and thick like syrup. Now we take three leaves from the basil plant that grows in the pot on the window ledge. We slice these into narrow ribbons and breathe the scent. Now add the basil to the strawberries and balsamic vinegar.' It is a recipe, but sometimes it sounds like a spell.

We let it sit for a few minutes, so the flavours can mingle. We use this time to think, or watch the sky, or just be ourselves.

When I feel it's ready I say, 'I'm putting the strawberry, basil and balsamic mixture on a slice of bread.' The bread smells brown and nutty. 'I grind black pepper over. It's time to go outside.'

The sky and trees are flooded with birds. The song flows and ebbs around us, on the air. Lauren gives a little sigh as the sun warms our skin.

'Now,' I say. 'We eat.'

Afterword

If you haven't finished *The Last House on Needless Street* yet, please don't read on – what follows is one long spoiler.

This is how I came to write a book about survival, disguised as a book about horror. In the summer of 2018 I was writing about a cat and I couldn't work out why. I had always been fascinated by the apparent ease with which those who lack empathy form strong, passionate attachments with their pets. Serial killer Dennis Nilsen's dog, Bleep, was the only creature he could be said to have had any functional relationship with. He loved Bleep and the fate of the dog was the only thing he was concerned with after his arrest. So I thought, *Maybe this is the right story, the one I should be working on.* Olivia the cat, who lives with Ted and gives him comfort, even though he took a young girl named Lauren and keeps her captive. But it wasn't working. Ted didn't seem like a murderer, or a kidnapper. I kept finding pockets of compassion for him. His story felt like one of suffering and survival, not like that of a perpetrator. And Olivia didn't really behave like a cat. She did have cat-like qualities but her voice seemed neither human nor feline, but something other. She seemed like a part of him. So did Lauren, the girl who was ostensibly Ted's prisoner.

I was researching the effects of childhood abuse when I came across a video online of a young woman named Encina, who has dissociative identity disorder, discussing her condition. She talked with great frankness and compassion about her younger alter. She treats her as her child, adopting a maternal attitude, taking care of her, making sure she's not scared, or faced with activities she can't accomplish, like driving. The younger alter came forward, for a time, and spoke. She talked about how lonely she is, because no other children want to play with her, because the body she's in is big and they don't understand. I felt that my outlook on life changed as I watched them talk. The video is listed in the bibliography (*What It's Like To Live With Dissociative Identity Disorder (DID)*). I realised that the book I was writing had never been about a cat named Olivia, a girl called Lauren and a man named Ted. It was about someone who had all these personalities within them. It wasn't about horror but about survival and hope, and how the mind copes with fear and suffering.

I had heard of DID before. It's the staple of many a horror plot. But watching Encina's system describe how their personality had diverged in order to deal with abuse, I felt that a piece of the world I had never understood had fallen into place. The world felt stranger now, but also more real. It was a kind of miracle, but it also made perfect sense, that the mind should do this.

I rang a friend of mine who is a psychotherapist. She has worked with, among others, survivors of trafficking and torture. 'Is this real?' I asked. 'I mean, is this a real thing?' I wasn't very articulate.

'In my experience it's absolutely real,' she said.

For over a year I went down a long rabbit hole, reading everything I could get my hands on to do with DID. I suddenly understood what the book was, and where it needed to go.

There are people in the therapeutic community and the world at large who firmly believe the disorder doesn't exist. DID seems to threaten people's worldview. Maybe it's because it interferes with the concept of the soul – the idea that there can be more than one person in a body is somehow terrifying. It certainly disrupts the underlying tenets of many religions.

The stories that accompany this disorder are without exception horrific. It's the mind's last resort, when faced with unbearable pain and fear. I am particularly grateful to First Person Plural, one of the major support groups for people with dissociative identity disorder in the UK, for helping me better understand this intricate condition. Their website and online resources are listed at the back of the book.

I spoke with someone who has dissociative identity disorder and works with others who have it, over the course of a long afternoon. They have asked not to be named. We met for the first time at a train station and went to a café nearby to talk. We were both flustered and shy at first. It's an intimate thing to discuss between strangers. But they laid open their past, and their life, with unflinching honesty.

They talked about how DID isn't a disorder when it first comes into being. It saves a child's mind from unendurable strain; it performs a life-saving function. It's only later in adult life, when it's no longer necessary, that it becomes a disorder. They talked about one of their alters, 'Legs', who doesn't talk. Legs' only function had been to get them back to bed after the abuse. They described how, while the abuse was happening, they would send all the different parts of their body away. All they held onto was the big toe, which they used to draw the body back together again afterwards. They told me that some alters used to despise the parts who experienced the abuse. Some of them don't understand why they're in a body that doesn't reflect who they are in age, gender or appearance. It makes them angry. Some of them have tried to hurt the body. Other alters try to maintain a distance, 'vacuum-packed', sealed off from the rest of the system. They want to live a separate, parallel life. The purposes of the different alters are clearly defined. The alter who goes to work will be cold towards family or a partner if they ring or come to see them during the day. The work alter does the job, just that.

They described how differently memory works for them. Each alter holds certain experiences. Memory is not linear, but nested in a series of compartments. 'I will never know what it feels like to remember things like you,' they told me. It can make seemingly simple tasks difficult. When following a recipe, for instance, they can't remember more than four ingredients at a time. Retaining too much information is dangerous because it means they might have to remember other things too. Sometimes they leave a gap between switches, leaving the body vacant for a moment, so that alters don't have to share knowledge. They described how difficult it is to pack for a holiday; remembering to put everyone's different things into the suitcase, clothes for all the alters of different ages. They described their own inner worlds, where their alters convene: a farmhouse at the centre of a crossroads, where approaching enemies can be seen from any direction; a playground guarded by armies; a beach.

They told me that they were healing. The alter who used to rip up photographs, trying to destroy the past, has stopped. After years of therapy and with a family of their own, they are learning to live together as one.

Towards the end of our meeting I asked, 'What would you like people to know about the disorder, that you don't feel is understood?'

'I'd like people to know that we are always striving towards the good,' they said. 'We are always protecting the child.'

It could take a lifetime to understand this complex disorder. There seem to be many variations between cases, and a multitude of different ways in which dissociative identity disorder can manifest. Ted is not based on a particular case. He is wholly imagined and any mistakes are all my own. But I have tried to do justice in this book to the people whose lives are touched by DID – to hold onto what was said to me that afternoon, over our cooling cups of coffee. Dissociative identity disorder may often be used as a horror device in fiction, but in my small experience it is quite the opposite. Those who survive, and live with it, are always striving towards the good.

Acknowledgements

To my wonderful agent Jenny Savill whose faith in Ted, Olivia and Lauren kept me going, and who fought for them all the way, I can only say thank you. The stars must have been aligned the day we met. My amazing US agent Robin Straus and her colleague Katelyn Hales worked tirelessly to bring this book to the US. I am eternally grateful.

The tireless, redoubtable Miranda Jewess edited this book firmly and gently into its final form. It must have been like driving a team of octopuses down Piccadilly. I am full of admiration for her, Niamh Murray, Drew Jerrison and all the Viper team who have worked so hard to support this book. *The Last House on Needless Street* found its perfect US editor in Kelly Lonesome O'Connor, and the best US home with Tor Nightfire. It is so rewarding to work with these wonderful publishers.

Love and thanks go as ever to my mother Isabelle and my father Christopher, for all their help since the very beginning. Their support sustains me, as does that of my sister Antonia and her family – Sam, Wolf and River.

To my shining, good-hearted and very impressive friends, thank you. I am so grateful to Emily Cavendish, Kate Burdette, Oriana Elia, Dea Vanagan and Belinda Stewart-Wilson for their willingness to listen, a place to lay my head in tough times, many words of comfort as well as more caustic observations, wine and much wisdom. Natasha Pulley has my deepest gratitude for our long talks, for her excellent ideas and endless wit. Gillian Redfearn's support and friendship has been a lifeline. My earliest readers were Nina Allan, Kate Burdette, Emily Cavendish and Matt Hill — their encouragement spurred me on. Eugene Noone's joy, creativity and friendship inspired me for many years and his memory will continue to do so. He is deeply missed by me, and many others.

I am profoundly thankful for my endlessly talented, wonderful partner Ed McDonald — for his support, generosity of spirit and keen editorial eye. I am so very lucky. I can't wait for more adventures together.

The charity First Person Plural provided me with invaluable resources on DID and gave me insight into what it's like to live with this complex disorder. They helped to bring dissociative identity disorder to life for me; I hope I have done them justice.

Bibliography

American Psychiatric Association, 2013. *Diagnostic and Statistical Manual of Mental Disorders: DSM-5*, Arlington, VA: American Psychiatric Association

Anonymous, no date. 'About Dissociative Jess', *Dissociative Jess* [blog]. https://dissociativejess.wordpress.com/about/ [accessed September 2018]

Barlow, M.R., 2005. *Memory and Fragmentation in Dissociative Identity Disorder* [PhD thesis], University of Oregon. https://dynamic. uoregon.edu/jjf/theses/Barlow05.pdf [accessed 2 November 2018]

Boon, S., Steele, K., and van der Hart, O., 2011. *Coping with Trauma-related Dissociation: Skills Training for Patients and Therapists*, London: WW Norton and Co.

Chase, Truddi, 1990 (1987). *When Rabbit Howls*, New York: Jove

Dee, Ruth, 2009. *Fractured*, London: Hodder & Stoughton

DID Research, 2017. 'Cooperation, Integration and Fusion'. http://did-research.org/treatment/integration.html [accessed 9 August 2018]

DID Research, 2015. 'Internal Worlds'. http://did-research.org/did/alters/internal_worlds.html [accessed 5 July 2017]

DissociaDID, 2018. *Inner Worlds (Debunking DID, ep. 8)* [video]. https://www.youtube.com/watch?v=CB41C7D7QrI [accessed 5 January 2019]

DissociaDID, 2018. *Making Our Inner World! – Sims 4* [video]. https://www.youtube.com/watch?v=gXLhEWSCIc4 [accessed 5 January 2019]

DissociaDID, 2018. *Why We Won't Talk About Our Littles (Switch On Camera)* [video]. https://www.youtube.com/watch?v=ZdmPlIjIrBI [accessed 11 November 2018]

Hargis, B., 2018. 'About Alter Switching in Dissociative Identity Disorder', *HealthyPlace* [blog], 14 June. https://www.healthyplace.com/blogs/dissociativeliving/2018/6/about-alter-switching-in-dissociative-identity-disorder [accessed 11 March 2019]

Jamieson, Alice, 2009. *Today I'm Alice*, London: Pan Macmillan

Johnson, R., 2009. 'The Intrapersonal Civil War', *The Psychologist Journal*, April 2009, vol. 22 (pp. 300–3)

Karjala, Lynn Mary, 2007. *Understanding Trauma and Dissociation*, Atlanta: Thomas Max Publishing

Kastrup, B., Crabtree, A., Kelly, E. F., 2018. 'Could Multiple Personality Disorder Explain Life, the Universe and Everything?' *Scientific American* [blog], 18 June. https://blogs.scientificamerican.com/observations/could-multiple-personality-disorder-explain-life-the-universe-and-everything/ [accessed 13 March 2019]

Matulewicz, C., 2016. 'What Alters in Dissociative Identity Disorder Feel Like', *HealthyPlace* [blog], 25 May. https://www.healthyplace.com/blogs/dissociativeliving/2016/05/the-experience-of-alters-in-dissociative-identity-disorder [accessed 12 March 2019]

MedCircle, 2018. 'What It's Like To Live With Dissociative Identity Disorder (DID)' [video]. https://www.youtube.com/watch?v=AokLjsY4JlU [accessed 3 August 2018]

Mitchison, A., 2011. 'Kim Noble: The woman with 100 personalities', *Guardian*. https://www.theguardian.com/lifeandstyle/2011/sep/30/kim-noble-woman-with-100-personalities [accessed 3 June 2017]

MultiplicityandMe, 2018. 'Dissociative Identity Disorder Documentary: The Lives I Lead' [video], BBC Radio 1. https://www.youtube.com/watch?v=exLDx09_ta8 [accessed 11 December 2018]

Noble, Kim, 2011. *All of Me*, London: Hachette Digital

Nurses Learning Network, no date. 'Understanding Multiple Personality Disorders'. https://www.nurseslearning.com/courses/nrp/NRP-1618/Section%205/index.htm [accessed 3 December 2019]

Paulsen, Sandra, 2009. *Looking Through the Eyes of Trauma and Dissociation: An Illustrated Guide for EMDR Therapists and Clients*, Charleston: Booksurge Publishing

Peisley, Tanya, 2017. 'Busting the Myths about Dissociative Identity Disorder', *SANE* [blog]. https://www.sane.org/information-stories/the-sane-blog/mythbusters/busting-the-myths-about-dissociative-identity-disorder [accessed June 2018]

Psychology Today, 2019. 'Dissociative Identity Disorder (Multiple Personality Disorder)'. https://www.psychologytoday.com/gb/conditions/dissociative-identity-disorder-multiple-personality-disorder [accessed 7 September 2019]

Steinberg, Maxine, Schall, Marlene, 2010. *The Stranger in the Mirror: Dissociation, the Hidden Epidemic*, London: HarperCollins ebooks

Truly Docs, 2004. 'The Woman with Seven Personalities' [video]. https://www.youtube.com/watch?v=s715UTuOoY4&feature=youtu.be [accessed November 2019]

Van de Kolk, Bessel, 2015. *The Body Keeps the Score*, New York: Penguin Random House

West, Cameron, 2013 (1999). *First Person Plural: My Life as a Multiple*, London: Hachette Digital

Online resource libraries

https://www.aninfinitemind.com/

http://didiva.com/

http://did-research.org/index.html

https://www.firstpersonplural.org.uk/resources/training-films/

https://www.isst-d.org/

http://www.manyvoicespress.org/

https://www.sidran.org/essential-readings-in-trauma/

https://www.sidran.org/recommended-titles/

About the Author

CATRIONA WARD was born in Washington, DC and grew up in the US, Kenya, Madagascar, Yemen and Morocco. She read English at the University of Oxford, and spent several years working as an actor in New York. Her first novel, *Rawblood*, was published in 2015, and was a WHSmith Fresh Talent title. Ward won the August Derleth Award for Best Horror Novel in 2016 at the British Fantasy Awards for *Rawblood*, and again in 2018 for *Little Eve*, making her the first woman to win the prize twice. *Little Eve* also went on to win the prestigious Shirley Jackson Award for best novel, and was a Guardian Best Book of 2018. Her next novel, *Sundial*, will be published by Viper in 2022.

🐦 @Catrionaward
🐦 @ViperBooks
📘 Viper Books